GUY FAWKES

Or Gunpowder, Treason, and Plot.

GUY FAWKES HELD THE SOLDIERS AT BAY WHILE VIOLET AND HAROLD ESCAPED THROUGH THE WINDO

GUY FAWKES;

OR,

GUNPOWDER, TREASON, AND PLOT.

CHAPTER I.

A WILD RIDE—THE MESSAGE OF LIFE AND DEATH—A DESPERATE ENCOUNTER—THE SCAFFOLD IN SIGHT—TOO LATE—THE AXE FALLS—THE VOW OF VENGEANCE.

"Out of my path! Back! back! on your lives! Away! away!"

Such were the cries hoarsely shouted by a panting horseman as his flying steed clattered through the stony streets of Manchester early one July morn in the year 1604.

Windows were thrown up and doors flung open, from which wondering heads eagerly protruded; while the startled pedestrians had barely time to catch a glimpse of the fleeing pair ere they disappeared in a cloud of dust, like the phantom figures of some wild and appalling dream.

On, on! through the early sun-lit streets they flew, as though they sought, in very truth, to outstrip the wind.

The horse takes a southern course, in the direction of the old Collegiate Church, the tall spires of which could be seen above the house-tops.

The clock in the belfry now chimes the three-quarters, and the pale, anxious, haggard face of the horseman lights up with eager, savage joy at the sound.

He has yet fifteen minutes to reach the gate.

"The Virgin be praised, I shall yet be in time!" he murmured, fervently.

His dress, that of a Spanish trooper, is travel-soiled and covered with dust. He has lost his hat in the long wild ride, and his flowing black hair and waving cloak streamed behind in the wind.

With eager, frantic haste he still urges on his nearly exhausted steed, plunging his spurs into the animal's quivering flanks till they reeked with blood.

"On, on! brave Jewel!" hoarsely cried the traveller. "'Tis cruel to serve thee thus, my faithful beast, but 'tis for thy dear young mistress's sake!"

The sagacious animal seemed as though it understood the purport of its master's words, for, giving an answering neigh, it bounded forward with renewed speed, ringing out showers of red sparks with its clattering hoofs.

Every obstacle in their path is cleared with lightning rapidity, and all regarded the flying horseman and his frantic steed as mad.

Now an ominous murmuring falls on his ear, like the distant roar of the mighty ocean.

He turns a bend in the road, and gives a great, gasping sob.

In the far distance he beholds a dense moving mass of up-turned heads crowded round a platform covered with black.

It is the scaffold!

He can see the tall pikes and halberts of the guard that surround it, glistening in the sun, the grim block of death, and beside it the masked executioner, with his gleaming axe.

A moment later, amid the loud murmur of the surging crowd, a beauteous girl, with long sunny hair, and robed in spotless white, slowly ascends the scaffold, followed by an aged priest.

"Esmé, I come—I come to save thee!" exclaimed the horseman in a frenzy of excitement, drawing a paper from his doublet, and holding it on high.

He is now rapidly approaching the place of execution—nearer and nearer the gallant beast takes him at every stride.

But its breath is short and rasping, its glossy coat dark with sweat and flecked with foam, while its wild glaring eye-balls seem starting from its head and its nostrils appear to breathe forth living fire.

"A reprieve! pardon, pardon!" he shouts, waving the paper frantically aloft.

But his voice is becoming croaky and husky as a raven's. The mob hear him not, but others have heard him, and heeded him, too.

Oliver Blackstock, an officer in the King's Guards, with a couple of his men, suddenly start from out a recess in the thick walls to bar his passage.

"Ah, villain!" cried the advancing horseman, drawing his sword, "was not your rancorous hate glutted when you consigned yon maiden to the scaffold on a false charge because she refused your loathsome addresses, that ye now seek to separate her from her only friend in an hour like this?"

Blackstock, his sinister features ablaze with evil passions, darted forward and made a sweeping side-stroke at the speaker with his heavy sword.

But the horseman received the cut upon his finely-tempered blade, adding as he did so—

"But I have foiled you, vile heretic! See, here is her pardon!" holding it on high.

"Down with the base traitor!" roared the officer, livid with rage.

The words had scarce left his lips, however, when with a swinging stroke of his flashing blade the horseman cut through Blackstock's steel cap, and he reeled backwards with a cry of agony to the ground.

Now the guard rushed forward to impede the daring horseman's progress, charging at him with their long halberts.

But he skilfully parried their deadly thrusts, and, with a couple of slashing blows, cut clean through the pike-heads, leaving the useless wooden staves in their hands; then bounded on his mad career.

"Secure the traitor!" shouted the soldiers after him.

The wild cry was taken up, and another possé of guards rushed forward with levelled partisans to stay the bold rider.

But they fared even worse than their luckless comrades, for the stranger's ready blade passed through the throat of one and wounded another in the sword-arm.

And now he is free once more, with his cursing foes left far behind.

But he deeply regrets the loss of those precious moments which their ill-timed interference has cost him.

If he should yet be too late! The thought almost unmans him.

A few hundred yards more and his purpose of life and death is accomplished.

It was a moment of terrible suspense.

He can now plainly discern every lineament of the lovely victim upon the scaffold.

She is kneeling beside the block in an attitude of prayer, and the venerable father stands before her with the crucifix upraised.

"Oh, for the wings of the wind! On, on, brave steed; but a few roods farther and she is saved."

The panting, sinking steed makes a final effort.

The horseman flourishes the pardon in the air, and endeavours to articulate the words—

"A reprieve!"

But his tongue cleaves to the roof of his mouth, and the words die away in his burning throat.

At that moment the horse gives an unearthly shriek, stumbles blindly forward, and falls stone dead.

Its rider is thrown far into the roadway bruised and bleeding.

But in an instant he is on his feet again, and with the paper still clutched in his right hand he staggers on.

He reaches the edge of the crowd, who, attracted by his wild and excited appearance, instinctively fall back to make a passage for him.

At that terrible moment there is a long, low, gasping cry of horror.

The stranger sees the axe of the executioner gleam in the sunshine for an instant, then descend upon the snowy neck of the kneeling victim.

A spasm of direst agony convulses his deathly pale features as he hears the sickening thud; and tottering to the shelter of a neighbouring tree he murmured, huskily—

"Too late, Esmé, my poor martyred sister; too late!"

He buried his face in his hands, and the convulsive heaving of his stalwart frame tell the agony of his soul.

Starting up suddenly he exclaimed, with appalling vehemence—

"But, by heaven! I will be terribly revenged on her wolfish, inhuman murderers; I swear it by the blessed Virgin! Henceforth I dedicate my life to the cause of restoring the true faith in this misguided land, and of freeing it from the tyranny and oppression of these false, accursed heretics, on whom I will wreak a most terrible retribution!"

"And I will join you, heart and hand," whispered a voice in his ear.

The traveller turned, and beheld a tall, muffled figure, with his broad-leaved hat pulled low to conceal his face.

"Your name, sirrah?" demanded the traveller, suspiciously, placing his hand on the hilt of his sword.

"Robert Catesby; and yours?"

"GUY FAWKES!" was the ready reply.

"Come!" whispered the muffled figure, "and I will lead you where a thousand strong arms and willing hearts are ready to march forth at the call of such a leader as thou."

And linking his arm in that of his companion they disappeared under the shadow of the old town walls.

CHAPTER II.

THE CROSS OF CHARING—THE DANCING GIRL— A TYRANT TASKMASTER—GUY FAWKES SHOWS HIS METAL—A DARK PROPHECY—THE SECRET ASSOCIATION.

A YEAR has passed since the events described in the foregoing chapter. It was towards the close of a long summer day that two travellers drew bridle at the top of Highgate-hill.

The scene which spread before them in the mellow evening light was a lovely one, and both paused a moment to contemplate it.

Wooded slopes and scattered oaks, rich meadow fields, and green hills dotted with sheep, met the eye for miles.

While in the distance London lay, with its scattered spires pointing up in the pure, unclouded air. The silvery Thames glided glittering on, and the sweet sound of the bells of St. John's came in silvery clangour over the valley.

Both travellers were in the prime of youth. One was handsome—eminently so.

His aspect was gallant, his figure commanding, and his countenance open and noble.

Rich nut-brown hair curled about his neck, his broad-leaved hat with its drooping feather was worn—as was the fashion of the day— slightly on one side, a light cuirass of steel was over his doublet, and he wore long silver spurs.

Such was Harold Rookby; while the steed he rode was a powerful roan, bright-eyed and spirited.

His companion, who was of a somewhat slighter stature, was equally well mounted and attired. His face was pale, though not devoid of beauty, and a flitting expression of deep melancholy occasionally overshadowed it, whilst in the depths of his dark, dreamy eyes slumbered a hidden fire.

Commenting on the beauty of the scene, the travellers, putting spurs to their horses, galloped over the country in the direction of Westminster.

At length they turned towards Charing-cross, where, in the ample space, groups of templars and gallants of the court were in the habit of sauntering, amusing themselves by observing the shows, jugglers' feats, and other performances of which this part of London was the established haunt.

As the horsemen drew nearer they perceived a crowd collected round a man playing a sort of mandolin, to the sound of which a young girl was dancing on a tight-rope.

The musician was a sinister-looking man, with dark bushy hair and moustache. His doublet was of green velvet with faded lace, scarlet hose, and he wore Spanish roses in his shoes.

He was handsome, but had a kind of brigand look, which was increased by the sham jewels he ostentatiously wore, whilst in his girdle was stuck a richly-mounted poniard.

He kept the crowd back from intruding upon the magic ring he had formed, and a large, savage-looking wolf-hound lay at his feet, watching his eye, as if prepared to second his efforts by flying at the throat of anyone who should approach too near.

The girl who danced could hardly have been more than sixteen.

She was strikingly beautiful, and this, perhaps, was the reason of the unusual crowd.

There were no tears in her eyes, and yet there was a timid sadness in their expression that looked as though she were used to weeping.

Her movements continued, but they were hardly delicate, as was the fashion of these feats, and she forced a faint smile to linger on her rosy lips.

It was a strange union of gentleness and immodesty, of smiles and suffering, and everyone seemed interested in the beauteous dancing girl.

The travellers dismounted and gave their horses to a groom, who suddenly emerged from a hostelry hard by, and the two young men passed through the crowd and took their stand close to the surly musician.

"Nay, by the rood, Guy," whispered the taller of the two cavaliers to his companion, "we do ill to linger here. Sir Everard and Catesby expect us both; let us mount again and hasten to the meeting-place."

"Tush, man, they leave not Greenwich till curfew," answered Guy Fawkes—for he it was—keeping his fine dark eyes fixed thoughtfully upon the girl, whilst an involuntary sigh escaped his labouring breast. "How like my sainted sister," he murmured to himself, "my murdered Esmé."

"Now, by St. George!" cried Harold Rookby, after a short pause, "it were no small shame to us to tarry here to see a merry-making, after having ridden ten miles with hot haste to bear a message of such moment. Trust me, we are acting most rashly, most indiscreetly."

"I tell you they are not yet arrived," muttered Guy, seeming scarcely to heed his companion's warning. "'Sdeath! Rookby, the poor girl will faint. See how feebly she is moving now! 'Tis a cruel deed to task her thus!"

As he spoke the girl lost her balance and fell from the rope.

She alighted, however, on her feet.

The saturnine musician seized her angrily by the shoulder, and seemed about to strike her.

"Shame! shame!" cried twenty voices at once, whilst Guy Fawkes sprang forward, and with the grasp of a tiger seized the savage musician by the throat.

The wolf-hound started up, and paused in the very act of flying upon the daring intruder, awed for a moment by the bold resolute eye that sought his own.

"Well done, grey doublet! Well flown, battle hawk!" burst from all parts of the crowd, as they eagerly pressed forward to witness the fray.

But the young soldier in an instant let go his hold.

The angered musician had just time to lay his hand upon his poniard hilt, where he kept it, looking with some surprise at the puny figure of him whose grasp had given such rough evidence of superior strength.

"Were I to cudgel thee for thy cruelty, ye would get but thy deserts, but as I know ye would repay it upon the poor wench whom ye were just now about to strike, I will e'en give thee gold that ye may use her well."

"There," continued Guy, taking out a piece of gold, "remember, 'twas the dancing girl that brought ye that."

The man took the gold sullenly.

But the girl came forward and knelt, then clasping her hands and raising her soft eyes, streaming with tears, to our hero's face, said—

"I will read your fortunes, fair sirs," and, rising suddenly up, she threw back the golden ringlets that had fallen over her brow.

"Your hands."

The two young soldiers smiled, but surrendered them to her.

The graceful being first fixed her eyes upon Guy's open palm, which she regarded intently a moment, then said—

"Yours, young sir, is a dark and clouded destiny. You are embarked in a great—a perilous undertaking—one requiring the most determined courage and skill."

Guy Fawkes started slightly, then said, with a grave smile—

"And think ye, fair one, I shall prove equal to the emergency?"

"Of a surety you will."

"And shall I prove successful in this great enterprise?"

"That remains hidden in the great book of mysteries, for see, the lines here break off abruptly."

"But could you not hazard a guess, sweet Sybil?"

"I would rather not speak my thoughts, for your sake, good sir," said the girl, with sudden seriousness.

"Nay, but I insist," urged Guy Fawkes.

"Then I fear me you will fail—more I will not say."

The smile faded from Guy's lips, and was replaced by his old gloomy look.

Turning lightly to Harold Rookby, the girl said, gaily, examining his hand—

"But you love, Sir Cavaliers, you love, and you are rivals."

The two suddenly withdrew their hands as if something had stung them.

The blood rose to the brow of Harold, while Guy turned deadly pale, and his keen eyes flashed again.

"Beshrew me, wench!" said Harold, striving to hide his confusion under a smile. "Ye read fortunes rarely. Now, prithee, is our lady-love young and fair, noble and true; is her hair sunny like thine or the colour of a raven's wing, and the suit of which rival does she favour most?"

"She is both good and beautiful," answered the girl, "yet one whom it is a crime to love. Her description I need not give, it is now present in both your hearts; the suit she favours most I may not tell."

"Marry! this is barren tidings, my fair oracle of Charing," said the young soldier.

"And thine own fortune?" inquired Guy Fawkes, addressing the girl. "Methinks it seems a hard one. Is yon stern man your father?"

"Father! Oh, no, no!"

"Brother?"

"Alas, no!"

"Thy husband, then?"

"No!" cried the girl, covering her face, and sobbing as though she would burst her bodice. "Ask me no more! ask me no more!" she added, removing her white hands from her flushing cheek, while her eyes sparkled angrily through her tears.

"'Tis a wayward girl, by my life," said Harold Rookby. "But to horse, Guy, we have tarried long enough."

By this time the dark-featured musician had removed the two poles to which the rope was attached, and throwing them upon his shoulder was preparing to depart

The girl suddenly grasped the arm of Guy Fawkes, and whispered hurriedly—

"At twilight come hither again; I would serve you."

Then, joining her gloomy companion, she disappeared through the crowd.

The two young soldiers called the groom, and, mounting their horses, rode off in the direction of Westminster.

CHAPTER III.

THE SECRET MEETING—A FAIR CONSPIRATOR— THE ATTACK—GUY FAWKES TO THE RESCUE— A WELL CONTRIVED ESCAPE.

"WELL met, gentlemen; I see, like myself, ye have but just arrived. How fares the mission?"

The speaker was no other than the zealous Catholic and notorious conspirator, Robert Catesby.

It was Guy Fawkes and his companion, Harold Rookby, whom he addressed.

For reply Guy placed a letter in his interrogator's hand.

"Help yourself, I beg," added Catesby, motioning them to the well-spread board, then prepared to peruse the missive. The young men, who were both thirsty and hungry, readily availed themselves of the invitation.

The room in which Robert Catesby and his brother conspirators secretly met to discuss their plans was one of a suite of noble rooms at Hamlyn Hall, the princely residence of Sir Godfrey Hamlyn, a rich and worthy Catholic gentleman, which stood in its own grounds on the banks of the Thames.

"Humph! more converts to our cause!" muttered Catesby, when he had ceased reading. "Though I regret to find ye have failed to prevail on Sir Godfrey to join in our plot, for his princely wealth would have been of inestimable service to us, still I do not wholly despair of winning him over."

At this juncture Violet Hamlyn, a lovely girl of seventeen, tall, and graceful as a lily, entered. She was followed by father Woodruff, a venerable silvery-haired priest.

"I give you good e'en, gentlemen," said the young heiress. "Can I count on my dear father returning to-night?"

The rich colour mounted to her fair cheek as she caught sight of Guy Fawkes and his companion.

Both bowed, but while Harold's handsome face glowed with undisguised pleasure, Guy's went the hue of death, and he involuntarily pressed his left side, as though to suppress some inward pain, though the action passed unnoticed.

"I regret to say, Miss Hamlyn," returned Catesby, courteously, "it may be many days ere your honoured sire returns; indeed, I have written him to remain where he is for the present, for I have strong reasons to believe that our party is suspected and watched by the Privy Council."

"Alas! these are grievous times for our poor persecuted Church," said the lovely girl, sighing deeply.

"You speak truly, Miss Violet," observed Guy Fawkes, earnestly. "The hopes we had indulged in on the accession of King James were false ones—false as the despot himself—false as his promise of tolerance to the Catholic party. He is a godless, bloodthirsty tyrant, who has deprived us of our rights and liberties, persecuted us with overwhelming taxation, fire, and sword, desecrated our altars, and slain our priests. Then who shall wonder when, crushed, insulted, down-trodden, we should seek out means to redress our wrongs?"

Violet shuddered, and seemed about to speak, when she was interrupted by Father Woodruff, who said—

"You reason well, my son; the hour of retribution is approaching. The one appointed by an all-merciful Providence to deliver our fallen and persecuted Church is even now at this moment amongst us," and he fixed his eyes meaningly on Guy Fawkes, who now wore the dreamy, fanatical look of one inspired. "The avenger, chosen by heaven itself, has arrived, and his work, done in secret and darkness, will appal one-half of the enemies of our faith and wholly and utterly exterminate the rest."

The aged priest paused from mingled emotions, and Guy Fawkes said—

"It is past the hour. Where are our brethren?"

"They seek a safer asylum far down the river, whither I would advise you, Miss Hamlyn, to repair," said Catesby, turning to the fair girl; "after to-night it would be unsafe to meet here. The wolfish searchers of the King are abroad to watch our movements."

"Are matters so truly desperate?" asked Violet, fearfully.

"They are indeed, fair maid."

"Then must I indeed leave the cherished home of my childhood? But if 'tis heaven's will it were ill of me to murmur. Come, reverend father; if you will join me I will go at once."

"Alas! my dear child, I will not endanger

your safety with my presence, for know you not that the law hath decreed that it is a crime to harbour a priest, the punishment for which is death?'

"Ye are well informed, thou hoary-headed Papist rogue!" cried a loud, gruff voice, which caused all to start and the three conspirators to place their hands upon their swords.

The same instant Oliver Blackstock, the pursuivant of the Privy Council, with half a dozen soldiers at his back, rushed into the room.

"I arrest you, Miss Hamlyn, in the king's name!" said the villainous pursuivant, pointing at her with his naked sword, "for harbouring and giving shelter to yon Catholic priest, known as Father Woodruff," and he made a motion to secure the terrified girl.

"Stay, vile murderer of my sister!" cried Guy Fawkes, throwing himself between the officer and his pale, shrinking victim. "So, Oliver Blackstock, we meet at last. Defend thyself, for I have a terrible reckoning to settle with thee!" drawing his blade as he spoke.

"I will settle with thee anon!" hissed the pursuivant, with a murderous gleam in his evil eyes. "Stand aside, and let me secure my lawful prey."

"Never, fiend!" cried Guy Fawkes, with swelling breast. "Only over my dead body shall you lay your polluting finger on her fair form."

"A truce to this balderdash!" yelled Blackstock, fiercely. "Hack the vile caitiff to pieces!"

And with a mighty sweep of his sword he rushed to the attack, followed by his pikemen.

But he found no easy antagonist in Guy Fawkes, for he was fighting for the idol of his secret affection—measuring swords with the remorseless villain who had robbed his beloved sister of life.

Catesby, brave as a lion, and Harold Rookby, also equal in valour, immediately joined in the fray.

The ring of their flashing blades filled the chamber with its deadly music, while the overturning of furniture, and the savage cries and oaths, added not a little to the horror of the scene.

Oliver Blackstock was an expert swordsman, or he must have succumbed to Guy Fawkes's desperate and determined onslaught.

The conspirators had purposely backed further into the apartment to afford Violet, whom they carefully shielded, an opportunity of escaping by the open door.

Observing the stratagem, a couple of the men-at-arms rushed forward to intercept the fair fugitive, when Harold, who was nearest, threw himself in front of Violet to protect her from their violence.

Both thrust at him with their pikes at the same moment.

The undaunted youth deftly received one on guard, but missed the other, which struck him in the knee-joint, and Violet uttered a piercing shriek as she saw Harold fall heavily to the ground.

The soldier raised his pike to despatch him.

But quick as thought Guy Fawkes, who had just disarmed his opponent, drew his petronel and fired at the ruffian.

The man uttered a deep groan and fell back into the arms of his companion.

"Fly, Violet, fly!" exclaimed Guy Fawkes.

The fair girl—seeing Harold in the act of rising to his feet, for his wound was more sudden than severe—darted through the doorway like a glancing sunbeam.

"Up the stairs, Violet, to the window over the stables," called out Harold, and he made a move for the door himself, with a hope of following Violet, when he was met by the comrade of the dead soldier.

But instantly seizing the pointed pike-head, he sent his keen blade through the fleshy part of the fellow's shoulder, then darted up the broad staircase after the fleeing girl.

Guy Fawkes had fought his way to the foot of the stairs, which passage he intended to hold until Violet had made good her escape.

And though hotly pressed by two sturdy men-at-arms he gallantly stood his ground.

To Catesby was left the task of defending the priest, which he did with the most accomplished skill and heroic bravery, though fiercely beset by the furious pursuivant and a couple of men-at-arms.

But on observing the probable escape of his fair victim and his hated foe, Guy Fawkes, Oliver Blackstock abandoned his attack upon Catesby, and rushed to the assault of Guy Fawkes.

Catesby's assailants, being thus thrown off their guard a moment, enabled the wily conspirator to touch a knob in the wainscot.

Instantly a panel rolled back.

"Enter, father, quick—to the river!" said Catesby, hurriedly pushing the worthy man through the aperture, then darting through himself, just as the pikes of the baffled soldiers came thundering upon the closed panel, which they quickly beat in, and started off in fruitless pursuit.

Meanwhile Guy Fawkes had been compelled to retreat step by step, under the desperate charge of Blackstock and his men, till he reached the top step of the landing, when suddenly, through the open window in the corridor, he heard the clatter of horses' hoofs.

"They have escaped," he cried, triumphantly, as he turned and beheld Violet and Harold galloping madly across the park.

Taking advantage of his momentary distraction, one of the soldiers, whose pike-staff had been shattered by the blade of Guy Fawkes, at once rushed forward and seized him.

But he had no common foe to contend with.

Guy Fawkes caught the fellow round the waist, and, exerting his herculean strength, threw him with terrific force against the ancient balustrade.

It gave way with a crash, and the unfortunate wretch was precipitated below, where he lay a shattered corpse.

All started back with a cry of horror, while Guy Fawkes, darting along the corridor, was in the act of climbing through the window, by which Violet and Harold had effected their escape, when the pursuivant sprang forward, and, grasping him by the cloak, exclaimed—

"Devil! I have thee!"

"Take that, presumptuous villain!" cried Guy Fawkes, striking him a violent blow between the eyes with his clubbed petronel. "When next we meet beware! for I will show thee but little mercy."

QUICK AS A TIGER'S BOUND THE ASSASSIN STARTED BACK AND PREPARED TO DEFEND HIMSELF.

And, springing through the window, he dropped to the ground, just in time to escape a deadly volley fired at him from the matchlocks of a fresh body of men-at-arms, who had suddenly burst upon the scene.

CHAPTER IV.

GUY FAWKES KEEPS HIS APPOINTMENT WITH THE DANCING GIRL—A COWARDLY ATTACK AND A FIERCE ENCOUNTER—FLIGHT AND PURSUIT OF THE WOULD-BE ASSASSIN.

AFTER his escape from Hamlyn Hall Guy Fawkes urged on his willing steed till he came in sight of Westminster Abbey.

Then turning his horse's head in the direction of Charing-cross he now remembered for the first time the dancing girl and her request to see him again at midnight.

Reaching the spot just as the clock of the palace of Whitehall tolled the hour of twelve, he drew rein and glanced hastily around.

All was silent as the grave.

The scattered houses lay glittering in the moonbeams—the whole place was deserted.

Suddenly his eye caught an object at the foot of the cross.

He approached it.

It was a female form seated there, solitary and alone, with her golden head drooping upon her bosom.

The sound of the horse's hoofs aroused her.

She raised her head, and Guy Fawkes, to his surprise, recognised at once the sweet, pensive features of the dancing girl.

Guy drew in his impatient steed, saying—

"Good e'en, sweetheart; why tarry ye here so late? Beshrew the horse! He plunges as if the devil switched him! Why keep ye so lone a watch, my fair fortune-teller? Saint Agnes! what hails the horse?" continued Guy Fawkes, holding a tight rein, while the fiery animal snorted as if with fear, and made desperate efforts to dash off.

The girl rose and looked fearfully round.

No one appeared in sight.

She approached nearer, but the horse now swerved from the cross, and, maddened by the check with which his rider held him, reared suddenly.

Guy Fawkes barely had time to fling himself from the saddle when the animal, who had lost his balance, rolled on its side.

Then, starting up, it galloped off without its rider.

Again the girl looked anxiously around, but still no one was in view.

Both stood for a moment or two without speaking, until the sound of the retreating horse died away on the stillness of the night.

"I have waited for you," said the girl, in those touching accents which so vividly reminded Guy of his sainted sister. "I have waited until my eyes grew heavy with watching. Twice I rose to go away. Yet something always whispered me that you would come. And now," continued she, with animation, while an expression of joy shot over her pale but beautiful countenance, "now you are come—you promised you would meet me here."

Guy Fawkes looked puzzled.

"My eyes searched for you everywhere, but I saw you not," resumed the girl. "The long hours passed away, and at curfew they made

us leave the cross. I went home; but something told me you would yet be here. I crept out unperceived and came hither again. 'Tis a fair night, Sir Cavalier; my watch has been lonely, but not sad."

"Nay, by St. Agnes!" exclaimed Guy Fawkes, "it must have been an irksome and a dreary one, and I grieve that ye have held it for me. Hark, the abbey bell chimes the half hour. It is a warning I must needs heed, not for myself, but for the missive which I bear."

He paused to listen a moment, then added—

"Quick, then, my gentle watcher, and tell me why ye sought a meeting. Your words to-day showed that ye know more of my fortunes than the stranger speaks. St. Mary! Why weep ye?"

"I would watch long days and sleepless nights," replied the girl, her eyes sparkling with tears, "to greet again a kind look and a gentle tone."

"And are these so rare with thee, sweetheart, that ye rate them at so high a price?"

"I have rarely known them," answered the girl. "I have seen a scoff on every lip and heard reproach from every tongue. Marvel not, then, Sir Cavalier, that a kind word is dear to me."

Guy looked at her keenly.

"There are some," he said, "who would interpret your language different from me, and yet, by my soul, I think they would read it wrong."

The girl blushed to the forehead.

"I have a favour to ask of thee," she said, "for one who is dear to me. Wilt grant it, Sir Cavalier?"

"Marry! let's hear it first."

"I have a brother, a noble-hearted and a gallant boy. He is about to commence a life of misery and crime. He is yet pure in heart, generous, kind. Oh, save him! save him!" she cried, clasping her hands and raising her eyes earnestly to his.

"But how, my fair pleader? Tell me how I can do this, and if I may compass it I will."

"Make him your foot page," she continued. "He will serve you truly. He will attend your steps, watch your couch, and bear a message to your lady-love. He is bold and fearless, and faithful as the steel ye wear."

"Before I answer ye, my pretty prophetess," returned Guy Fawkes, musingly, "I must crave your favour to tell me of my own fortunes. This evening your words showed that ye knew more of them than I deemed was known to any but one."

"I know more of them than ye wot," said the girl, "and more, Sir Cavalier, than would gladden thee."

"What!" exclaimed Guy Fawkes, bitterly. "Are they then so dark that even the mummer's legend will not cast a hope upon them?"

The girl was silent.

"Come, child, time presses," added Guy Fawkes, with a bitter sigh. "I bear a letter, which, if it fell in to strange hands, might change the destinies of the realm. Ah, what noise was that?"

They both looked anxiously around them, but no living object appeared in sight.

The very shadows lay dark and motionless, for the moon was without a cloud.

"I heard nought," said the girl, who had turned suddenly pale and approached closer to her companion.

Guy Fawkes laid his hands on her shoulders and gazed on her beautiful countenance with an expression of admiration; then he murmured to himself, "How like Esmé's living image."

Aloud he continued—

"Quick, my sweet one, what saidst thou of this boy? Though, in good sooth, I have small need for pages."

"Nay, but the boy hath need for thee," she said, archly.

"Fairly answered, kind heart; but how dare I trust one, educated as you hint he has been, with secrets that would bring peers to the block?'

"Oh, he will be no spy," cried the girl, with enthusiasm; "his nature is candid and bold; poor boy, he will serve you faithfully and well. Oh, then, save him from the dreadful life which is in store for him—from the craft and snares of base and wicked men, who in time will make him as base as they—a brawler and a thief, a common stabber and a fiend—oh, save him from such a fate, I implore ye!"

She covered her face with her hands and sobbed aloud.

"'Tis enough," said Guy Fawkes, deeply moved; "your suit is granted, though it perilled my head. But why quit ye not a life that has such associates!"

"I may not—cannot quit it now."

"You speak in riddles. That your life is a hard and cruel one I myself was witness of. Your own words give it a darker character even than my fears forboded. Why, then, do you not abandon it?"

"I tell you I cannot—dare not!"

"Dare not! You love it, then?"

"You question but to scoff me," said the excited girl.

"Nay, my poor wench, nay."

"Then question me no more." She paused a moment, then added, "but my brother, my brother, let us speak of him."

"I will do what ye ask, my poor girl," said Guy Fawkes, sadly. "To-morrow let him come to me at"—and he whispered in her ear—"and if I cannot give him service myself I will find it for him amongst those who will treat him as their own."

The girl seized his hand and pressed it passionately to her burning lips.

"Now mark me," she said, in a trembling whisper, "you are beset with enemies on all sides."

"Faith! I had good proof of that not an hour since at the hands of the minions of the king, and barely escaped with my life."

"'Tis not the officers of the crown alone whom ye have to fear—there are others," said the girl, in a cautious, meaning tone. "Others who profess to serve the same dark and dangerous cause ye yourself are embarked in. Traitors, who—"

But the words were cut short.

A dark figure sprang suddenly from the other side of the cross, and, grasping Guy Fawkes, struck a blow at him with a long, keen dagger.

But the girl, with a wild scream, had bounded to Guy's neck and interposed between the assassin and his intended victim.

The blow fell, but Guy was untouched.

It struck the girl under the shoulder, and she fell bleeding to the earth.

Ere the assassin's arm could be raised again Guy Fawkes had seized him by the wrist and wrenched the murderous weapon from his grasp.

Another instant and he had struck it into the villain's throat.

Quick as a tiger's bound the assassin started back, and, drawing a long Spanish rapier, prepared to defend himself.

With the instinct which bold minds possess in those moments when cowards shrink, the sword of Guy Fawkes was already bared, and sprang to that of his assailant with hearty good will.

Then the clash of steel resounded.

The passes were rapid and deadly—the bright blades flickered like lightning in the clear moonlight—eye, with the keen glance of the basilisk, was fixed on eye, and both burned with the fellness of the thirst for blood.

Guy's mind at that terrible moment told him that the face before him was one which he had seen before—but it was no time to go in quest of memories.

His soul was frenzied with the wish to kill, and while his strong wrist felt his thirsty sword-point turned aside he almost yelled with madness.

Both were men of fierce passions—the one, indeed, had many noble qualities which the other did not possess—but these were forgotten now. They met with the equality which hate confers—their rapid swords flashed with the same rancorous thrusts, and the features of both had the same demon look of death.

With the one it was the wild, exulting passion to destroy; with the other, the fiendish echo with which man's bosom still promptly responds to the vengeful hand of justice—blood for blood.

Both were good swordsmen.

Guy Fawkes's assailant had the longer blade, but this advantage, when men fight within fearless distance, is but a slight one.

The clash of their swords rang clearly on the calm night air, and these were soon blended with the thick-breathed threat and the savage cry of baffled revenge.

Guy, whose excitement continued to increase, began gradually to heed less his own defence than the frenzy to assail, and made several desperate efforts to close with his adversary.

But these, from their maddened rapidity, served him also as a guard. His opponent retreated, with cooler skill, to allow this fury to exhaust itself.

Then the sound of approaching horsemen—in a momentary pause of the combat—rang loudly in their ears.

The assassin started at the sound, and guessed that a rescue was at hand.

Making one desperate lunge at his assailant, which pierced his doublet and slightly wounded him in the side, almost in the act he bounded past him and dashed forward towards Temple Bar. Guy Fawkes followed hotly.

Down they rushed through the long, wide Strand, the high stone houses standing out boldly on either side, with the moonbeams falling on the fantastic ovals, niches, and angles.

The streets were now perfectly deserted.

The night watch had heard the clash of steel, and wisely wandered towards St. Giles's-fields.

The peaceful citizens, whose dreamy ears heard Guy Fawkes's maddening shout as he rushed past their windows, only turned petulantly on their couches and breathed a curse on the Templars, to whom they ascribed every disturbance of the times.

The fugitive turned at length from the open street, and darted down a narrow lane leading towards the river.

The ground was damp and miry, and on both sides were garden walls.

A house, or rather a court of houses, appeared at the extremity of the lane.

They were high and gloomy-looking, and clustered within a narrow space; a dark passage formed their common entry.

Down this passage the fugitive rushed with a fleet and fearless step Guy, without pausing to consider whither he was entering, also plunged into the darkness, waving his naked sword.

Guy Fawkes proceeded at full speed along the vaulted passage, which seemed to be of unusual length.

The air felt damp and oppressive, and the sound of his heavy boots and long jingling spurs fell on the ear dead and hollow.

Still the fugitive passed rapidly on, followed by his excited pursuer.

Guy Fawkes now saw that instead of going in the direction of the issue from the archway into the interior court he had been led into another, probably a branch of the former, and evidently running towards the river.

The dampness of the place seemed greater, and the earthy, tomb like sensation was increased by the silence and the darkness of of this suspicious retreat.

Although ignorant of every spot his footsteps covered, and conscious that he might be rushing on to his destruction, and might be attacked secretly in the position which the darkness and his ignorance of the place created, Guy Fawkes only thought of the blow which had struck the poor girl instead of himself, and had saved his life, perhaps at the expense of her own.

He pressed forward with unabated fury, guiding his steps by those of the fugitive; the thick air and his own exertions made him pant, but it was like the hoarse threatenings of a pursuing bloodhound baffled of its prey.

The man he followed was a bad one, and the bright gold which would be given him for the letter of the conspirators, which he knew Guy Fawkes bore, seemed to glitter before his eyes. He was near friends, also, and his antagonist almost in his power.

But he felt a sinking of heart; the sounds of rage which still hung upon his ear seemed like the omens of death.

He had raised in the bosom of another a devil fiercer than his own, and one which the instincts of his nature made him shrink from.

He was followed by one whom he felt was thirsting for his blood—who would fly at him like a tiger, heedless of his own safety, bent only on destroying.

His heart forsook him. Although a bold man and a villain, there was something in the wild death yell which in the fearful intensity of the hate with which he was pursued, fairly unmanned him.

And he fled as the coward flies, with a dread not only of what he might suffer, but of the very being that pursued him.

The fugitive hastily struck his sword-hilt on the iron bar of a grated door that opposed his progress until it rung again, then turned quickly round and faced his pursuer.

It was difficult to tell if the blow was occasioned by the impetuosity with which he had rushed against an unknown obstacle, or whether it was intended as a signal to anyone on the other side.

CHAPTER V.

RUSHING INTO THE JAWS OF THE ENEMY—BROUGHT TO BAY—A NARROW ESCAPE—THE MYSTERIOUS VISITOR.

GUY FAWKES did not pause a moment to consider the question that arose in his mind as to whether the blow which struck him was intentional or otherwise, but shouted—

"Villain, I have thee now!" and pressed in upon him hotly.

Their swords, with a ringing clash, crossed in the darkness.

It was a fiendish struggle!

Guy Fawkes was stoutly opposed; his fierce thrusts were turned aside by the sweeping parries of a strong arm. The sparks flashed from their dented swords, and he himself was furiously assailed in turn.

Skill was now of no avail!

They fought amid the most profound darkness, in a place like a funeral vault, damp and chilly as the grave.

A few moments more, and one or both must have fallen.

But now the sound of advancing footsteps was heard on the inner side, and a faint gleam of light shot through the crevices of the grated door.

Guy Fawkes, in spite of his efforts, was still pressed upon, and compelled to retreat a few paces, when the creaking door was hastily opened by a tall, bearded man, holding a lighted torch above his head.

Guy Fawkes's opponent retreated slowly, still facing his adversary; but no sooner had he passed the door than it was hastily shut, and Guy Fawkes was again in darkness.

He heard for a moment what seemed to be a sharp dispute between the two men, one of whose voices appeared to be familiar to him, on the other side of the door.

The words sank to a lower tone. This was followed by the sounds of retreating footsteps and the shrinking glimmer of receding light.

At length light and sound died away together, and Guy Fawkes felt he was alone.

He leaned against the wall—a sudden depression of spirits succeeding his excitement.

He thought of the dancing-girl whom a few minutes ago he had seen struck down at his feet; and now, for the first time, remembered that the face of his opponent was that of her tyrant taskmaster.

He instantly resolved to go in quest of her.

He was far from considering himself safe where he was; and now that the frenzy of passion had subsided, began to fear that he might be seized, and the letter, urging Sir Godfrey Hamlyn to join the plotters in their conspiracy against the King, might fall into the hands of their enemies.

Guy Fawkes now blamed himself for having rashly entered into such needless hazard, and reproached-himself bitterly for having left the poor dancing girl lying bleeding at the foot of the cross.

To reach the open air, however, was no easy task.

The labyrinth of passages was intricate, and led to an extensive communication with other buildings.

Guy Fawkes, however, groped his way, and, retreating with much slower progress than he had advanced, succeeded in coming in sight of the entrance, into which the moonlight was pouring.

He heard the creaking of bars behind him and the noise of many tongues, but he hurried on towards the spot where the light was shining, and in a few seconds stood in the open air.

He now breathed freer; but, still considering himself in danger of pursuit, he passed rapidly along the narrow lane, and reached the Strand.

He then hastened anxiously towards Charing-cross.

The neighbourhood was quiet and deserted; the moon shone brilliantly in the starlit sky.

All was open to its soft light here, and lay beneath it in quiet beauty.

The long fields stretched dreamily on one side, the dark green woods of St. James's clustered on the other, and here and there in the distance were narrow glimpses of the glittering Thames.

No one was near the cross—the dancing-girl had disappeared.

Not a living soul was to be seen. Yet stay!

Suddenly, as though it had sprung from out the bowels of the earth, a tall masked and cloaked figure caught his eyes, standing beneath the dark and forbidding portal of Zach Horlock, the astrologer's shunned abode.

From whence had he come?

Guy Fawkes was certain he was not there a few moments previous.

Unable to find a solution to this suspicious and mysterious circumstance, Guy Fawkes concealed himself in the deep shadow of the cross to watch the stranger's movements.

The masked figure, after looking cautiously about, and finding the coast clear, knocked in a peculiar manner on the stout oaken door.

Then, retreating into the roadway, he looked up at the black and weather-stained casement.

He waited a few seconds, and a light appeared in the misty pane. He approached the door once more and knocked again.

On the appearance of a second light in the window he darted down a narrow passage, which led to the rear of the abode of mystery, and disappeared.

But even as he did so the loosened mask slipped from his face, and his strongly-marked features became plainly discernible in the bright moonlight.

"Sir Sidney Wildbrook," exclaimed Guy Fawkes, in amazement. "There is some evil brewing, of that I am convinced. I will watch, or our great plan may yet be defeated."

And, approaching stealthily in the direction taken by the mysterious midnight visitor, Guy Fawkes followed in his footsteps like a tiger which scents its prey.

CHAPTER VI.

THE ABODE OF HORLOCK THE MAGICIAN—A DIABOLICAL PLOT—THE BLACK ART—A SCENE OF TERROR—AN UNEXPECTED ATTACK.

THE magician Horlock's sacred retreat was a dark Gothic chamber, in the centre of which was a large table, containing a number of cabalistic characters, charms, retorts, phials, &c., surmounted by a magic mirror, or glass of fate, which, through a strange mystic light, from some unknown source, emitted a weird, preternatural halo over every object on which it glanced.

In this grim abode of mystery and wickedness sat two persons, Sir Sidney Wildbrook—a wily Catholic nobleman, and a favourite with King James, though secretly plotting with the conspirators, whose cause he professed to serve—and the magician Horlock himself.

The magician was a short and meagre figure, with small red eyes, a sharp aquiline nose, black beard and brows, and a somewhat repulsive and malignant expression of countenance.

"Have no fear for me, good sir," said Sir Sidney, in answer to some remark of the magician's. "There is small chance of my courage failing me, though as yet I have not been present at these orgies. Sayest thou the Witch of the Marsh is here, and assisted by Owen Rainham?"

"They have been busily engaged, your grace, since noon," said the magician. "At that hour the waxen image was completed and the fatal fire lighted. From that hour shall King James begin to waste and wither away, and continue so to do, until the throne of England shall be left vacant for a worthier occupant."

"Thanks, good Horlock," said Sir Sidney, giving the man of mystery a well-filled purse. "Do I not well? Our Blessed Lady knows that it is not for the sake of gratifying any ambitious thoughts of my own that I enter on this seemingly unhallowed work, but in compassion of the miseries which my unhappy brethren endure under the sway of the tyrant James."

"Thou dost indeed well," said the obsequious conjurer, "your grace is but to blame for having so long delayed to avail yourself of that knowledge and those arts into the mysteries of which your poor servant has been the unworthy means of initiating you, for the purpose of putting an end to the evils with which this misguided country is overwhelmed."

"True, true, good Horlock," said the nobleman, with an anxious brow; "yet I fain would receive some more certain assurance as to the King's and my own future destiny. When wilt thou invoke to my presence the spirit who is to answer such questions as I shall propound?"

When the unscrupulous but superstitious nobleman asked these questions he determined in his own mind that, if the spirit raised should prophesy that the King would fall a victim to the deadly plot which Guy Fawkes and his companions had laid for him, he would remain true to his oath of allegiance to them, but if they should fail he would espouse the cause of the King.

"Your grace," said the magician, after a pause, "it is by severe and painful penance, anxious watching, and long fasting alone, that I could prevail upon the invisible power whom I serve to gratify your grace's desire."

Whereupon the knight took a rich and massive collar of gold from his neck and gave it to the magician, adding—

"Hasten the period at which my desires may be gratified, good Horlock, I pray thee."

"Your bidding shall be done!" said the magician, waving his wand thrice round his head. "Behold!"

Suddenly a lurid red light appeared on the hearth at the further end of the room.

Over it cowered two misshapen forms. One was a woman, bent nearly double with age and infirmity—her yellow cheek was sunken and hollow, her lips dry and withered. This was the Witch of the Marsh.

She seemed to be mumbling some diabolical prayer or incantation, while her right hand, resting on a stick, moved to and fro in accompaniment to the spell she was uttering.

Her companion, who was a lean and shrivelled old man, knelt by the fire, attentively perusing a large black volume.

The nobleman, bold of heart as he was, could not help shuddering, especially as, although they stood in the full blaze of the fire, their figures cast no shadow on the floor of the apartment.

At a given signal the witch drew a cover from off a muffled form upon a low couch, and revealed a life-size waxen image, which needed not the crown upon its head to tell him that it was intended to represent King James, so faithful a portraiture of the monarch did it present.

The figure, wasting beneath the heat of the fire, now presented the appearance of a man emaciated by illness, and fast sinking into the grave.

"Rare artists," murmured the plotting nobleman; "accept the thanks of Sir Sidney Wildbrook, and doubt not that you shall be substantially rewarded. But tell me, I pray thee, when the work shall be accomplished."

"When yonder image sinks to the ground," said the witch, in a discordant shriek, "destroyed and dissolved in the flames, then will the spirit of James of England melt beneath the influence of his disease and mingle with the elements."

"Ah! sayest thou so?" cried the nobleman, triumphantly. "That is well—that is well. Yet," he added, gravely, "these signs and symbols may be delusive. Horlock, I claim the performance of thy promise; call up a spirit that shall give answers to such questions as I may propound."

"Your grace," said the magician, "shall be obeyed. Yet, pardon me, but I fear your courage may fail."

"Nay, nay, dotard!" exclaimed the nobleman, wrathfully; "fear not my courage. I have gone thus far, and will not now recede."

The magician bowed respectfully, and taking a white wand in his hand, advanced into the centre of the apartment.

With his wand he described a circle on the floor, which he traversed three times, pouring from a phial the while a blood-red liquor, and chanting in a low and solemn tone something utterly unintelligible to Sir Sidney.

He then threw himself upon the floor and groaned bitterly for several seconds.

Then starting up he rushed towards the fire, seized the volume which Owen Rainham held in his hand, and, returning to the circle, began to read loudly and rapidly from it, but still in an unknown language.

At length he closed the volume, bowed reverentially three times, and retreated backwards out of the circle.

At that moment came the solemn tolling of a bell.

Then a noise like the sound of distant thunder was heard, the door of the apartment opened, and a strange, ghostly, grotesque figure, which could not be distinctly seen, appeared before them.

A wild cry burst from the lips of Sir Sidney at the sight of the dread apparition, and even from those of Rainham and the witch.

"For the love of the Virgin be silent!" said the magician, in a whisper. "Waste not these precious moments in idle alarm. Demand what ye will of the spirit, but be courageous and brief."

"Tell me," said Sir Sidney, advancing tremblingly towards the magic circle, "what fate awaits King James?"

He gazed with anxiously straining eyes upon the unearthly being, as, in an awful voice, the spirit answered—

"King James from earth shall fly
Swiftly and speedily as I."

"Ah! that is well," cried Sir Sidney, "for now I can keep inviolate my oath of assistance and secrecy to the supporters of our holy Church."

"But had the prediction been reversed thou wouldst have embraced the cause of the King, vile traitor," hissed an unknown voice in a subdued tone.

"Now, one question more," continued the knight.

"In heaven's name be speedy, your grace!" cried the magician, gazing anxiously on the magic mirror, on which the red rays of the fire fell at that moment, "for the midnight hour is approaching, and my power over yon spirit is fast waning."

"Tell me, then," said the nobleman, half-fearful to put the question—"tell me of my own future fate."

The answer was given in a speedy and peculiarly impressive tone:—

"The secrets of thy future fate
Let my attending spirits state,
Tell the Lord of Wildbrook's doom,
Come, attending spirits, come!"

The spirit, as he finished his prediction, was seen to apply something to his lips; no unearthly sound was heard to proceed from them, but the loud blast of a bugle.

All started back in affright.

A responsive shout was heard, the doors were burst open, and a number of masked men, with drawn swords, and carrying lighted torches, rushed in.

"Base traitor and villain!" thundered the pretended spirit, throwing aside his disguise and revealing the stern, relentless features of Guy Fawkes; "your hour has come!"

At the sudden and wholly unexpected appearance of Guy Fawkes and his followers, Sir Sidney Wildbrook stood speechless and transfixed with amazement.

With a vengeful cry of "Down with the base traitor!" they rushed furiously upon the recreant knight, their flashing swords gleaming fiercely in the mystic light, and he would

GUY FAWKES

Or Gunpowder, Treason, and Plot.

GUY FAWKES CAUGHT UP A FLAMING BRAND AND STRUCK THE MONK A STUNNING BLOW WITH THE FIERY WEAPON.

assuredly have fallen a victim to their wild fury but for the timely intervention of the magician.

Drawing a phial from under his robe, Horlock instantly sprinkled its contents upon the floor in front of the advancing conspirators.

Like a flash a wall of dense, stifling vapour rose between them and their foes, through which the conspirators found it wholly impossible to pass.

Several minutes elapsed ere the blinding, choking fumes had cleared, and then it was found that Sir Sidney and the magician had vanished, although there appeared to be no way of escape possible except through the stout oak flooring.

The witch, too, and her companion had also disappeared ; but how the conspirators were utterly at a loss to conjecture, as they were convinced they had not escaped by the door.

"Let us instantly search this ill-omened abode of sorcery and crime till we discover the false, perfidious wretch !" cried Guy Fawkes, sternly ; "leave not a hole or corner unexplored."

A deep murmur of assent was returned to this appeal.

His followers consisted of Ambrose Rockwood, Thomas and Robert Winter, and John Wright.

While Guy Fawkes and Rockwood examined the carved panelling in the hope of finding some secret spring or sliding-panel, their companions were similarly engaged upon the floor, in the expectation of discovering some hidden traps or other outlet.

But their efforts remained unrewarded by any such discovery.

In vain they searched the many and curious little rooms, presses, cupboards, cellars, and laboratory, sounding the walls, and piercing the wainscoting and beds with their swords.

The fugitives had vanished as though they had been mere creations of the shadow.

"That the wizard Horlock deals in the black art and has spirited away the traitor, Sir Sidney, I am convinced," said Guy Fawkes, gloomily, coming to a halt. "Further search were vain, and to tarry here longer would be fraught with direct danger."

"Do ye apprehend, Guy Fawkes, that Sir Sidney would betray us?" observed Robert Winter.

"Faith ! 'tis difficult to say what the arch-traitor may not do," responded Guy Fawkes, knitting his brows fiercely.

"Marry ! while he is at large our very lives hang by a thread !" said Ambrose Rockwood.

"He must be captured or silenced at any hazard," vociferated John Wright.

"He must !" exclaimed Guy Fawkes ; "let that task be mine ! Come, we must be gone !"

And they secretly and silently left the grim abode of the wizard by the private way.

Threading their way cautiously along in the darkness, under cover of the hanging trees in St. James's Park, Guy Fawkes hastened on in the direction of a famous hostelry, where they were sometimes wont to meet in secret.

"Whither would ye go?" said Rockwood.

"Back to the Black Dragon, where I found ye awhile since, when I sought thine aid," answered Guy Fawkes

"Nay, let us go not there ; I mistrust the place," rejoined Rockwood. "Had ye been

but a few moments later ye would not have found us there. Our suspicions have been aroused against the host, and we have resolved never to hold another meeting there."

"Have ye then fixed on any other place of rendezvous ?"

"In good sooth that have we," returned the former speaker. "Robert Winter has secured for us a house at Southwark, on the banks of the river, which, it is said, formerly belonged to a small merchant, but which he suspects is in reality the property of a prosperous river pirate."

"Good !" said Guy Fawkes ; "let us repair thither at once."

By this time they had reached Westminster-stairs, and, hailing a wherry—for the waterman lay asleep in his own boat—the conspirators stepped in, and soon after were being rowed rapidly towards their destination.

They landed some distance from the house by the riverside. Having paid their fare, they cautiously made their way to the rear of the curious old dwelling.

A dim light was burning in the back casement, as though they were expected.

Finding the coast clear, Guy Fawkes approached the door, and tapped softly and in a peculiar manner upon the panel.

A moment or two later the door was silently opened by a man bearing a guarded light, and all passed in, one at a time, unobserved by anyone.

The conspirator, Mark Swinton, who awaited their coming, having placed wine and eatables before them in the long room at the back of the house, they readily sat down to the welcome repast and talked over their plans.

It was finally arranged that Guy Fawkes should proceed to Westminster on the following evening to direct that the powder, with which it was intended to blow up the Parliament House, and which he had bought of a smuggler, should be secretly conveyed to the old house at Southwark.

Guy Fawkes then early retired to his room, for he was anxious to be alone.

Removing his hat and cloak, he opened his doublet, and drew a small miniature from his bosom, which he pressed to his lips.

He threw himself into a seat, and, still holding the portrait before his eyes, gazed fondly on it.

It was a beautiful countenance. The eyes, of deep hazel, were pensive and sweet, the little mouth was full and exquisitely formed, the whole being expressive of winning grace and rarest loveliness.

In short, it was no other than the miniature of Violet Hamlyn.

Guy's fine features glowed with admiration and passionate love, and his bosom heaved tumultuously.

His dark eyes drank in the look of that beautiful face as though it gazed upon him ; he kissed again the miniature, and placed it with fond gentleness in his bosom.

It was one of those moments when love, by its own intensity, triumphs over the fact that it is not returned.

Suddenly he started, for there was blood upon his hand—it was that of the poor dancing girl.

Then the gloom again came over his soul.

He pressed his hand to his throbbing brow, and muttered aloud, in passionate bitterness—

"Fool! fool! What have I to do with love?"

CHAPTER VII.

THE THAMES BY NIGHT—THE MYSTERIOUS MESSENGER—STARTLING NEWS—VIOLET'S PERIL—GUY FAWKES'S DESPAIR—A DEADLY RESOLVE

IT was early in the evening of the following day that Guy Fawkes ventured forth on his dangerous mission.

A boat was near at hand, into which he instantly sprang, giving the waterman instructions to land him at Westminster-fields.

The evening was a lovely one—the rich rays of the declining sun was flashing on the smooth waters of the Thames, and the city bells were sounding dreamily through the dim, hazy air.

On his left lay the green fields of Lambeth, studded with noble trees, while to the right the scented breeze came over a hundred lovely gardens filled with fragrant flowers.

Flags with emblazoned arms floated on high from the housetops, gaily painted barges were bearing richly-dressed gallants to scenes of midnight revelry, and the sounds of mirth and music that issued from the water showed how heartily those on board were disposed to laugh away the hours.

While nearer, in deep swelling tones, came the sound of the organ and the chant of monks as they sang their matin hymn.

Guy Fawkes became deeply impressed, and, as the solemn strains fell upon his ear, the thought that he was the chosen of heaven for the restoration of his unhappy Church became more firmly rooted than ever in his superstitious mind.

When alone, in the silent hour of night, he seemed conscious of a shadowy presence ever urging him on to the path of glory—a dim, mysterious, spectral form—that haunted his lonely footsteps, and that ever pointed in the direction of the Parliament Houses.

Starting from the deep reverie into which he had fallen, Guy Fawkes suddenly looked up and beheld a cloaked figure standing in the shadow of Westminster-stairs.

The figure made a sign, intelligible only to Guy Fawkes, who, ordering the wherry to stop, instantly sprang upon the landing-stage, and disappeared in company of the stranger.

When they reached the shelter of the tall, overhanging trees in Westminster-fields Guy Fawkes turned towards his companion and said—

"Well, Redman, why seek me thus unexpectedly?"

"To tell you that Miss Hamlyn is in the hands of the accursed heretics!" returned the conspirator Redmond.

"Merciful heaven! Violet in the hands of our wolfish foes?" gasped Guy Fawkes, turning deadly pale, and staggering as though he had received a mortal blow.

But almost instantly recovering his stern, imperturbable demeanour, he added—

"But I thought she had, in company of Harold Rookby, successfully effected her flight from Hamlyn House when besieged by the minions of the King."

"That is correct," returned Redman; "they reached Battersea in safety, but Miss Hamlyn's horse here cast a shoe, and she took refuge in the cottage of a peasant, while Master Harold Rookby went in quest of the village smith in order to get the horse re-shod. During his absence the cottage was attacked by the soldiers of the King, and Miss Hamlyn carried off."

"This is terrible!" cried Guy Fawkes, deeply agitated. "In the hands of her fiendish captors—her fate will most assuredly be a fearful one."

"She will be questioned, and, if she refuses to betray us, tortured! Holy Mother of Mercy, the thought of her fair form being contaminated by the rude touch of those ruthless butchers, and her beauteous limbs torn asunder on the horrid rack, almost drives me mad."

"Oh, would that I could suffer in her stead; by the rood, I would even forego my great and holy purpose rather than she should suffer such a frightful doom."

"There will be no necessity for that, I hope," returned Redman. "Our agent, Paul Jerome, the young priest, secretly wrote to Harold Rookby, informing him that Miss Violet is incarcerated in the vaults of the old monastery of Chelsea."

"Well, man; and did he not instantly fly to her rescue?" cried Guy Fawkes, with impatience.

"He did, with a score or more followers at his back, and fully armed."

"What then?"

"They have attacked the church," continued Redman, "but axes, hammers, pikes, and stones fail to break down the barrier by which ingress is gained to the vaults in which, it is said, Miss Violet is confined."

"Ah! I understand. You would remove the obstacle by the same means as it is decreed that the great enemy of our cause shall be removed—gunpowder! 'Tis well—ye could not have sought me at a more fitting moment. Follow!"

And, making towards a long, low, rambling building, on the borders of The Marsh, having the appearance of a granary, they became lost to view under the drooping yews by which it was surrounded.

CHAPTER VIII.

THE ATTACK UPON THE MONASTERY—A FIERCE ENCOUNTER—THE MONASTERY IN FLAMES—A THRILLING SCENE.

MEANWHILE let us hasten to the old and picturesque monastery of Chelsea, which rose grey and venerable through the tall trees encompassing it.

About the principal entrance a fierce and excited crowd was collected, headed by Harold Rookby, who, sword in hand, struck long and loudly upon the stout, iron studded door, demanding admittance.

A barred wicket suddenly opened, at which the harsh, forbidding face of the bishop appeared, who said, angrily—

"What is the meaning of this riotous, unseemly conduct? What is it ye seek in this lone and sacred place, and at this solemn, silent hour?"

"Violet Hamlyn," said Harold Rookby, in

his clear, ringing tones, "whom have ye here unjustly confined."

"You mock us, bold, presumptuous boy!" cried the priest, vehemently. "Ye know full well the foot of woman never crosses these sacred precincts. Begone instantly and in peace to your homes, or I will call down heaven's bitterest maledictions upon ye all. We have no such maiden here."

"You lie, false priest," said Harold, passionately. "I know ye have concealed within these foul, sin-stained walls, the sweet maiden in whom my every earthly hope is centred, and I swear, by all that is sacred, either to liberate her or die in the attempt."

"Begone, all of ye!" exclaimed the priest, wrathfully; then, as he observed a sudden rush towards him, he shouted, "Sound the alarm—let the righteous hear of our distress!"

At that moment a loud peal burst forth from the belfry, and as the crowd heard the sounds they uttered a wild shout of derision.

"Let every arm be nerved with the consciousness of doing an act of justice," said Harold Rookby, as he struck a heavy blow upon the door with a battle-axe.

"To the rescue, friends, to the rescue! He whose heart has beat with affection for his own true love will answer with a will."

The spark of chivalry which Harold's words kindled in their breasts caused their enthusiasm to burst forth, unrestrained by danger or death.

Now the air is filled with wild shoutings, and heavy blows resound far and wide as the mob, with hammer, axe, and pike, batter and hew vigorously the oaken door.

Immediately the whole building appeared to be lighted up.

Then numerous monks were to be seen hurrying to and fro, actively making preparations for defence.

Soon the contest became terrible.

Without a dense mob is striving to gain admittance, whilst on the parapets of the holy pile the monks were hurling stones upon, and directing other implements of destruction against, their clamorous assailants beneath.

The sacred temple is now the mark of vengeance to an infuriated populace, and the sky is covered with a blackness, as if heaven shrouded itself from the unnatural conflict that was raging beneath.

The iron cressets were planted in the ground, and in a moment the resinous and pitchy substance within them blazed forth, from the glare of which they had ample light to prosecute their work of ruin.

Many amongst that wild, infuriated band were for burning the entrance down.

But Harold Rookby was strenuous in his opposition to the scheme, for he feared that such destruction might encompass the very victim they were so anxious to rescue.

Again the besiegers rained shower after shower of heavy blows upon the door, soon making the oaken panels chip and fly into a thousand splinters.

The monks above, however, were not idle.

Several of the belligerents were struck down by their missiles, and many an insensible form strewed the ground.

Suddenly a huge stone, thrown with unerring aim by one of the monks, struck a powerful, stalwart man, who was foremost amongst the besiegers, upon the knee, nearly crushing the bone.

Maddened by the excruciating agony, he seized a flaming cresset, and, with a wild cry of revenge, hurled it at the body of monks from whom the missile had come.

Swift as a fiery meteor it rushed through the air.

But, missing its mark, it sped past the group of monks and lodged upon the roof, composed of ornamental wood-work.

A shout of derision escaped the brotherhood as the fiery missile passed them. Then, as the deep execrations of the mob below, while bearing their wounded companion away, reached their ears, they answered it with a roar of laughter.

In a few moments, however, a thick smoke arose from the place where the cresset had rested. A dense cloud enveloped the roof. Upward, upward it curled, and then a fierce lurid flame burst out.

The lighted brand had burnt through the wooden roof, and, unobserved, drops of flaming pitch, falling through the rafters, had set fire to the building within.

What dismay now reigned among the hitherto exulting monks as they observed the fury with which the fire raged!

The assailants ceased from their toil, and stood gazing upon the burning pile with a look of triumph.

Not so Harold Rookby; his mind appeared tortured by the unforeseen event, and for a moment he clasped his temples between his hands, lost in anxious thought.

Hostilities now ceased as if by mutual consent, and the monks seemed paralysed at the rapidity with which the fire spread.

But not a hand was offered by those without to save the building from destruction.

Harold Rookby, however, now stood before them, and as his eagle eye glanced rapidly over their features he said—

"Uprouse ye, my brave friends! We came here not to destroy this place—it was to rescue the oppressed within its walls. Assist!—assist to subdue the fire we have kindled, or the maiden we have come to save will perish!"

At this appeal the eager mob joined heart and hand to save the very building they would a while since have gladly seen in ruins.

As the monks heard the words of Harold Rookby they threw open the portal that had so long defied the attempts made to hew it down.

Then a body of them came forth, and they called upon their late assailants to help them in extinguishing the flames.

CHAPTER IX.

HAROLD ROOKBY AND PAUL JEROME — THE TREACHERY OF FATHER HUBERT—A SEARCH THROUGH THE FIERY FURNACE—VIOLET'S LIVING TOMB—THE CELL IN FLAMES—HAROLD TO THE RESCUE—UNEXPECTED APPEARANCE OF GUY FAWKES.

HAROLD ROOKBY was the first to rush into the burning edifice.

But scarce had he crossed the threshold when a figure in the garb of a monk rushed from behind a dark pillar, caught him by the arm, and pulled him into a recess, where, for a while, they spoke unobserved.

"This has been a terrible and unexpected event," whispered the young priest, hoarsely; "and your greatest energies must be exerted to rescue the girl."

"Do you fear danger of any other description than this accident could cause?" asked Harold, anxiously.

"Heaven knows! The worst may already be passed, but I bade you in my hurried message to hope much, yet dread all. She whom ye seek is here, but so imprisoned that your heart will sink indeed at the hope of recovering her while the fire lasts."

"Oh heaven! what madness this is!" exclaimed Harold, pressing his hand to his brow; "but tell me," he added, striving to be calm, "tell me, have they attempted—have they dared to torture that beauteous girl?"

"Not bodily, but mentally."

"How, how? Oh tell me quick, or I shall go mad with suspense."

"Speak lower; should any of the inmates hear us the scheme we have planned would be foiled. Be calm as possible, and I will tell thee all. Miss Hamlyn is in this place, confined within a stone coffin. Nay, hear me; of such contrivance is it that she cannot move from her upright position even to reach the morsel of bread or the drop of water that is placed at her feet!"

"Oh, horror! horror! and thou——"

"I have been prevented from giving her aid. With you now remains the rescue!"

"Where is she at this moment? What part have they confined her in?" asked Harold, breathlessly.

"She is in that part where the fire rages most. Follow me, I'll——"

But before the priest finished speaking a crowd of men, carrying water, rushed by, bearing along with them the priest in their wild confusion.

Having at length extricated himself from those who encompassed him, he was about to return to where he had left Harold Rookby, when he was suddenly confronted by a tall monk, who seemed to throw himself purposely in his way.

"Whither so fast, brother?" said he, "has the strange youth, so lately our assailant, spoke aught that interests ye so greatly that ye wish to confer again in secret with him?"

"I do not understand you aright, brother Hubert," returned the young priest, calmly. "Your language has a sinister meaning in it which I cannot fathom."

"And yet it is not deeper than ye considered thine own cunning," replied the other, sneeringly. "Tell me, what was the conference ye held with the stranger?"

"Let me pass, brother; I will not hold words with thee. You cannot expect that the confidence placed in me shall be confided to another."

"Out upon such talk! It is well for fools to hear. We are one fraternity; what secrets should we have from each other?"

"You forget yourself, brother," returned Paul Jerome, with dignity. "Whilst we stand cavilling here the place burns. Let us join those who are striving to overcome the flames."

"Else will our victim die sooner than our master hoped," said the monk Hubert, fixing his piercing eyes upon his companion's pale face.

"Why do you speak of that unhappy girl?" inquired the young priest, suddenly.

"To remind ye of our royal master's vengeance. Mark me, Paul, I have watched your conduct of late, and I fear your heart is not wholly in the cause we serve."

"What reason have I given you to suspect me?" inquired the young priest, uneasily. "Think you I would have been one of the four who put that poor girl in the horrid place, where she now suffers the torments of the damned, if I had been an impostor. Doubt me not! no one serves our cause with greater zeal than I."

"Well, I was hasty; but it was to try ye, brother. Step into this ante-room—the heat and turmoil will not assail us there, nor shall we be overheard. I would speak with thee about the dreadful fate which awaits the girl now in our power."

"Most readily," replied the young priest.

And, unconscious of the other's villainy, he passed into the chamber, without betraying the uneasiness he felt for Harold Rookby.

Scarcely, however, had he crossed the threshold than the perfidious monk without swung the door to, and, taking a key from a bunch at his girdle, locked the other in.

"I shall be free from thy officious meddling," muttered he, as he strode away.

But whilst the monk Hubert thought that the other was so secure in the chamber the room was empty and the young priest free.

The instant the door was closed upon him he proceeded to where a painting of the Madonna appeared fixed, and, moving it aside by some secret means, he passed along a narrow passage leading to the place where he had so suddenly been separated from Harold Rookby.

But the excited youth had not waited for his return.

He had heard that his beloved mistress was near the fiercest of the flames, and thither, where the fire raged most, sped the gallant youth.

He rushes wildly along a narrow passage, through which the smoke is rolling with stifling force, and hurries down some steps, the wood of which is already blistered; his hair, streaming behind him, is scorched and burned.

The heat is intolerable, but still he hurries onward.

What shall stay his steps? The fire may rage, death in its most hideous shape may stand before him, but the knowledge of Violet's fearful danger has nerved him unto deeds of desperation bordering on madness.

Harold Rookby's headlong career, however, could not last for ever, and at length he stood, breathless and exhausted, uncertain where to go in quest of her he would so gladly save.

Passing rapidly through the vault, he shut a door which, fortunately, was at the far end, and for a few brief moments the fire was stayed by this slender barrier.

Again he was free to catch a breath of air, and though it was but an instant's respite, it infused fresh energy into his flagging frame.

But now the slight door is burnt down, and, like the mouth of a yawning volcano, the flames burst through with a wild roar upon the hapless youth.

Onward he fled, but oh! in what agony of mind.

His own life now required that energy of purpose he would fain have given to his beloved, and the thought that he knew not whether her dungeon was far or near drove him well-nigh to madness.

Yet he gained upon the fire, and, notwithstanding its fury, got beyond its power.

With his hands blistered and the soles of his boots burnt through he reached a flight of steps. Ascending them at the top of his speed, he came to the end of a passage, from which no outlet ran.

Oh! the horror of retracing his steps, to face again the danger he had passed, to brave once more the stifling heat of that raging fire!

The alternative was a terrible one, but it must be that or death in its most fearful form —to be burned alive.

Instantly his resolution was taken.

Pressing his scorched doublet over his mouth he dashed madly down the steep stairs.

He paused a second at the foot, uncertain where to go.

Then, remembering a passage he had before passed, he again entered it, although it was filled with dense smoke and flames.

And now, as he stood in a low vaulted corridor, at the end of which a steep well staircase began, he shouted lustily the name of her he so feverishly longed to find.

Was it fancy or did he indeed hear a smothered moan by his side?

Or was it merely the sound of the fire which, apparently, was raging fiercely on the other side of the vault he was in.

Heavens! how he rushed to a large door that now caught his attention, and with what frantic eagerness did he attempt to unfasten it.

Bolts, bars, locks are rapidly forced back, but yet the door will not yield.

Again the frenzied youth strove with herculean strength.

Another tremendous effort, and he wrenches one of the bars from off the door.

Possessed of this powerful lever, he applied it to the mouth of the ponderous lock.

A vigorous jerk and the iron wicket gives way with a loud crash.

Then, dashing down the lever, he rushes madly through the open door, shouting wildly—

" Violet, Violet!"

Great heaven! how his voice rings through his own ears.

How his own cries seem thrown back without penetrating further than a few feet.

He has reached the strange and horrible chamber where the maiden is confined!

A chill shudder passed through his frame as he observed the character of the place!

It is the torture-chamber—the room where he knows she must be—the very spot which he has so earnestly endeavoured to reach!

But his eager, searching eye saw her not.

The room was empty; nothing but flames and smoke, and the charred and blackened roof, meet his tortured gaze.

Suddenly his ear caught indistinct sounds, and again his parched and heated throat hoarsely screamed—

" Violet, Violet! where art thou? Violet, Violet, in heaven's name, speak!"

The place echoed back the startling cry.

"Who calls on Violet?" thundered a voice, and Hubert, the tall monk, rushed into the dungeon. "Who calls on Violet here?"

"I!" cried Harold, as he sprang furiously towards the monk, like one who has recognised a deadly foe. "I! Who has a greater right?"

"Thou!" replied the monk, starting back in affright."

"Ay, villain! I. You little expected me here!"

And as the red glow from the flames played upon the youth's face his rage impressed it with a horrible look.

"Dastard!" he added, "where is she? Where is Violet—the victim of your vile treachery? Where is she, thou base panderer to a tyrant's will? Quick, answer me, or, by my soul, this moment is thy last!" with passionate vehemence.

But the monk for reply only uttered a cold, mocking laugh, when, with the fierceness of a tiger, Harold sprang upon him.

"Dare to mock my agony!" shrieked he. "Hell-hound, I will tear the secret of her charnel-house from your black, fiendish heart!"

"Off, madman! What need is there for *your* roaring? A few minutes and your death is certain Behold, the flames are even now within a few feet of us; already they scorch your clothes."

"Be it so—you, at least, shall die also; and heaven be praised that I have met thee to give thee the punishment ye deserve! Die, dog!" shrieked Harold.

And, clutching the monk fiercely by the throat, he hurled him violently to the ground, adding—

"Die! Thy vile frame shall first be consumed by the fierce fire, and then, but not till then, will I—"

"Release me!" gasped the monk, as he struggled desperately with his determined assailant.

"Never till death—barbarous, heartless wretch!" exclaimed Harold.

Then for several minutes a deadly, terrible struggle ensued, but the youth held his foe too firmly for him to escape.

"Release me!" again panted the monk. "I have had no hand in the girl's imprisonment."

"Liar!" thundered Harold. "Would you die with so foul a lie upon your soul?"

"Die!" shrieked the monk; "who dares to die amid such horrors as this?"

"Who? Myself and thee!" cried Harold, exultantly. "And," he added, impressively, "the angelic victim of a fiendish plot—Violet Hamlyn!"

"No, no, no!" yelled Brother Hubert, frantically. "It cannot—must not be! Let me go—let me go out of this place; the corridor is of stone and will resist the flames. See see how yon pile smokes and crackles!"

"The burning building will be a rare requiem over thy blistered body, false monk," taunted Harold Rookby.

"Madman! have you become a demon already?" returned the monk.

"Ha, ha! 'Tis my turn now."

"Release me, and I will tell thee the spot where Violet is. She is in this chamber—amid this fire—this horror!"

"Where—where? Quick, the spot!"

But as Harold relaxed his hold the false

monk suddenly released himself from his grasp, and attempted to escape.

As swift as lightning Harold dashed in pursuit. Seizing him, ere he reached the door, by the waist, he flung him savagely against the heated wood.

With a wild cry the monk fell heavily, and as the wood panelling was thrown down by his sudden weight a stifling black cloud of smoke arose.

Nearly suffocated by the dense vapour of the igniting mass, the youth, overpowered and exhausted by his trying efforts, fell fainting upon the hot floor.

Denser and denser becomes the rolling, choking, blinding smoke, and the heat is now almost unendurable.

His brain reels, he feels his senses fast leaving him.

Ah! What was that magic sound that had power to rouse him?

How wildly his eyes roll in their sockets! What a horrible tremor seizes his frame!

What fresh life and vigour springs into his weary limbs, and with what delirious haste does he rise and totter forward on hearing that low moaning cry of—

"Help! help! Mercy! mercy!"

"Violet! Violet!" shouted Harold, frantically, as he rushed to a small aperture in the rough stone wall in which the fiendish wretches had entombed poor Violet.

And, as the well-known voices struck each other's ears, a wild joy-note of recognition was given by the ill-fated pair.

But how short is the bliss of the lovers!

Again Harold staggered back, the thick stifling smoke once more overpowering him, and with a gasping, choking cry, he sunk at the foot of the horrible coffin of his beloved mistress.

There he lay, to all appearances, dead, unable to raise an arm to rescue her whom he had now found, but, alas! too late.

No other sound was heard save one last cry from Violet—no sob, no gasp, no sigh.

The fierce raging fire had all the place to itself, to fill with its roaring, destructive fury.

But surely such a terrible fate is not reserved for two so young, so fond and true to each other as these!

Surely Providence in its mercy will send some guardian angel to save them from this frightful death!

The eleventh hour has arrived and all hope of escape seems gone!

Where, oh where, are those stout hearts who assisted the swooning youth outside?

Have they forgotten him in the distracting excitement of the fire?

And where is his firm and fearless friend, Guy Fawkes?

Hark! what shout is that?

Now the roof is being hewn to pieces—men are attempting to gain admittance.

But will they arrive in time?

A moment is now an age; an instant lost and they will be too late to save those they so eagerly seek!

Just then there is a loud crash and wild shouts of triumph.

The same instant a stout rope comes dangling down like a huge writhing serpent.

And almost simultaneously a form descending it comes whirling through the clouds of black smoke and sheets of flame with fearful velocity to the ground.

It is Guy Fawkes.

He takes in the scene at a glance.

Quick as thought he goes on one knee, and, raising the head of Harold, pours some liquor from a flask, which he took from his doublet, between his friend's lips.

Then, placing him gently back, his eagle eye caught sight of an iron bar upon the floor.

In another instant he is working with it upon the wall in which the object of his secret adoration is entombed alive.

But he must be speedy, or all will yet be in vain!

This thought spurs him on to almost superhuman exertions.

In a few seconds he has made a breach large enough for Violet to pass through.

A wild cry escapes him as he beholds the unconscious form of Violet.

His bosom is racked by mingled emotion, and, with gentle, reverent touch, he lifts her lovely head, and gently forces some of the potent drink between her sweet lips.

Then suddenly he felt himself seized forcibly from behind.

He turned and found himself in the grasp of Brother Hubert.

The monk's sinister features were ablaze with fiendish malignity as he hissed—

"Fool! thinkest thou to gain so easy a victory over me? Ye came to save my hated enemies; far better for thee hadst thou thought of thine own safety more, for I have sworn by all the saints that ye shall perish with them."

"Thou vain, prating braggart!" said Guy Fawkes, with a dangerous gleam of his dark eyes. "Ye little know me if ye think I would abandon my purpose at thy puny bidding! Release your hold, or, by heaven, I'll hurl thee a shattered corpse 'gainst yon wall!"

The priest gave utterance to a taunting laugh, whereas Guy Fawkes grappled with him like a fury-roused animal, and a short but terrific struggle took place.

Meanwhile Harold Rockby, having in a measure recovered under the influence of the powerful stimulant Guy Fawkes had administered to him, staggered to his feet.

He looked around, and, catching sight of Violet's pale, still form, through the broken wall, uttered a glad cry and darted towards the opening.

As the excited youth took her in his arms to bear her from her living tomb, she opened her lovely eyes, and, murmuring his name, her fair head sank upon his bosom.

At that moment Guy Fawkes succeeded in dashing the monk to the ground.

He was on his feet, however, in an instant.

But, with the speed of electricity, Guy Fawkes caught up a flaming brand, and as the monk again rushed forward he struck him a stunning blow with the fiery weapon.

The monk uttered a shriek of agony and sank senseless upon the stone floor.

"Quick! quick!" cried Guy Fawkes. "In a few minutes the rope will be burnt through."

Then, taking the slender, graceful form of Violet across one arm, and seizing the rope with the other, he placed his foot in the noose at the end and gave it a violent shake.

The signal was immediately understood by those willing hearts and ready hands above.

In an instant more Guy Fawkes and his lovely burden were rapidly ascending through the rolling smoke and roaring flames to the steep roof.

Suddenly a wild cheer announced their safe arrival.

The rope was then lowered a second time.

Not a moment too soon; for Harold Rookby again felt that choking, death-like faintness fast stealing over him.

He had just sufficient sense, however, to grasp the rope firmly, and place his foot in the loop.

The next instant he felt himself flying through space.

His brain reeled and swam, fiery meteors flashed before his bewildered vision, his nerveless hands relaxed their hold, and he felt himself falling!

Then suddenly he became dimly conscious of being seized upon by a hundred eager hands, and, whilst the wild burst of triumphant shouting was still ringing in his ears, he fell back in the arms of his deliverers insensible.

CHAPTER X.

THE CONSPIRATORS' HAUNT BY THE RIVER—HAROLD ROOKBY'S GRATITUDE—THE MEETING BY THE OLD FERRY HOUSE—GUY FAWKES'S PAGE—THE DANCING-GIRL'S WARNING—A NEW ACQUAINTANCE—AN UNEQUAL ENCOUNTER—GUY FAWKES IN THE POWER OF HIS FOES

IT was late in the afternoon of the following day ere Harold Rookby recovered consciousness.

On opening his eyes he was greatly surprised to find himself lying upon a rude bed in the old house by the river at Southwark, with Guy Fawkes by his side.

"How came I here?" he asked, gazing curiously around, then up at the darkened windows.

"In a hired conveyance I was fortunate enough to procure after your providential escape from the burning monastery at Chelsea," returned Guy Fawkes.

"An escape, indeed!" exclaimed Harold, shuddering visibly at the recollection. "Never was mortal in more deadly, more fearful peril. Never did the truest friend man ever had display such noble self-sacrifice—such lion-hearted bravery and devotion, as thou, good Guy."

He was unable to proceed for emotion; but, grasping the hand of his deliverer, he pressed it fervently to his lips; then, recovering himself, added—

"Guy, brothers-in-arms we have been for many years, and good and staunch friends always, but this noble deed of thine has filled my heart with life-long gratitude—given birth to an affection within my breast such as is rarely felt by dearest brothers."

"Think not but that I am truly proud of thine esteem, good Harold. "But do not overrate my services, I beg, for I would do the like deed for any whom I deemed my comrade or friend," rejoined Guy Fawkes, warmly returning the pressure of his companion's hand.

"Now tell me of Violet!" pursued Harold, eagerly.

An expression of pain passed over Guy Fawkes's features, but he answered readily—

"Violet is safe in the room above; she is greatly recovered, and has been inquiring for thee."

"Violet here, and recovered! Oh, this is unlooked-for happiness!" cried Harold, in an ecstasy of delight. "Let me instantly hasten to her."

And, rising from his couch, he staggered towards the door.

"Farewell," said Guy Fawkes, gently placing his hand upon his friend's shoulder, while the o'd look again overshadowed his features; "I am about to go to Lambeth-marsh respecting the conveyance here of the gunpowder, my mission there yester e'en being a bootless one. Our friends are assembled in the long room adjoining, and should they inquire for me tell them of the errand on which I have gone."

Harold promised compliance, and ascended to the room above, while Guy Fawkes, having donned his hat and cloak, ventured forth by the back way, after first seeing that no one was about.

Keeping well in the shadow of the hedgerow that bordered the Surrey side of the river, though darkness was falling apace, Guy Fawkes reached the old ferry-house at Blackfriars.

He was about to pass on when a figure started up from a wooden seat, and hastened after him. Guy Fawkes suddenly turned and confronted his pursuer.

He was a swarthy, dark-eyed youth of fifteen, his features were small but handsome, and he had a look of acute intelligence.

The youth was poorly but neatly clad, his manner, without being assuming, had a degree of confidence, and his bright eyes glanced towards Guy Fawkes's sword as if he longed to wear one.

"Now, sirrah, what seekest thou?" Guy Fawkes demanded, sternly.

For reply the boy presented him with a sealed letter.

It was written in a neat but unsteady hand, and was as follows:—

"HONOURABLE SIR.—The bearer is the boy whom your goodness of heart made you promise to take into your service. I commend him to you with a sister's gratitude. I pray you make no further inquiries about me. My hurt was but a slight one, and has been cared for. Stir not abroad after sunset—your own life is in danger.—EVELYN."

"By the mass! but the warning comes somewhat late, my pretty Evelyn," said Guy Fawkes, folding the letter, "and I may not heed it. How fares your sister, boy?"

"I know not," answered the boy, curtly.

"Or will not tell," rejoined Guy Fawkes, with a grim smile. "Well, I seek not to know what may be a point of honour with you to conceal."

Then, writing on his tablet, he added—

"Go ye to this written address; they will find ye more fitting raiment and attend to thy wants. Remain ye there till I seek ye out."

After placing the missive in the lad's hand he hastened on, and was lost to sight in the gloom of the evening.

Guy Fawkes walked along in thoughtful silence towards the wooded fields by the river side, his mind still busy with the scene he had left.

Suddenly he heard a low whistle at no great

distance from him, answered by two others on different sides of the damp pathway on which he moved.

He also saw a dark shadow flit through the trees.

For the first time he remembered the warning of the dancing-girl.

He now heard hurried whispers and the sounds of advancing footsteps.

He paused, and laid his hand upon his sword-hilt.

At this moment his attention was distracted by hearing the advance of someone else from an opposite direction, but who evidently made no secret of his approach, as he was singing—

> "A gallant man was Robin Hood,
> A noble wight was he !
> He ranged and rode in merrie Sherwood
> All under the greenwood tree !"

"What ho, Cavaliero !" exclaimed the singer, issuing from the trees, whose round beard and flat cap well-suited his jolly English face. "What ho, Sir Cavalier ! I give you good e'en.

> "I give ye good e'en and I give ye good morrow,
> Away with all care and away with all sorrow,
> For a tankard that's full——"

"Peace, you noisy knave !" interrupted Guy Fawkes, in a low, angry whisper, "and have thine eyes about thee, if ye would not have a dagger stuck in thy throat to aid thee to sing withal."

"A quart of spiced ale would suit it better," answered the yeoman, who seemed to have been partaking of the beverage he spoke of. "But who art thou who callest me knave ? Dost thou think because ye wear a looped feather in thy cap that thou mayest come quips on me ? Marry, come up ! My mother was a honest woman and my father a grave man, who ate pancakes on Shrovetide.

> "Oh, my father was a yeoman bold,
> A yeoman stout and true,
> He——"

"Hold that tongue of thine that ye wag with the devil's licence !" again interrupted Guy Fawkes, "and look there——"

"Where ?" inquired the songster, starting back at the sight of the shadowy forms between the trees.

"Now cut thee a cudgel," said Guy Fawkes, "and follow me. If we escape these men, whom I guess are cut-throats, thou shalt have at the Maypole yonder as much ale as will drench the small wits which heaven hath given thee"

"It was the devil's luck that sent me hither," said the songster, drawing out a large clasp-knife, and cutting off a bough, which he stripped and prepared with dexterous rapidity. "Yet," continued he, "if these fellows had seen me wrestle on Friar's-green, or play at quarter-staff with Mark Mealy Mug last Whitsuntide, they would think twice ere they attacked us. Pray heaven that they may not have matchlocks with them !"

There was no mistaking the intentions of the men who lurked among the trees.

The gleam of a bare sword shone clearly from among the green boughs.

The pathway through which Guy Fawkes advanced now became narrower and more retired.

The skulking ruffians in advance slowly retreated, and he found himself reluctantly approaching a spot in which his assailants would possess every advantage of treachery and unequal combat.

The glimmer of cold steel had not escaped his companion.

"These be no true men," he said. "'Tis a blessing I have but a silver James in my pouch !"

"But you have a throat," muttered Guy Fawkes ; "and if you value it have thine eyes about thee. If they attack us we must fight back to back."

"Aye, marry, will I, and strike with hearty good will—just the same as if Dolly Rosebud was looking at me ;" and the speaker, grasping his cudgel tighter, walked as if he were treading on eggs. "Canst guess, Sir Cavalier, who these villains be ?"

"One of them—the dark shadow you see peeping from behind that oak—I think I have once crossed swords with, though why he seeks to attack me again, unless it be for my purse, I am as ignorant as thee."

"I had never good luck since I wore a friar's gown at a masking," rejoined the other, "and it is certain death to strike in another man's quarrel ; yet here I am, as likely to be killed in fighting or running away as stabbed for looking on. Would that I had stayed at Mother Swillwell's—— See, Sir Cavalier, our friends are gone !"

"Follow me," said Guy Fawkes, darting down a narrower path, in the direction of the river.

His companion obeyed, and was instantly at his side.

"There is a wicket-gate at no great distance," resumed Guy Fawkes ; "could we reach it we are safe."

"I should like to give the villains one buffet with this stout sapling," said the yeoman, brandishing the tough weapon as he strode along.

"The keeper has bloodhounds," muttered Guy Fawkes ; "he shall loosen them, and we will follow their track. I will know why this hell-dog haunts me thus."

As he spoke he came in full view of the glittering river, but saw an object there which, in spite of his haste and danger, made him suddenly pause.

His companion uttered an expression of alarm.

A long, dark boat, well-manned, sharp-bowed, and of a form denoting speed, floated, snake-like, under the shadow of the green bank on which he stood.

The villainous crew lay noiselessly on their oars ; the very ripple that bubbled on them was not heard, and the tall trees that rose on the higher part of the bank shot their long shadows far over the dim shelter in which this suspicious-looking craft swam motionless.

Guy Fawkes's active mind forgot fear and his own danger at the sight, and for a moment he was off his guard.

It was fortunate, however, his companion was not the same.

Three men on the instant darted into the path.

One of them made a fierce lunge at Guy Fawkes with his sword, which, but for the quick interposition of his companion's cudgel, would have cloven his head in twain.

Then came a blow like the kick of a horse—a sob, and the dull sound of a heavy body falling on the ground, followed in the succession of seconds, and, ere Guy Fawkes had drawn his sword, the first assailant lay stunned at his feet.

But his sword-arm was instantly seized.

Two ruffians simultaneously grappled with him. Their object, however, appeared different from that of the first, as they endeavoured rather to disarm than to injure him.

The struggle was a fierce and determined one.

Guy Fawkes was on the point of being overpowered, when another stunning cudgel blow, dealt from behind, made one of the bravoes stagger, and Guy Fawkes, shooting out his foot, sent him reeling to the ground.

He had only now the third to deal with, for several of those left in the boat had rushed to the scene of conflict and occupied themselves with his companion.

The fellow Guy Fawkes struggled with was a strong, muscular man, who held him with a grasp of iron.

"Yield thee, rash, stubborn fool!" he hissed hoarsely and savagely.

But Guy Fawkes still refused—his blood was up.

He felt the tightened grasp upon his throat, he saw his sword lying idly on the ground, his eyes met the fierce insulting glance of his opponent, and the fiery passions of his nature burned again.

He suddenly caught hold of the hilt of a dagger in the ruffian's belt.

His fingers instantly closed on it, and, quick as thought, he drew it and dealt him a heavy blow.

The fellow uttered a maddened growl of pain, for the strong sharp point had cleft his lip, struck out several of his teeth, and filled his mouth with blood.

The villain let go the hold of Guy Fawkes's throat, and attempted to seize his arm.

But in this he did not succeed.

They grappled and closed again, and rolled on the earth together.

The heavy pant of exhausted nature, the deep, excited sob of baffled rage, when the wild blood flows burning through powerful limbs, gave a wild desperation to this tiger-like struggle, which exulting devils might have shrieked to witness.

Guy Fawkes's adversary, maddened with the pain of his wound, made frenzied efforts to wrench the weapon from his grasp.

But in this he was defeated.

Strong and muscular as he was, he had to contend with one who wanted neither strength nor the fiery will to use it.

Guy Fawkes's right arm was free again—his knee was now on the villain's breast.

He raised the dagger swiftly on high to bury it in the wretch's throat, when suddenly he felt himself seized from behind.

His arms were instantly pinioned to his sides, a bandage thrust over his eyes, and he himself was violently dragged down the river's bank.

Then he was forced into the rocking boat.

He heard fierce muttered oaths and hurried words of altercation on the shore; others jumped into the dancing craft, and one or two were lifted heavily into it.

The next moment the plash of oars and a sudden bounding motion showed that the boat had left the shore.

For a few minutes there was not a word spoken.

Nothing was heard but the dipping of the oars and the long, sweeping swish of the blades, as the light boat darted fleetly along.

But by and by low moaning sounds issued from the bottom of the boat, mingled with wrathful imprecations in a foreign tongue.

"Holy St. Peter, they must be Frenchmen!" ejaculated a voice at Guy Fawkes's side, which he at once recognised as that of his late companion.

"How fare ye, my friend?" demanded Guy Fawkes, addressing him.

"What! are you here too!" exclaimed the other; "I thought I saw you on the ground?"

"Men fail and rise again in this world of ours," rejoined Guy Fawkes. "Are you hurt?"

"I have a cut on the back of my head," replied his fellow-captive; "but how deep it is I cannot tell, for my arms are pinioned, and, by the mass, stiffly too."

"Canst guess, worthy sir," he added, "what these miscreants mean to do with us? Tell me, is the king at war with France?"

"They are no Frenchmen," muttered Guy Fawkes, "but Scotchmen, I strongly suspect, and the foreign tongue is merely assumed as a blind."

"Then Holy St. Mary have mercy upon us! We shall be flayed alive!"

"Let us hope better things," returned Guy Fawkes, "although what they mean to do with us, or why they have dared to commit this outrage, I cannot tell more than you. Yet, trust me, it will not pass unavenged."

"That is but small comfort," rejoined the other. "I would give all the revenge in the land for a clear start of twenty yards from the river side, with this cursed bandage taken from my eyes."

"We cannot be far from London Bridge," said Guy Fawkes; "could we know when we come near it I would alarm the watch——"

"Silence!" cried a voice, authoritatively. "Another word and we will pitch you into the river."

Guy Fawkes chafed with renewed rage, and had difficulty in restraining an angry reply.

His companion, on the contrary, began to mutter an inaudible prayer.

They now proceeded silently at the same rapid rate.

The cold night breeze played upon their faces and the motion of the boat became perceptibly greater.

And, from the long, measured strokes of the oars, it was evident that the tide favoured them.

After rowing some distance further they spoke a suspicious-looking vessel in the middle of the stream.

The boat then turned to the shore, her bow struck without grounding, and they landed on a kind of wooden pier.

Guy Fawkes, still with his eyes bound, was led through what seemed a long vaulted passage.

Ere he had proceeded many steps he heard the boat leaving the beach and the loud demand of his late companion to be set on shore.

The passage through which Guy Fawkes was led was paved with stone, and the air, although it was a sultry night, was cold and damp.

He passed through various doorways—the stubborn locks and creaking hinges denoting they were seldom used.

At length his guides or guards paused. They knocked softly at another door, which was opened, and Guy Fawkes was led into an inner room.

The bandage was suddenly taken off his eyes, and he looked in astonishment around him.

He was in a large, dark, vaulted room, the roof, the walls, and floor of which were of stone.

Behind him was an iron-grated door, solid and massive.

Before him, on a raised wooden bench, sat an individual, whose guise ill-accorded with the rude cavern-like place around him.

He wore a small half-mask, through which his eyes restlessly glistened like a snake's.

From what could be seen of his face he was of middle age, of a dark and handsome countenance, the expression of which was callous and forbidding.

His dress was sombre but costly, his doublet being of rich velvet, his sword and dagger hilts of burnished gold.

A splendid jewelled order on his breast sparkled brightly in the dim light, and a black feather drooped from his broad Spanish hat, under which his long, dark hair, fell in luxuriant tresses, giving additional dignity to his imposing aspect.

On both sides of him stood a few hirelings, dressed like men-at-arms or functionaries of justice.

They were all uncovered, and turned their eyes towards Guy Fawkes with a look of deep interest.

"Unbind him!" said the cavalier, who sat on the bench.

In an instant Guy Fawkes's arms were free.

"Uncover!" said one of the men, "you are in the presence of a peer of the realm."

Had the man known Guy Fawkes, he would have spared himself such a request. As it was it passed unheeded.

"I believe you are the head of a party secretly organised for the avowed purpose of re-establishing the Catholic faith in this country?" said the English nobleman.

"If so, how comes it," said Guy Fawkes, "that you carry me hither a prisoner, and now interrogate me like a criminal?"

"These are bootless questions," said the masked cavalier. "Your own quick wit will tell you that this is no place for a discussion of rights; you will learn more anon.

"Now, mark me," he added, with impressment. "There was a despatch sent, at the instigation of the Pope, by one of the most powerful Catholic noblemen on the continent to a brother Catholic of equal rank in this country, making certain proposals, which we strongly suspect deeply concerns the welfare of our sovereign James.

"What these proposals were are known only to three men in Christendom. The Pope, the nobleman in question, and thee. The first is in Rome, the second in Manchester, but the third, as thou knowest——"

"Is your prisoner!" muttered Guy Fawkes.

"Even so! Now, the honour of England and the interests of the world are concerned to know what those proposals were.

"It is for this I have sent for thee. My messengers were rude, I grant you, and one of them, I know not wherefore, thirsts for your blood; but so do not I.

"Deal frankly with me, and the gold of the Indies will be your reward. You are young, bold, and ambitious; wealth will buy you rank and distinction. Gold, my brave gallant—bright gold! The cross of St. George on thy breast, and the choicest steeds under thy bridle hand.

"These shall be yours for friendly communication with the power I serve."

Guy Fawkes laughed outright.

"Presumptuous heretic," he said, haughtily. "You little know us. There is not one among the meanest of our insulted, persecuted Church, but would treat your offer with scorn. Traitor to my sacred cause! Spy to the accursed heretic! Base minion of thine! Would to heaven we were alone on a green hill-side!" he cried, with flashing eye.

"It is boldly worded, fair sir," answered the masked cavalier, calmly; "but reckon not that such a venture as this is perilled rashly or lightly abandoned. From these vaults you cannot pass alive but as a partisan of James."

"Then," said Guy Fawkes, firmly, "I must needs abide in them. I will die a thousand deaths rather than betray the cause I serve."

"Death," said the disguised nobleman, laughing coldly, "is easily braved. The young scoff at its terrors; it is only the dotard that clings to life. Your death would ensure your secrecy, but further not the cause for which present danger has been incurred. Wise men know other means to tame the obstinate; yet I wished to spare you this!"

He raised his hand as he spoke.

Then a black curtain, which Guy Fawkes had not hitherto perceived, was drawn aside, revealing a darker portion of the gloomy cell.

Here a pale, ghastly light was feebly burning, and two hideous men, with sacks over their heads, which formed a grotesquely ugly point at the top. Two large holes were made, through which their sinister eyes sparkled redly, and close by stood a strange, weird-looking instrument.

A shudder pervaded Guy Fawkes's bold soul at sight of it.

Horror! It was the rack!

CHAPTER XI.

THE VAULT OF DEATH—THE MASKED CAVALIER —A BOLD REQUEST—GUY FAWKES'S REFUSAL —DRAGGED TO THE RACK—A FEARFUL MOMENT —THE EXPLOSION.

GUY FAWKES instinctively looked around him to find some means of escape.

But the cold stone walls—the strong, iron-fastened door, the gloomy, cavern-like place, and the appearance of those in whose power he was, mocked the thought.

His eyes again fell on the fiendish instrument, rendered more ghastly and awe-inspiring by the uncertain light.

His cheek, in spite of himself, became ashen white, he felt the blood running coldly through his veins, and the horror of bodily torture triumphed for the moment over the native fearlessness of his character.

"Time presses," said the masked cavalier, in the same cold tone; "shall I bid the rack-wheel turn or not?"

"What would you have?" inquired Guy Fawkes, scarcely able to conceal the tortuous thoughts which racked his agitated bosom.

"The letter containing the secret instructions of the power ye serve."

"I have it not," returned Guy Fawkes, openly. "Search me if ye will, and prove the truth of my words."

"What have you done with it, then?"

"It has been delivered to whom it was addressed."

"It boots not," returned the cavalier, impatiently, "since of a surety ye must know its contents ye can e'en tell us by word o' mouth."

"Think ye I would stain my manhood by an act so base as to surreptitiously acquaint myself with the contents of a missive entrusted to me in all good faith for its safe deliverance, or betray the confidence of those to whom I am bound by no ordinary tie. It is evident ye little know me, Sir Cavalier!" cried Guy Fawkes, with passionate vehemence.

"This is trifling," said the nobleman, sternly; "and the moth that flutters round the taper flame has as much wisdom as he who trifles by the side of the rack. Speak out. This is no place to employ the slippery arts of the wily Papist priests ye serve, and whose blind, besotted tool ye are!"

"Ye have had my answer," said Guy Fawkes, firmly and defiantly.

"Ah! you refuse then——"

"To betray the councils of our sacred league I do!"

The swarthy features of the disguised nobleman glowed.

He started to his feet, but suddenly checking himself almost in the act of giving a hasty command to his ready satellites, exclaimed, excitedly—

"You are tampering with more than life—with more than death-pangs—it will leave your body blasted—a curse on your miserable existence. On that iron bed," he continued, pointing to the rack, "your bold mien will change to yells of agony—you will leave it with disjointed limbs—with a body incurably distorted, that will make life a curse and torment to you! Mark me, young sir. It may be that woman's love is dear to thee. Her heart loves heroism, but not in a palsied body. She will pity the helpless cripple, but her bright eyes will wander to him whose soul, although less noble, is better housed.

Guy Fawkes's thoughts instantly reverted to Violet, and he shuddered visibly.

"I wish to spare you," went on the cavalier; "but, believe me, from no kindness towards yourself. I could crush you like a worm, nor think once again on your lingering agony. But I wish to spare ye, because your sufferings would serve me less than your enforced aid might do.

"The king, did he but know, would buy the knowledge of the contents of the despatch in question with his fairest province. Gold has been lavished to discover it, but in vain.

"The secret is now within these walls—

locked, indeed, in your bosom. But there"—and he again pointed towards the rack—"there is a key of iron that will open it."

Guy Fawkes was silent—stunned and overwhelmed with conflicting thoughts.

"You still hesitate," resumed the crafty nobleman, watching him narrowly. "It may be that your honour pricks you, but will it render you insensible to torment? The madness of enthusiasm itself is quelled by one turn of that grim wheel!

"There is nothing to stir the blood, nothing to dare, here. It is no battle front, no crossing of blades, no conflict with your kind; one look of the strong man's agony, one shriek of he whose fearless soul would have confronted death unmoved, would tell you that here you have not even the exultation of despair."

He waited, but still Guy Fawkes replied not.

"And whom do you betray?" pursued the masked tyrant, sternly.

"A faithless priest, a base deluder of his misguided followers—an ambitious knave, that masks guile under the purple robe, a very villain, although the head of the Church, that——"

"It is false!" cried Guy Fawkes, fiercely; "base heretic. You lie! you——"

"To the rack with him!" yelled the indignant noble, in a voice of fury.

Quick as the words were uttered Guy Fawkes was seized.

He made a desperate resistance, but all in vain.

His foes were too many for him. He was forcibly dragged to the rack and bound firmly hand and foot upon it.

"Proceed with the torture," cried the noble, passionately.

The grim executioners immediately thrust their iron-tipped levers into the rollers of the rack and gave them a turn.

Another moment and Guy Fawkes's limbs would have been torn from their sockets.

At this critical juncture, however, a wild scream rang out loudly in the vaulted cell, and the frenzied face of the dancing-girl appeared, though unseen, at the grated window.

Simultaneously came a stunning shock, a wild, roaring sound, like the peal of a hundred cannon.

The stone walls shook and trembled, and the very earth seemed moving.

The tapers and torches fell down and were extinguished. The air was charged with fumes that made the breathers gasp.

Captive and captors, prisoner and judge, stood in the darkness and ruin, aghast and panic-stricken.

Then instantaneously a thick sulphuric vapour filled the place.

Guy Fawkes heard one of the ruffians near him mutter in a hurried, terrified whisper—

"There is treason in the camp. We have been betrayed by one of our own people."

They all stood in trembling expectancy of something still more fearful to follow.

Presently, however, the sounds of angry voices without broke upon them, among which were the excited tones of a female voice, which Guy Fawkes fancied he recognised as belonging to Evelyn, the dancing-girl.

The stout door was open again, and a

GUY FAWKES

Or Gunpowder, Treason, and Plot.

"THE SECRET IS NOW WITHIN YOUR BREAST, GUY FAWKES, BUT THE RACK IS A KEY OF IRON THAT WILL UNLOCK IT."

No. 3.

ruffian trooper entered, pale and agitated bearing a torch.

The fellow addressed a few words to the masked nobleman, who burst into a torrent of angry imprecations.

"Release yon stubborn idiot from the rack, but leave him firmly bound ; then follow me."

Seeing that the men faithfully obeyed his orders, they quitted the cell in company of their tyrant lord ; whilst Guy Fawkes was left a prisoner in the bolted and barred chamber, in utter darkness, and with no companion—but the rack.

Deepest silence followed their departure.

The sulphurous odour still remained and made the damp air oppressive, but the stillness around him was perfect and unbroken.

He became convinced that a powder magazine had blown up, and his heart throbbed with a sudden hope that it might lead to his escape.

He could not guess where he was, but knew enough to be confident that he was immured in one of the secret strongholds which in those days abounded on various parts of the river-side, originally prepared for the purposes of contraband merchandise and the spoils of piracy, but now and then applied to purposes of State.

"They must mean to destroy me," muttered Guy Fawkes, "so here I must remain, with powerless limbs, a helpless and a hopeless prisoner, until death relieves me of my misery."

He seated himself by the side of the rack. Both arms were painfully fastened, and his temples throbbed feverishly.

He thought of Violet and his hopeless passion for her—he thought, too, of his rival, Harold Rookby, whose condition he compared with his own ; yet never once did he think of betraying the agents of the cause he served, and of which he deemed himself the chosen of heaven.

Then he remembered the scream he had heard immediately before the explosion, and the evident dismay of the ruffian who rushed in with the torch.

Thus his wandering thoughts ran on until his brain grew dizzy and his wearied mind sank into a kind of stupor.

It was not sleep—nature has a species of lethargy which is not repose.

With his tired head resting against the oaken post, his eyes shut, and his features wearing their accustomed melancholy expression—for he was dreaming of his sainted sister, Esmé—Guy Fawkes lay, unconscious of time.

From this state, after a long interval, he was suddenly aroused.

He felt a soft hand laid gently upon his shoulder.

On opening his eyes the graceful form of a woman stood before him, with a small lamp in her hand.

Guy Fawkes uttered an ejaculation of surprise, for his visitor was none other than Evelyn, the dancing-girl

She was pale as marble, but the expression her beautiful countenance was earnest and full of life.

Her gaze met his, but only for a moment.

Making a signal of imploring silence, she drew a bright keen knife from her girdle, and with trembling hands cut the cords that bound Guy Fawkes's stiffened arms.

Then, raising the lamp again, and repeating the signal of silence, the dancing-girl beckoned him to follow her.

She led the way with the utmost caution to a narrow iron door immediately behind the rack, which had hitherto escaped Guy Fawkes's attention, and proceeded with noiseless steps to an apartment in which two rough, seafaring men were standing, as if waiting for him

Not a word was spoken by anyone, and here he was again compelled to have his eyes bound.

After passing, or being led, through what seemed to him a detour of similar passages, he felt the cool refreshing breeze of the river once more playing on his face.

He could now hear the lapping of the tide, and, from the swaying motion, knew that he was entering a boat

The next moment it glided from the shore.

Guy Fawkes breathed freer, and the spirit of adventure again rose strong within him

Still uncertain whither he was going, he was about to tear the bandage from his eyes when he felt his hand gently seized.

The soft fingers that clasped it, however, told him that it was no unfriendly grasp, and a sweet, earnest voice, whispered—

"If you uncover your eyes we are lost."

"Then be it as it is," replied Guy Fawkes, the buoyancy of his spirits returning. "I care not how far I sail since I travel with such a companion."

"Peace—peace ! for heaven's sake, peace !" said Evelyn, in an imploring whisper, suddenly withdrawing her hand.

On they rowed in silence.

But Guy Fawkes found with increasing uneasiness that the boat, instead of returning towards Southwark, was running down the river

He began to fear that he was to be put on board some outgoing foreign vessel, which would utterly prevent him carrying out, at least for a time, the great purpose he had in view.

He heard the Greenwich clock strike four, and the hail of vessels on the river, to which, however, no answer was made.

After a considerable time Guy Fawkes worked up to a high pitch of desperation, tore the bandage from his eyes, resolving, if need were, to plunge into the stream and swim to the shore.

A muttered curse and a long steel pistol—the bright barrel of which glittered in the moonlight—pointed towards his head now greeted him.

Evelyn suddenly interposed, and, addressing the man in Romany with a fluency which rendered her words unintelligible to Guy Fawkes, stayed his arm, while the rowers rested on their oars.

The man put the pistol sullenly into his belt, and, giving a sharp and angry word of command, the light boat bounded on again.

Guy Fawkes had now leisure to notice this person, who seemed to be the commander of the boat

He was not, as he had at first anticipated, the former companion of the dancing-girl, but a person of older appearance, though still in the prime of manhood

He wore the dress of a sailor—richly, even

gaudily embroidered—his thick curling hair and bushy moustache were black, and his small bright eyes of the same colour.

His aspect was reckless and sensual, indicative of the indulgence of passion. Without being dignified he was commanding.

"Whither are you taking me?" demanded Guy Fawkes, who felt a sudden repugnance, he knew not why, against the individual who commanded the boat.

The question was unheeded by the party addressed, but the girl answered—

"You will be landed anon."

Guy Fawkes, on the impulse of the moment, took the dancing-girl's cold hand in his, and pressed it to his lips.

Again the hand of the sailor crept to his pistol hilt, and Guy Fawkes saw he had changed countenance.

The girl covered her face with her hands, and her long fair hair fell over her shapely arms like a veil, baring her beautiful white neck, the rich ringlets resting on her knees.

Guy Fawkes looked on her with undisguised admiration.

Her extreme loveliness, her devotion to himself, and the rude companions with whom her lot seemed to be cast, awakened in his breast an interest of the most intense and passionate character.

CHAPTER XII.

EVELYN AND GUY FAWKES—A SAD PARTING.

THE more Guy Fawkes gazed on Evelyn, the dancing-girl, the more enamoured he became of her.

A vessel of foreign build now appeared some distance before them, whose high spars rose over a long black hull, and her form, unlike the clumsy vessels of that day, was sharp, clean-shaped, and fitted for speed.

The boat in which they were seated was now rowed to the shore.

A pleasant green bank, sloping towards the river side, covered with trees, some of whose drooping branches dipped into the stream, was the spot where the boat struck her bow.

Guy Fawkes needed no signal to leap ashore.

No sooner had he done so than, taking the hand of Evelyn—who, turning round, addressed a few words in a strange language and in a plaintive tone to the commander of the little vessel—she also landed.

Guy Fawkes led her from the spot, but the boat waited for her.

"Stop!" said she, pausing when the trees shrouded them from the river-side. "I dare go no further ; stay and listen to me."

"I pause at your bidding, sweet one," said Guy Fawkes ; "but, by the mass, with no good will. Let us on and leave this place. By my life, I will repay this masked villain his courtesy of to-night ;" and his fine eyes glittered ominously.

"Nay!" cried Evelyn, quickly ; "you will not do so. You must promise—you must swear —that what you have seen and heard to-night shall be locked for ever a secret in your bosom, and that you will take no steps to find out the place again from which you have now escaped. You will do this?"

"Not so, sweetheart. But let us on, and I will answer thee. St Mary! I have no sword Let us leave this place!"

"No!" said the dancing-girl, grasping his arm. "I dare not stir. Oh, promise me— promise me! I have pledged my word for thee!"

"And on that slender bond I was permitted to escape!"

A smile so sad, so expressive of conscious bitterness, came over the beautiful features of Evelyn, that Guy Fawkes saw his question had touched a chord that was painful to her.

"Beshrew me, sweetheart," said he, in a lighter tone, "I will do anything you ask me in reason, but these ruffianly heretics are villainous spies, and, if I mistake not, pirates to boot."

"They will be gone to-morrow," said the dancing-girl, pleadingly. "I tell you to search for them would be useless. The hiding-place ye know of is now a mass of ruins—to search for them would only injure yourself and one who is dear to you."

Guy Fawkes smiled, and laid his hand lightly on her fair shoulder.

"Wouldst destroy for ever," continued Evelyn, "your hopes of Violet Hamlyn?"

Guy Fawkes started and withdrew his hand from the shoulder of the dancing-girl.

She saw it, and a pearly tear came suddenly to her eye.

"You promise me, then?" said she, looking timidly up in his face.

"I do," said Guy Fawkes, whose thoughts for the moment had wandered from the scene.

"And swear?"

"No oath is needed when men promise willingly."

"Be it so—I will trust you. Now hear me——"

"First tell me," interrupted Guy Fawkes, "what thou knowest of Violet Hamlyn."

"I may not answer that ; but listen to me——"

"This is a scheme in which the partisans of the king play a dishonest part," muttered Guy Fawkes ; "but, mark me, a day of retribution is at hand. The masked stranger told me that treachery to the Holy Church would aid the king——"

"Nay, do listen to me," repeated Evelyn, this time reproachfully, "for I have aided thee."

"'Tis true, my sweet one, and I acknowledge it but churlishly," said Guy Fawkes, humbly. "Twice have ye saved my life—aye, this last good act of thine hath rescued me from worse than death. Say how I can recompense it—if the gratitude of a life—if the protection of a true heart and a willing arm—if all I possess——"

"Do not speak thus," said the girl, indignantly. "Give your gratitude to heaven, your gold to your hirelings, and your protection to her you love. I ask not these. There is no barter made in what I have done for thee this night.

"It was this weak hand," continued she, with excitement, "which fired the train and saved you from the torments of the rack. It was I who made your keeper faithless, who now, at the jeopardy of his life, has brought you hither. Dost hear me?"

"And how," demanded Guy Fawkes, "hast thou compassed this? The man that waits for thee in the boat below has the stamp of Cain upon his brow. It was no generous impulse that made him do thy bidding, fair one."

The dancing-girl blushed crimson

"Is it just," said she, with sparkling eyes—"is it manly to question me thus, Sir Cavalier?"

"Hear me now, my kind one," said Guy Fawkes. "Had we met in a scene of revelry—had I known thee but as one young and beautiful, though the companion of base and lawless men—had I seen thee but as the dancing-girl, whom a hundred gallants passed rude jests upon, then, indeed, might you have spurned my questions with scorn.

"But now," he added, with emphasis, "twice, owing to you, my life has been spared. I am not ungrateful, Evelyn, knowing that but for thee at this moment I should have been lying with distorted limbs under the torture of the rack. I ask you—as you are my saviour—is it a marvel that I should demand to know the sacrifice at which you have saved me?"

"I cannot, will not, answer you," said the girl, impetuously. "What boots it you to know? No power on earth can recall it now."

And she again covered her face with her hands and wept.

"Say not so," cried Guy Fawkes, with increasing emotion; "you are too young to despair. What is past——"

"Name it not," said the girl, shuddering. "Had I gold to buy thy rescue? Had I power to bid your keepers turn aside? Would the iron doors turn at my bidding? Would the stone walls open to give thee liberty?"

Guy Fawkes essayed to speak, but she went on without heeding him.

"Were't better that I leaned over thy couch in all the purity of a cold but innocent heart—over thee mangled, helpless, lifeless; or that now, standing here without a fetter or wound, you should ask *me* what sacrifice I have made."

"Your words are riddles," said Guy Fawkes, "and yet they rouse fears worse than the rack you have saved me from. Heavens!" he continued, powerfully exercised, "are you then—you, whom a cynic might adore—are you, my beautiful and generous one, the victim of——"

"Peace, peace!" cried the dancing-girl, wildly—"I could bear revilings from all the world, but not from thee."

"Revile thee," said Guy Fawkes, reproachfully; "no, but I would pity—I would save thee—I would——"

"Pity—I ask it not," said the dancing-girl, throwing back the long scattered ringlets from her brow, "and to save me exceeds your power. But see—the morning already dawns, and I tamper with danger."

It was as she had said.

The east was grey, and a faint cold light was struggling with the moonbeams.

The girl's pale face and the deep melancholy of her aspect were in keeping with the cheerless light that now threw a pallid glow on every object.

Yet she was exceedingly beautiful, perhaps more touchingly so for the simplicity and poverty of her guise and the ineffable sadness of her countenance.

The light bodice that bound her graceful bust was of white, like her robe—poor, but unsullied; and the faded cloak which she had thrown over her shoulders could not impair the luxuriant beauty of the silken hair that fell on it, nor hide the round white arm and hand that peeped beneath its folds.

Guy Fawkes gazed on her with passionate admiration.

"She is mate for a king," he muttered to himself. "Angel is written on her sweet countenance, and yet——"

Evelyn appeared to read his thoughts.

She laid her hand again upon his arm, and, raising her starry, eloquent eyes to his face, said, in a voice of touching plaintiveness—

"Think not harshly of me."

"Harshly of thee, kind heart? No, no."

"But I know," added the dancing-girl, sadly, "we cannot help our thoughts; but remember, whatever I am, I would have suffered a thousand deaths—infamy, scorn, your own reproaches, rather than have had cause to mourn for thee.

"Hark, they whistle," she added, as the shrill sound came from the river below; "I dare not stay."

Guy Fawkes made a movement as though to remonstrate.

"Nay, brave sir, you can do nothing for me," she continued; "think of me as one lost—as a poor flower crushed almost before it blossomed—as one unworthy the concern of thy heart, which I know is a feeling and a noble one.

"You despised not my first warning—forget not my second. I pray thee to remember that there is no heroism in being heedless, and needless danger is a braggart's boast.

"You are—you still will be—an object of pursuit, of crafty design, of untiring watchfulness, to those from whom you have this night escaped.

"Men steeled by poverty and callous by unpunished crime will haunt your path. Gold, in a heavy sum, is set upon thy capture, and there are ready hands to seek to accomplish it.

"Stir not abroad at nightfall, or travel without a sure guard. Avoid the pathways by the river-side, and, if you value your dearest hopes, and those of her you love, be silent as to what you have seen to-night.

"Trust the page your kindness has sheltered. He is faithful, Sir Cavalier, and will serve you well."

At this moment the call from the river again fell on their ears.

"I must be gone. Again they call me."

"But answer them not," urged Guy Fawkes, drawing her to him. "Answer them not. Go not there again. Your lot, whatever it is, may brighten yet. Nay, by heaven, you shall not go from me!"

"I must!" exclaimed the dancing girl, with her wonted impetuosity. "The chains that bind me I cannot break, though they gall my very soul."

"But others may," observed Guy Fawkes, meaningly. "Nay, I will not, cannot suffer you to go thither again. Let them do their worst, I will defend you while I can raise an arm. There is a hostelry at no great distance, let us hasten to it and there seek refuge. By heaven you shall not go back!"

"Unhand me, Sir Cavalier," cried Evelyn, vehemently. "Hark! they whistle again! I cannot, dare not—understand me—*would* not refuse to answer!"

"And yet it is a thraldom," said Guy

Fawkes, "which even now I mark you shudder at!"

"But one I will not be questioned for obeying. Farewell, farewell. Once more they call for me. Follow my warning, and forget poor Evelyn the dancing-girl."

She seized his hand as she spoke, pressed it passionately to her cold lips, then swiftly glided from his side.

Guy Fawkes followed to the top of the bank and saw her dart like a fawn into the boat, which the next moment shot out into the stream.

It rowed rapidly down the river and was soon out of sight.

The dark, suspicious-looking vessel, already mentioned, had disappeared.

CHAPTER XIII.

THE VISION—A PROPHETIC WARNING—IN THE HANDS OF THE ENEMY—LEO THE PAGE TO THE RESCUE.

GUY FAWKES stood alone.

The chill morning breeze played upon his fevered cheek, the quiet river rippled at his feet, and the early songsters sang merrily in the welkin.

The strange events which, since sunset, he had passed through appeared miraculous—his parting with Harold and Violet at the old house by the river; his assault and seizure; the threatened rack, at which even now his blood ran cold; his rescue and escape, and the extraordinary means by which these had been effected; while the singular, wayward bearing of the dancing-girl and her mysterious surroundings perplexed and impressed him more than all the rest

The whole seemed to him as a dream, from which he was but partially awakened.

He gazed around him with a vacant eye; then, leaning against a tree, fell into a train of thought.

The scenes he had recently been engaged in passed in succession across his mind, until every image and thought became painful to him.

The early morning mists still lay over the silent landscape.

A dense white cloud suddenly rose before his straining vision, and he became conscious of a dim, shadowy presence, that ever haunted him when alone and in moods like these.

He advanced towards it with hands outstretched, like one labouring under the influence of magnetism.

As he approached it still nearer he perceived that the vision had resolved itself into the angelic form of his sainted sister Esmé

With his lips partly open and his eyes wildly starting from their sockets, while his whole expression was that of one whose senses were momentarily paralysed by fear or awe, Guy Fawkes sank reverently upon his knees.

A solemn stillness filled the air, and even the voices of the birds became dumb.

At length, as though recovering from the spell which enchained him, Guy Fawkes suddenly raised his hands imploringly towards the vision of seraphic beauty, and thus addressed it—

"Spirit of my beloved sister, wherefore hast thou appeared to me? Is it to reproach and admonish me for letting other matters of a less sacred nature weigh with and turn me aside from my oath—my vow to avenge thy cruel death?"

The lovely vision shook its head firmly but sorrowfully.

"Art thou, then, come," continued Guy Fawkes, "to confirm me in the opinion that I am the elect of heaven to be the chief agent in destroying those who oppress us, and the instrument through which our forlorn and fallen Church shall be restored?"

Again the beauteous form mournfully shook its head.

"Speak, saintly shade of my revered and idolised Esmé," pursued Guy Fawkes, in a dreamy, fanatical style. "This sacred enterprise in which I am embarked, and which so engrosses my every sense—my every thought—will it succeed? Is it approved of by high heaven?"

As he ceased speaking the figure seemed to glide towards him, for he felt the touch of its rosy finger, lighter than the thistle's down, placed upon his bent and trembling head.

Then an angelic voice, in accents of wondrous sweetness, said—

"Desist, my brother, desist! Be warned—be warned!"

The musical, harp-like sounds vibrated and died away with the low hum of the scented breeze, and a deep and holy stillness reigned around.

For some moments Guy Fawkes remained with his head bent low and his form heaving with suppressed emotion, scarcely daring to raise his eyes.

But when at length he did so the fairy form had vanished, as though it had melted into the fleecy mists of morning.

"It is an omen—a prophetic omen—that our cause will fail," mused Guy Fawkes, reflectively; "but I must not deter nor dishearten my brethren by telling them what this day I have seen and heard. Furthermore, I am ready to spill my last drop of blood if it will ever so lightly aid our project or benefit the Church!"

The early sun now shone warmly on the green summer fields, the smooth wide river, and the beautiful country around.

Guy Fawkes roused himself and proceeded towards a hostelry, which he knew was at no great distance from the river side.

It was snugly situated under the shelter of a wooded hill, and not far from a rough, broken pathway, which in those days formed the only road for some miles on that side of the Thames.

The picturesque little inn was kept by a man named Luke Lovelark, a jocund knave, who Guy Fawkes remembered had served in his regiment abroad, and who now, out of respect for his calling, named it The Jolly Trooper.

As Guy Fawkes approached the inn he heard the sound of voices, the noise of trenchers, and now and then a loud laugh, as of men who jested at their ease.

He entered the little paved court that joined the house to the stables, and approaching the open door, at which a huge mastiff was slumbering in the sun, paused a moment and heard as follows—

"I repeat it, Master Luke," said a solemn voice. "These are sorrowful times that see our fellow-townsmen given to the flames. Poor Master Oakley! I had hoped the days of fire and faggots had expired with Mary of cruel memory."

"Why is good Master Pearce Oakley to be burned like a common felon at the stake?" asked a second one.

"Because," replied another speaker, "he dares to follow the faith of his fathers, and chooses rather to part with his blessed life than sin against his conscience by turning Protestant."

"The devil's benison on all such, say I!" exclaimed a voice, which Guy Fawkes, to his joy, knew at once as that of his late companion.

"Marry! and thou art an honest man!" continued the host. "Thou shalt have thy ale double, and this is beef that should be served on a silver trencher. Eat, man—when thou camest hither you seemed as if——"

Here Guy Fawkes's entrance put a stop to further conversation.

The host, who knew him at sight, threw down the huge knife with which he was cutting off large juicy slices of beef from a smoking joint, and, whipping off his white cap, bowed with profound urbanity to his new guest.

Guy Fawkes's late companion in adversity and hard knocks, who had done such execution with the sapling he had cut, started up and exclaimed—

"Holy Virgin! Then do dead men walk the earth!"

"Get me a stout horse, mine host, that will carry me to London," said Guy Fawkes, addressing Luke.

Then, turning to his confrère in misfortune, who stood gazing upon him in open-eyed astonishment, added—

"I am glad to see you, my friend."

The honest fellow seemed doubtful whether he were dealing with mortal man or not, and reluctantly took Guy Fawkes's proffered hand.

"Thou wilt breakfast ere ye ride, most honourable sir," said the host. "A morsel of beef or venison pasty and a stoup of burned sack will brace you for the journey, and I have as gallant a roan at thy service as ever a brave man bestrode."

"Hast thou another good steed, mine host?" said Guy Fawkes's companion, "for, by the saints, I took this voyage down the river as little on my own business as any journey I ever made, and I am due elsewhere."

"I have," said the worthy host, spreading a snowy cloth on the table before Guy Fawkes; "and the best is heartily at your service. I would I had a better for thee, for thou art a worthy man, and hast a wholesome horror of heretics."

"Wilt join me?" said Guy Fawkes, to his companion of the fight, as he seated himself at the board.

"Marry, that will I, Sir Cavalier!" rejoined the other, readily taking a seat, "for I am as hollow as the dome of St. Paul's, and thirsty to boot, though I have taken more water in two minutes than I ever hope to swallow again all the rest of my days."

The inn kitchen in which Guy Fawkes sat was large and lofty, well-furnished with oaken seats and tables of the same material.

Implements of cookery, oddly mingled with a few weapons of warfare and the chase, glittered on the walls.

Before a blazing fire stood a bright-eyed, rosy-cheeked girl, and a serving-man.

The men that occupied the adjoining seats had the dress and appearance of travelling yeomen, though there was one who sat apart, with his features concealed by the hood of his garbadine, whose bright, piercing eyes—the only feature visible—Guy Fawkes momentarily thought he had seen before.

"Well, how fared ye, my friend?" said Guy Fawkes, in a low voice, as he slowly dispatched his meal.

"In good sooth but ill, my master," replied his companion, in the same low tone; "I was kept a prisoner, and then—dost note my clothes are yet but poorly dried?—I was thrown, bound hand and foot, into the river."

"What!" said Guy Fawkes, pausing in the act of drinking, "did they then——"

"Aye, marry, did they not; but it pleased Providence and a young priest——"

"How, sirrah; what mean ye?"

"Even what I say," rejoined the other. "I snapped the cords that tied my hands, and nearly managed to reach the bank, where I lay exhausted, and should have been drowned after all, but for the young priest and a bright-eyed page he had with him."

"How were they named?" asked Guy Fawkes, eagerly.

Here the muffled figure leaned forward, apparently to listen.

"I bethink me the young priest was called Jerome; I caught not the name of the page."

The muffled figure rose unnoticed, and departed from the room.

Guy Fawkes looked surprised, but muttered an unintelligible ejaculation of satisfaction.

The meal being finished, the clatter of horse-hoofs on the paved doorway told that the steeds were ready.

Guy Fawkes rose, while his companion took a small gold chain from under his doublet, and presenting it to the landlord, said—

"My pouch is empty, mine host, but take this chain, and keep it till I pay thee. Lose it not, if thou art an honest man, for it was given me by Dolly Rosebud, the fairest maid in broad Surrey. Thy horse this good gentleman will see housed with his own."

"Nay," said the host, "I will e'en trust thee without thy chain."

Guy Fawkes handed the host a gold piece.

"This," said he, "will pay for my companion and me. Your steeds shall be safely stabled in Westminster."

The landlord bowed and Guy Fawkes mounted the horse that stood waiting for him.

His companion followed his example.

Guy Fawkes—his dress soiled, his sword-belt empty, and the feather in his cap crushed and broken—began to arouse the curiosity of the idlers in the courtyard, and he and his companion were anxious to be off.

There was good need they should be so, though they were unsuspicious of immediate danger.

At last they were about to set spurs to their impatient steeds when a loud, stentorian voice shouted—

"Hold, in the king's name!"

And the same instant Oliver Blackstock appeared at the head of half a score of men-at-arms, filling up the entrance to the gateway of the inn yard.

"Ha!" exclaimed Guy Fawkes, starting back at this unexpected apparition. Then, as though to himself, "This is the work of that muffled villain who left awhile since. Curses light upon him, for I strongly suspect he is that false priest, Brother Hubert."

"Yield thee, bold traitor," cried Oliver Blackstock, advancing, sword in hand. "I have thee now, mine enemy; escape is impossible." And his sinister features, ablaze with vindictiveness, were rendered yet more repulsive by the gash upon them inflicted by Guy Fawkes's petronel at Hamlyn House.

Guy Fawkes uttered a defiant laugh, for, despite their overwhelming numbers, and weaponless though he was, he would have made a dash for it, and ridden them down.

But as though Blackstock had divined his intention he exclaimed suddenly—

"Present! Fire upon him if he attempts to resist!"

And in an instant half a score of matchlocks were pointed at Guy Fawkes's head and heart.

Seeing that resistance was useless Guy Fawkes dismounted at once, as also did his companion.

Of course the greatest consternation prevailed in the old inn yard, and Master Luke Lovelark, the worthy host, seemed more perturbed than all the rest put together, for he entertained a deep regard for Guy Fawkes (his former officer and comrade in many a hard-fought fight), and it hurt him greatly to think it was beyond his power to help him in his hour of need.

In an instant the troopers surrounded their prisoner, and, with an expression of demoniac triumph on his ugly visage, Oliver Blackstock strode up to Guy Fawkes. Shaking his gloved hand in his face, he hissed rather than said—

"It is my turn now braggart!"

"Make the most of it, then, for it will be short-lived!" cried Guy Fawkes.

And before they could divine his intention he broke away from the loosened hold of his captors and dealt the luckless officer a vigorous blow in the chest.

With a howl of rage and pain he staggered back, and, all unconscious of the well-hole behind him, fell headlong to its deep and slimy bottom.

A shout of loud laughter from some of the bystanders greeted the surly officer's mishap, while the troopers, with a roar of savage fury, pounced upon their prisoner and brutally bore him to the earth.

One gigantic fellow raised the butt of his matchlock to strike the struggling conspirator, which, had it reached its mark, would have effectually put an end to his adventures.

But a terrific blow from the hammer-like fist of Guy Fawkes's companion lay the huge trooper groaning in the dust.

Meanwhile some of the troopers and a few of the idlers about the yard were busy assisting the unfortunate Oliver Blackstock out of the well.

And a pretty figure he cut as he sat gasping for breath on the low wall of the well, his dripping clothes hanging about him in folds, all over mud and green slime.

Indeed, his appearance was so ludicrous and mirth-provoking that few present could prevent themselves laughing, the worthy host not proving an exception.

"Aye, laugh away, ye witless knaves!" cried the discomfited officer, vengefully, through his grinding teeth; "but, mark me, I'll turn thy tears o' mirth to those of bitterest sorrow an I prove any of ye to be Papist rogues."

And he looked pointedly at the red, swollen face, of the worthy host, who seemed in instant danger of bursting in an endeavour to suppress his laughter.

"As for thee, thou spawn of Antichrist," added the dripping Oliver, turning with fiendish hate to Guy Fawkes, "thou hast least cause of all for merriment, for 'tis a ghost of a smile that will sit on thy ill-favoured face when 'tis spiked, as it will shortly be, on Traitors' Gate."

He then rose, and, advancing towards Luke Lovelark, demanded of him a piece of rope with which to fasten Guy Fawkes's hands.

"Marry, brave sir," rejoined the merry host, "were I of a mind to hang myself I lack the means, for, by my faith, I've not a piece of rope long enough in the place."

"Beware how ye trifle with me, sirrah, for should I prove that ye speak falsely I may e'en be tempted to turn executioner myself and hang ye by your own fireside," said Blackstock, with a black scowl. "Search the place at once, men!"

"Nay, it were bootless," cried the host, standing in their path. "But here is a bell-pull that will doubtless answer the purpose," he added, reaching one from a press as he spoke, which in truth looked strong enough but was in reality useless.

The officer took it with a significant sneer, and bade his men bind the hands of Guy Fawkes and Ralph Roley, Guy Fawkes's companion, behind their backs.

This was speedily done, and four of the troopers were told off to keep guard over the prisoners in the adjoining room.

Oliver Blackstock then retired for a short time to make himself presentable. This done, he ordered some ale for his men and a flagon of burnt sack for himself, for which he did not pay.

Then saying, in a tone just loud enough for the astute host to hear, that they must hasten with all speed to Heron Abbey, he quitted the house with six troopers, leaving the rest in charge of Guy Fawkes and Ralph till his return.

No sooner had the retreating footsteps of the king's officer and his men died away in the distance than the host busied himself making a huge bowl of spiced ale posset, accompanying the task with sly winks and knowing grins, while he ever and anon looked furtively about as though in fear of being watched.

When the steaming savoury potion was ready he went to the door of the room where the troopers kept guard over Guy Fawkes and his companion, and, gaining admittance, set the flowing bowl upon the table, saying that he had brought the liquor according to their master's orders.

The host then, in a side whisper, told Guy

Fawkes that Blackstock and his men had gone to Heron Abbey.

The troopers were delighted at the good cheer set before them, and as soon as the host left the room fell to a-drinking with right good will.

The chamber in which they sat had a diamond-shaped lattice in it that overlooked a charming fruit garden, which was partly open to admit the fresh air.

Near to this two of the troopers were seated, with their loaded matchlocks resting against the window-frame.

Guy Fawkes and Ralph sat near the old-fashioned fireplace, while the other two soldiers rested between them and the door.

Soon the bowl was empty, and one of the troopers, going to the door and opening it, shouted down the passage—

"What ho, landlord! Fill again the flowing bowl; our master will pay the merry reckoning when he returns."

The bowl was refilled and emptied, and refilled a third time. The potent, fascinating liquor begun to tell even on the hard-drinking soldiery.

One, with his head upon his arms, was already snoring loudly on the oaken table, whilst the others gave evident tokens of shortly succumbing to the drowsy god.

Guy Fawkes watched the proceedings with a grim smile of satisfaction.

Suddenly the shadow of a figure fell across the window.

He looked quickly up, and beheld the form of a boy standing in the opening.

It was his page Leo, Evelyn's brother.

The boy was in the act of stealthily drawing the nearest trooper's matchlock through the window.

Guy Fawkes recognised him on the instant, and the boy put his fingers to his lip to enjoin silence.

A meaning look was exchanged between Guy Fawkes and Ralph, and Leo swiftly and silently possessed himself of the other trooper's gun, both of which he placed outside against the wall.

By this time two more of the troopers were asleep with their heads upon the table, while the fourth was obstinately trying to keep himself awake.

But at length his nodding pate rested upon the board, and he, too, appeared to sleep.

Then it was that Leo the page stole softly through the window into the room.

One glance at the sleeping troopers to assure himself that all was safe, then, drawing a sharp knife, he severed first Guy Fawkes's then his companion's bonds at a stroke.

"Secure that fellow's matchlock," whispered Guy Fawkes to Ralph, pointing to the soldier nearest the door, "while I take charge of this one's."

Ralph obeyed with alacrity, and, gun in hand, made for the window through which Leo had just clambered.

Guy Fawkes was not quite so successful with his man.

He had drank less heavily than his companions, and seemed to be dimly conscious of what was going on, for as Guy Fawkes attempted to take the weapon from his hand his grasp all at once tightened upon it, and, starting to his feet, he exclaimed—

"Aha! prisoners escaping!" and he raised the matchlock to his shoulder as Guy Fawkes, with a swift bound, sprang through the open window.

The trooper's aim was unsteady and the ball flew harmlessly over Guy Fawkes's head.

The report had aroused the troopers and all was now consternation and confusion.

They staggered to their feet and blundered about in a vain search for their weapons.

All at once, however, their attention was directed towards the garden, where they beheld Guy Fawkes struggling in the grasp of the muffled traveller.

"Help! help! Quick—secure the prisoner!" he called, frantically.

The trooper again raised his weapon and fired.

A flash of fire, a loud report, and a shriek of agony followed.

All rushed to the window, and as the smoke cleared they beheld the muffled figure writhing upon the ground, while the blood flowed in a red tide from his shoulder.

It was the monk—Brother Hubert!

The troopers, without heeding the wounded man, made instant search for the fugitives, but in vain. They had escaped and taken the weapons of their foes with them.

<hr/>

CHAPTER XIV.

SIR SIDNEY AND THE MAGICIAN—A DARK SCHEME OF VENGEANCE—THE ATTACK UPON THE CONSPIRATORS' HAUNT—ABDUCTION OF VIOLET.

RETURN we now to the mystic abode of Zach Horlock the astrologer and to Sir Sidney Wildbrook.

It will be remembered that when the magician invoked the supposed spirit to reveal the fate of King James and the destiny of the unscrupulous knight Sir Sidney himself, Guy Fawkes, disguised, appeared in the place of the base agent of the wily astrologer.

This successful ruse on the part of Guy Fawkes had first been conceived by his having seen Sir Sidney Wildbrook enter the house of the magician.

Suspecting the dark and sinful nature of the depraved nobleman's visit, he had hastened for the assistance of his companions, and together they had secretly entered the abode of sorcery and sin. They seized the base tool and partner of Horlock's duplicity, who was waiting to ascend to the room above as the spirit, and terrified him into a confession of his master's black secrets, with the result already described.

The sudden and mysterious disappearance of the magician and his companions had been effected in this wise.

When Horlock caused the wall of fire to rise between him and the conspirators, to save himself and party from their fierce attack, he touched the knob of a hidden lever in the thick rough wall, which caused a portion of the masonry to open and reveal a secret chamber.

The magician and his party hastily entered, and the door closed silently and sharply upon them.

And before the mystic flame, which Horlock had raised to save them from their foes had expired, the wall had resumed its solid and immovable appearance.

On the departure of Guy Fawkes and his companions, after their fruitless search, the magician and Sir Sidney ventured forth from their place of concealment.

"The bold, presumptuous villains," cried Sir Sidney, with knitted brow and flashing eye; "one word of mine would bring all their lawless heads to the block."

"Yet methinks it would serve thy purpose better, Sir Sydney, to leave that word unsaid," observed the wily astrologer, with hidden meaning.

"True, Horlock, true," returned the nobleman, musingly, and then, in a more modified tone, "marry, 'twas a narrow escape we had from the hands of those rebellious rogues."

A contemptuous sneer curled the thin lips of the magician—though unnoticed by Sir Sidney—and he replied, with just a tinge of sarcasm—

"For thee, Sir Sidney, mayhap there was good cause to apprehend danger, but for myself, my divine art places me above the fear of such puny foes."

Sir Sidney frowned slightly, though he appeared not to notice the inference of the crafty astrologer, and said—

"Wilt despatch me one of thy serving-men, good Horlock, to dog the footsteps of these audacious traitors, for their rendezvous will now be kept secret from me, and I would give much to know their hiding-place."

"Your grace's request shall be instantly obeyed," said the astrologer, with fawning humility.

And, quitting the room, he gave the required instructions to a menial.

The man instantly departed on his unworthy mission, while the magician returned to his distinguished guest.

"Harkee, friend Horlock," said Sir Sidney, motioning the other to a chair, "as thou art skilled in so many matters, perhaps it hath come under thy cognisance that I am deeply enamoured of that fair and beauteous wench, Violet Hamlyn?"

"That hath it, your grace," returned the magician, "and furthermore, that she hath refused thy addresses on the score of thy profligacies and thine over-ripe years."

"Ah! varlet, dost thou dare to mock me——"

"Pardon, your grace, I echo but the voice of rumour——"

"Then do you lack wisdom as well as courtesy, for rumour, as of old, is both liar and fool!"

"Trust me, your grace, I will e'en be more circumspect in the future," said the astrologer, cringingly.

"See that thou art, or it shall fare ill with thee, despite thy vaunted power," said the nobleman, with a dark, meaning scowl.

The magician turned ghastly pale, but there was more of resentment than fear in the quiver of his lip as he bowed him low.

In an altered tone Sir Sidney proceeded—

"That the maiden looks coldly on my suit, and that her sire, Sir Godfrey Hamlyn, regards the probability of my being his son-in-law with ill-favour I freely grant ye; though to further me in my wooing I e'en joined myself to a cause, which, apparently Sir Godfrey himself is on the eve of espousing."

"And the nature of which——"

"Is a secret," interrupted the plotting nobleman; "and one which will pay thee far better to preserve than reveal, friend Horlock!"

Bright promise and dark menace were expressed in these covert words

The magician fully gauged the strength of their meaning, and again made obeisance before the knight, who continued—

"The true cause of Sir Godfrey's antipathy to me is, I strongly suspect, because in former years I was the favoured suitor of the fair lady Eleanor, now his wife, but whose highly excessive and too demonstrative affection for me made me suspect the purity of her motives, and, in a moment of pique and despair at my coldness, gave her hand to my eager but despised rival."

"False, calumniating slanderer," thought Horlock.

"Well do I know the spotless purity and angelic modesty of the gentle being whom in your venomous malice ye seek so vilely to traduce—well do I know that she ever held ye in abhorrence and rejected your detested offer with the scorn it merited; and further, recreant knight, thy vow to be revenged on her, though they be blood of thy blood and bone of thy flesh.

"And is her innocent child to be the first victim of thy fiendish vindictiveness towards that hapless house? No, by the stars, whose humble slave and devoted student I am, not if Zach Horlock can prevent it; though I must act with extreme caution, for already doth he hold the rope round my neck, which one false step would cause him to pull tight, and thus cut me short for evermore."

"Thou art strangely silent, sirrah," said Sir Sidney, noticing the magician's preoccupation; "I would know the purport of thy secret thoughts."

"I was pondering on the perversity of fate and the incompatibility of the sexes," replied the astrologer.

"And have ye found a remedy, most learned pedant, for the last-named complaint?"

"That have I in good sooth, Sir Knight."

"How, sirrah? Explain——"

"For incompatibility of thoughts, sentiments, and feelings," went on Horlock, "I have love philters that will soften the heart of lover or mistress though it were as hard as adamant."

"Speakest thou seriously?" said the superstitious knight.

"Aye, by the twelve mystic signs of the Zodiac, do I; and she, who was as cold as frozen snow before partaking of the magic draught, will be ready to fall into the hitherto despairing arms of he whose hand shall have administered the potent philter."

"Then, by the mass, will I barter with thee for one. I would win this proud girl for mine own, by means fair or foul, for I owe her parents a grudge I would repay with weighty interest."

And the expression that accompanied these words would have put to shame an exultant fiend's.

"Quick, give me the philter," added Sir Sidney. "I am impatient to try its efficacy; moreover, 'tis growing late, and I would be gone."

"Thinkest thou, Sir Knight, than a draught of such potency and magical power could be produced or obtained like the ordinary drug of the leech?" said the wizard, with offended dignity.

"How mean you, seer?"

"That every love philter is so constructed as to fit the peculiar circumstances of each case, and to work the spell one would require two whole days and nights of extreme toil, unremittent attention, and assiduous care."

"Marry! sayest thou so in good earnest. But perhaps the magical influence of extra gold might hasten the brewing of it. "Take this," he added, handing Horlock a well-filled purse, "and do ye bring me the philter to-morrow night I will double the gift."

"I will do all in my power to expedite the work," said the astrologer, impressively; "but I make no promise of its completion before the given time."

"I shall expect it at my residence to-morrow e'en, nevertheless. Adieu, thou subtle knave, adieu."

Waving his hand gaily, the high-bred ruffian, attended by a servant, bearing a lighted flambeau, descended the stairs, and, wrapping his cloak round him, ventured forth into the stilly night.

The magician, as he watched him unseen from the window, muttered curses on his unworthy head, and with the words "Fool!" and "Villain!" trembling on his quivering lip, he entered his secret chamber to prepare the magic charm.

Despite his rich patron's injunctions to hasten the compounding of the love philter, Horlock could not, or, more probably, in order not to lessen the dignity of his art, would not, hurry its completion.

Whatever the cause, it was not until the second night from Sir Sidney's visit to the astrologer's abode that the knight received the much coveted potion from the hands of Horlock's attendant.

It was the same rascal who had been sent to dog the footsteps of Guy Fawkes and his companions, and, though he started like a bloodhound on the scent, he had failed to discover the conspirators' hiding-place until that same evening.

Sir Sidney was delighted at the news, and liberally rewarded the fellow for his information.

An hour later, having got together some half-dozen armed retainers, and enlisted the sevices of as many men-at-arms, Sir Sidney led them, under cover of darkness and the rising storm, to the secret haunt of the conspirators on the banks of the Thames.

They commenced their attack upon the rear of the premises, and so secret and silent had been their approach that it was only when they were beating down the stout oaken door that the conspirators were awakened to a sense of their danger.

Taken thus by surprise their situation was rendered still more alarming by the fact that several of their members had gone in search of Guy Fawkes, among whom was Harold Rookby, so that the odds they had to contend against were considerable.

But the conspirators fought bravely and well, with a courage born of desperation, and several of the foemen fell maimed and bleeding, or sank to rise no more.

But ultimate victory over their determined foes they dared not hope for, and the word was given for flight.

The conspirators immediately beat a hasty retreat, and, rushing in a body to the room above, succeeded in placing a heavy wooden bar across the closed door just as their assailants came thundering upon it with their heavy weapons.

This was the apartment in which Violet Hamlyn lay concealed after her rescue from the burning monastery.

Terrified and alarmed at the awful sounds of strife below, the pale but beauteous girl stood in the centre of the room trembling and speechless, and clasping the page Leo for support.

The brave boy had drawn his dagger—with it firmly clutched in his right hand, and his left clasping the slender waist of Violet, he swore to defend her against the violence of their ruffianly foes.

Despite their imminent peril a murmur of admiration escaped the conspirators, as, dashing into the room, they beheld the bold and fearless attitude of the boy.

"Come, Miss Hamlyn, quick, to the roof!" cried Ambrose Rookwood, who acted as leader "'tis our only hope of escape!"

A ladder was placed instantly against the roof, the bolt of the trapdoor drawn back, and Rookwood and John Wright stepped out on to the roof in order to assist Violet through.

The deeply agitated girl was being handed up the ladder by Mark Swinton and Robert Winter, while Leo was standing at the foot, when suddenly the door gave way with a terrific crash.

The next instant Sir Sidney Wildbrook, with his men at his back, dashed into the chamber.

Swinton and Winter turned to meet their opponents, whom they attacked with tiger-like ferocity.

Violet, thus suddenly deprived of their support, and not near enough to reach the hands of those on the roof, slipped in a half-swooning state down the ladder again.

"Ha! Violet here," cried Sir Sidney, with savage joy, on beholding her; "this is a prize unexpected. Seize the girl," he added, to a trooper hard by, for he was busy defending himself against Mark Swinton's bold and fierce attack.

The man rushed forward to secure the shrinking terrified girl.

His rude grasp was upon her outer garment, when, quick as thought, Leo plunged his weapon deep in the ruffian's shoulder, and he fell back with a groan.

"Fly! sweet mistress, fly!" cried Leo, trying to force Violet up the steps.

"Quick, or you are lost—lost!" shouted Rookwood from the roof above.

But Sir Sidney at that moment ran his sword through Mark Swinton, who sank weltering in his blood.

Springing over his fallen body, the high-born villain struck Leo a blow that felled him to the earth, and, seizing hold of Violet, who had nearly reached the top of the ladder, dragged her forcibly back again.

"Mine at last!" he cried, with devilish triumph, clasping her in his hated embrace, and pressing his loathsome kisses upon her pure, sweet lips.

"Take that, profane, unmanly villain," loudly ejaculated Robert Winter

And, striking the profligate noble a fearful blow in the face, that sent him reeling against the wall, he darted up the ladder and on to the roof, just in time to escape a shower of missiles aimed at him by Sir Sidney's followers.

Chase was instantly given, but the conspirators contrived to make their escape over the housetops owing to the increasing darkness and their knowledge of the locality.

Violet had swooned, and lay motionless and death-like upon the bare floor, while those of Sir Sidney's followers who had not joined in the chase of the fugitives crowded round their stunned and smarting lord to tender him their assistance.

"To rescue the lady now is hopeless," thought Leo, dejectedly.

But it suddenly flashed across his bright active mind that he could better help Violet, to whom he was devotedly attached, by being at liberty than a prisoner.

So, taking advantage of the confusion and consternation which now prevailed, he slipped out of the room unperceived, and was soon speeding along the river bank on the wings of the wind.

CHAPTER XV.

HAROLD ROOKBY MAKES A TERRIBLE DIS-COVERY—DEATH OF MARK SWINTON—THE AFFRAY AT THE INN—A VALUABLE ACQUAINT-ANCE—ON THE TRACK.

IT was nearly daylight when Harold Rookby returned, weary and dejected, from an unsuccessful search after his cherished friend and companion, Guy Fawkes.

As he approached the old house by the river the broken door and other palpable evidences of recent strife caused his heart to give a sudden bound of fear and quicken almost to suffocation.

What if some terrible danger had befallen his beloved Violet!

The thought seemed to turn his very blood to ice and paralyse his every sense.

In a state bordering on distraction he dashed into the house, now all battered and bruised, and with broken weapons and patches of blood in every direction.

That a fierce and deadly conflict had taken place was plainly evident at every step he took, and in his effort to reach the room above his painfully-swelling heart almost failed him.

But with a resolution borrowed of coming despair he mounted the stairs.

The shattered door, the broken panes and walls, the gory stains upon the floor, all mutely told of the terrible tale of destruction and death

Harold glanced hastily round the room, but it was empty.

"Gone! stolen from me, perhaps for evermore!" he exclaimed, clasping his hand to his brow in a paroxysm of deepest anguish "Oh, had I but been here they should never have torn her from my arms—not though they numbered legions! My poor, persecuted darling, let me but know the name of thy dastardly

abductor, and not all the power in the land shall save him from my vengeance!"

Just then a low moan fell on his tortured ears.

Harold turned with a start, and, glancing searchingly around, now noticed in a deep recess the recumbent form of a man.

With a feeling of inexpressible dread and dire foreboding he cautiously approached.

A straggling ray of early light fell upon the upturned face of the prostrate figure, over which the grey shadow of death was fast stealing.

"Great heavens, Swinton!" cried Harold, starting back in horror at his companion's ghastly white face and the gaping wound in his side, from which the life stream was slowly ebbing away.

Going on one knee, and raising the head of the fast sinking man, the young soldier said, with deep feeling—

"You are wounded, my poor friend.'

"Aye, unto death," said Swinton, slowly and faintly.

"Oh, that a leech were at hand!" cried Harold, in a distressed tone. "What can I do for you, Mark—poor Mark?"

"Nothing, Rookby," he answered; "my sands of life are ebbing fast—all will soon be over; but do not ye tarry, lest our enemies return and you too fall a victim to their treacherous machinations."

"But tell me, Mark, if ye have still the power, what has happened, and where is Violet?"

The narration was a tedious and a painful one, interrupted as it was by the dying man's struggles for breath as the occasional rush of blood to his throat choked his utterance.

"But the name of this ruthless fiend—this vile abductor of my darling Violet," panted Harold, when the sad story was told.

Swinton rolled his glassy eyes helplessly, for his rigid lips seemed powerless to utter a sound.

"Merciful Providence, am I to be robbed of the prospect of wreaking vengeance on the heads of the dastardly perpetrators of this foul crime?"

And then, in accents of agonised appeal, he again craved to know the name of their despoiler.

The dying conspirator strove hard to reply, but, for a time, was unable to do so. At length, by a supreme effort, he managed to articulate, in a scarcely audible whisper, the name of Sir Sidney Wildbrook, then fell back—dead.

Harold Rookby forced back the curses and execrations that rose to his lips at mention of him who had wrought such suffering and sorrow. He was in the presence of death.

Taking off his cloak he reverently drew it over the rigid form of his lifeless comrade, and, muttering a brief prayer for his soul's welfare, left the house with hushed and solemn step.

Without, the whole face of nature was changed—black, angry clouds filled the sky, a tearing, shrieking wind rushed hurriedly by, violently agitating the surface of the river, and a fine penetrating rain was beginning to fall.

With bitterness in his heart and fury in his mind Harold set out for the residence of Sir Sidney Wildbrook.

It was situate in Hatton-garden, then an elysium of green fields and waving trees.

Harold remembered, as he was being ferried across the freshening river, that his mother's late handmaiden, Jane Wiles, had taken service under Sir Sidney, and if he could only obtain a glimpse of her he would soon be able to learn whether Violet was a prisoner in the power of the recreant knight.

By the time he reached Hatton-garden the rain descended in torrents, and he was glad to seek shelter in a hostelry hard by, which he had good reason to suppose Sir Sidney's serving wench would visit about noon.

But the rain still continued its ceaseless downpour, noon came and went, but it brought not Jane Wiles.

Consumed with anxiety and burning impatience at the delay, Harold Rookby, when he had finished his measure of sack, determined to wait no longer, but to go straight to the house and try and get a glimpse of the maiden.

In the inn parlour where he sat was a mixed company, drinking ale, or sack, or the metheglin which the house afforded.

In a corner near the blazing fire sat a jolly-looking minstrel, quaffing the contents of a capacious horn.

At length setting down the cup he passed his rapid fingers over the small harp, or lyre, which he carried by a strap at his side.

The hum of conversation ceased, and all assumed an attitude of attention.

The minstrel again dashed his hand over the strings, and after a short and masterly prelude, sang in a plaintive tone these lines—

"Where has the maiden gone?
    Far from her lover.
Sad, sad will he be
    Till her fate he discover.

"Down with the stream she's gone,
    Tearing her tresses,
And shrieking for aid
    From the spoiler's caresses."

At the first words of the song Harold started and coloured hotly.

"Was there a significance in the quoted words which the singer meant for him, or was it merely one of those marvellous coincidences so common in life?" thought Harold.

He listened eagerly for the next verse, when a low-bred ruffian, in a spirit of utter callousness, drew his knife across the strings of the lyre.

The action passed unnoticed by the minstrel himself, who, again striking his hand across the instrument, caused the half-severed strings to part with a snapping, jarring noise.

The minstrel turned and beheld the grinning ruffian returning his knife to his girdle.

"Thou scurvy rogue!" cried the minstrel, suddenly seizing him by the throat in a vice-like grip, "thus to deprive a man of his means of livelihood. I would throttle ye where ye stand but that I am an honest man and would not rob the hangman of his rights!"

And he flung the ruffian with such violence from him that he stumbled against a table at which his scowling companions were seated. In an instant all were sprawling and struggling upon the ground, at which the other guests became convulsed with loud laughter.

With a yell like a pack of infuriated wolves the savage horde rose to their feet, crying—

"Down with the malapert beggar! Slit the old reptile's throat!"

And with murder gleaming in their evil eyes they drew their knives and rushed upon the minstrel.

But the fearless old man laid hold of a chair, vowing he would brain the first man who approached.

The cowardly crew shrunk back a pace, awed for the moment by the determined front of the old minstrel.

But it would have fared badly with him had not ready succour been at hand.

Harold, who was a lover of fair play, could not stand idly by and see the old man ruthlessly butchered.

Drawing a pair of petronels from his belt, he threw himself between the old minstrel and his ill-favoured assailants.

"Back, ye cowardly, murderous curs!" he exclaimed, in clarion tones, presenting the gleaming weapons at them. "Nigh a half-score against one, and that, too, an old and defenceless man. Get ye gone, or, by the blessed Virgin, I swear I'll make carrion of your ugly carcases."

The cursing, scowling crew saw at a glance that he was not the sort of man to threaten in vain, so they slunk off like whipped curs.

"I owe ye many thanks, young Sir Cavalier," said the minstrel, shaking Harold's hand with a hearty grip, "which I one day hope to repay. Pray accept this call"—giving him a silver whistle—"and should danger threaten you in your travels by the river or among the green woods, blow upon it, and if a score of stout hearts and willing hands be not ready to respond dub me knave and rogue."

Another hearty shake of the hand and he was gone.

Harold walked towards the old-fashioned porch, pondering deeply on the many and singular events in which he had played so prominent a part, when he suddenly observed a pretty damsel, displaying a pair of exquisitely neat ancles as she daintily picked her way over the watery pools facing the inn.

The maiden raised her shapely head at sight of the handsome traveller, and at a glance Harold recognised in her the object of his quest, sweet Jane Wiles.

In an instant he was by her side.

The girl's bright eyes sparkled with mingled pleasure and respect at the sight of Harold, and her damask cheek became more rosy than ever.

Conducting her to a retired nook, the young soldier inquired of her if her master were at home.

The girl replied that he was not—that he went out late the previous night and had not returned.

"And can ye not hazard a guess, fair Mistress Jane, where he may be found?" said Harold, with assumed gaiety.

"Aye, marry! that can I, and a shrewd one too," replied the girl. "Miles Hopkins and Lambert Goff, two of my lord's retainers, came home some two hours since in a sad plight, and I overheard them say that Sir Sidney had gone by water to his castle on the Kentish coast, and they made some mention of a lady young and fair bearing him company."

"Then was the minstrel a true prophet!"

GUY FAWKES
Or Gunpowder, Treason, and Plot.

"TIED ME UP THE MAIDEN," CRIED GUY FAWKES, "OR MY BULLET SHALL RIDDLE THY FOUL HEART!"

No. 4.

exclaimed Harold, hastily, "and I may not tarry a moment longer. Fare thee well, sweetheart, we shall meet anon," and, pressing a piece of money into the blushing girl's hand, he hurried away through the pelting storm.

Reaching the river's brink he, by the aid of a well-filled purse, secured the service of a fast-sailing cutter.

The oarsmen scrambled into their places, the sail was hoisted, and, aided by a favourable breeze and their powerful strokes, the little vessel sped merrily through the dancing waters, whilst Harold Rookby's heart beat high with hope at the prospect of snatching his beloved Violet from the toils of her base and unscrupulous abductor.

They hailed the crews of the several vessels they met to know if they had seen anything of a skiff containing several men and a young lady.

These inquiries were for the most part greeted with bursts of merriment, in which Harold Rookby was far from joining.

All the description he could give of the boat and its occupants was so vague that he could gain no tidings whatever of the object of his anxious search.

They inquired also at the various landing-places on both shores of the river, and here, at least, they acquired some negative information which was valuable, namely, that no boat containing more than two persons, and those not of the softer sex, had put in at them during the past two days.

This news, such as it was, made Harold all the more anxious to continue down the stream, for it never struck him for an instant he might be on the wrong track.

When they reached Woolwich they again inquired of a waterman on board a small fishing vessel whether he had seen anything of a boat containing several men, who were conveying a young lady away against her will.

"No, yer honour," replied the fisherman, touching his hat. "I aint seen nor heard nothing of no young lady, though, some hour agone or more, I picked up a hankercher which mayhap had fallen from some craft, and which might have belonged to the young lady yer honour's in search on."

"Let me see it," said Harold, with eager impatience.

"Well, yer see, yer honour," replied the man, in a sly, shifty way, "I happened to stow it snugly away, and, by St. Nicholas, I can't for the life o' me think where," scratching his head in a perplexed fashion.

"Try and think, my honest fellow, in heaven's name," said the young soldier, in a torment of suspense. "Make instant search, for more than life itself may depend upon the issue."

The fellow turned out his pockets, looked into his hat, went into the little cabin and searched, but all to no purpose—it was not to be found.

"For the love of the blessed Virgin," exclaimed Harold, nearly distracted, "I pray thee search more closely, and if ye find it I will reward ye."

And he held a silver crown between his finger and thumb, as an incentive to the man's exertions.

It operated as money invariably operates,

and in less than two minutes the crafty rogue discovered the kerchief in an inside pocket.

Harold Rookby no sooner beheld it than he exclaimed, excitedly—

"Holy St. Mary, 'tis hers! Here, take thy guerdon, fellow, and give me the kerchief."

And tossing the piece of silver to the fisherman, he snatched the dainty lace trifle away from the man and pressed it passionately to his lips.

"Ah, Violet, my darling!" he murmured fondly, "this precious token tells me that I am on thy track at last, and, Heaven willing, I trust that ere long I may hold thee to my heart as close as I do this dearly-cherished trifle of thine," thrusting the handkerchief into his bosom as he spoke.

Then, turning to the boatmen, he added, with startling energy—

"Row, my brave fellows, row with might and main. Our prey is scented, and I will give each man five silver crowns above the promised reward an' ye run the abducting robbers down!"

The men, encouraged at the prospect of extra reward, went to work with a will and a cheer, and the little vessel fairly shot through the leaping wavelets, as the hurrying wind was all in her favour.

Night, however, was fast approaching, and the owner of the skiff began to cast his eyes wistfully around him, to scan the appearance of the sky.

"What is it ye apprehend, skipper—a storm?" inquired Harold Rookby, closely watching his movements.

"Aye, yer honour," returned the old sailor, "and a right tough and lusty one, too, from the look of yon cloud. Axing yer honor's pardon, I would advise that we put in at the nearest port."

Just then, however, the young soldier caught sight of a boat in the distance, which appeared to be swiftly moving in the same direction as their own.

"Zounds, man, yonder goes the skiff we are in pursuit of, unless I am sorely mistaken!" cried Harold, indignantly, "and think ye I would forego the chance of overtaking her because of a bit of a squall? No, by the mass, not though all the elements were to wreak their fury upon me in the attempt."

The man demurred, looked surly and unwillingly, but the promise of additional reward again quickly silenced his murmurings.

The rain now fell in huge drops, ominous clouds were driving rapidly over the sky, and the ghostly grey of twilight was fast deepening into the darker hue of night.

The anxious, impatient young lover paid no attention to the wind or the rain, however, but the boatmen, who were somewhat less eager, ventured to give a hint or two on the impolicy of braving the coming storm.

The young soldier looked at them so imploringly and appealed so eloquently, aiding his eloquence by the promise of reward, that they also held their peace.

"Perhaps some of ye have sweethearts or sisters yourselves," he urged, in conclusion. "Think, then, what would be your feelings were the dear one in the hands of the spoiler, and aid me as you would have me help you, if such were the case. All I ask of ye is to do your utmost to overtake yon boat."

The men answered the appeal with a ready cheer, and pulled vigorously in pursuit of the skiff, which was skimming rapidly over the water about three-quarters of a mile ahead of them.

In spite of the terrific speed at which they were going, they did not seem to gain sensibly upon the object of their pursuit.

The driving vapours had now formed into one immense cloud, which covered the whole heavens, and from whose bosom the rain fell down in vast, drenching showers, whilst the shrieking wind wailed like a lost spirit among the tall bulrushes along the shore.

The men once again exhibited signs of discontent.

Wound up to a pitch of the wildest excitement by the chase, the young soldier offered to triple their reward if they would but continue till they overtook the boat, which was now not half a mile distant.

They made another supreme effort.

And by the time they reached Northfleet the strenuous exertions of the men enabled them o come abreast of the vessel which had led them so weary a chase.

Bitter was the mortification of Harold to find that it was no more than a fishing boat containing only one man and a boy.

And, to add to his disappointment, the man could give him no information.

The storm now howled about them in good earnest, and the fast-descending rain was drenching them to the skin.

The skipper, after bestowing a hearty curse on the fisherman and his boy, now recommended that they should seek refuge on shore.

Though deeply chagrined, Harold could no longer refuse a request so reasonable, especially when the old seaman swore by all the saints that no boat could stay out in such weather.

"Moreover, yer honour," he added, "as the craft we're in pursuit on aint passed this fisher rogue—the devil's benison on him, say I—the chances are that it has landed its crew on t'other shore."

This was a ray of hope for Harold, and thitherwards the rowers accordingly turned the head of their boat.

They soon effected a landing at Greenhithe, which was even then a village of considerable importance.

Dripping with rain, the young adventurer sought admittance into the first dwelling he came to—a wretched hut, inhabited by a mariner, his wife, and family.

They had, however, a comfortable fire, and this was the one thing needful, under the present circumstances, to Harold.

While he was drying his garments the mariner's wife, in answer to his inquiries, informed him that some hours previously a party of men, with a lady closely muffled, had landed from a skiff, and, having procured horses, had ridden southward.

Harold resolved to pursue them without delay, despite the darkness and the wild storm. He could not be persuaded even to stop the night, in order to set out again with renewed vigour on the morrow.

But asking where he could procure a fleet horse, and being told that he might obtain one at the Owl's Nest, a queer little old-fashioned inn on the borders of a wood, Harold threw some money upon the table, and, having thanked them for their kindness, hurried out into the wild night.

The inn spoken of was not far distant, and as the young soldier entered the room set apart for travellers, he at the first glance thought it was empty, but soon discovered that another man was there besides himself.

This person appeared to be a wandering pilgrim, from his cassock and hood, the latter of which was pulled over his face so as to entirely conceal his features.

He appeared to be drying his damp garments as he sat in the shadow of the huge fireplace; but he turned suddenly as Harold entered, and had the young soldier been able to see the glances of his restless eyes he would have read in them mingled triumph and astonishment.

Having ordered some wine, Harold asked the rosy-cheeked maid if he could have the loan of a stout horse.

But the damsel replied she was sorry they could not oblige him, for the only beast they had in their stable had been borrowed by a gallant cavalier, about an hour since, for his lady, whose palfrey had fallen lame

"Was the lady old or young?" asked Harold, eagerly, "and was she dark or fair? Was her companion young also and comely, or was he turned of manhood's prime—stern and sinister of visage?"

"Marry, Sir Cavalier," said the pretty maid of the inn, holding up her hands, "how shall I answer thee all these questions in a breath? To begin, however. Firstly, was she old? Faith! seventeen summers could scarce have crowned that bonny, winsome head of hers, and she was more sweetly fair than the pearly hedge-rose—her eyes a purer, richer blue than spring's earliest violets."

"'Tis she!" exclaimed the young soldier, with fervour. "It was to those lovely-hued, soul-lit orbs ye have so fitly described that she owes her sweet name."

The pilgrim, who had been intently listening, now glided from the room unobserved.

"Take thou this, my pretty poetess," added Harold, giving the blushing girl several silver pieces, "and a thousand thanks to boot. And now, as a parting favour, tell me which road did these same travellers take?" turning to depart.

"The path through the woods to Stoney Dene, where I overheard the cavalier say they might stop the night, gentle sir," answered the girl. "But stay a moment, I pray. I have not yet told ye what the cavalier was like."

"There is little need, I fancy," returned Harold, "for I suspect he was nearly old enough to be the maiden's grandsire, and was also proud, fierce, and haughty."

"Marry, thou art a wizard, for the knight was all these"

"I thought as much," replied Harold. "I may not tarry another moment. Farewell."

"Nay, 'tis an ugly road to travel on such a night. I pray thee rest here till daylight," said the girl, earnestly.

"I am a soldier and wear a sword, and fear not danger nor darkness. Adieu, my pretty one" And he was gone.

"Beware of the swamp——"

The young soldier failed to catch the

remainder of her last words as he hurriedly turned the corner of the old building.

With his eyes well about him he hastened along the wild rugged track till he reached the bridle-path in the wood.

Here the waving, swirling trees overhead shut out the dim light and compelled him to pick his way with greatest caution.

It was a long and weary task.

Twice he thought he heard footsteps between the pauses of the storm, once in advance of him, then again they appeared behind him.

He listened intently, and loosened his sword in its scabbard, ready for instant use ; but the startling sounds were not repeated, and, pushing boldly on, he at length emerged from the thicket.

In front of him was a vast boggy track, one of the most dangerous marshes in the whole county.

A dense mist lay over its treacherous bosom, hiding from the young soldier's anxious gaze the deep black chasms and gaping water-holes with which this dismal quagmire was intersected.

Unaware of the dangerous character of the locality he was approaching—that there were only a few narrow paths across this dreary swamp, and these known only to the turf-cutters and a few others, and ignorant that the slightest deviation from the proper track would cause the venturesome traveller to be swallowed up for ever in its black oozy bed—Harold slowly advanced, uncertain which direction to take.

Greatly perplexed, he paused a moment, and tried to penetrate the gloomy blackness before him.

Suddenly a bright light like that of a lantern rose, as it seemed, out of the earth.

"The saints be praised !" exclaimed the young soldier, "there is at least a human dwelling in this lonely wilderness, and at no great distance either."

Woe to him did he but trust to the delusive gleam of that terrible *ignus fatuus* or will-o'-the-wisp.

The plaintive cry of the plover, the thrilling shriek of the bittern, and the doleful croak of the bull-frog, coming across the desolate morass, sounded unusually ominous to Harold's ear.

"Holy St. Mary, perchance this is *not* the path to Stoney Dene," he said ; "it hath a far from inviting look," and he turned to retrace his footsteps.

He found himself confronted by a tall, cowled figure, who seemed as though he had suddenly risen from the bowels of the earth.

Harold started and clapped his hand to his sword-hilt ; he had thought himself utterly alone in that silent place.

"Ah, Sir Pilgrim," he exclaimed, recognising his fellow-traveller of the inn, "what would ye with me that ye dog my steps ?"

"I heard ye but now say," said the pilgrim, in a voice which Harold thought he had heard before, "that ye were uncertain of the way to Stoney Dene. The road lies straight before thee"—pointing to the swamp.

"Art sure, Sir Pilgrim ?" said the young soldier, dubiously.

"See you not the lights of it yonder ?" said the pilgrim, with some asperity.

"I do," Harold replied, "but deemed not that the place was so near."

"Nor is it, my son—that light is deceiving, and far more distant than ye think," returned the pilgrim.

And the young soldier had just a suspicion that there was a hidden meaning in his tone.

"It may be as thou sayest, good father, but the road hath a gruesome, uncanny look, which I am far from liking."

"Go to, my son, do ye shrink when one old and infirm like I am fear not to brave its dangers, if dangers there be. In truth it so haps that I also am journeying to the Dene, and if ye care to follow I will e'en be thy guide, but if ye lack the courage, why then——"

"Enough, old man !" exclaimed Harold, stung by the implied taunt, "lead on—I follow."

The pilgrim picked his way slowly along, and the young soldier thought he exercised undue care and unnecessary caution.

But as they proceeded Harold felt the quivering, groaning marsh shake and yield beneath his every step, and a strange feeling of dread misgiving suddenly took possession of him.

Moreover, the pilgrim himself, who was some paces in advance, suddenly came to a full stop, as though he also was in doubt of the right path.

And at that moment the light, that had hitherto burnt steadily and brightly, now assumed a ghastly hue, then it burst, scattering a thousand lesser lights—dancing, contracting, and expanding—all over the plain.

"Ah ! false guide," cried Harold, on beholding the fatal sight ; "you have deceived me !"

"I know it, my hated enemy till death," shouted the pilgrim, with fiendish glee, throwing back his hood and disclosing the sinister features of Hubert the Monk.

"Base traitor and apostate !" exclaimed Harold ; "I have discovered thy black-hearted villany in good time !"

"Not so, blind, boasting braggart," laughed the monk, scornfully. "In thine ignorance of the path ye can only escape being swallowed up in the fathomless depths of this terrible swamp by a miracle. I have led thee here, like yon will-o'-the-wisp, to compass thy destruction."

"Have a care lest I compass *thy* destruction," cried Harold, sternly, drawing a pistol.

"I fear ye not, wretched imbecile !" scoffed the monk ; "thy powder-flask I secured at the inn. The charges in thy weapons are damp and useless, so I can laugh to scorn thy vain and empty threats !"

Roused to frenzy, Harold presented his petronel at the monk's head, and pulled the trigger, but no discharge followed.

"Ha, ha !" laughed the monk, with demoniac triumph. "Ye are entrapped—escape is impossible. Ye cannot advance or retreat, or turn to right or left. Darkness is around ye, and death in its most fearful—most hideous form—stares ye in the face on every hand. Ha, ha ! who triumphs now ?"

"Not thou, vile assassin !" cried Harold, presenting his remaining petronel at the traitor, but it missed fire as the other had done.

And, goaded almost to madness by the monk's mocking laugh, he advanced a step forward and hurled the heavy weapon with unerring aim at his head.

It struck the monk a terrific blow full in the face.

He uttered a fearful shriek, and, staggering back, lost his balance.

There was a floundering plunge, followed by a horrible, stifled cry, and he disappeared from mortal sight for ever.

At the same moment the young soldier felt that he himself was sinking, for the wet, spongy earth was giving way beneath him at every step.

He struggled desperately to extricate himself, but in vain—at every movement of his body he sank deeper.

He tried to clutch at the verge of the narrow path, but the soft, yielding bog crumbled in his frantic grasp.

And down, down, he went—deeper and deeper—till the heavy slush rushed into his ears and eyes.

Then, with a loud, frenzied appeal to heaven for help, and a last despairing prayer for his beloved Violet on his lips, the seething, choking mass closed over his head, and Harold Rookby knew no more.

CHAPTER XVI.

LEO THE PAGE GIVES HIS MASTER SOME START-
LING INFORMATION—THE ADVENTURE IN THE
WOOD—VIOLET FOUND AND LOST—ON THE
RIVER—RESCUE.

"THOU art a faithful lad and a good one, Leo," said Guy Fawkes, as they paused to take breath on the border of a pine thicket after their escape from Oliver Blackstock and his men. "Tell me, boy, by what wonderful means did ye discover our place of confinement?"

" 'Twas in this wise, good master," returned the boy. "After the attack of Sir Sidney Wildbrook and his followers on the secret meeting-house of those brave gentlemen—your friends—at Southwark——"

"Our secret meeting place discovered?" interrupted Guy Fawkes, with startling vehemence, "and by that remorseless fiend? May heaven's lightnings wither him! Why told you me not this before, boy?"

"Marry, your honour," interposed Ralph Roley, "the brave lad hath had little chance of wagging his tongue till now."

"True, true," returned Guy Fawkes; "I had forgotten. Proceed, good Leo."

"On the defeat of your friends, worthy sir," continued Leo, "and the capture of Miss Hamlyn, whom, single-handed, I was powerless to defend——"

"Violet in the power of that abandoned monster?" again interrupted Guy Fawkes, greatly agitated. "Oh, heavens, this is terrible! But where were my companions?—where was Master Harold Rookby?"

"Thy gallant companions, good master," said Leo, "sought to defend her like the brave and noble gentlemen they are, but they were outnumbered by Sir Sidney's men, and were forced to seek safety in flight."

"These are ill-tidings that ye bring me, boy," said Guy Fawkes, gloomily. "It were bad enough that our rendezvous has been discovered, but Violet in the hands of that base villain is ten thousandfold worse."

He pondered deeply for some seconds, then added, with flashing eyes—

"But she must be found. Aye, though we have to search the kingdom through—she must be snatched from the arms of her ruthless abductor, though a hundred lives were imperilled in the hazard."

"I sought to find her whereabouts, but failed," pursued Leo. "Something seemed to tell me that by following the windings of the river I should find thee, my master, and I did," concluded the boy, proudly.

"Ye forget to tell how ye fished me out of the stream, thou malapert page," said honest Ralph, with mock anger, "as though it were not worth the narration."

"Certes! an' I had almost forgotten to tell," said the brave youth, smiling, "that I overheard, whilst loitering in the hostelry yard, Blackstock bid his men prepare themselves to accompany him to Heron Abbey after he had effected thy capture, my master."

" 'Sdeath," ejaculated Guy Fawkes, passionately. "This wolfish trooper villain, who seems to bear a charmed existence, for my blade hath been turned aside from his base black heart half a score of times, has scented his prey even in that peaceful retreat, and meditates an attack, for he suspects, and rightly too, that Catesby and Father Woodruff is in hiding there."

"Then let us hasten to Heron Abbey," said Leo, "and swell the small list of its defenders against this gutter tyrant Blackstock."

"I am with ye, honourable sire," exclaimed Ralph, "though when I shall again press the red lips of my Dolly, whom I vowed to meet two moons agone in Lambeth-walk, the devil and St. Anthony only knows."

As they journeyed on Leo acquainted his master with the particulars of Sir Sidney's attack upon the conspirators, the absence of Harold Rookby, and the death of Mark Swinton.

They rested for a brief space when mid-way on their journey to partake of refreshment, and at the close of day sighted the grey spires of Heron Abbey.

Guy Fawkes pushed eagerly on, some distance in advance of his companions, and presently he discerned a light twinkling in the wood on his left.

Examining his arms, to be in readiness if needed, he hurried along the base of a hill, then, diving into the wood, pursued his way along a broken, rugged track, now guided by the moonlight.

In a few minutes he saw that the light proceeded from what appeared to be a ruined cottage, while at that instant the long deep howl of a wolf-hound fell ominously on his ears.

Any enemy was better than a contest with such a savage adversary, he thought.

And pulling a steel pistol from under his cloak he advanced boldly towards the cottage with the glittering weapon in his hand.

A deep voice was heard calling on the hound, and as Guy Fawkes dashed on a man, whose face seemed to be familiar to him, appeared in the path.

At the same time his eye fell upon the open casement, and he saw within the cottage a female form lying upon a humble couch, with a girl, whose features he could never forget, supporting her head.

It was Evelyn, the dancing-girl.

Heedless of danger, Guy Fawkes saw, with a wild thrill of joy rushing to his heart, that she who reclined upon the couch was the pale, but beautiful young heiress, Violet Hamlyn.

He uttered an ejaculation of rapturous astonishment.

The stranger had started back, and seemed disposed to dispute his advance.

But, reckless of the dagger thrust to which his rashness exposed him, Guy Fawkes rushed forward and entered the cottage.

Violet started from the couch, and, uttering a cry of joy, sprang towards him.

Guy Fawkes clasped her to his bosom, when a shriek, loud and thrilling, made him look the other way.

And he beheld Evelyn clinging wildly to the bearded ruffian who, with a drawn dagger, had followed him in.

The wolf-hound now burst from an inner apartment, in which he had been badly secured, and the next instant would have fixed his fangs in Guy Fawkes's throat.

But the strong voice of the man, whose arm Evelyn had stayed, brought the hound to his heels.

Guy Fawkes turned again to Violet, and passionately kissed the sweet white brow that now rested on his bosom.

The strange man passed out gloomily from the cottage, followed by the savage hound.

The dancing-girl crouched in a distant corner, and, drawing her faded mantle over her beautiful shoulders, fixed her mild soft eyes upon Guy Fawkes with a look more eloquent than words can express.

"Thou art safe—fear not, my own sweet Violet. Raise your eyes and look upon me," whispered Guy Fawkes, yielding to the blissful temptation, his own heart throbbing as wildly as the bosom that rested upon it.

"Save me, Guy! save me!" muttered the agitated girl.

"Fear not my sweet one, none shall harm thee while I am near; but tell me where is the heartless robber who carried thee off, and his base followers."

"Gone to procure fresh steeds, and they may return at any moment," said Violet, in trembling alarm.

"Then let us instantly hasten to Heron Abbey, which is not far distant, and where thy father and friends are assembled," said Guy Fawkes, hurriedly. "'Tis a sweet night, and under the harvest moon we shall travel merrily."

"I will at once prepare me for the journey," returned Violet, in trembling response.

She turned to pass from the chamber, when a dark figure stood at the entrance, as if to oppose her egress.

Violet uttered a cry of alarm.

Guy Fawkes, who only then recognised the features of the man who had attacked him at Charing-cross, grasped his sword-hilt.

But ere he could draw the blade his wrist was suddenly seized, and, turning towards his new assailant, he saw to his utter surprise it was the dancing-girl.

Her mild eyes were bright with tears, her face was pale, and its expression one of agony.

Still she grasped and hung upon his wrist, though her burning hands trembled while they held it.

"Stand!" cried the bravo, now addressing Guy Fawkes, as he coolly levelled a long-barrelled pistol at his head. Advance a step and I fire! Ye entered unbidden, Sir Cavalier; but ye depart not without leave."

Violet, who had started back on the first alarm, shrieked at the sight of the levelled weapon, and threw herself into Guy's arms.

Guy Fawkes himself stood as if spellbound. The man continued to confront him in the same threatening attitude, and the dancing-girl, still clasping his sword-arm, remained kneeling at his feet.

"Whose prisoner am I?" demanded Guy Fawkes, haughtily, "or by what authority do ye dare to detain me here?"

"We have met before, Sir Cavalier," replied the other, "and it may be we shall meet again. You are no prisoner but at liberty to depart with my leave. The lady must remain until those who confided her to me return, and it may not be well for thee to meet them."

"Remove your pistol!" said Guy Fawkes, defiantly.

"No, by the mass! One footstep nearer and I fire!"

"Remove your pistol, dog! Dost think to frighten me?"

The dark eyes of the swarthy spy flashed at the concentrated scorn with which his intimidation was met.

He cocked the weapon. The click of the lock fell on Guy Fawkes's ear, and the bright Spanish barrel glittered and scintillated before his eyes.

For a moment he hesitated.

The sound of approaching footsteps at this moment broke upon their ears, succeeded by the savage bay of the hound.

The dancing-girl started to her feet. Her male companion changed countenance, while Guy Fawkes turned his eyes to Violet, who, dizzy with alarm, had sunk swooning upon the humble couch.

"Hullo! ha! down hound!—aye, spring if ye dare, and I will put an ounce of lead through thine ugly head. What ho, within there!" shouted a voice outside.

The moment the person outside the cottage, in which was being enacted such exciting scenes as those just recorded, had concluded his demand for admission, the spy, by way of answer, uttering an exclamation of rage, ran his bright eye adown his pistol, levelled it at Guy Fawkes, and fired.

The sound rang and tingled on the ear, and a cloud of smoke, mingled with a startled shriek, burst upon the narrow chamber.

But Guy Fawkes, although almost stunned, neither winced nor fell.

"You've drawn the shot, ye cursed jade!" fiercely exclaimed the would-be assassin, as he threw the heavy weapon at the dancing-girl and disappeared.

It struck her head—blood streamed down her pale features, and she staggered fainting out of the room by the backway.

"Poor girl," muttered Guy Fawkes, deeply moved; "she may be wounded unto death. I could not leave her thus—perhaps to perish—after this further proof of her devotion to me.

It was Ralph's voice I heard, and Violet is reviving, so all will be safe till my speedy return," and he hastened out of the cottage in pursuit of Evelyn.

A minute later the sound of horses' hoofs—a scuffle, oaths, and execrations—a heavy blow, and a deep groan might have been heard.

Then "bang!" went the butt end of a pike, striking the door with such force that it burst open—shivered and splintered.

Meanwhile Guy Fawkes had gone in quest of the dancing-girl. He called her by name, passed through an adjoining chamber, where he perceived arms and disguises, but saw nothing of her he sought.

Continuing his search he left the house and entered the wood already mentioned, in which the cottage was embedded.

Presently he arrived at a thicket of hazel boughs, densely clustered, forming a concealment as perfect as the sheltered nook the wood-bird builds her nest in.

On the trunk of a felled oak, where her feet were almost touched by a noisy brook which ran white and winding through the wood, poor Evelyn sat. She had twined a kerchief round her head, her slight back was bent, and her forehead was resting on her hands.

The babbling of the stream prevented her hearing Guy Fawkes's approach, and he had to touch her on the shoulder ere she regarded him.

She sprang to her feet, and a sudden look of alarm changed on her expressive features to one of melancholy as she recognised Guy Fawkes, then she sat herself on the oak again.

"Evelyn, you must leave this place and come with us. Poor child," said Guy Fawkes, gazing on her, "what a life is yours!"

Evelyn did not speak, but a look of still deeper melancholy came over her beautiful features

"Come, my poor girl, I will find thee an asylum, as I have done for thy brother. Thrice now you have saved my life, and, what hath imposed on me a deeper debt, ye have shielded her I love."

"That is no debt calling for thanks," said Evelyn, quickly. "I did no more for her than I would have done for any other woman. Speak not of the services I have done for her in the same breath with that which I have done for thee."

"I know how much I owe thee, my poor Evelyn," said Guy Fawkes, noticing her sudden excitement with surprise, "and it were base in me to leave you exposed to the tyranny of the ruffian with whom your fate seems so strangely united."

He paused, then continued—

"The first time I saw thee the villain who a moment ago fired, assassin-like, at my head, threatened to beat thee like a hound in a public square."

"But you stepped forward!" cried the dancing-girl, with enthusiasm; "you stepped bravely forward and stayed his arm. Oh! shall I forget that hour—those words of thine —the look of noble kindness and pity you cast upon me? They were the first I ever knew. No, they will not be forgotten."

She covered her face and wept.

"Let us hence, my poor Evelyn. I will repay your kindness with the active gratitude which deals not in studied words. Come with me, kind heart—you shall go to Heron Abbey with Violet Hamlyn."

Evelyn started to her feet, her fair brow curled into wrinkles, and her white lips writhed again.

"No!" cried she, in a voice of frenzy, "I travel not with thee or her."

"Nay, I leave thee not here."

"Yet here I will remain," she said, impetuously.

"Hear me, Evelyn! I have twice seen thee struck to my feet in your efforts to save me— I owe ye thrice a life. I see you under the thraldom of cruel tyranny. Were I a man if I left thee here? No!" cried Guy Fawkes, forgetting his own immediate danger in his zeal to rescue the unfortunate girl. "I cannot leave thee here! I should be baser than the scowling churl who struck thee bleeding to the earth if I left thee the victim of such a doom. No—you saved my life and the honour of her I love"

"Speak not of that!" cried Evelyn, almost in a shriek.

"Then this, by the heavens above us! I will say and act upon. You shall not stay. I will procure thee an asylum. I will save thee!"

"Save me? No! no! The cruel world has blasted my life—the buoyancy of this poor heart has gone!"

"Say not so. Those bright eyes that now flash upon me have heaven's own purity in their glances. Those features that look upon me with fervour have——"

"Spare me, spare me!" cried Evelyn, in agonised accents, which echoed again through the silent wood.

"Why linger, then, in a lot that may not be spoken of without horror? Come with me, my beautiful one. I will find thee a home where the errors of thy former life——"

"You do me wrong—cruel wrong!" cried Evelyn, raising her delicate form to its fullest height, while her wild eyes flashed indignantly.

"Then come with me," urged Guy Fawkes. "Have I not seen thee stricken with a savage hand? Have I not witnessed the ribald scoff of crowds when ye danced to pleasure them at the Cross of Charing? Have I not known those whom ye associate with to be villains of the deepest dye? Say, Evelyn," he added, with tender pleading, "can I leave thee here when I love thee?"

"Love me?"

"Aye, as a sister—a dear, dear sister——"

"Oh! mock me not! Hie thee to her you *do* love, for remember your lot is still beset with difficulty if mine is accompanied by crime."

"Crime!—that sweet countenance—those pure, deep eyes! No, no!"

"You so charged me."

"Then were I base to do so. Crime lurks not in guise like thine without polluting it more."

"You speak not as you think!"

"Hear me—hear me I may not leave ye to a lot like this. It chains ye to cruelty, it exposes ye to infamy, to the tyranny of— of——"

"Oh, heaven!" cried Evelyn, wringing her hands convulsively.

"Evelyn!"

"You wrong me!" exclaimed she, impetuously, "and your generous nature, which prompted ye to search me out."

"Not so, my proud and beauteous one. I have seen enough to know that thy lot is wretched, and that I were craven, indeed, if I relieved it not."

"And can a heart's wish," said Evelyn, "a generous deed, an impulse of a noble mind, rid this bosom of its load of misery ? Alas, no !"

"But it may change the destiny of a life, Evelyn—we trifle with precious time."

"You do—you do !" cried the dancing-girl, clasping his arm with both her small hands. "Fly from this spot—onward—onward ! If you are found here your fate is sealed."

"But not alone, sweet Evelyn," said Guy Fawkes. "I cannot leave thee here."

"I thank thee for thy proffered escort," she replied, with a melancholy smile, "but here I must remain."

"Not so—no. Your lot here the vilest of your sex would spurn—the meekest nature would rebel against. By heaven ! I leave thee not !"

"Then it must needs be that I leave *thee*. Farewell ! If you tarry, your life and the honour of her you love are placed wantonly in the power of fiends. Farewell—it may be that we shall meet again."

She started from his side like a fawn, and the next moment the thick bushes hid her from his sight.

Guy Fawkes gazed wistfully after her a moment, but he had no choice left.

The danger she had warned him of roused his fears for Violet, and he turned to regain the cottage, where he concluded Ralph and Leo held impatient watch.

He was about to enter the house when the page came running towards him. Alarm and consternation were depicted on his pale visage.

"I have been seeking for ye everywhere, my master," he cried, breathlessly.

"Sayest thou so ?" said Guy Fawkes, apprehending danger from the boy's looks. "Speak quickly. Hath ill befallen Mistress Hamlyn ?"

"She hath fallen again into the hands of Sir Sidney Wildbrook," gasped the trembling boy.

Guy Fawkes started back as though he had received a sudden stab.

"Merciful heavens !" he exclaimed, "is it always to be thus ? Am I ever to be thwarted by this fiend incarnate ? But let him look to it when next we meet. Oh, fool and villain that I was, to leave her even for a single moment !"

Then, turning to the agitated boy, he added—

"But did ye not carefully mark the road they took, boy ?"

"I did, my master," answered Leo, "though the risk of discovery was great."

"Doubtless it was, my brave lad," said Guy Fawkes. "In my own selfish grief I had forgotten thy difficulty and danger. Proceed, I pray ye."

"As I followed cautiously in their track behind the roadside hedges," continued Leo, "I overheard their leader order them to shape their course towards the river side, and there procure a boat to convey them over to the other shore."

"Thou hast done bravely and well, good Leo "—shaking the boy warmly by the hand—

"and doubt not but that thou shalt be amply rewarded for thy services."

"I need not reward from thee, my dear master. I seek only thy friendship and affection," said the boy, with kindling eye.

"Doubt not but ye hath both, good Leo," returned Guy Fawkes. "And now let us hasten to the river. I know the country well, and by a near cut methinks we can reach the water almost as soon as our enemies. Summon Ralph —quick !"

"Alas, my good master," returned Leo, sighing deeply, "I fear me he is badly hurt, for, though he strove to defend Miss Violet with lion-like courage, the merciless robbers were too many for him and beat him down, and he now lies in yon cottage scarce able to lift his suffering head."

"Ye speak without reckoning, Sir Page," said a voice that caused them both to start. "Marry, it were a good fifteen minutes agone since I were in that bad condition, and think ye it takes a man of sense and determination that time to recover from a mere crack o' the crown ?"

And the same instant honest Ralph Roley, looking as invincible as ever, stepped from the porch of the cottage and stood before them.

"Thou art a brave man and a true, good Ralph," said Guy Fawkes, grasping his hand with fervour, "and I am proud to call thee friend. Already am I deeply thy debtor, but thou wilt find me no niggard when settling-day comes."

"Ye honour me, worthy sir," returned Ralph, delightedly. "Marry, I only wish ye had been by my side when that brazen rogue, Sir Sidney, and his ruffianly crew came to carry off the young lady. By old Nick's bones they would have found it no easy victory, though they did outnumber us by three or more."

"They should never have carried her hence, good Ralph, save across my dead body," said Guy Fawkes, with swelling breast. "They are hastening to the river. Art well enough to journey thither, Ralph ? 'Tis scarce a league distant."

"Aye, that am I, Master Fawkes," returned the faithful fellow, "an' were it twenty instead of one I would travel there cheerfully to strike a blow for bonny Mistress Violet."

"Hath thou arms ?"

"That have I," said Ralph, touching his belt. "Yon cottage is reeking with them."

"Then let us hie in pursuit, and may heaven and the blessed Virgin aid our efforts," said Guy Fawkes, uncovering.

"Amen !" murmured Ralph, raising his cap.

Guy Fawkes leading the way they plunged into the heart of the wood and were soon on the track of their foes.

As they approached the river Guy Fawkes turned off into a deep gully which cut its way though the heart of a huge cliff.

A few minutes later they reached the shore, the silvery wavelets glittering like countless diamonds in the moonlight.

"Ah, see, they are here," cried Leo, pointing down stream.

Guy Fawkes looked in the direction indicated, and a startled cry left his lips as he beheld a boat in the act of leaving the shore.

Seated in the prow of the little vessel was

Sir Sidney Wildbrook, with his arm clasped about the slender waist of Violet, who was vainly endeavouring to free herself from his loathsome embrace, while four sturdy ruffians were working lustily at the oars.

"By the soul of my fathers!" cried Guy Fawkes, with terrible earnestness, raising his hand on high, "if I can but place my grip on the throat of yonder base persecutor of helpless woman I swear I will never release it till I have rendered his vile blackguard body for ever powerless to wreak further harm."

Then, casting a rapid glance around, he resumed—

"I can see no boat on the shore. Oh for a light skiff and a pair of oars!"

"Both are here, master," said Leo, coming forward.

As Leo spoke Guy Fawkes noticed a fisherman's hut built deep in the shelter of an overhanging cliff, and beside it his boat, pulled up high and dry.

"Shall I summon the boatman, sir?" asked Ralph.

"There is no time for that," returned Guy Fawkes. "This will pay for the loan of it," giving Leo some money. "Do you, boy, thrust it under the threshold."

Leo instantly did as he was desired.

"Now, quick, bear a hand, and let us get the boat afloat."

They all bore a hand and soon ran the little vessel down the sloping beach.

Guy Fawkes took his seat in the stem and seized a pair of oars, Ralph followed suit, while Leo, seating himself in the stern, took charge of the tiller.

In another instant they pushed off in hot pursuit of their foes.

The swell of the jutting cliff had hitherto prevented Sir Sidney and his party from seeing the movements of their pursuers. In fact, they were wholly unaware that they were being followed at all.

But now, as they beheld Guy Fawkes's party in the bright moonlight bearing down upon them in full chase, Sir Sidney gave utterance to a startled oath and ordered his men to fire upon them.

"There is only one charge amongst us, your grace," answered the dusky spy, "thanks to the stubborn lout at the cottage, on whom we wasted so much powder, and that, too, I fear, in vain."

"Then let that last charge be directed at the foremost miscreant's heart," added the false knight, "and see that ye take steady aim, Paulo."

The man addressed clasped his matchlock to his shoulders and took careful aim at Guy Fawkes as his skiff came skimming over the freshening waves.

"Beware, sir!" suddenly shrieked Leo, as he beheld his beloved master's peril and gave a fierce tug at the tiller.

Only just in time.

A second later and the shot of the assassin would have passed through Guy Fawkes's body.

But through Leo altering the vessel's course the bullet intended for his master struck the devoted boy.

He uttered a piercing cry and throwing up his arms fell heavily into the bottom of the boat.

Ralph ceased rowing and instantly caught Leo up in his strong arms.

"Great heaven! is he dead?" asked Guy Fawkes, his voice husky with emotion.

"No, sir, he has only fainted," replied Ralph; "'tis merely a flesh wound—he'll be better anon."

"The vile robbers and assassins!" shouted Guy Fawkes, fiercely. "Upon them, brave heart, and, remember—no mercy!"

"Aye, aye, sir," responded Ralph, with a tug at the oar that made the little craft fairly leap through the hissing water.

The boats of the pursued and the pursuers were now within a few yards of each other.

At this juncture Violet, with a vigorous effort, tore a silken gag from off her face, and exclaimed, in loud and thrilling accents—

"Save me, Guy! In mercy's name save me from this dreadful man!"

Guy Fawkes answered the frenzied appeal by instantly springing up in the boat and presenting a petronel at Sir Sidney, crying—

"Shameless, cowardly villain! yield me up the maiden free and unharmed, or by the blessed Virgin my bullet shall riddle thy foul black heart!"

Before Guy Fawkes could define his opponent's intention Sir Sidney started up with lightning swiftness, and, seizing the terrified girl, held her over the tossing flood, thus shielding himself from the ball of his antagonist.

"Fire, rash fool, if ye will!" cried Sir Sidney, mockingly, "but thy bullet shall only reach me through the heart of my victim."

Guy Fawkes uttered a cry of dismay as he beheld the terrible danger of his beloved Violet, and instantly lowered his weapon.

"Now begone, presumptuous meddler!" added Sir Sidney, sternly, "or, by the Holy Cross, I swear that on the slightest show of violence I will hurl this fair maiden into the rushing tide!"

Violet uttered a shriek of horror as she hung suspended over the heaving waters, and shuddered so violently that she nearly slipped from her abductor's grasp.

Sir Sidney stooped down to save her, when, quick as thought, Guy Fawkes raised his oar and brought it crashing down upon the scoundrel's head.

With a groan of agony he staggered blindly forward, and one of his followers, sword in hand, rushed to avenge him.

A timely shot from Ralph's pistol, however, laid him lifeless across the gunnel of the perilously-rocking boat.

With a piercing scream Violet slid from her captor's loosened hold and sank into the moonlit waters, while Sir Sidney clung like grim death to the edge of the boat.

The combined weight of the two men upon the side of the frail craft caused it to capsize, and the next moment its yelling crew were struggling with the mad, racing tide.

The water had scarcely closed over Violet's fair head when Guy Fawkes leaned forward and caught her in his eager arms.

Then, assisted by Ralph, he lifted her into the boat.

Guy Fawkes pressed Violet's beloved form to his wildly-beating heart and sought to restore her to consciousness, while Ralph, all heedless of the prayers and entreaties of the drowning wretches in his rear, seized the oars and pulled boldly and gallantly for the opposite shore.

CHAPTER XVII.

THE RESULT OF A GOOD DEED—HAROLD IN A MAZE—THE FREERANGERS—THE SUPPER IN THE FOREST—A DANGEROUS ORDEAL.

WHEN Harold Rookby opened his eyes again to the light of this world he looked about him in the uttermost surprise and wonderment.

He was lying upon a bed of dried moss in a deep glen in the heart of a forest.

The sun was sinking down in the west, and the lengthened shadows cast by the tall trees proclaimed the near approach of another night. Already the breeze began to blow with a more refreshing breath, and the wild flowers of the woodlands to emit a more fragrant perfume.

Harold found that his clothes had been cleansed from the black mud of the swamp and carefully dried, and the scene that presented itself to his wondering gaze was picturesque in the extreme.

A fire, made of large branches of pine and fir, was burning brightly in the midst of an open space, emitting a dense pillar of smoke, which rolled away in black folds above the tree tops.

The whole place was redolent of a savoury smell, which the young soldier soon ascertained proceeded from the body of a fat buck, which was roasting whole by the huge fire.

But what mystified him most was there was not a solitary soul to be seen.

He was contemplating the scene with all the interest which its novelty was so well calculated to inspire when he suddenly became aware of the presence of someone beside him.

He looked up and in speechless astonishment beheld the old minstrel of Hatton-garden.

"How fare thee now, my son?" said the old man, kindly. "Hast thoroughly recovered from thy immersion in the swamp?"

"In good sooth that have I," returned Harold, "thanks to the wondrous kindness of some unknown friend."

"Not unknown, young sir," said the minstrel. Gad-a-mercy, man, we have met before!"

"Then 'tis to thee I owe this priceless debt!" cried Harold, seizing the old man's hand with fervour.

"Ye owe me nothing, in faith," returned the minstrel. "If I fished ye out of the marsh did ye not save me from the drunken fury of the rabble at the inn? Therefore are we quits."

"But I was at my last gasp," said Harold.

"The more fool thou, when thou hadst round thy neck the silver call, which I told ye to blow on in thy hour of need. Hadst thou obeyed my instructions thy palate had never been polluted by the mud of the bog. Marry, twas more than a marvel I chanced to be that way."

"Doth it, indeed, possess such magic?" asked Harold.

"Trust not my word, Sir Cavalier," said the minstrel, "but when next ye need help put its power to the test," and he turned to depart.

"One word, Sir Minstrel," observed the young soldier, staying him. "That song ye sang at the inn—didst compose it thyself?"

"Aye, did I, and what of it?"

"Why this—that you must know something of a fair maid, who hath been carried away by a false villain," replied Harold.

"Nothing, by our lady," said the minstrel. "Nothing but what I heard and what thou wouldst have heard, too, if thou hadst made proper inquiries. But whither art thou bound? Art still in pursuit?"

"I am. And where go you, Sir Minstrel?"

"Oh, I live as the birds do," replied the old man, "wherever they can get corn for their singing. But I can tell thee this, if thou dost not know these parts well they are not very safe for lonely travellers, and my protection would be worth that of twenty men to thee 'gainst the fierce bands of gipsies and freebooters who roam these wilds."

"I doubt it not," said Harold, "seeing thou art of a race whom all respect. But I'm not afraid. I've a good sword at my side, and while I've that I fear no man."

"As thou likest, young sir. Thy bones are thine own, and thy head too, at least for the present. Fare thee well."

"Nay, stay, I——" but the old man had disappeared through the trees, though Harold could hear him singing in a stentorian voice an ancient ballad, the last lines of which ran thus—

To the knight his sword, to the monk his hood,
But freedom to us in the merrie greenwood.

Scarcely had the singer finished when several lusty voices shouted it back in chorus, and the next instant a dozen sturdy fellows, in half-gipsy, half-forester costumes, and armed with stout staves, came leaping through the brushwood and from behind the trees.

"A goodly company, i'faith!" exclaimed Harold, in open-eyed surprise. "I pray thee tell me who and what art thou, my brave fellows."

"It boots little who we are," said one of the new-comers, "or what we are. Thou art a trespasser, and therefore our prisoner, so put down thy sword and come with us."

"Not till I have had it taken from me will I be any man's prisoner!" cried Harold, desperately, maddened at this fresh delay in his pursuit of Violet.

Some of the rangers immediately set upon him from behind with their long staves, and speedily knocked the sword from his grasp, without doing him much injury, then they made him their prisoner.

Harold, thus powerless, remembered the whistle, and instantly resolved to see whether it would bring anyone to his aid.

He blew it lustily, and as the sounds echoed through the mazes of the forest he noticed that his assailants looked confused and gazed inquiringly into each other's faces.

In another minute half a dozen more men, clad in the same strange fanciful dress, and armed with the almost-exploded cross-bow, appeared on the scene, to the no small surprise of Harold.

"Zounds!" he cried, resigning himself to his fate. "I'm in a worse plight than ever. I call for friends, and I have brought more enemies upon me."

"Didst thou blow that call?" said one of the new arrivals.

"Aye, marry, that did I," answered Harold.

"And who gave it thee and told thee how to use it?"

"Wandering Willie, a minstrel, one of the best friends I have. I would give a hundred marks to see him at this moment."

"Then why, in the name of Old Nick, did you not tell us so at first?" cried one of the first comers.

"How could I?" said Harold, as it instinctively flashed upon him that these were the minstrel's men. "But, since ye know it now, I pray thee lead me to him and give me my sword again."

The weapon was instantly restored, and the young soldier was treated with the utmost courtesy as he was led towards the rude seat near the fire, which he had not long left.

The next instant he beheld the minstrel, and received a hearty shake of the old man's hand.

"Welcome to our home in the forest and to our hearty cheer," he cried.

And throwing aside his false wig, beard, and gown, he disclosed a handsome young man of five and twenty, dressed in black and green like those around him, only of a finer quality, and wearing a sword at his side, a dirk, and a silver whistle.

"Long live our chief, Will-o'-the-Woods, the Freeranger!" shouted the men as in one voice, raising their hats from their heads and waving them on high.

A few moments later the astonished Harold was seated by his new friend's side enjoying a dainty repast of roast buck, washed down by many a horn of old sack, which was handed to him ever and anon by the attendant Freerangers.

It was a wild and singularly picturesque scene, that barbaric supper party in the forest, well worthy the pencil of the painter.

"And now, friend Harold, get thee to thy couch," said Will-o'-the-Woods, rising from the feast, "and I will think ere morning how I can best aid ye in thy search after this fair maiden."

"But no—I had forgotten," he quickly added. "Thou art not yet a freeman of our company, and canst not be trusted longer with us until thou art duly enrolled amongst the members of our ancient fraternity. Wilt thou become one of us?"

"Aye, that will I," said Harold. "Is the ceremony a lengthy one?"

"Somewhat so," replied the Freeranger chief. "Hast thou a strong heart and a discreet tongue?"

"I think I possess those virtues in a degree, though a rogue would vouch the same."

"Canst thou bear pain and never flinch?"

"Try me!" answered Harold.

"The ordeal is a hard one," said Will-o'-the-Woods.

"I care not. Thou hast gone through it," said Harold.

"Aye! that have I, and every one of my men."

"Then why should not I? Am I not as good as any of them?"

"Good! I like thy courage. It augurs well—thou shalt this night be enrolled in our company, initiated in all our mysteries, and take the oaths, which none ever yet broke and lived many days afterwards."

As the Freeranger finished speaking he drew a small silver call from his bosom, and applying it to his lips blew a shrill blast, which reechoed among the glades of the forest.

It was immediately repeated on every side of them, by twenty or thirty similar instruments

A minute afterwards the young soldier found himself surrounded by a score of Freerangers. His arms were seized and pinioned before he could say a word, and a bandage passed over his eyes and firmly tied.

Somewhat startled by this rough treatment, he was about to protest against it when as suddenly a gag was clapped into his mouth, and he was rendered completely powerless—unable to struggle, to call out, or to see.

He had, it is true, the use of his legs, but they were of little service, except to bear him whither his conductors pleased.

He was led rapidly forward, the crowd of foresters shouting with loud mirth in the rear till the brown woods rang again with the echoes of their lusty voices.

The face of Harold was flushed and hot, and the cool night breeze that played upon it was refreshing to his whole frame.

He had boasted somewhat of his patience, and it had now to be put to the test.

Coarse jest, obstreperous laughter, and the loud huzzas of the Freerangers came at intervals upon his ears, and he was altogether puzzled to imagine the intentions of his companions.

To him it seemed as if they were walking for miles amid the forest, turning sometimes to the right and then to the left.

Now in open glades and now amid thick brushwood, that tore his garments and pierced into his flesh, and now over swamps and boggy ground, where he sank up to his ankles.

At last he heard the voice of Will-o'-the-Woods, for the first time that he had been able to distinguish it amidst the din and confusion, giving the command to halt.

The noisy crew were silent immediately, and a halt was made, evidently still in the open air, for the young soldier could feel the light breeze blowing freshly into his face and hear the leaves of the trees rustling as it passed.

An instant afterwards the gag was removed from his mouth and the bandage from his eyes, and Harold, looking about with as much alarm as bewilderment and curiosity, found himself in the midst of a group of Will-o'-the-Woods' men, all looking upon him with the utmost gravity, while a deep silence prevailed.

The young soldier was about to speak when the Freeranger chief waved his hand and the gag was immediately placed in his mouth again.

"Hallo, Dan-o'-the-Dale—come forth!" said the chief, and one of the Freerangers stepped forth with a crossbow in his hand. "Be thou hoodwinked and stand thou there," added his chief.

The man was blindfolded accordingly and placed exactly opposite the spot where Harold stood.

At the same instant another forester who was behind the young soldier repassed the bandage over his eyes, and he was once more utterly helpless.

"Turn thou round to the east and to the west," said Will-o'-the-Woods to the man whom he had designated as Dan-o'-the-Dale, "and having said thy prayers take aim at this bold youth who wishes to be introduced into our company."

A deadly paleness overspread the face of the young soldier, and it was well perhaps for his reputation that his mouth was gagged and his arms bandaged, or he might have betrayed that he was not quite at his ease.

"Thou blinded archer," said a clear, sonorous voice, which Harold did not recognise, "make ready thy bow and endeavour to strike the heart of this aspirant. Aim, Dan, as if thine own life depended on the result."

The young soldier involuntarily muttered a curse upon them all as his troubled ear caught a sound as if the archer was bending his bow.

The next instant he breathed a prayer for his lost and beloved one's safety, then recommended his soul to heaven, for he thought his last hour was come.

"Arrow of the blinded archer," said the disguised voice, "if the man against whose breast thou art now directed be a brave man and a true, if he hateth oppression and loveth justice dearer than his life, if he prefer cold water in freedom to rich wine in slavery, if he never refused to share his roof and his crust with the weary and the hungry, spare him, and touch him not! But if he be a coward, a slave, a fawner, or a churl, may thy pointed steel pierce deep into his heart!"

A loud "Amen!" was uttered simultaneously by all present, and Dan-o'-the-Dale once more prepared to discharge his shaft

There was a moment of deep and solemn suspense as the forester lifted his bow.

The young soldier bit his lips and held his breath, feeling that he would like to compress his frame into half its ordinary compass.

In another instant the shaft sped from the twanging bow.

The flying arrow whizzed past Harold's ear, and a loud huzza rose from every one present, so loud that it almost deafened him

He was at first so confused by the suddenness of the uproar that he could not tell whether he was hit or not.

But he thought he could hear the arrow quivering above his head.

Then, to his great relief, his eyes were immediately unbound, and looking at a tree which was close to him he saw the arrow firmly embedded in its trunk, still shaking and trembling from the velocity of its recent flight.

"A true man!—a true man!" was the cry that now arose.

And his arms were immediately unpinioned by order of the Freeranger chief.

"Hail, brother!" said the latter, advancing, his bright, cheery face all covered with smiles, and shaking the still bewildered soldier cordially by the hand. "Hail, brother! Thou hast passed the ordeal, and may now, if thou wilt take the oaths, be enrolled as one of us. Thou hast stood the trial well, and our band will be proud of thee."

"By the Holy Virgin!" said Harold, "I thought myself a dead man. Did that sturdy rascal yonder really take his best aim at me?"

"Marry! that did he," replied Will-o'-the-Woods, "and if thou hadst been false-hearted, a coward, or a churl, the world would have been rid of thee by this time. There is wonderful virtue in Dan-o'-the-Dale's arrows—

they never touch the brave and the true-hearted."

"Is there no deviltry in them?" inquired Harold, with the superstition of the age.

"Pooh, pooh, man!" said Will; "but wilt thou take the oaths?"

"I will. Administer them."

A circle of about fifty Freerangers was immediately formed.

Then each man drew his sword and pointed it at the young soldier's breast.

Harold did not flinch or even wink at the circle of cold, sharp steel, that glittered in the pale moonlight, but met it all with a steadfast glance of his fine fearless eyes.

He then swore to uphold the ancient rights of the chase, enjoyed from time immemorial, and not to submit to all those harsh and stringent rules enforced by the present monarch, King James.

He also swore to do justice and love mercy, and to obey the laws of the realm in all things consistent with conscience—never to see the poor want if he could relieve them; never to suffer a woman to be injured, or a strong man to oppress a weak one if he could prevent it.

Harold willingly took the oaths, the swords were dropped, and every man of the band successively shook hands with him.

He was then honourably escorted back to Will-o'-the-Woods' home in the forest, where another sumptuous feast was prepared, and where copious libations were drank to the health and prosperity of the new member.

The Freeranger chief, remarking that his guest must be tired and weary with the fatigues of the day, begged him to seek repose.

"No, I thank thee," returned Harold. "I could not sleep were I to lie down. I shall never rest till I have gained news of her I seek"

"If that be the case," observed Will-o'-the-Woods, "I will see if I cannot help you in your search."

Then he communed with the different groups of his band, conversing with them apart in low tones.

At length he returned to the young soldier, with a look of pleased intelligence upon his comely face.

"One of my men tells me," he said, "that the party ye seek passed the borders of this wood some hours ago, taking the direction of Heron Abbey."

"A thousand thanks for the news!" said the young soldier, joyfully. "I will hasten on at once, and I may yet reach them ere they can get a vessel to take them across the river, if that be their intention."

And he prepared to depart.

"Nay," returned the Freeranger chief, "not so fast. The prospect of pressing the sweet mistress of thy affection to thine heart may fill thee with a world of valour, but surely thou art not mad enough to dream thou couldst rescue her single-handed? There were five or six of them, I am told."

"In my eagerness I had forgotten that," said Harold, with a thoughtful, troubled look.

"Marry! I should think thou hadst," said Will-o'-the-Woods, laughing. "You are like all lovers—they think that nothing is impossible."

GUY FAWKES

Or Gunpowder, Treason, and Plot.

AS GUY FAWKES FIRED ONE OF THE PURSUING SOLDIERS WENT CRASHING DOWN OVER THE PRECIPICE.

No. 5.

"I know how to meet the difficulty," said Harold, brightening up. "I have friends at Heron Abbey who will most readily give me aid when I have sighted the villainous lordling who has stolen my betrothed. To them will I go for assistance should I need it."

And seizing the Freeranger's hand he shook it fervently.

"Adieu for a space," he said. "Again and again I thank you."

"Stay," said Will. "Will you not take a score of our fellows with you? They will go willingly, though their heads hath not touched a pillow for two or more nights."

"Nay, I would not impose so heavy a task upon them—they must be worn out"

"Then, by the mass!" said the Freeranger chief, emphatically, "a couple of them shall be your guides to lead ye through the mazes of the forest."

This offer the young soldier gladly accepted, and having taken a hearty leave of the Freeranger chief and his band he trod the sylvan windings of the bosky wood close in the footsteps of his blithsome guides.

CHAPTER XVIII.

HERON ABBEY—ILL NEWS—THE MEETING—THE CONSPIRATORS' OATH—DANGER.

IT is now time we returned to that bold and fearless plotter—Robert Catesby—and his companion, Father Woodruff.

On escaping from the riverside residence of Sir Godfrey Hamlyn, when attacked by Oliver Blackstock and his followers, the twain made their way along the secret passage, which ended beneath a summer-house in the garden near to the water's edge.

By removing a heavy slab in the floor of the arbour they were able to gain the surface of the earth again.

Replacing the stone they hastened to the river's brink, and from amongst the tall reeds and rushes drew out a skiff, which lay well under the shadow of a spreading willow to which it was moored.

Requesting Father Woodruff to step in, Catesby took the sculls, and under cover of the darkness speedily placed himself far beyond the reach of his pursuers, and by break of day he and the priest arrived at Heron Abbey.

After some delay in rousing the sleepy warder the portcullis was raised and they managed to gain admittance. At an early hour they had an interview with Sir Godfrey Hamlyn, to whom Catesby communicated the news of the pursuivant's attack upon the house and the flight of their party and his child.

The old knight was greatly perturbed on hearing this, and said—

"How fatally unfortunate! A few hours later and my poor dear Violet would have been free of the terrible charge which now hangs over her. A month ago I left the ill-omened house resolving never to enter it again. Violet was away at the time, and on her return here expressed a fervent desire to go and take a last farewell of the beloved old home in which she was born. Alas! fatal hour——"

"Fatal indeed!" sighed Father Woodruff, "since my presence there on that lamentable occasion should be the means of bringing down upon her young and innocent head the awful charge of having harboured a priest."

"But she had no idea when she started on her journey that you would be present at the old home," said the sorrowing father, "so the charge is a false one. Think not, however, holy father, that I should regret her having imperilled her young life in giving thee, a minister of our beloved Church, needed shelter; but you were there prior to her arrival, with those who could protect you if need were. Therefore I say she is innocent of the charge with which she is accused."

"True," observed Catesby; "yet I fear me it would be dangerous to test the matter before the Privy Council, for that bloodthirsty wolf, Blackstock, is ever prowling in search of fresh victims, for whom he receives special guerdon, and if the base, villainous spy sets up a charge it is rarely that his word is gainsaid."

"Thou art right, my son," said the priest, gravely shaking his head.

"But my child!" interposed Sir Godfrey, anxiously. "Is she in the power of this remorseless fiend or is she free?"

"That she 'scaped I know," said Catesby, "and that, too, with those who are trusty and true, and who if necessary would defend her with their last drop of blood."

"Of whom do ye speak?" asked the old knight.

"Of the youth Harold Rookby, whose prowess hath already been proven on many a well-fought plain, and the moving spirit of our great cause, Guy Fawkes."

Sir Godfrey looked troubled a moment, then said—

"'Tis well—I know none braver, and heaven grant that ere long my darling child will be restored to her anxious parent's arms."

A few days later the party at the abbey was considerably augmented by the arrival of a large band of the conspirators, embracing Sir Everard Digby, Francis Tresham, Ambrose Rookwood, the Winters, and John and Christopher Wright.

As Catesby greeted them he requested each in a low voice to say nothing of Violet to Sir Godfrey unless they had good news to impart concerning her.

His injunctions were strictly obeyed by one and all.

A disused room with a double exit, in a remote part of the west wing of the quaint old building, was set apart for the conspirators.

"Are we all assembled?" said Father Woodruff, looking around when the stout door had been securely bolted and barred.

"No, good father," replied Ambrose Rookwood. "There are several absent, and notably so Guy Fawkes."

"Knowest thou aught of his abiding place, my son?" said the priest.

"I cannot tell, holy father," replied Rookwood "He took his leave of us several days ago to visit the powder-maker on the marsh, and has not been seen or heard of since. We've grown uneasy at his absence."

"Fear not," returned Catesby, assuringly; "it will not be long ere he is again amongst us."

"I hope it may be so, my son," returned Father Woodruff. "However, we can at least proceed in this matter without him, for there is no fear of his swerving in the cause or proving disloyal."

Then taking a primer from his robe he addressed the conspirators, saying—

"I will again administer the oath to you, my brethren."

All instantly uncovered, and bending the knee the priest, in a solemn, impressive tone, pronounced the following oath—

"You shall swear by the blessed Trinity, and by the sacrament you propose to receive, never to disclose, directly or indirectly, by word or circumstance, the matter that shall be proposed to you to keep secret, nor desist from the execution thereof until the rest shall give you leave."

At this point all drew their swords, and, pressing the blades to their lips said, fervently—

"We swear!"

The priest rested the open book upon the points of their gleaming weapons a moment, then spreading his hands above their heads blessed them.

As the holy father ended his blessing on the conspirators on their resumption of their oath of secrecy and perseverance in the cause they arose and silently resumed the seats they had vacated.

Catesby now stood up and addressed the meeting.

"Brethren, the despotic and tyrannical monarch by whom we are persecuted and oppressed we could quickly remove, but we should gain little towards righting the wrongs of the Catholic party by his death alone. No!— all our enemies shall die with him!"

"But how?" asked Tresham.

"The matter hath been well discussed by Guy Fawkes and myself," continued Catesby, "and he himself hath proposed that we should hire a cellar under the Parliament House and place therein a large quantity of gunpowder and other ready combustibles, then, when all our detested adversaries are assembled above, fire the train that shall hurl this baneful nest of heretics into eternity. Do ye all assent to this plan?"

"I myself, for one, do not," said Sir Godfrey, rising, "and had I suspected the diabolical nature of your scheme I would never have taken the oath that made me one of you——"

"Ah! a traitor!" cried the assembled conspirators in a breath, placing their hands upon their weapons.

"Not so," returned the old knight, unflinchingly, "and, though I regret to say I am one of you, fear not. No power on earth would make me betray you."

"Dare we trust him?" whispered Sir Everard Digby to Tresham.

"I think we may safely do so," returned his companion.

"Yet where there is the shadow of a doubt there is danger," returned Catesby, "and in a case like this, brethren, such a fault should be punished with instant death."

"Stay!" said the priest, authoritatively; "act not rashly. I will answer for Sir Godfrey's silence with my life!"

"Just hear me rightly, gentlemen," continued the old knight. "Know that though I joined ye and will keep your secrets inviolate I refuse to assist you even in the slightest in this matter."

The conspirators looked troubled and conferred together for some moments, while the priest stood apart gently remonstrating with Sir Godfrey.

But nothing he could urge would shake the old knight's resolution.

Catesby, then addressing him, said—

"Sir Godfrey, though we are bitterly disappointed in this thy strange resolve, for we looked to thee for great pecuniary aid to further the cause, yet will we hold thee free from harm under promise that you keep inviolate our secrets."

Just at that moment there was a loud knocking at the door, and a sweet, refined voice said—

"Godfrey—husband! a king's officer, calling himself Oliver Blackstock, with several men-at arms, is at the outer postern, and demands in his Majesty's name that you deliver up to him our child Violet, Father Woodruff, Robert Catesby, and lastly yourself, for giving shelter to the priest."

All started and placed their hands upon their swords.

"What's to be done?" said the priest and Catesby in a breath.

"Follow me," observed Sir Godfrey, "and I will put ye where they will never find you."

CHAPTER XIX.

HAROLD WARNS GUY FAWKES OF DANGER—THE FLIGHT THROUGH THE RAVINE—THE BIRDS OF ILL-OMEN—GUY FAWKES DEALS DESTRUCTION TO HIS FOES

ON the recovery of Violet to reason Guy Fawkes ordered Ralph to turn the boat's head and row back to shore lower down stream, his object being to reach Heron Abbey as soon as possible, in order to restore the anxious girl to her bereaved parents.

Ralph instantly complied with his chief's request, whilst Leo, who had been more stunned than injured by the bullet graze, gradually recovered, and did his best to assist in getting the boat as quickly as possible to shore.

Meanwhile Harold Rookby, having been escorted as far as the cottage in the wood by the two Freerangers, bade them a courteous good-night.

He was about to press forward when his attention was arrested by the sound of voices and the jingle of arms and accoutrements.

Eagerly he peered between the intervening bushes, and beheld a *posse* of mounted troopers in front of the cottage, whilst through the open window he saw the captain of the troop interrogating a suspicious-looking individual whom it was evident was fresh from an immersion in the water.

It so chanced that in the position Harold stood concealed he was nearer to the window than the troopers, and by straining his powers of hearing could catch all that passed between the inmates of the cottage.

And in less than a minute he learnt the position of Guy Fawkes and his companions and the imminent and immediate danger in which they stood.

He waited to hear no more, but set off at his fastest speed for the river side.

Arriving there he discerned those he was in quest of in the act of landing, and as he hastened towards them he raised his voice, and exclaimed, hurriedly—

"Ah ! Violet—Guy, I greet you well "—clasping a hand of each. "We are pursued by Captain Merridon, with a score of mounted troopers at his back. Not a moment is to be lost !"

"What is to be done ?" cried Violet, despairingly.

"Let us make for the boat again, your honour," suggested Ralph, "and row to the opposite shore."

"And thus expose ourselves to the fury of their fire," returned Guy Fawkes. "No, their bullets would reach us long ere we reached the other side. I have a better plan than that, in faith. At the summit of yon gap there is a cavern, where in my youth I——"

"Ah ! see, they are upon us !" suddenly interrupted Harold, sighting the glittering armour of the troopers as they broke from cover and came galloping along the sands towards them.

Violet uttered a terrified cry, but Guy Fawkes caught her up in his arms, exclaiming—

"To the ravine !" and dashed forward, quickly followed by his companions.

Entering the dark, winding gorge, they sought their way along a rugged side-path, fit only for a wild cat, and having reached a sort of cavern or recess in the rocks they paused to take breath and sat down on a rude bench of stone.

"Here for a while, at least, we are safe," said Guy Fawkes, with a sigh of relief, and wiping his heated brow.

"How green the trees are ! How pure yon falling water !" murmured Violet, admiringly, despite her peril. "How rich the wild flowers blossom, and how bright the sweet moonlight is seeking to find us out amid the thick boughs which encircle our cave of refuge !"

"Aye !" returned Guy Fawkes, with kindling eye. "Look ye down the vale and look ye up to heaven. He who rules above spread out this beautiful land beneath our feet and hung yon marvellous canopy over our heads, and gave unto us the fowls of the air, the fish of the stream, and the beasts of the fields for our inheritance.

"But the wickedness of man mars the bounty of heaven. We are deprived of our patrimony, we are hunted to the desert places, and are forbidden to sing the praises of Him who dwells on high under penalty of life and limb.

"But let us retire farther into this wild and seldom-trodden glen and prepare to do battle with the relentless enemies of our deeply-wronged Church."

They arose and continued their journey along the rude paths which the foot of man and beast had fashioned in that wild ravine.

Sometimes the way scaled a steep and fearful crag, sometimes it crept among the fantastic roots of the oak and the beech, and sometimes it went to the very margin of the brink, where the rock was cleft, as it were, in two, disclosing the foaming stream at the depth of fifty or a hundred fathoms.

Guy Fawkes often had to use all his skill, though he well knew the path, in conducting Violet along this dangerous way.

At length, however, they reached what appeared to be their abiding place, and which was called the Friar's Cell.

This was a rude but not ungraceful sort of temple formed out of the freestone rock.

The entrance was wide, and overhung with ivy and honeysuckle, and the interior was recessed, presenting what to anchorites might appear both seats and couches.

"This is the place," said Guy Fawkes, "where our warriors of old found refuge when they warred for the independence of their country, and in this place will we fight the good fight without fainting. Might and cruelty must prevail in this land for a time, and we are driven for a season to the heaths and desert places, to be wounded by the shafts of the hunter."

"And all this should we patiently endure," added Violet, "for freedom from the yoke of the enemies of our Church."

"Aye, Violet," responded Harold, "it is for freedom of life and limb, freedom for our souls, freedom to worship our Maker according to our conscience, that we are hunted from place to place, from rock to rock."

"And woe to him who seeks to harm us in this place of refuge !" said Guy Fawkes, taking a loaded matchlock from Ralph. "With this kind of weapon I never miss my aim, and this sword at my side was never by my whole strength thrust in vain !"

So saying, Guy Fawkes stood within the ivy-draped porch of the cavern, and lent an ear to every sound and an eye to every bird that flitted from bough to bough.

Meanwhile Captain Merridon and his men had dismounted, and, led by a false clue, had plunged into the winding mazes of the glen on the opposite side.

And when they, at risk of life and limb, had reached the upper gorge of the deep defile, almost facing the Friar's Cell, where Guy Fawkes and his companions lay hid, they were met by one of Sir Sidney Wildbrook's half-drowned myrmidons, who told them that he had traced the footsteps of the fugitives to the cave in the summit of the other cliff, where Guy Fawkes stood with loaded matchlock in hand, from which the fleetest eaglet could not hope to escape.

"Out upon thee, man !" exclaimed Captain Merridon, with scorn. "Thinkest thou *I* fear this fanatical firebrand ? I'faith ! if we meet and I fail to feed the ravens—there's a pair o' them looking at me now—with his vile Papist carcass may the fiend make my ribs into a gridiron for my soul !"

"Whist, captain !—for heaven's sake whist !" said a veteran trooper. "Not that ye frighten me with such wild words, but devil take me if I like the presence of these hooded crows. They look at us as they look at a sheep that's doomed to die on the mountains."

"An' I were you, captain," said another trooper, "I would e'en take their counsel and keep out of this dark glen—it lies not in our line o' march, and——"

The captain silenced him with a motion of his hand, and said—

"Corporal Helstone, take ten men and station them privily in the ruins of the old hunting-tower. There they stand," pointing higher up the glen.

"They command from the upper windows the entrance of the Friar's Cell, where this fighting conspirator is. It is a long shot, but you are skilful. The rest of the men will enter the ravine at both ends. The moment you have a full view of him at the entrance take deliberate aim—if he falls here is my purse and you are a sergeant."

Corporal Helstone stationed himself and his men according to orders, whilst his captain went deeper into the ravine, on the desperate service of dislodging a practised warrior, whose place of refuge no one could approach without peril of his life.

"I think, my lads," said the corporal, "our captain has shaped out a garment for himself he will find some danger in sewing."

"And I think," observed a soldier, "that our corporal speaks more like a tailor than a soldier. 'Sdeath! I don't like to be packed up in this crumbling old tower when there's game in hand, but no doubt the captain thought we were all tailors, and that our courage was but small."

"I will show my face, Gaston, where yours dare not be seen," exclaimed the corporal, standing full in view.

And, pointing his musket straight towards the entrance of the Friar's Cell, he fired.

A stifled cry of pain followed the shot, and Harold fell wounded upon the floor of the cell.

With a cry of fear Violet threw herself on her knees beside him.

"Quick, Leo, load me another matchlock," softly cried Guy Fawkes, with calm determination.

And while the page was in the act of sending the bullet home with the ramrod his master calmly advanced towards the mouth of the cavern.

Peering warily through the screen of honeysuckle and ivy which covered the entrance he instantly discharged his weapon.

The ravine echoed loudly to the report, whilst Corporal Helstone dropped forward from the precipice, and his helmet was seen to glitter for a moment as he fell headlong into the fearful chasm below—dead.

Then, turning towards Violet, Guy Fawkes said—

"How fares it with Harold? Not seriously hurt, I hope?"

"Alas! I cannot tell," replied the anxious and terrified Violet. "His wound bleeds so freely I can scarce discern his features."

"I am better now," answered Harold, recovering. "The shot grazed my temple and stunned me—it will quickly heal," and he rose to his feet.

"I have avenged the shot," said Guy Fawkes. "But the heretical dogs are closing fast around us."

Violet uttered a slight ejaculation of fright.

"Fear not, Violet," he added; "they have yet to learn the secret of the Friar's Cell. It commands both the upper and lower approaches. But where is Ralph?"

"He has penetrated farther into the recesses of the cavern to try and find some other outlet," observed Leo.

"'Twere not required," remarked Guy Fawkes; "but hist! there is another son of Satan in the act of presenting his engine of death at us. Give me the matchlock, boy."

Leo handed him the gun, and, raising it to his shoulder, he took steady aim.

The sergeant that conducted the party who were to penetrate from the lower gorge received the ball in his brain as he gained the summit of the rock, and immediately fell over the cliff.

It fared no better with a second adventurer, and the remainder, believing that the fugitives were in force, halted, and were undecided what to do.

"Now, my lads!" exclaimed Captain Merriton, "the game has begun—the old tower is sending shot after shot, and there will be nought left for us to do but to march to the Friar's Cell and report on the dead bodies."

So saying he descended into the ravine and wound his difficult and adventurous way wearily with foot and hand.

"Captain," said the veteran who had formerly addressed him, laying his hand on his arm and pointing upwards, "there's our black forerunners. That man never had luck that they took a fancy to yet; but I'll follow you to the red-hot doors of perdition before I'll flinch. Only I have no faith in things if these blood birds don't believe they are to feast atween your breastbones and mine."

The captain was observed to turn a shade paler as he looked on those dark companions of his march. Still he went boldly forward.

One of the uncanny creatures uttered a croak and peered into the chasm below, where the roaring stream was invisible for mist and spray, and appeared as if it saw something.

At that moment the captain took off his helmet and waved the long plume to scare the birds away, and at the same time continued to advance.

Suddenly there was a startling report.

The ball from Guy Fawkes's piece almost grazed his cheek and struck the veteran who followed him on the forehead.

The latter, in a death-pang, clutched hard the arm on which his palm was laid, then dropped heavily back, and the living and the dead, locked in a fatal embrace, were precipitated some thirty fathoms into the awful depths below.

The rest of the troopers were struck with dismay—their leaders were slain. No one volunteered to advance, and as they stood irresolute they heard a shot ring again from the dreaded place, and saw the body of one of their comrades sink down on the window-sill of the tower, while his musket, dropping from his relaxed hands, went rattling down the rocky ravine.

"All the Papists are come from hell," cried a trooper, "to defend this cursed glen. Let us march out, place sentinels at the passes, and dispatch two of our fleetest horses to the town for an officer to command us and for foot soldiers accustomed to such warfare—curse it! For my part I can only fight on horseback."

This sentiment, as it promised security, was embraced by all.

They retired to the extremities of the ravine, placed sentinels, and despatched two troopers to the town for assistance.

When the day dawned they penetrated unmolested into the Friar's Cell.

But the fugitives had gone.

They had escaped through a secret entrance, and then scaling the almost perpendicular side of the ravine, had sought shelter in a distant glen on their way to Heron Abbey.

CHAPTER XX.

THE SECRET HIDING-PLACE—OLIVER BLACKSTOCK BAFFLED—LADY HAMLYN SURPRISED BY SIR SIDNEY—A DESPERATE STRUGGLE—THE ATTACK UPON THE ABBEY—FLIGHT

IN a former chapter we left Sir Godfrey Hamlyn and his brother conspirators in a state of considerable consternation on learning that Oliver Blackstock demanded admittance in the name of the king.

On Sir Godfrey receiving the information from his wife he proposed to effectually conceal those whom the officers had come to arrest.

"This way, gentlemen," he concluded, walking towards the beautifully-carved mantel-piece.

And pressing his two fingers on the eyes of a hideous carved head of a satyr, which formed part of the supports of the huge shelf, a clicking noise succeeded

Then the massive hearth began to sink.

"Holy father, an you, Mr. Catesby," said Sir Godfrey, "do you both step on to the slab and descend to the vaults beneath. Not all the combined army of King James could ever find ye there."

Catesby conducted Father Woodruff to the slowly-sinking stone, and, standing thereon, they shortly disappeared from sight.

Then Sir Godfrey removed his fingers from the face of the figure, and the slab speedily rose into its place again.

"My lord, my lord," said a servitor, rapping on the panel without, "the officer below demands instant admittance in the king's name."

"Admit him," returned Sir Godfrey. Then turning to the conspirators, he added, "Gentlemen, pray be seated—appear wholly unconcerned and at your ease."

The conspirators, in various attitudes of careless grace, seated themselves around the table. Some sipped their wine, some smoked others assumed an indifferent air, and all, more or less, engaged in an easy, desultory conversation.

They had scarcely composed themselves, however, when Oliver Blackstock, followed by his men-at-arms, entered the room.

"Now, sirrah!" cried Sir Godfrey, starting from his seat. "What is the meaning of this intrusion?"

"My mission here, Sir Godfrey," said Blackstock, slightly quailing under the old knight's dignified demeanour, "is to arrest your daughter, Miss Violet Hamlyn, for having harboured one Father Woodruff at your honour's residence on the banks of the Thames."

"The charge is a false one, fellow," said Sir Godfrey. "My daughter was not cognisant of the worthy father's presence there previous to her journeying thither."

"That is a matter which ye will have to settle before the justices, Sir Godfrey," returned Blackstock. "I bear a warrant for the arrest of Miss Hamlyn, and I command you in the king's name to deliver her up into my keeping."

And he produced a paper as he spoke.

"It is far from my wish to resist the law," said the knight, "but were I disposed to comply with your demand it would be wholly beyond my power. It grieves me to say my daughter is missing, and I know not where she is."

"That is exactly the reply I expected," said Blackstock, with sneering incredulity; "but I will e'en satisfy myself upon this point anon."

"Malapert knave!" cried the old knight, red with anger and clapping his hand to his sword, "dare you doubt my word?"

"I am told that she is here hid," said the fellow, stolidly.

"Then, sirrah, you were wrongly informed."

"It is further stated that ye have given refuge to Father Woodruff and one Robert Catesby, a suspected traitor to the State, both of whom I have a warrant for," continued Blackstock, insolently.

"You will find no such persons under my roof," replied the old knight, with emphasis.

"At any rate I shall make a careful survey of the premises."

"You are at liberty to do so."

"I must also place you under arrest. Your sword, Sir Godfrey."

"You must first show me your warrant ere I deliver up my sword!" cried Sir Godfrey, indignantly.

"I arrest you on suspicion, Sir Godfrey, of having harboured the aforesaid Father Woodruff and Robert Catesby," said Blackstock, "and I will take the responsibility of the act upon my own shoulders."

"Search the house, fellow, if ye please, but unless you find here those whom ye seek I shall resist ye to the last!" cried the old knight, standing on the defensive.

"And we will support you, Sir Godfrey, to the bitter end," cried the assembled conspirators, starting up and drawing their swords

"Beware, gentlemen, lest in your zeal to serve a State prisoner ye put not thine own necks in the halter!" cried Blackstock, furious at being baffled in his fell design.

"We will abide the issue should you proceed to extremes," said Ambrose Rookwood, meaningly.

With a muttered imprecation the officer turned away, and, addressing his men, said—

"Search the place—leave not a stone unturned or a corner unexplored at your peril!"

The order was obeyed with alacrity. But after a long and most diligent investigation they signally failed to find those they sought.

With rage and bitterest disappointment burning at his heart Blackstock called his men together and took his departure, greatly to the relief of Sir Godfrey and his guests.

Meanwhile a scene of a very different nature was being enacted in the private apartment of Lady Eleanor Hamlyn.

Sir Sidney Wildbrook, having been defeated in his attempt to successfully carry off Violet, made his way to Heron Abbey, determined to try his arts upon her mother, the Lady Eleanor; for, be it remembered, he still retained possession of the love-philter intended for Violet.

As a relative of the family he found no difficulty in gaining access to the mansion, then, concealing himself amid the many shadowy recesses of the winding passages, he quietly awaited his opportunity, and as he saw Lady Hamlyn enter her chamber he stole softly in after her.

Her back was towards him, and, being unconscious of his presence, she threw herself upon her knees before a beautifully-sculptured shrine of the Virgin, and became absorbed in prayer.

Sir Sidney approached on tip-toe, and was about to touch her on the shoulder.

But he suddenly paused in the very act, his handsome face aglow with sinful triumph, and taking the philter from his doublet he suddenly pounced upon her like a tiger upon its prey, and, forcing back her shapely head, strove to pour its contents between her lips.

But Sir Sidney had not calculated on the extraordinary will and strength of the Lady Eleanor.

Though taken by surprise she closed her teeth firmly, and the dark, subtle liquor was upset and marred the purity of her snowy neck and fair panting bosom instead of being forced down her throat.

She resisted him right bravely, and the struggle that ensued was a desperate one.

Again and again did she cry aloud for help during that wild, exciting contest, but her shrieks seemed not to reach those who would have flown eagerly to her assistance.

So fierce and desperate had been the encounter that her dainty clothes hung almost in ribbons about her beautiful form. Still she did not relinquish her grasp of her heartless persecutor, who, finding his base ends could only be accomplished by violence, resorted to the most cruel and ruffianly means to effect his purpose.

Her strength was fast giving way under his furious attack.

A moment more and she sank down exhausted, uttering a last despairing cry, and she would have fallen an easy victim had not the door been burst suddenly open, when Guy Fawkes, Harold Rookby, and a servant, all fully armed, hastened into the room.

Lady Hamlyn started to her feet with a sob of hysterical joy at sight of her preservers, and darted towards them.

"Ah, villain! think not to escape!" Guy Fawkes exclaimed, dashing after Sir Sidney, and making a cut at him with his rapier.

At that moment the crafty nobleman threw something on the floor.

Instantaneously a wall of living, leaping flame arose—as on a former occasion at the abode of the magician—and held Sir Sidney's pursuers in check.

When the fire had subsided it was seen that Sir Sidney had escaped through the window.

"Let us pursue the villain to the death!" cried Guy Fawkes, waving his sword and springing forward.

Just then, however, the ringing clash of arms, shots, and sounds of loud strife told that a desperate encounter was going on in the west wing of the abbey, and Guy Fawkes instinctively knew that the conspirators were hotly engaged with the king's troops.

He was on the point of going to their assistance when a panting servant rushed up, exclaiming, breathlessly—

"Save yourselves, my masters; the place is besieged by a considerable force of troopers and men-at-arms—your only hope is in flight!" and he passed on.

Then, with a wild shout, a number of troopers came dashing up, and before Guy Fawkes could prevent it had surrounded and seized Lady Hamlyn.

To contend against such unequal odds Guy Fawkes saw at once would be sheer madness.

Parrying, therefore, the many blows that were aimed at them, Guy Fawkes and Harold darted through the window which opened out on the ramparts.

Guy Fawkes knew every inch of the place, and, pursuing their way under cover of the deep embrasures, they reached the wing where they had left Ralph Roley and Leo in charge of Violet.

"Quick, Violet! we are pursued!" cried Guy Fawkes, taking her trembling hand. "Not a moment is to be lost!"

He led them round a winding corridor, then, descending a flight of steps, opened a door in the wall, which looked out upon the moat.

A flat-bottomed boat was drawn up close under the step.

"Thine hand, quick, Violet!" said Harold, seizing the fair girl's hand as he spoke to help her into the boat.

"But my dear parents?" urged the weeping girl, pausing.

"Are in the hands of a merciful Providence," returned Guy Fawkes.

Violet still hung back.

But now a loud, triumphant shout fell on their ears, and, turning, they beheld a dozen troopers in full chase of them.

The fugitives instantly scrambled into the boat.

The wicket was slammed hastily to, and Guy Fawkes, taking the long boat-hook, propelled the punt across the moat just in time to escape the deadly shower of shot that was fired at them by the baffled and cursing soldiery.

CHAPTER XXI.

FLIGHT OF THE FUGITIVES—THE FREERANGERS TO THE RESCUE—THE FOREST RETREAT—EVELYN AND LEO—THE DANCING-GIRL'S SECRET LOVE—GUY FAWKES AND RALPH START ON A DANGEROUS ERRAND.

NOT satisfied with the result of his search, for he still felt convinced that his victims lay hid somewhere in the old dwelling, Oliver Blackstock bade one of his men conceal himself in one of the many recesses of the ill-lighted corridor, then took his departure across the drawbridge, which the stalwart warder eagerly lowered for him.

The trooper remained in his hiding-place nearly an hour before he deemed it prudent to venture forth.

Then, observing that the unsuspicious warder showed symptoms of drowsiness, he pounced upon him with cat-like step and drove his dagger through his heart.

The warder fell to the ground without a sound—dead!

The murderer then set the machinery in motion, and a few seconds later the drawbridge was lowered, when Blackstock and his men, now considerably increased in numbers by the remainder of Captain Merridon's troopers, were secretly admitted.

Meanwhile the conspirators, deeming it safe for Catesby and the priest to come forth from their place of concealment, had reassembled, when the wily Blackstock and his men stole unexpectedly upon them.

A fierce and deadly conflict ensued, but nearly all the conspirators managed to escape by means of a secret passage, with which the curious old place abounded.

Lady Eleanor, however, as we have shown, fell into the hands of the enemy.

Guy Fawkes and his party were determinedly pursued by Blackstock's men to the border gf Bleam Wood, and it was painfully evident by the little band of fugitives that they would not be able to hold out against their relentless foes much longer, for the soldiers were gaining on them fast, and Violet, overwrought oo the conflicting scenes she had passed through, was rapidly becoming exhausted.

Suddenly, however, Harold remembered the Freeranger's gift, and, raising the silver tube to his lips, he blew a shrill blast.

A minute later and the forest re-echoed with many shrill answers.

Then, crashing and plunging through the bushes and brushwood, came a score or more of Freerangers, all fully armed.

"A rescue, brothers! A rescue!" cried Harold, at the sight of them.

They took in the scene at a glance, and, recognising the voice of their new member, rushed to meet the foe with a wild, ringing cry.

The king's men found they had no ordinary foe to contend with, so they hastily beat a retreat, though not before several had been mortally wounded.

Harold, unfortunately, was again wounded in the fray, and, in company of Guy Fawkes, Violet, and the page, was conveyed to the romantic abode of Will-o'-the-Woods in the forest.

By the evening of the following day the young soldier was consumed by a raging fever, while the anxious and devoted Violet and Guy Fawkes were watching by his side.

Leo had gone for a ramble through the merry brown woods, delighted with the wild gipsy-like life and the stalwart and romantic bearing of the blithesome and roystering band of Freerangers.

About to turn down a deep, shady glen, where the game abounded, he was suddenly confronted by the dancing-girl.

"Evelyn, my sister!" cried the boy, in pleased surprise.

"My brother!" said Evelyn, and the next instant he was clasped to her bosom.

"What of thy master?" she demanded, hurriedly.

"He is well, sister," replied Leo, "though he hath imperilled life and limb a score of times since last we met."

"He is entering on a career of great danger," said the dancing girl. "You will follow him, guard him, shield him with your life, and suffer him not to sleep unwatched, nor to walk unattended. Hands will be raised against him and spies compass him about; but be you faithful, Leo. Oh, should you betray him!"

"Betray him!" repeated the boy. "Evelyn, why speakest thou thus?"

"Should you falter in your fidelity," said the girl, with rapid emotion, "should you waver a moment between your duty and your life, play coward in the hour of danger, or traitor when your faith was trusted, then may a sister's curse——"

"Evelyn! Evelyn!" cried Leo, "why do you use such words to me? Not for all the gold in England would I betray a trust, or strike faintly in——"

"Yes, yes," said the dancing girl, abruptly, "but the lady—Miss Hamlyn—thinkest thou, Leo, that he loves her fondly?"

"Aye, sister, with all his heart. I had not thought a bearded man could pine so for a woman."

"How mean you, brother?"

"I have heard him whisper her name in sleep," went on the boy, "and seen the tears start from those dark eyes of his when——"

"Peace, peace!" cried Evelyn; "why tell me this?"

"Marry, because thou asked me," answered Leo.

"He loves her!"

"Thou hast lost thy wits, gentle sister, and always seemest to do so when we speak of Master Fawkes and the lady he loves. How fares Paulo?"

"Name him not!" cried Evelyn; "speak not his hated name if ye would not drive me mad. Do you not loathe me? Do you not feel my touch contamination? Yet I am your sister, Leo."

"My kind, good sister, what mean you, Evelyn?"

"A day will come when you will blush for me —when you will wish that I had never lived!"

"Evelyn, my own gentle Evelyn!" said the boy in astonishment, "what mean you by words like these?"

"He loves this Violet Hamlyn!" continued the dancing-girl. "Saidst thou that he loved her?"

"I have said so a hundred times. It was you yourself first told me that he did."

"She is beautiful—yes, very beautiful—and pure, too, as the white robe she wears. I have never seen a fairer woman—a sweeter face. Her nature must be kind and true, and yet——"

"Evelyn, someone approaches."

"It is Paulo!" muttered the girl, shuddering. "Farewell, Leo!"

She raised his head and kissed his cold brow passionately with her burning lips, then glided from his side, and the next moment was lost amidst the mazes of the wood.

* * * * * *

Violet, deeply distressed to know the fate of her beloved parents, found in Guy Fawkes a ready knight-errant.

Cleverly disguised as a court gallant, with fair wig, moustache, and skilfully-painted face, he set out on horseback in company of his faithful attendant, Ralph—who was also disguised—for the town, inwardly resolved to gain some tidings of the parents of her whom he loved so fervently, and yet, he feared, so hopelessly.

As they reached the crowded streets the busy hum of voices filled the air, and there seemed to be some more than ordinary event in the minds of men.

There was a busy abstracted look of interest

and importance on each face—a want of that idle curiosity that generally pervades the multitude—which could not fail to attract Guy Fawkes's attention.

Words of strange import fell upon his ear, and oft the repeated mention of the name of Hamlyn arrested his attention.

He reined in his steed beside one who, from his dress and demeanour, seemed to be a burgess of repute.

"Friend," said Guy Fawkes, as he leant over his horse's neck, "there seems to be somewhat of commotion in the town. May I ask the cause?"

"Ye may, Sir Cavalier," was the concise reply, "for there's like to be a foul affair sifted this day, but I do ill to bide gossiping here else the court-house will be filled."

"The court-house!" exclaimed Guy Fawkes.

"Aye, the court-house," said the man, glancing at the hilt of his long and somewhat rusty rapier; "ye hath doubtless heard of the great trial that's to depend before the Justice-General."

"Trial! What! Who?" exclaimed Guy Fawkes, trying in vain to conceal his fear and agitation.

The man looked earnestly at him for a moment and shook his head.

"A foul conspiracy has been detected, Sir Cavalier, the likes of which was never heard tell of in this unhappy country since the days of the bloody queen. The Lord preserve us from such evil doings."

CHAPTER XXII.

LADY HAMLYN TRIED FOR WITCHCRAFT—PUT TO THE TORTURE—A FEARFUL SCENE—GUY FAWKES'S RASH DEED—A NARROW ESCAPE.

"TELL me and my friend Ralph," said Guy Fawkes, "what are these same foul doings of which thou speakest?"

"Treason, Sir Knight—a vile conspiracy against his majesty's life."

"A conspiracy against the king's life!" said Guy Fawkes, greatly relieved, for he never dreamt of the vile accusation Sir Sidney had made against the beauteous Lady Eleanor.

"You may well grow pale with terror, young sir," said the stranger, mistaking the cause of his emotion, "and if ye saw, as I have done, in what a bonny disguise sin and sorrow come, ye would forswear the sex for aye."

"Is there, then, a lady implicated?" asked Guy Fawkes, his apprehensions returning with redoubled force.

"Aye, that there is, Sir Knight, and when did ye ever see mischief without a woman at the bottom on't? But such a woman! No living being e'er saw one more beautiful, gentle, and sweet. But the devil 's good to his own, and well knows how to spoil his children, till he lures them on to their destruction."

"But who—who, I pray ye, is this lady?" asked Guy Fawkes, in a fever of agitation.

"The lady?" replied the traveller, in surprise. "Ye must be a stranger indeed that ye have not heard of the beauteous Lady Hamlyn."

With difficulty Guy Fawkes repressed a cry of alarm.

He waited to hear no more, but, dashing his spurs into his horse's side, galloped down the street, followed by Ralph.

Having reached the Abbey Inn, Guy Fawkes and Ralph left their horses in charge of the host, and quickly retraced their steps towards the Justice Court.

Hurried forward, and impelled by the crowd around him, Guy Fawkes entered a low and narrow door, situated at the end of an obscure passage. One or two mace-bearers stood near it, but they were powerless to resist the rushing crowd. Guy Fawkes was carried onward, and passing through another door found himself at once in the presence of the assembled members of the High Court of Justice.

The room or hall into which Guy Fawkes was so suddenly ushered was not of large dimensions, and was but indifferently lighted. Round two sides of it a narrow gallery was erected, intended principally for the accommodation of the lower orders.

At one end, on a bench somewhat elevated, sat the Lord Chief Justice Popham, and beside him were the lord justice's clerk and two deputy-justices in their robes of office.

A serious sympathetic concern appeared upon their countenances as they spoke together in low, suppressed tones.

At a table beneath them the counsel for the Crown, the deputy-clerk and his assistants, and a number of other members of the court were placed.

At the lower end of this table, and a little on one side, stood Deverell the Doomster.

He was a tall, raw-boned, and haggard-looking ruffian, whose forbidding features were almost hidden by the huge bushy whiskers and moustache he seemed to take a peculiar pride in cultivating.

His ragged red locks escaped from beneath a black skull cap, and his huge hand rested on a glittering axe—the symbol of his terrible office.

There was a deep—a breathless silence in the court.

The whispered consultation of the judges ceased, and almost at the same moment that Guy Fawkes entered from one side of the court the unfortunate Lady Hamlyn was led in from the other. Guy Fawkes could scarcely suppress a cry of surprise and pity as he gazed on her pale features.

But her step was firm, and the calm, untroubled expression of her sweet blue eyes showed that even the horrors of her situation could not appal the well-regulated soul that dwelt within her breast.

She was placed in a chair, and so seated that while the judges and her accusers could observe the workings of her pensive, innocent face, she could scarcely discern a trace of their features.

The light streaming through the long, narrow stained-glass windows fell upon her pale face, and perhaps the sun never shone upon a more lovely or a sweeter countenance.

She was still young, and bore her years so well—even in sorrow and affliction—that Guy Fawkes could have imagined her the sister and not the mother of his beloved Violet.

The clerk of the court read the indictment or accusation, which was of the usual form.

It set forth that Eleanor, Lady Hamlyn, of Heron Abbey, on the faith and testimony of certain witnesses, had been accused of conspiring to cause the death of his most sacred majesty King James, by poison and witchcraft. Moreover, that she had entered into a compact with the Powers of Darkness, and, setting aside the fear of Heaven and the Christian faith, had sold her soul to Satan, by whose aid and assistance she had frequently endangered the lives and prosperity of his majesty's liege subjects through practising the foul art of witchcraft —a crime abhorred by Heaven and man.

"Eleanor, Lady Hamlyn," he concluded, in his cold and passionless tones, "what say you? Are you guilty or not guilty of the crimes laid to your charge?"

"Guilty or not guilty, Eleanor, Lady Hamlyn?" repeated the Doomster, in a harsh tone, but without turning his head or moving a muscle of his sinister face.

"Not guilty, my lords!" answered Lady Hamlyn, in a voice of thrilling sweetness, that vibrated to the heart of every hearer.

Another short whispered consultation took place amongst the judges, the jury was sworn in, and the trial proceeded.

The jury consisted of fifteen men, who, whatever their education might have been, were deeply impressed with the popular belief that if the unfortunate culprit should escape they themselves, by her power, would die. So that scarcely a chance of life remained to the accused.

After a few other preliminary arrangements the deputy clerk cried out—

"Call Sir Sidney Wildbrook, his Majesty's Minister and Knight of the Holy Order of St. John!"

As she heard these words a visible but momentary tremor passed over the countenance of the unfortunate Lady Hamlyn.

In an instant, however, she had recovered her calmness and self-possession.

"It is true, then," she murmured, and then patiently awaited the result of his examination.

Sir Sidney entered with a slow and steady step.

All gave way before him, and Guy Fawkes fairly gasped for breath when he beheld him so villainously calm and unmoved.

"Miscreant!" he muttered to himself, "this, then, is thy fiendish work."

In the mad frenzy of that moment he would have darted forward and seized him where he stood, but a strong detaining arm was suddenly laid upon him.

Looking round he beheld the faithful Ralph, the expressive seriousness of whose face at once recalled him to a sense of the place and presence in which he stood.

The examination of Sir Sidney proceeded.

His testimony was apparently clear and distinct—no doubt could remain as to the identity of the party by whom the materials for the accusation had been furnished.

He swore to his own knowledge of her having used incantations, verses, and spells, and also of having laid goat's flesh on the threshold of a room where a waxen image of the king was laid, thus designing, by slow and wasting means, to accomplish the death of the gracious monarch.

He even bore witness that one so fair and beautiful had obtained a personal interview with the Prince of the Powers of Darkness for the furtherance of her hellish schemes.

With well-affected sorrow he bent his head to the ground, and as he spoke the tears streamed from his eyes.

His hands were crossed upon his breast, and with every appearance of humility he averred that the holy symbol of the cross which he bore, and of which he was a poor but unworthy champion, had on his approach dissolved the unholy conference and forced the Prince of Darkness to retire.

When he had finished his testimony a general groan resounded through the assembly, though there were some in whose eyes tears glistened at the appalling show of guilt established by the evidence of one the purity of whose principles and character could as little be doubted as the guilt of a being so gentle and so lovely.

Zach Horlock, disguised as Sir Sidney's steward, was the next witness who appeared, and Guy Fawkes was dumbfounded to behold him in such a guise and in such a place.

He corroborated the testimony of his coadjutor in everything, even in the most trifling detail.

Popham, the Lord Chief Justice, leant his head on the bench as the disguised magician concluded. The last ray of hope—if hope had ever shone—now seemed to flit away before the mass of positive evidence adduced.

But rising with a calm and undisturbed air Lady Eleanor bowed to her judges and said—

"My lords, may I request that Sir Sidney Wildbrook be recalled?"

"Assuredly, lady, and Heaven grant that his testimony avail thee!" answered Lord Popham, while a gleam of something like hope brightened his mild, benevolent grey eyes a moment.

The deputy-justice, however, knit his brows and darkly frowned.

He was on the point of opening his lips to oppose the recall when Sir Sidney again appeared.

"Sir Sidney Wildbrook," said Lady Hamlyn, "are you not related to my unfortunate lord?"

"I am, lady," replied Sir Sidney, in surprise.

"In what degree?"

"I am his first cousin," answered he, in increased astonishment.

"And when he has been cut off from the cares of this world, and I, too, have perished under the hands of the executioner, who will be considered the representative of his noble family?"

The nobleman bit his lip angrily and was silent.

A solemn feeling of anxiety pervaded the court, making it as still and silent as the grave.

"I ask you," repeated Lady Eleanor, fixing her soft but penetrating eyes upon her accuser, "who, in that event, would succeed to the princely inheritance of Hamlyn?"

"Lady," replied the deep-toned voice of Sir Sidney, "methinks you need not that I should enlighten you upon that subject."

"Sir Sidney, I would hear it from thy lips," she said, calmly.

"Then," observed the knight, "I believe the honour and dignity of supporting that noble house would descend to a very unworthy representative."

Lady Eleanor nodded her shapely head in emphatic acquiescence.

"It would be mine, lady," he added. "But Heaven forbid that in aught this should influence my testimony against thee this day."

"I said not that it would, Sir Sidney," she rejoined, while a slight smile passed over her calm but pale features. "I said not that it would, but methinks your imagination runs before *my* words."

And she kept her eyes fixed upon his countenance, as though she were reading the inner workings of his mind.

Though inwardly enraged he looked around with calm and dignified assurance.

"Thou art silent, Sir Sidney," she continued. "No matter. But, tell me, hast thou not in anticipation been enjoying our possessions and marking out their wide boundaries?"

"I have not," answered Sir Sidney, unblushingly.

"Hast thou not," pursued Lady Eleanor, "traversed each foot of its goodly ground? Hast thou not pointed out where thou wilt bestow increased splendour upon its beauties? Aye!—the very spots where thou wilt pull down and where thou wilt build up. And hast thou not——"

"Lady," interrupted the false knight, "I have done none of these things, nor can I conceive to what end thy questions are proposed. Long years have now passed since I beheld the princely residence of Hamlyn."

"And yet, Sir Sidney," she resumed, quietly, "you have borne testimony as an eye-witness to events which are said to have occurred there within the past few days."

A momentary burst of applause resounded from the multitude.

Guy Fawkes's dark eyes flashed with eager joy, and Ralph's jolly face wore a delightful look as he whispered—

"Her ladyship will be acquitted—of a surety she will. His testimony is not worth the paring of a horse's hoof."

"I said not," exclaimed Sir Sidney, when the tumult had somewhat subsided, "that these events had occurred at Hamlyn."

"True, Sir Sidney," remarked Lady Eleanor, "but your able steward and assistant hath said it for you."

Sir Sidney bit his lip in palpable confusion, and the murmurs of the multitude increased.

The justice-general's kindly features gleamed with pleasure.

But the justice-clerk arose from his seat, and, in a voice of thunder, commanded the witness to be removed.

"What, my lords!" he exclaimed, "shall we who sit in judgment here, for a slight mischance—an unimportant slip—throw aside the whole mass of positive evidence we have this day received?"

A deep murmur of disapprobation swelled throughout the court; but the stern visage of the advocate for the Crown as he arose quelled the rising storm.

He was a thin, spare man, upon whose features not a single gleam of feeling or compassion ever rested.

He then addressed the jury, assuming to trace witchcraft to its source, to convince them of the existence of such a crime, of which not one of them was disposed to doubt.

He brought forward historical and classical references, and quoted Scripture, in which is written, "Thou shalt not suffer a witch to live;" and again, "A man or woman that hath a familiar spirit, or that is a wizard, shall surely be put to death. Thou shalt stone them with stones, their blood shall be upon them."

And finally he wound up by adverting to the evidence in the case under consideration as thoroughly establishing that the unfortunate Lady Eleanor at the bar had been guilty of every branch of the crime that the most noted of the Persian, Assyrian, or Indian magicians could possibly have committed.

"In conclusion, good gentlemen of the jury," he exclaimed, "I am under the full conviction that I am not doing more than my duty when I ask from you a verdict of guilty against the prisoner at the bar!"

Lady Hamlyn now rose, while a slight flush tinged her pale cheeks. Her manner was still calm, firm, and dignified.

She stood in silence for a few seconds to collect her thoughts, then in her soft, sweet voice addressed the court.

"My lords and gentlemen," she commenced, "after the learned and most eloquent discourse you have but now heard, it would be vain on my part to attempt to convince you that the crime of which I have been accused has no existence save in the imagination of men.

"I do not wish, gentlemen, by any ill-judged appeal to your feelings, to injure the justice of my cause. Weak and feeble as I am I must grapple with the fearful accusation which has been adduced against me this day, and endeavour to prove that, if not absolutely false, it is at least marked with a stain of suspicion so deep as to render it totally unworthy of the slightest credit or respect.

"I shall not dwell upon the days when my honoured lord cherished this viper in his bosom, nor shall I now trouble you with adducing any evidence rebutting the many dark and cruel hints thrown out by Sir Sidney. It is sufficient that you gentlemen should know that the information which forms the substance of this investigation was furnished by him. He, then, is the accuser, and, like the serpent in the fable, has turned his envenomed sting against the breast which sheltered and protected him.

"From his own lips, gentlemen, you have heard in how near a degree of relationship Sir Sidney stands to my respected lord. You have also heard that he is heir apparent to the princely inheritance of Hamlyn, and to you I appeal, as I would to those acquainted with the impelling motives of a depraved heart, and ask if the prospect of being rewarded by possession of the many honours and wide domains of that ancient house be not sufficient to bias, if not wholly to corrupt, the testimony of so interested a witness and informer? Remember, too, gentlemen, he is a party to the cause. He was not dragged forward from his secret hiding-place by the strong arm of the law—but freely and voluntarily came forward to bear testimony against his near and dear relatives.

"Furthermore, gentlemen, you have the testimony of the suborned and prejudiced servant of this honourable knight, to those circumstances having taken place at Hamlyn, and finally you have the positive assurance of this same honourable knight that he had never visited the domain for years. How then, I would ask, is it possible that he could have been an eye-witness to events which are said to have occurred at Hamlyn, when, by his own confession, he had of late years never been near it?"

She paused, and a loud murmur of applause sounded through the court.

The justice-general again smiled, and his grave countenance lighted up with pleasure. The deputy-justice frowned and shook his head, while the jurors, one and all, were absorbed in silent attention.

Meanwhile Lady Hamlyn had covered her eyes with her hand for a few minutes, and when the tumult had somewhat subsided continued—

"The crime, gentlemen, wherewith I am charged, is of attempting the life of his sacred majesty, which may Heaven long preserve! And what, gentlemen, I would ask, is the scope and substance of the testimony brought forward in support of this very heavy inquisi-tion?

"Simply this—that to accomplish so iniquitous a design I have used spells, verses, incantations, and laid goat's flesh on the threshold of a room wherein a waxen image of the king was laid.

"Absurdly false as it is, I would blush for my country could I find fifteen intelligent men so weak as to be led astray by evidence such as this. Moreover, gentlemen, as the most convincing proof of my innocence I would ask you this simple question: Were I endowed with those immeasurable mystic qualities wherewith I am supposed to have been vested, think you I could not, even now, at once free myself from the strong grasp of power whereby I am restrained?

"Dwell upon this, gentlemen, I entreat you. Ponder it well, and be convinced that you will best discharge your duty to your country, your conscience, and your God, and fulfil righteousness and justice, by acquitting me of all guilt or participation in the crimes with which I have been so falsely charged!"

She sat down, and there was silence in the court—the deep, breathless silence that betokens an agony of suspense.

The judges looked towards the jurors. The jurors, evidently moved, looked towards the judges.

But, with one exception, *their* looks were stern and resolved.

Then a whispered consultation next took place amongst the judges.

The Lord Chief Justice Popham was observed to shake his head, as if rejecting some proposal that had been made.

The deputy-justice-general appeared to press the matter. The dispute grew hotter and hotter, and the words "question" and "torture" were overheard.

But the deputy-justice-general at length appealed to his brother judges, who, by a silent nod, seemed to approve of the proposal he had made.

The mild features of Lord Popham became more and more clouded, and he bent his head upon the rich pillow before him, as if to conceal feelings which all the dignity of his character and situation could not enable him to overcome.

The deputy-justice whispered a few words to one of a pair of familiars, who conferred with his brother spirit, and both the black-shrouded, evil-looking messengers of cruelty and death disappeared.

The anxiety of the spectators had now risen to its utmost height, and vented itself in low and broken murmurs.

The jurors put their heads together and the judges laid back in their seats and preserved a deep and gloomy silence.

A slight bustle was now heard at the entrance of the hall, and the two familiars reappeared, leading between them the noble form of Sir Godfrey Hamlyn.

He was told to be seated in a chair of peculiar construction, close to the bar at which his unfortunate lady stood.

No sooner was he seated than, through the action of certain springs, he was immediately fettered in such a manner as to leave only his legs and arms at liberty.

Lady Eleanor turned her soft blue eyes upon him—filled with tears.

"Lady," said the deputy-justice, addressing her, "the law is merciful, and though the proof of your guilt is sufficient, it gives you another opportunity to retract your hardened plea. Say, will you confess?"

The lady faltered, but a look from her husband reassured her, and she answered, firmly—

"My lord, I have nothing to confess, and never shall a daughter of the house of Hamlyn be pointed at as a forsworn and perjured woman."

"The consequences then, lady, be upon your own head," said the questioner, as he handed a paper to the clerk of the court.

It was an order authorising the torture of the Lord of Hamlyn to compel confession of the crimes whereof his lady was accused.

"Do you still persist in asserting your innocence?" demanded the justice.

"I do!" replied Lady Eleanor, firmly.

A signal was given to the Doomster, and various instruments of torture were displayed, that would have struck terror into a less firm and innocent mind.

An involuntary shudder ran through the spectators, and Guy Fawkes was only restrained by the strong grasp and entreating look of Ralph from bursting forward.

For one moment the features of Lady Hamlyn became as pale as death, but the manly countenance of her noble husband remained unblanched.

Another signal was given and then the grim Doomster proceeded to the execution of his office.

An iron boot was fitted to the leg of the unfortunate nobleman, and a heavy wedge was then inserted between it and the shin-bone

The Doomster stood with his huge mallet over his shoulder, prepared on the slightest signal to strike.

"Innocent or guilty, lady?" said the judge.

"Innocent," came the words, in a low faltering tone.

Simultaneously descended the heavy mallet on the wedge, with a sound that struck like a knell upon the heart.

A wild shriek burst from the lips of Lady Eleanor, and she pressed her quivering hands over her eyes.

The excess of pain forced the blood from the poor sufferer's cheeks, and a cold perspiration broke upon his brow. No change of feature betrayed his agony, and he stretched forth his hand to his beloved wife with a firm and

GUY FAWKES

Or Gunpowder, Treason, and Plot.

INSTANTANEOUSLY A WALL OF LIVING FLAME AROSE, WHICH HELD SIR SIDNEY'S PURSUERS IN CHECK.

No. 6.

reassuring look. She clasped it, and pressed it to her lips and heart again and again.

A silent tear stood in many an eye, but the harsh countenance of the Doomster was unmoved. He stood with his mallet suspended in the air.

At a given signal it again fell upon the iron wedge, and a half suppressed cry of agony burst from the lips of Sir Godfrey.

His lady fell back, her eyes closed, and to all appearance her pure spirit had escaped from sin and suffering.

Not a breath was heard throughout the crowded court—not a sound, as with redoubled force the awful hammer descended on the iron wedge.

The bone was crushed to splinters, and a shriek of agony that no human fortitude could suppress burst from the lips of the suffering nobleman.

The wildness of the cry recalled his unhappy partner to consciousness.

She started with ashen face and dishevelled hair, and the word "Guilty" had half-escaped her bloodless lips.

When even in this dire extremity of pain Sir Godfrey cast an entreating glance towards her that at once sealed those lips which had so nearly pronounced her own and her husband's doom.

The Doomster hesitated and looked towards the bench for instructions.

The justice-clerk gave a silent nod.

"The limb is crushed!" said the Doomster, in reply, and with stoical indifference.

Another whispered consultation then took place, and at a given signal the fetters of Sir Godfrey were loosed and the instruments of torture removed.

But they were removed only to give place to another of a more refined description.

The iron boot, pilikins, and thumbikins were then in common use. But the instrument in question had only been recently imported from foreign parts under the auspices and direction of the justice-clerk.

In appearance it resembled a large trough, having sundry iron bars sharpened on the upper edge stretched across its surface.

Guy Fawkes had never seen or even heard of such an instrument, nor could he devise its accursed use.

It was brought forward, and soon the maimed and suffering man was seized and stretched on his back at full length across the sharp iron bars that were fastened on the trough.

To these he was bound, to prevent the possibility of his rising from, but not of his turning or moving horizontally upon them.

A thick napkin was then placed across the lower part of his face, in such a manner as almost to prevent respiration.

Another instrument was then erected by the Doomster, from which a small stream of water flowed, at the height of several feet.

This stream was so directed as to pour right into the mouth of the tortured man, by means of which, and of his own inhaled respiration, the napkin was forced altogether down his throat.

The functions of his lungs, consequently, were so far suspended as to create the most intense and cruel agony.

A suppressed cry of horror arose from every throat in the crowded court.

It was by main force alone, added to the energetic action of Ralph, and an inward consciousness of the uselessness of his interference, that withheld Guy Fawkes from bursting forward to the rescue.

Fortunately, in the confusion that ensued, his agitation was not observed.

Strange as it may appear, Lady Hamlyn seemed the most calm and collected of anyone amid that fearful scene, but it was the calmness of despair.

At first Sir Godfrey endured his new and refined species of torture with an almost imperceptible struggle.

But as the stream continued slowly to pour upon his mouth, and the difficulty of respiration was more and more increased, his struggles became greater and greater.

The agony at length appeared to be insupportable.

His eyes almost started from their sockets, the veins in his forehead were swollen almost to bursting, and the forehead and face, so far as uncovered, assumed a black and swarthy hue. Suffocation was fast approaching.

It was more than mortal man could endure, and his struggles became dreadful and appalling. It was then that the full merits of this horrid instrument of torture were displayed, for the struggles of the unhappy victim, acting upon the sharp-edged bars of steel on which he had been extended, caused his back to be cut and lacerated in a frightful manner.

The blood streamed in torrents from his many wounds, and this sight recalled his unfortunate wife to a degree of consciousness she had not for many minutes felt.

She clasped her hands before her eyes and screamed, in wild agony—

"Oh, spare him! spare him! *I am guilty!*"

All present had been deeply interested in the fate of the beautiful accused, but the appearance of so unlooked-for an engine of torture and its awful operations had for the last few minutes totally withdrawn their attention from Lady Hamlyn.

The confession came upon them like an electric shock, and a wild cry of disappointment and dismay burst from every lip.

Guy Fawkes, in the pent-up madness of his indignation, tore himself from Ralph's grasp, and, reckless of the presence in which he stood, shouted furiously—

"My curse upon thee, thou foul monster!"

And with one terrific blow he stretched the villainous Doomster senseless and bleeding upon the ground.

The deed done, Guy Fawkes instantly became aware of the folly and madness of his act.

"What ho!—seize him there!" exclaimed the justice-clerk to the black-robed familiars.

But the confusion and dismay into which the court had been thrown by so unparalleled an act of audacity prevented them from at once comprehending even so plain an order.

And ere there was time to repeat it the strong grasp of the faithful Ralph, at every hazard to himself, drew Guy Fawkes quickly back and pushed him into the very centre of the crowd.

"Fly, friend, fly!" was whispered in his ear from every side, as a space was opened out and room made for him to pass. "Fly, if ye would save your hand!"

"My head as well," thought Guy Fawkes, "if they only knew who it belongs to."

So the admonition did not require to be repeated. Like lightning Guy Fawkes, followed by Ralph, darted towards the door.

"Seize him, I say—seize the malapert villain!" furiously shouted the justice-clerk. "What ho, guards! guards!"

The frenzied cries followed them along the echoing passage down which Guy Fawkes and his companion fled for dear life.

Suddenly the tramp of armed men approaching told them that the guard had heard the justice's cry and were hastily responding to it.

"Mask quickly, and let us conceal ourselves behind yon pillars—'tis our only chance," whispered Guy Fawkes, as he caught the gleam of arms in the semi-darkness.

Instantly they slipped on their masks and softly stole behind the massive stone columns.

Only just in time, however, for the next moment the guard came trooping up, while Guy Fawkes and his companion, in a fever of dread alarm, stood with trembling hearts and bated breath till they had gone by.

It was a moment of terrible suspense.

But no sooner had the last soldier passed their place of concealment than they darted along the corridor through which they had come, into the open air, and were free.

CHAPTER XXIII.

GUY FAWKES MEETS WITH A FRIEND IN HIS HOUR OF NEED—SURROUNDED BY PERILS—A FEARFUL SPECTACLE.

SEPARATED from his companion, Guy Fawkes fancied the cries of his pursuers increased upon his ears, and their hurrying steps pressed almost immediately behind him.

Fearful of being overtaken, he flew along the almost deserted high-street, and a sudden projection hiding him from their view a moment, he darted into one of the many low-browed shops and disappeared.

It was a desperate step, but in the terrible agitation of the instant it was the only place of concealment that presented itself to his anxious gaze.

A 'prentice boy, who raised his shrill voice as Guy Fawkes darted into the innermost recesses of the shop, appeared to be the sole occupant of the rich but well-nigh deserted mansion.

"Hush, thou noisy varlet!" said Guy Fawkes. "Shelter me but a short space and here's a silver crown to buy thee comfits."

But the boy was not to be appeased. He continued his alarm in a yet louder strain, and discovery must have speedily followed had not an elderly man entered at that moment—thought upon his countenance and gravity in his step.

"Ye graceless loon!—ye ne'er-do-well!" thus he saluted his apprentice. "If thou screamest after that fashion I will make thy back and my cudgel acquainted. Had the Evil One himself come to melt my gold and silver in his own infernal crucible thou couldst not have given tongue to a louder strain."

"Mayhap he hath come, master mine," replied the lad, pointing towards Guy Fawkes, "an i'faith, if he would only blow your bellows too, he may stay where he is!"

"Certes! thou art a clever lad, and may yet come to preferment," said the goldsmith, advancing towards Guy Fawkes.

The conspirator immediately recognised in him the portly burgess who had that morning afforded him information of Lady Hamlyn's trial.

The recognition on his part was as instantaneous.

"Ha! ha! Sir Cavalier!" he exclaimed, "ye gave me the top of the morning, methinks. The noon to thee! By my faith, I little thought to meet thee here so soon!"

"I crave thy pardon for this unseemly intrusion, worthy sir," interrupted Guy Fawkes, "but would ye grant me concealment for a space from those bloodthirsty wolves of the law?"

And Guy Fawkes told the worthy fellow what had happened.

"Aye, that will I," returned the old goldsmith. "Ye did a bold and worthy deed, young sir, and it shall ne'er be said that Martyn Goldpurse was the man to betray good blood for felling such a monster as that cold-blooded wretch Deverell the Doomster.

"It was rash—nay, mad of me to act as I did," said Guy Fawkes, "but I could not stand idly by and witness such fiendish cruelty any longer."

"Ah, young sir, 'tis a sad business," said the goldsmith, shaking his head. "Had the poor dear lady been a Protestant instead of a follower of our deeply-persecuted faith this foul day's work had never been."

"Thou art right, friend," returned Guy Fawkes. "This false king has deceived, plundered, and persecuted us till our great wrongs cry aloud to heaven for vengeance!"

"Verily he hath much to answer for!" cried the goldsmith, gloomily.

"Aye, but the day of retribution is near its dawn—the hour is approaching when the blow shall be struck which shall fall upon the head of this heartless, godless tyrant, and stamp him out for ever!"

Meanwhile the worthy goldsmith employed himself in pushing aside a variety of implements and articles of his trade.

"Down! down! young sir, for by my faith here is the hue and cry at the door," exclaimed the old man, raising a trap-door and signalling Guy Fawkes to descend.

The conspirator did not need to be told a second time, but instantly leaping into the abyss the trap-door closed above him.

He could distinctly hear the goldsmith replacing the scattered articles in their original place, while he addressed his apprentice thus—

"And you, ye reckless unthrift, see that ye keep a calm face and your tongue within your teeth, and may be ye shall have this silver piece and Saturday e'en to yourself to play upon the green."

"I would rather it were a crown piece, good master mine," responded the hopeful youth. "An' as for Saturday e'en to myself I hath that by my indenture as it is."

"Well, well," said his master, "we'll not quarrel about that, Nicky, for ye are a clever spark, although there be a spice of Satanas about ye."

The place of concealment in which Guy Fawkes had been unexpectedly stowed might have vied in riches with an El Dorado, Mexico, or Peru. It was stored with gold and silver—melted and unmelted—ingots, bars, and ore, together with huge quantities shaped into the various chalices and utensils then in use.

But Guy Fawkes had neither inclination nor light sufficient to admire the richness and beauty of their manufacture.

An increased noise overhead attracted his attention, and he heard the voice of the worthy goldsmith seemingly in contention with some-one now present.

"Good e'en to ye, Master Goldpurse," said a voice of no pleasing sound. "We have been in every shop but thine, and I doubt me but this malapert gallant hath given us the slip-by."

"And no great matter neither, methinks, Saul Holdcraft, if he has," replied the goldsmith.

"No great matter i' faith," echoed the other. "It will be the matter of chopping off a right hand, methinks. Call ye that no great matter? They that be so ready to use their hands should lose them."

"What!" said the goldsmith, "for giving ugly Dan Deverell a flooring? That would be scarcely fair, methinks, Saul Holdcraft."

"No, no, Master Goldpurse," replied the officer. "Not because the man was Deverell the Doomster, although he has got a thump that will scarcely mend this month or more, but because of the place and presence in which the blow was inflicted. But blood and gallows! I am wasting time when I should be searching through your house, master. So here goes!"

"Search my house, ye ne'er-do-well vagabond," exclaimed the merchant, in great wrath. "Think ye that I, the second magistrate of the borough, would harbour any vagabond that breaks the law, ye uncondemned knave? I warrant me ye'll have an eye to the gold and silver, and any small thing that will stick to your tarry fingers, or that pouch of thine can conceal. Out upon ye! ye untried thief—ye marauding villain!"

"Come, come, Master Goldsmith," said the officer, "speak civilly, or mayhap your hands may be fitted with a pair of wristikins of a baser metal than your own glittering ornaments are made of. This is a Privy Council affair, and ye wot they like ill to be meddled with."

"Well, well, Saul Holdcraft," said the goldsmith, in a subdued voice, "take your own way. But hark ye, Saul, stick ye to the Privy Council and ye may bid farewell to the advancement to any post that may happen to drop through in the borough. Owen Norris is old and frail now, poor fellow, so remember."

This hint was not lost upon the officer, for after some indistinctly muttered words, the import of which Guy Fawkes could not discover, Saul Holdcraft and his myrmidons departed, to the no small relief of the prisoner.

Guy Fawkes, however, had plenty of time left him for reflection.

The sound of feet treading backwards and forwards in the shop was heard, also the voices of the incomers and outgoers. Everything appeared to be going on in the usual routine of business, but the worthy goldsmith seemed in no hurry to pay him a visit.

Guy Fawkes's patience was well-nigh exhausted, but there was no help for it.

So, wearied with listening for that which came not, he at last lay down upon the floor and vainly tried to snatch a brief repose.

The shades of night had descended upon the earth before the goldsmith deemed it prudent to release Guy Fawkes from his place of concealment.

When the goldsmith released Guy Fawkes from his hiding-place it was with many well-meant and oft-repeated cautions that he should make the good town quit of him with all possible speed.

There was little need of such advice, for now that his sole object of coming there had been defeated in so melancholy a manner he had already determined to make his way back once more to Bleam Woods to comfort and support poor Violet in her terrible bereavement—to be near her, to render any service or aid that lay in his power.

His cautious benefactor having enveloped him in a great cloak, noiselessly undid the bolts and bars of a well-secured door, which Guy Fawkes had not before observed. After a firm pressure of his hand and a hearty benediction, he showed his quondam guest into the open air, then, closing the door replaced each bolt and bar with his wonted care.

Wrapping his cloak around him Guy Fawkes made the best of his way across what appeared to be a cemetery, then, leaping a low wall, he found himself near an open space, and in the midst of a large crowd, which appeared to be moving in one direction.

A few minutes brought him to the castle hill, and there, for the first time, he became aware of the awful scene which he was about to witness.

Short indeed had been the single step between life and death, the preparations for the execution of the fair but unfortunate Lady Hamlyn being even now complete.

She had been found guilty and condemned upon the evidence of her own extorted confession, and, without being allowed even the short space usually granted to the worst of criminals to prepare for eternity, had been led forth from the place of trial to suffer the punishment due to her imagined crime.

Guy Fawkes could scarcely believe his eyes when he saw her standing in the centre of the open space in front of the castle, more like the being of another and purer world than a creature of this lost and ruined earth.

There she stood, clothed in a flowing robe of the purest white, from the rich lace around the breast of which her beautiful neck and bosom arose as if they had been fashioned by the hand of some cunning artist from a block of the fairest marble.

Indeed, her beauty and innocence were such as almost entirely to draw the attention of the spectators from the scene of terror by which she was surrounded.

But one glance sufficed to show that the unhappy lady was firmly bound by a band of iron to a long upright stake, and heaped around her feet were a number of huge faggots dipped in oil, pitch, and other combustible matter.

Guy Fawkes's eyeballs almost darted from their sockets as the reality of the dreadful scene before him was forced upon his mind.

But the love of self-preservation, and a bitter consciousness of his inability to afford the hapless mother of his beloved Violet the smallest aid, withheld him from darting forward to the relief of the doomed lady.

For should he so involve himself he knew not what might become of the equally unhappy Sir Godfrey, whose rescue depended in a measure upon his exertions. And what, too, would become of the innocent and deeply-tried Violet?

Around the place of execution there was a strong and well-armed guard.

Each soldier supported in his left hand a large lighted torch, the red dusky glare of which—cast upon the sea of fixed and eager countenances, the variety of dresses and glint of weapons and armour, and the horrible apparatus of death—added a hundredfold to the terror of the scene.

Guy Fawkes would have turned away—he would have fled—he would have done anything to escape the soul-haunting sight—but he was so hemmed in by the dense crowd around him that he could scarcely move a single limb.

At the side of the unfortunate lady a priest, habited in the vestments of his holy order, stood.

He held a crucifix to her white lips, and for some minutes she was engaged in earnest and most heartfelt prayer.

Her lovely eloquent eyes were turned towards that heaven where her hopes were centred, for every earthly object was now fast fading from her sight.

A silence, which was most intense, breathless, and painful, hung over the vast multitude. The night was calm and beautiful, and the silvery moon glided on its way as brightly and as pure as if no such scene of black iniquity and guilt was being enacted beneath its pale light.

It was at this moment that the lips of Lady Hamlyn were observed to move, and Guy Fawkes distinctly overheard her speak the following sentence—

"Bless thee, my Violet, bless thee!" uttered in low, distinct tones.

There was then a minute's pause, after which, in a firm, collected tone of voice, her hands clasped and her eyes raised to heaven, she exclaimed—

"Sir Sidney Wildbrook, I summon thee to appear before the judgment-seat of heaven to answer for the evil deeds and perjury of this day!"

These were the last words the unfortunate sufferer was heard to utter.

A burning torch was thrown among the faggots, and a long, tremulous, dancing stream of light rose like a meteor towards the sky.

Guy Fawkes's eyes were fascinated as by the gaze of a basilisk. He could not turn from the dreadful sight.

The flames advanced—a faint cry was heard —and after that a long suppressed shout of agony burst from the lips of the assembled multitude.

They bewailed the fate of one so fair, so beautiful—one who was now beyond their reach, whether for good or evil.

Her mild and gentle demeanour throughout the whole of the trying time had made a deep impression upon the minds of all, and, notwithstanding the superstitious dread and horror with which her fancied crime was regarded, they could not help looking upon her as a martyr in a bad cause.

Many a tear rolled down the rough cheeks of those assembled and deep suppressed sobs burst from among them.

The sufferer—she who stood before them— conscious of her own innocence, was perhaps the most unmoved, the most collected of all.

The mad, leaping, devouring flames had caught her thin white robe, and, rolling around her, rose in bright and flickering beams towards a bosom purer far than their own light.

A wild cry of horror burst from the surging, excited crowd.

But no symptom of suffering or terror appeared on the poor victim's angelic countenance. Her eyes were turned towards the starlit sky, and there was an expression of seraphic beauty in the aspect of her calm, holy face.

But this is a scene upon which the mind cannot dwell.

Ere the leaping, roaring flames could reach a vital part, even the grim Doomster, exercising the mercy of his office, advanced behind the stake, and with one blow of his heavy hammer terminated the poor victim's sufferings and life.

The blow fell upon her fair head, instantly crushing those once beautiful and transparent features.

At the same moment the fierce flames, stirred and increased by some combustible matter thrown upon them, rose rapidly around the stake, and all that remained of the unhappy lady was hid from view for ever.

The horrid spell which had so long chained the faculties of the spectators being so fearfully and so suddenly dispelled, they now broke forth into a wild, simultaneous shout, and, attacking the guard, who were fain to seek safety in flight, darted forward and tore away the faggots that still blazed around the stake.

But their aid was too late.

Nought but a heap of scorched and blackened ashes was presented to their view—neither the form nor the semblance of a human being remained. Their wild burst of passion at once subsided as the multitude recognised this fact, and there they stood, calm and sorrowful, contemplating the wreck of all that had once been so beautiful and fair.

Guy Fawkes, even while in his heart he blessed the mercy of the executioner, with a half-suppressed cry of anguish turned from the shocking sight, and, exerting his great strength, pushed aside every obstacle. He darted down the steep street as if the frantic rapidity of his movements would leave behind the remembrance of a scene which neither time nor distance nor speed could ever efface from his memory.

There was but one muttered observation that fell upon his ears as his progress was for a moment obstructed. It was this—

"Heaven be with us! 'Twas an awful sight! If our king had not broke faith with his subjects this would ne'er have been. Heaven forgive him and soften his heart towards the poor lassie, her daughter!"

Guy Fawkes could have blessed the speaker, and, turning round, tried to get a view of his features, but in the darkness of the night he could only obtain a very imperfect glimpse.

In the pause of that moment a shout broke upon his ear, but he heeded it not, or, fancying it only the precursor of some other scene of cruelty, hastened to escape the sight.

CHAPTER XXIV.

UNEXPECTED SUCCOUR—A DARING SCHEME—THE MIDNIGHT WATCH—THE SIGNAL—THE CATAS-TROPHE—THE FIGHT AND THE ESCAPE.

GUY FAWKES's dreams were far from those of a pleasant nature, nor did his sleep partake much of the sound repose of youth—it was restless, feverish, and brief.

He rose at an early hour and quitted the hostelry—to which chance had guided his steps the previous night—wearied alike in body and in mind.

He wandered on, scarcely mindful of the direction in which he was proceeding, till, raising his eyes, he was instantly recalled to a sense of reality and life by the sight of the dark and blackened spot on which the dreadful execution of the preceding night had taken place.

He turned from it with shuddering horror, and fled from a spot burdened with the remem-brance of so painful an event.

He ran in the direction of the castle, and did not diminish his pace till its proud, haughty bulwarks stood before his eyes.

Then he paused and gazed on them with a dreamy sort of interest, for the castle was the prison of the unfortunate Sir Godfrey.

As his eyes scanned its broad ditch and raised drawbridge, its overhanging battlements and embrasures, its massive ribbed gate and grated portcullis, together with the many watchful guards surrounding it on all sides, and then roamed over the steep, dizzy height, and inaccessible rock on which the grim fortress stood, Guy Fawkes sighed to think how hope-less the attempt to communicate with any prisoner within must be—how fruitless the effort to aid or effect an escape from its walls.

Wrapt in these meditations he did not observe his near approach to one who for some moments had been watching him, till the soft strains of a harp, struck by a masterly hand, fell upon his ear.

Guy Fawkes turned quickly round, and under the shelter of a small projecting turret at the northern extremity of the castle gate he beheld an old harper seated, wrapped in a palmer's cloak, while a slouched hat concealed the greater part of his features from view.

Guy Fawkes thought he recognised the voice of the Freeranger chief, Will-o'-the-Woods, but when he beheld an old harper, apparently blind, and habited in worn and tattered garb, he was about to turn away with a feeling of disappointment at his heart.

But the old man, after a quick and appre-hensive glance around, ventured to raise his hat, and disclosed the intelligent and comely features of Will-o'-the-Woods.

One glance told him he had been recognised, then, by a signal of his hand, he made Guy Fawkes understand that he wished him to leave the place. He again replaced his hat, and, striking the chords of his harp, began a wilder and more warlike strain.

Guy Fawkes retired slowly and sadly, casting many a lingering look behind.

Like a second Blondel at his master's prison gate, the disguised Freeranger chief continued playing for some time, striving by repeated and various strains to draw the attention of those within.

This he seemed at last to effect, for in a short time Guy Fawkes, from his place of watching, saw a small wicket in the castle gate slowly open, and several musketeers, emerging from it, sauntered towards the minstrel.

They stood in conversation for some time, during which the old man, seemingly by their desire, tuned his harp more than once, and sang the wished-for lays.

At length he rose, and after a short apparent hesitation on the part of the soldiery the whole party moved towards the castle gate and passed through the wicket. It closed behind them, and they were hid from the con-spirator's view.

Being ignorant of the Freeranger's inten-tions, but suspecting that they must be con-nected in some way with the imprisonment of Sir Godfrey, Guy Fawkes determined to await his return.

He therefore continued to linger near the spot, so as not to be observed himself, yet within sight of the castle gate, in order to command a view of the only way by which the minstrel could return.

Many hours passed away in this dull and tedious occupation, and it was not till the sun had risen high in the firmament that his eager eyes again beheld the wicket open and the form of the minstrel descend the step-way which led from the castle gate.

Guy Fawkes darted forward to meet him, but the old man passed on his way without bestowing a single glance of recognition, till, reaching a vaulted entrance, he turned quickly into it, signing at the same time to Guy Fawkes to follow.

The eager conspirator darted after him, and, guided by the sound of his retreating steps, followed him to the safe shelter of an old ruined chapel.

The perspiration stood in large drops upon the Freeranger's brow, but there was a glance of satisfaction in his bright eyes showing that his toil had been rewarded by a corresponding measure of success.

"Tarry not here, good Fawkes," said Will-o'-the-Woods, as soon as he gained his breath. "Tarry not, lest even the breath of suspicion should attach to our movements. 'Tis done, and I trust in the blessed Virgin success may attend our efforts."

"Good—friend!" said Guy Fawkes, pressing his hand. "It will be well if we can attain our object. Show me but in what I can be of service to thee or the father of poor Violet, and I swear to you nothing shall be lacking on my part. Quick, good Will, quick!"

Taking him into a retired corner of the ruin the Freeranger bent forward and whispered rapidly in his ear—

"You saw the old man enter the wicket, but you saw not the goodly coil of rope that entered with him.

"The governor of the castle feasts to-night. The weak and languid state of the prisoner has thrown him off his guard, and the single sentinel over him loves gold better than his faith. To-night he leaves the key unturned, when, Heaven willing, we will aid the deeply-perse-cuted Sir Godfrey over the lower bastion that

GUY FAWKES AND THE FREERANGER CHIEF HOLD THE TROOPERS IN CHECK.

overhangs the bell tower, near to which faithful hearts will be prepared to receive him.

"Guy Fawkes," he added, in a lower but emphatic tone, "be you there !"

Then, pressing his finger to his lips as a token of secrecy, he glided from his side and was gone.

"I will be there !" muttered Guy Fawkes, turning slowly from the ghostly-looking place, and he then returned to the retired hostelry in which he had passed the preceding night.

It appeared to Guy Fawkes as if the hours of that day would never pass.

Six, seven, eight, came, and still the busy hum of men was heard in the streets.

Nine o'clock, then ten, and all had become calm and silent.

Guy Fawkes now issued forth and directed his steps towards his destination.

As he passed St. Mary's Church the sacred spires and minarets were silvered by the moonlight, and the full mellow-toned voices of a numerous choir rose upon the stillness of the night as their vesper-song ascended like incense to the skies.

Everything beneath spoke of peace and goodwill to man—above, the dark battlements of the castle hung lowering like an evil spirit frowning on the fair scene below.

But Guy Fawkes stopped not to admire the fairness of one nor the grimness of the other.

He passed on, and gradually the strains of the evening hymn died away, the last notes trembling on the face of the waters as he stood below the narrow projecting battlements of the bell tower.

Here he looked up from a kind of natural impulse, but shuddered with a feeling amounting almost to horror when he beheld a small and almost invisible turret perched upon the topmost ledge of the cliff.

It seemed as if the superincumbent weight of the stone would have dragged the shelving rock from its root and hurled both the tower and its foundation upon the head of the unwary gazer.

Guy Fawkes was still gazing upwards when a strong grasp was laid upon his arm, and a deep but suppressed voice exclaimed—

"What ho, Sir Cavalier !—studying the courses of the planets ? Ah, well ! portend they fortune or misfortune to our venture, master mine ?"

To shake himself free from his assailant and grasp the hilt of his trusty sword was with Guy Fawkes but the work of a moment.

But ere he could draw it from its sheath his other arm was grasped, and the well-known voice of the minstrel, speaking in the same suppressed tone, exclaimed—

"Hold thee, good Sir Guy ! By the mystery of my craft the moon seems to rule the ascendant and have power in the house of life to-night. Wouldst thou slay thy faithful Ralph ?"

"Nay, by the mass !" cried Guy Fawkes, turning round and grasping his devoted follower's hand. "I knew not it was thee, good Ralph, and I should ill requite thy precious services were I to do thee the aught of harm."

"Aye, marry, thou wouldst indeed," returned the disguised Freeranger. "The boys, in the guise of sailors, are here mustered, and await but the signal."

"Hush ! stay, my masters," interrupted Ralph, suddenly. "It waxeth somewhat late, methinks, yet no light appears in the turret."

"Heaven grant that nothing ill hath happened to mar our goodly plans," murmured Guy Fawkes, anxiously.

"The saints forbid it !" responded the minstrel, fervently. "It must be nigh the hour."

As if in reply the clock of St. Mary's tolled forth the solemn midnight hour in deep and hollow tones.

Still no movement, no sound, no appearance betrayed that aught of interest was passing within the castle walls.

The minstrel began to show evident signs of impatience and anxiety.

Guy Fawkes beat the turf with a quick and feverish movement of his foot, while the disguised Freerangers stood with folded arms beneath the shadow of the grey walls, ready for instant action.

Suddenly a single pebble, as if coming from a crevice of the rock, dropped at Guy Fawkes's feet.

"Whist !" whispered the minstrel, as he laid a tightening grasp on the conspirator's arm.

A second pebble fell at their feet.

Relaxing his hold, Will-o'-the-Woods pointed upwards, and Guy Fawkes, following the direction of his arm, beheld first one and then a second feeble light appear at the window of the small projecting tower. These lights remained stationary for a few seconds and then disappeared.

A low indistinct murmur was immediately heard—like voices floating in mid-air.

It was a moment of deep, intense anxiety to those below.

The window of the tower was darkened, as if some intervening object had obscured the light. The next moment an indistinct mass was observed to swing itself over the grated bars, and, clearing the lower extremity of the tower, it hung for a moment suspended over the fearful chasm below.

It then slowly and gradually descended, and presently the form of a man became distinctly visible in the rays of the pale moon.

This proved to be the hapless Sir Godfrey Hamlyn, who, by the thin strands of a slender rope, hung suspended between life and death.

Even the breathing of Sir Godfrey's friends below was scarcely audible, and not a sound of any kind was heard.

The anxiety of Guy Fawkes at this moment was wound up to a pitch of most painful intensity.

The sailor-like Freerangers, forgetting everything else in their interest for the being whom their leader had called upon them to aid, gazed upwards with faces on which an expression of mingled uncertainty and fear was depicted.

One—the youngest and most active of their number—had climbed a considerable way up the jagged surface of the rock, dexterously availing himself of every projecting crag and shrub to aid his ascent and assist the object of their care.

But he was still far from him.

With a shuddering sensation the party below beheld the descending motion of the suspended nobleman gradually decrease, and at length wholly stop.

It was plainly evident that the rope was too short.

Once or twice it was drawn up a short distance and then let down again.

Then, from the slight commotion that was visible in the tower, it appeared as if those within were devising some means to increase its length.

In the meantime the unfortunate Sir Godfrey swung in mid-air.

It was a fearful and terrible position.

Far beyond the reach of Guy Fawkes and Will-o'-the-Woods below, and apparently also as far beyond the power of immediate assistance from those above.

A slight breeze, which barely rippled the surface of the water, swayed him gently backwards and forwards, and gave somewhat of the appearance of life to that which otherwise would have appeared only as a dead and senseless weight.

But that chill breeze bore death upon its wings.

Suddenly an ominous crack was heard in the stillness of the night.

And with a half-suppressed cry of horror Guy Fawkes and his companions saw that one twist of the treble cord, frayed by the continued rubbing on the sharp rock, had given way.

Almost instantaneously another sound was heard, and, ere a single thought of its import could pass through their minds, a third.

The rope had given way, and the body of the unfortunate nobleman, bounding rapidly from crag to crag, lay crushed and senseless at their feet.

Guy Fawkes and the Freeranger chief rushed forward to lift him from the ground, but the bruised and shapeless object scarce retained the likeness of a human being.

One glance sufficed to show that the noble spirit of Sir Godfrey Hamlyn had flown for ever.

A wild, despairing cry burst from the lips of Guy Fawkes.

At the same moment a flash was seen from the battlements of the castle, and the report of an arquebuse followed almost instantaneously.

The ball whistled over their heads, and the cry of "Away, away!" resounded from the tower above them.

Lights flashed backwards and forwards along the line of ramparts, and two or three armed soldiers, with torches in their hands, were seen rapidly descending the steep side of the hill towards the postern of the Well-house Tower.

There was not a moment for consideration.

The body of the hapless Sir Godfrey was lifted into a boat—kept for the use of the garrison—that lay chained to a small pier or abutment on the lake.

The Freeranger chief, Will-o'-the-Woods, who had now cast aside his disguise, followed.

Guy Fawkes's foot was on the gunwale of the boat when they discovered that the chain was secured by a strong and heavy padlock to the pier.

And now rattling of bars and keys was heard at the postern gate.

Guy Fawkes instantly sprang ashore, and, drawing his sword, with one tremendous blow severed the massive chain in two.

At that moment the gate flew open, and some four or five men-at-arms rushed upon the beach.

Before Guy Fawkes could regain the boat they were upon him. But he defended himself right gallantly against their fierce and desperate attack.

And the "Ring! ring!" "Clash! clash!" of their contending blades echoed among the neighbouring hills.

Seeing the great odds against which Guy Fawkes had to contend, Will-o'-the-Woods instantly leapt ashore to the assistance of his friend.

His sudden appearance threw the assailants off their guard for a moment, and Guy Fawkes and the Freeranger chief held the troopers in check.

The next, however, they rushed to the charge, and the combat waxed fiercer than ever.

Suddenly there was a sharp gurgling cry as Guy Fawkes's skilfully-handled sword passed through the throat of one of his enemies.

The mortally-wounded wretch clutched his near companion in a death clasp, and the living and the dead rolled to the earth together.

At the same instant one of Will-o'-the-Wood's adversaries fell to the ground in his death agony.

At this juncture the soldier on the ground, having extricated himself from his dead companion, seized Guy Fawkes's leg and tried to trip him up.

The Freeranger chief detected the fellow in the act and instantly pinned him to the earth.

But not before Guy Fawkes had lost his balance, however, which allowed the sword of the advancing captain of the guard to pass through the conspirator's side.

With a deep moan Guy Fawkes sank back insensible in the arms of his friend, who, with a lightning blow of his finely-tempered blade, cut through the officer's steel cap as though it had been made of tin.

The blow laid his skull open to the bone, and the swooning man fell like a log across the dead body of his comrade.

Then, with the same startling activity and ready tact that characterised all his proceedings, the Freeranger chief caught up the inanimate body of Guy Fawkes in his arms and leaped with him into the boat.

"Bear away!" he shouted to his men—"away! away!"

And the boat, impelled by the strokes of the powerful rowers, sped swiftly over the lake.

The remaining soldier was only armed with an arquebuse, and this he now raised to his shoulder and prepared to fire upon the flying fugitives.

Guy Fawkes or the Freeranger chief must have fallen a victim to his sure and deadly shot had not a figure suddenly sprung out from the darkness of the castle walls and diverted his aim by coming behind him and forcibly pushing him into the lake.

The weapon exploded in the air, and the unlucky trooper, in his heavy armour, was struggling the next moment at the bottom of the lake.

The new comer was no other than Harold Rookby.

His first impulse was to plunge into the water and swim after his friends.

But the consideration of an instant showed him the folly of this attempt, which would only have exposed him to the fire of his assailants.

And, quick as thought, darting behind a projecting angle of the tower, he fortunately escaped the notice of a fresh troop of men who were hastening to the spot, and whose attention was exclusively directed to the boat.

From his place of concealment Harold beheld several shots fired across the water, but apparently without effect.

The boat reached the opposite bank of the lake, the crew sprung ashore, and, lifting the melancholy remains of Sir Godfrey on their shoulders, the Freeranger chief and faithful Ralph Roley followed with the unconscious Guy Fawkes.

Rapidly ascending the rising ground they directed their course to the long-forgotten hamlet of Witchelm and disappeared from sight.

CHAPTER XXIV.

HAROLD ROOKBY FINDS FURTHER USE FOR HIS READY SWORD—A SINGULAR ADVENTURE WHICH WILL PROVE THE FORERUNNER OF A GREAT EVENT.

HAROLD now bethought himself of his own safety, and, availing himself of the shelter of the city walls, stole softly away under its friendly shadow.

The deep-muttered curses of the disappointed soldiers fell upon his ear.

But, wrapped in his dark cloak, he escaped their notice, and soon had the satisfaction of hearing these sounds exchanged for others of a much more welcome nature.

They were the grating of the huge postern upon its harsh hinges, and the sullen clanking sound of its bolts, chains, and bars as they were once more thrust into their wonted places.

The young soldier made the best of his way towards the eastern gate of the city, not with the hope of obtaining entrance that night, but with the desire of securing shelter in some outhouse, many of which were scattered around the entrance to the town.

Prudence whispered to him that he ought to avoid the city as a place where his own personal safety would be in rather a precarious position.

His beloved Violet had already learned the fearful fate of her idolised mother and the sentence of death passed upon her father, and, knowing herself to be a banned and marked person by the State for the supposed crime of giving shelter to a Catholic priest, the poor distracted orphan girl, when she knew her lover was on the road to recovery, sought safety in flight, and entered the holy Convent of St. Just.

On Harold becoming cognisant of these facts through a letter she had left, he resolved to go in quest of her, though he had no knowledge of her place of retreat.

Wrapped in meditation the young soldier proceeded cautiously along till, on approaching a straggling group of the outhouses we have before mentioned, he was startled and alarmed by a piercing female shriek, a crashing sound, muttered oaths, and the violent clashing of swords.

The sound to him was like that of the trumpet to the ear of the war-horse.

Quickly wrapping the skirt of his cloak around his left arm he drew his sword and rushed to the spot from whence it seemed to proceed.

Turning the corner of the quaint old street he beheld a wrecked and overturned carriage, and hard by the coachman lying stiff and stark from a gaping wound in the left breast.

In the centre of the roadway a graceful female form, richly-dressed and lovely as some sculptured saint, even in her death-like pallor, lay senseless and alone.

He saw at a glance that she was uninjured, though insensible, and whilst in the act of raising her from the ground he was arrested by loud and repeated cries for "Help!"

Placing his cloak under the lady's head he hastened towards a kind of gateway, where he beheld a single man being furiously set upon by three others, each apparently of a far stronger and more robust make than the person they assailed.

His back was placed against the wall, his foot was firmly set before him, and he defended himself with such incredible skill as showed him to be a perfect master of the weapon.

Harold did not stop to inquire into the justice of the cause, but instantly ranging himself on the weaker side, with characteristic impetuosity attacked the three assailants.

The vigour of his unexpected attack bore them back an instant, and the stranger, finding himself thus assisted, redoubled his exertions. Thus the two, seconded by youth, strength, and skill, in their turn became the assailants.

The contest was not of long or doubtful duration.

Numbers were on one side, but high and youthful blood, with a bold and reckless bearing and far superior skill, were on the other.

And in less time than we have occupied in narrating the story of the affray the three cowardly assassins turned their backs and fled.

Harold Rookby had now leisure to look at the person to whose succour he had thus unexpectedly arrived.

At a single glance he was irresistibly struck with a feeling somewhat approaching to awe at the expression of mingled intelligence and dignity that appeared on the countenance of the stranger.

He was about the middle size and appeared to be about forty.

Rather robust than otherwise, his form was by no means ungraceful or inelegant.

The contour of his face was a perfect oval, shaded by an abundance of light chestnut hair.

His eyes were blue, full, brilliant, and piercing, but at times they softened into an expression of the most arch and open humour.

Now and then, indeed, a slight shade of melancholy seemed to flit across his fine features.

But it was not of lasting duration and soon disappeared entirely.

These observations were rapidly made by the young soldier as the stranger quickly approached the spot where he had last seen the lady, but she was gone.

"Hark ye, friend," said the stranger, looking about, "didst see a lady lying upon the ground as thou passed?"

"Aye.

"Did she seem hurt, thinkest thou, or had she merely swooned from fright?"

"I'faith I can scarcely say," returned Harold. "But I should think she had only fainted."

"The saints be praised!" exclaimed the stranger, in a relieved tone. "But what hath become of her I marvel—she was too sick to walk away."

"See," suddenly cried Harold, "yon good people are bearing her into their house," and the young soldier pointed to the shop of a saddler, through the open door of which an elderly dame and her daughter were carrying the unconscious lady.

The stranger followed them into the house, and, having seen them lay his wife upon their humble couch, he placed a purse of money on the table, saying—

"I thank ye heartily, my good people, for your kindness and humanity. Do ye do your utmost to restore the lady to her senses, and should she be alarmed at my absence tell her to be of good heart, for I shall return anon with a fresh conveyance to bear her home."

And, kissing the pale brow of his statue-like spouse, he left the house and rejoined the young soldier.

"Hark ye, friend," he exclaimed, as he wiped his bright sword and restored it to his scabbard, "saw ye the arms or bearings of these rapscallions who attacked me? I doubt not the princely Godwin hath had somewhat to do in this matter."

"Indeed," said Harold, "your assailants vanished so quickly that I had scarce time to observe what device or cognisance they bore, but methinks I perceived something like a golden coronet glancing on the moonbeams."

"Aye, aye!—like enough, like enough!" exclaimed the stranger. "But, brave younker, I hope thou hast not met with aught of mischance in the affray. The readier at times gets the worst knock."

"No," answered Harold, "and I trust that in reply to the same question you will be able to give me a like assurance."

"What, man!" exclaimed the stranger, "hast thou taken leave of thy wits, or thinkest thou the best master of fence within the four seas of England would allow six such rapscallion tatterdemalions as these to come within his guard?"

"And yet methought I heard a cry for help," said Harold.

"True, man, true, I was sorely pressed, and by my halidome! but for the two helps, Providence and yourself, I might have chanced second best in the squabble. They were stalwart rogues, i'faith, and nae man can fight for ever—but this matter shall be looked into.

"Soul o' my ancestors!" he added, glancing in the direction of the castle, "it's like the day o' torches in them—lights here, lights there, glancing backwards and forwards like a will-o'-the-wisp on a murky night."

It will readily be supposed that the young soldier had no inclination to converse upon so delicate a subject.

He passed it off with some common-place remark, and, relapsing into silence, strode along by his companion's side.

A sudden thought seemed to strike the stranger, for, turning abruptly to Harold, he said—

"By my halidome! young sir, but we had almost forgotten to ask our preserver's name. We are somewhat acquainted with the butterflies that frequent the Court, but our recollection maun be somewhat faint, or we havena' seen the face o' you before."

"Very likely not," said Harold, "for the Rookbys have not of late been basking in the sunshine of their sovereign's favour. Evil tongues and false hearts have played them evil."

"The Rookbys!" exclaimed the stranger, a deep frown passing over his brow. "Are ye of that unhappy race who would ha' kept their gracious sovereign in the bonds o' thraldom? And ha' strangled him, too, for aught I know," he added, in a lower tone, turning his head aside.

"I am!" said the young soldier, firmly. "And this I will venture to assert—that there is at least one Rookby whose heart and hand will ever be alike warm and ready should his majesty continue to act uprightly and keep inviolate the promises he hath made to his subjects."

"Heaven's grace, man, an' what's your name! ye speak boldly for a younker."

"Harold Rookby is no coward," was the reply.

"What!" exclaimed the stranger, "are you the son of old Sir Andrew?"

"The same."

"And by my troth," replied the stranger, "he was a stalwart knight, young man. Ye come of the best o' the race. But what has become of Sir Andrew?"

"Dead!" answered Harold, sadly. "He died in foreign parts, more of a broken heart than of bodily disease. He had been banished for the crime of others—banished by a sovereign he loved and respected, and for the earthly and eternal weal of whom his last prayer was uttered.

"Banishment weighed upon the old man's heart like a weight of lead, and at length brought his grey hairs in sorrow to the grave. He now sleeps in a foreign land, far from those green English hills he loved so well."

"Aye, young man," said the stranger, with deep feeling, "and it was with a breaking and sorrowful heart that his most gracious sovereign was forced to banish his subject from his presence."

"'Twas a cruel act on the part of his majesty to judge my poor father on the bare word of his enemies," said Harold Rookby, with emotion. "It wrecked his prospects, broke my dear mother's heart, destroyed for ever my domestic peace, and sent me a sad and desolate wanderer over the world. So how can his majesty wonder that I am inclined to favour the cause of the malcontent Catholics, whose wrongs need speedy and lasting redress?"

"And by my halidome they shall have it!" cried the stranger, "an'—an' they have patience."

Then, as if suddenly remembering himself, he added—

"But, in Heaven's name, man, how came ye to venture here from across the seas wi' that unlucky name o' thine tacked to your doublet-skirt? By my troth it must ha' been a pressing cause, or—ha, ha! have I caught ye napping?—there's a damsel in the case.

"Ah!" he continued, jogging him with his

elbow, "I see it in that flushed cheek and sparkling eye. But ne'er be ashamed on't, man—ye couldn't tempt your neck in better cause; and he that risks all for a fair face, although it may be for a false heart, deserves to be weel repaid.

"Eh, younker? Was it the flaunt o' a jerkin or a merry glance from behind a muffler that brought ye spanking frae the sunny land o' Spain?"

The versatile powers of this extraordinary being struck the young soldier with astonishment.

One moment he gazed upon the stranger as he would have done upon the lightning's wild and vivid flash through the gloom of a dark and tropical storm. The next his open frankness of manner commanded Harold's confidence, and, won by his cordial warmth and kindness, the young soldier, without a moment's hesitation, gave an outline of the history of some of the scenes with which the reader is already acquainted

As Harold proceeded with his narrative the manner and appearance of the stranger seemed to undergo a complete alteration.

He listened with a deep, fixed, and attentive air, occasionally interrupting the speaker with a half smothered exclamation.

At Harold concluded he was silent for some time, and seemed to ponder within his mind upon what he had heard.

In this silent mood the two walked onwards for several minutes.

Neither spoke. The grey morning dawned in the east, and the slanting beams of the sun were seen in long tremulous rays darting from behind the high hills that lay before them, they having taken a considerable circuit from the northern extremity of the town.

Here the stranger suddenly stopped, and, looking at Harold with a grave and troubled countenance, said—

"This matter must be sought into. I doubt me this Sir Sidney Wildbrook is but a rotten kernel in a wholesome shell after all. But you an' I maun part now, friend. Your way is straight ahead, and mine," he continued, pointing down the sloping ascent leading away from the city, "lies there. But a word in your ear, friend. Don't let your best friend know what has passed between us this early morn. Awa' wi' ye, an' keep close for a space till this storm blows o'er. It may be that you an' I will meet again where ye least expect it. Meanwhile, fare ye weel and Heaven speed ye!"

As he spoke the stranger drew his cloak more closely round him, and with a light and active step hastened in the direction in which he had pointed.

The young soldier gazed for a few seconds after the receding figure, then, following his example, drew the folds of his ample cloak around his face and form, and once more bent his way to the gates of the city.

CHAPTER XXV.

THE STORM—THE WATCHERS—THE DANCING GIRL'S DARING DEED.

RETURN we now to London for a brief space. The old clock of Westminster Abbey had struck twelve and the porter had retired to rest.

The heavy rain was pouring on the ancient building, drifted in sheets by the tearing wind, and the tall trees in St. James's Park bent and waved restlessly as the fierce bursts passed over them.

The streets were deserted, the cry of the wassailer had ceased, the nightwatch had sought shelter, and the very dogs were silent even.

A loud peal of thunder reverberated sullenly above the other sounds of the wild storm and seemed for a moment to hush them.

Almost ere the sound had left the ear a vivid flash of lightning was followed by a peal louder than the first. Flash succeeded flash —the forked lightning darted through the black rolling clouds, the thunder became almost one continuous roll and the rain fell in heavy torrents.

"The devil's benison on the night!" muttered a voice from the great porch of the northern side of the abbey. "The storms of winter and summer strive for mastery. Heavens! what a flash was that! Did ye mark the features of the statues as the light played upon them?"

"Hush! for Heaven's sake hush!" replied a female voice, as a terrific peal of thunder broke over them and echoed with startling clearness within the lofty arches of the gloomy pile.

"Keep from the statues' bases!" exclaimed the first speaker. "The pavement trembles under my very feet. Some of them may rock over and crush you!"

"They will stir not," answered the other, plaintively.

"I could have sworn they glare at me with life—yes, with life—when the light flashes upon them. There, there again!" continued the speaker, pausing with a blanched cheek until the flash had died away.

"'Sdeath! how the rain falls! Marry, the cloistered monks may shiver in their cells. Methinks the old building is doomed. Would there were shelter elsewhere."

No answer was returned, and the speaker, wrapping his mantle closer round him, leaned his back against the wall and looked out upon the night.

The portico in which he stood was full of architectural beauty—the noble arch, fretted roof, sculptured saints, and delicate tracery. This, however, afforded little shelter from the cold—the wind rushed into it, and the rain struck against the inner walls.

"What keeps the boy?" exclaimed the first speaker, restlessly, looking without the porch. "No eye can pierce the darkness. This grave statesman loves long communing. How long is't, Evelyn, since you saw Leo?"

"Days. I cannot reckon them."

"But the time, wench? Was't the night those new friends of Master Guy Fawkes hunted me to the river and tore the old house down that had sheltered us so long?"

"The same," replied the dancing-girl. "You came up the stream and landed me at the palace stairs."

"The boy is changed since then," muttered the other.

A low sigh answered him.

"Ah! he comes at last!" cried the man, as Guy Fawkes's page glided into the porch,

GUY FAWKES

Or Gunpowder, Treason, and Plot.

JUST THEN MYRA APPEARED AT THE WINDOW AND WARNED HAROLD ROOKBY TO FLY.

No. 7.

anxious to escape from the storm. "Well, Leo, hast seen the mighty Lord Chancellor?"

"Aye, marry," answered the boy, "and 'tis a grave, grand man, I promise you."

"What said he to Master Guy Fawkes's message?"

"Not a word," replied the page, "but here is a sealed letter which he charged me to bear to him with all speed."

The man grasped it eagerly.

"We will break the seals and copy the words. By our lady, fortune smiles upon us! I would never seek a better paymaster than bold Sir Sidney. He is as open-handed as the day, and will buy the secrets of this letter with more gold than an usurer could tell and weigh in the running of an hour-glass. Come," he added, "I know the trick to take a seal's impress—to-morrow I will see this knightly statesman, and, it may be, make better terms than you could do. I have driven crafty bargains with ministers of the Crown before now, and know their ways.

"This letter of Sir Everard Digby's will not only prove the guilt of Master Fawkes but of his companions also. Sir Sidney would give half his wealth to have Guy Fawkes in his power, and now his wish shall be gratified. He knows too many of my amorous lord's secrets that he should wish him to live.

"You have done well, Leo—you have found a veritable gold mine," concluded the Spanish spy.

"Yes, and I claim the half of what it yields," said the page, promptly, "even were it a waggon full of gold."

"Ha! ha! you are apt. Go to!"

"Apt or no, quick or dull of wit, I go full risk in the venture, and shall expect a full share of the reward."

"Risk!"

"Aye. By Saint Mary! if Master Guy Fawkes knew that I had betrayed him my head were not readier to my bonnet than his dagger to my throat. This letter will bring him to Tyburn or the Tower. His own death——"

A cry from a distant part of the porch made the boy pause.

At the same moment Evelyn sprang forward, seized the letter, and tearing it to atoms scattered it to the wind.

"Leo! Leo!" she burst out, in terrible agony, "have you too become a traitor and a spy—a bidder for the price of innocent blood? Would you dare betray those who have trusted you—the master whom you serve, the friend who sheltered you?

"But it is you," she continued, turning towards the Spaniard—"it is you who have done this.

"False of heart and crafty-minded, was it not enough that I should be your victim, without dragging this poor boy down to the same hellish pit into which you have led me?

"But it shall not be," she added, frenziedly. "I will warn Guy Fawkes of this treachery. He shall not be betrayed."

"Hold! hold!" said the Spaniard, fiercely, seizing the white arm of the dancing-girl. "You have done enough without making vaunt of the mischief you will do. Base minion, you have plucked gold from my very grasp. Wherefore came you hither, you spaniel-dog—unworthy to crouch at a bold man's heel?"

"Aye, I have been a spaniel!" cried the poor girl, wildly, "and I have crouched like a smitten dog in face of the infamy that my own heart proclaimed.

"I have followed thee," she pursued, "watched thee, and read joy or sorrow in the look you gave me. For myself I will not murmur, but there is a new feeling in my breast—for another I will dare even thee!

"I am your slave—the sport and toy of your idle hour. I must bear all, but the other, though my heart crack, you shall not crush."

"False mistress!" cried the dark, handsome ruffian, casting her from him, "you speak of what your frail heart knows not how to practise. It is not many weeks since on board the Spanish vessel in the river——"

"Peace! peace!" shrieked the girl. "Whatever my sins may be it is not you who should reckon them."

"Then how came ye, in the devil's name, to act as you have done? The letter you have destroyed was worth a knight's ransom in yellow gold."

"But it would have been the reward of treachery," rejoined the dancing-girl, "and the price of innocent blood!"

"Treachery! And art not thou a traitress? Innocence, forsooth!" he added, with a mocking laugh, "what hast thou to do with that? And yet you thwart me like an evil genius, and hold up the cloak of honest virtue as a shield. The boy is wise and knows better."

"Oh, this is base!" cried Evelyn, in a voice that struggled with her sobs. "Leo, Leo, have I not warned you of doing such a thing?"

The boy spoke not a word, but turned his eyes towards the storm without, which now seemed to rage with increased fury.

Tall chimney-tops were blown down, and spires shook the bases that supported them.

The Thames flooded its banks, and the towers of religious houses crumbled under the red lightning's touch.

This storm has been chronicled in the legends of superstition.

It was the night of the attempted assassination of King James at his hunting tower at Royston, by one of the followers of Lord Grey de Wilton, of the "Rye" conspiracy.

Old St. Paul's, it is said, was struck by lightning and its square spire rent, vessels were shattered on the coast, and omens of some signal calamity were said to have been heard amid the terrors of the storm.

There was a deep pause in the thunder claps for a moment or two.

It was suddenly broken by the harsh voice of the Spaniard.

"Evelyn," said he, "you have done that which you will repent. But it is no night to tarry here. Leo, return to your master, and tell him Sir Digby's letter has been blown into the Thames."

"Stir not!" cried Evelyn, vehemently. "If you value your safety, brother, cross not your master's path again."

She passed quickly from the porch and was instantly lost in the darkness.

The Spaniard, surprised at her sudden retreat, was a moment ere he followed.

He did so at length, and paused to catch the sound of her footsteps, but these were lost in the noise of the pouring rain.

He called sharply to the page to follow him, and passed stealthily from the place.

Leo, since his sister had so passionately appealed to him, had not spoken a word.

CHAPTER XXVI.

THE MEETING BETWEEN HAROLD AND VIOLET IN THE OLD GRANGE—DANGER—THE SIGNAL—FLIGHT OF THE YOUNG SOLDIER.

THE same storm which burst with such devastating fury over the goodly City of London raged with equal violence among the wooded fens and wild, towering cliffs of Old Royston. Indeed, it was this very storm which caused Harold Rookby, during his seemingly endless search after the deeply bereaved and hapless orphan. Violet Hamlyn, to seek shelter in the deep dark porch of an old castellated building among the rugged Royston hills.

As there he stood in the deepening gloom of that grim entrance, listening to the pelting rain and the howling blast, he fancied he heard a quickened breathing proceeding from a deeply-curtained recess or chamber on his left.

He advanced towards it with a rapid pace, and, casting aside the heavy hangings, beheld a lovely sylph-like being lying upon a rich velvet couch, her face buried among the downy cushions as though she were weeping, her bright sunny tresses mingling like threads of richest gold with the crimson drapery.

She looked timidly up as Harold entered, and disclosed the beauteous but pale and sorrowful features of Violet.

"Found, my darling, found!" exclaimed the young soldier, in a tone of rapture.

With a quivering, sobbing cry Violet rose to her feet and threw herself into her lover's outstretched arms.

He clasped her lovely delicate form to his wildly-beating heart, and rained passionate kisses on her cheek, brow, and neck, while the grief of the hapless orphan's heart burst forth in a torrent of half-inarticulate sobs.

Slowly she awoke to a consciousness of her situation, and shrank trembling from Harold's embrace, her face and neck covered with rosy blushes.

The young soldier grasped her little fairy-like hand, and, drawing her gently towards him, said, with deep feeling—

"Dear Violet, how heavy is this blow that hath fallen upon thee—how terrible the trial! Let me share——"

"Name it not—name it not, I beseech ye!" she interrupted, hastily, her bosom heaving with intense emotion. "To dwell upon it would, I feel, drive reason from its seat. I have prayed for strength to bear it with fortitude and resignation, and, with Heaven's help, I will do so."

"My good, brave Violet!" murmured the young soldier, with fervid adoration. "But tell me," he added, "how is it I find you in this lone retreat of your foster-sister Myra? She is the kinswoman of your relative and enemy Sir Sidney Wildbrock, is she not?"

"There is some mysterious bond of relationship between them, I believe," answered the fair girl, "though I know not its nature."

"But was it not unwise, my Violet, to venture here, when perchance at any moment Sir Sidney may pay his kinswoman a visit?"

"On the contrary, Harold," replied Violet, with a faint smile, "Myra is devoted to me, and hath little love for this same relative, whose shadow hath never yet darkened her threshold."

"But are there no others save Myra," asked Harold, "to protect thee, my Violet, in thy hour of need?"

"There is a man-servant, his wife, and Myra's father, old Jacob Wentworth," said Violet.

"What! he—the whilom tool and slave of the base villain, Sir Sidney?" cried the young soldier, greatly perturbed. "Beware, Violet, of him. I pray thee beware."

"Nay, dear Harold, you wrong him. He has sheltered me when he could hope for no reward. He is faithful—he *must* be faithful."

"I trust that it may be so," returned Harold; "but why not entrust yourself, dear one, solely to my care? Surely the arm of Sir Harold Rookby—for I won my knightly spurs in Spain—were a better protection to the daughter of the house of Hamlyn than that of Jacob Wentworth? I doubt me the old dotard——"

"Nay, Sir Knight," said a stern voice near at hand, which caused them both to start, "do not abuse the old man. In his actions he may err, but his motives, I'll be sworn, are pure."

"Yes, yes, Myra," said Violet, taking the hand of the speaker—a tall, handsome, gipsy-looking woman—"he is your father. I am sure he could mean nought but good to me."

"What motive," continued Myra to the young soldier, "other than that of pure affection and generosity could have actuated him in protecting the innocent and persecuted lamb of the fold, or what advantage would it be to him that one hair of her sweet head should be injured? No, no, Sir Knight, your suspicions of the old man are unkind and unjust."

"Nay, blame him not, Myra. Believe me it was but the passing thought of a single moment," pleaded Violet.

"I do not blame him, dear one," answered Myra, in a subdued voice, as she bent to kiss the pale brow of the lovely suppliant. "I blame him not—nay, more, there lives not one to whose care I would more gladly consign thee than to that of Sir Harold Rookby.

"He hath both the strong and the willing arm," continued the speaker, "and my Violet stands in need of both. But, alack! alack! his means equals not his will. The stately tree of the forest affords but an evil shelter when the tempest is abroad and the blue lightning gleams."

"True," said the young soldier, gloomily. "But while the tree stands it affords both shelter and protection, and only ceases to yield these when the wild tempest and the lightning bolt have laid it scorched and blackened on the ground."

"Yes, and what *then*," demanded Myra, "becomes of those who have sought its shelter? Are they not also buried in the same ruin?

"But why," she added, interrupting herself—"why do I thus waste the precious moments? Sir Knight, I came to warn thee, but ask me not from whom my knowledge is derived. Believe me, thine enemies are on thy track like thirsty bloodhounds—therefore fly, if you would yet live to aid the Lady Violet."

"Never !" said Harold, firmly. "Violet, come what may we part no more."

"What ! Sir Knight," exclaimed Myra, "not when led to prison and the scaffold ?—for both will assuredly be thy fate shouldst thou tarry here."

"Hush, Myra, hush !" said Violet, shuddering, and pressing her hands over her eyes as if to exclude some terrible thought.

"I will watch without for a brief space," added Myra, "and warn you of the approach of your enemies." Then she hurriedly left the chamber.

"Harold," said Violet suddenly, raising her pretty head, "we must part. Had Violet been the rich and free heiress of Hamlyn Sir Harold Rookby would have been her choice, but the poor friendless orphan will never add her burden of sorrow and distress to the weight of trouble which her benefactor has already to endure."

"Violet !" exclaimed the young soldier, fervently, "dear Violet ! we must not part— there is madness in the thought. Be mine, and we shall——"

He stopped short, for a sense of his own forlorn condition dawned suddenly upon his mind.

Violet smiled faintly at his warmth.

"You forget, Harold," she answered, "that even now your very name is proscribed in the land—that you are almost a homeless wanderer, with nought but your sword to depend upon.

"Yet Heaven knows," she added, with deep emotion, "could I be of service to you, neither poverty nor sorrow should ever separate us again."

For a short space neither uttered a syllable.

Then at length, with an assumption of gaiety, to lessen the weight which the brave-hearted girl deemed must weigh upon her lover's mind, and in order to veil the real feelings of her aching heart, she said—

"I could not, you know, Sir Knight, enact the part of your page or esquire—this slender frame and feeble arm would but ill suit the boisterous scenes of war.

"But stay, do not interrupt me," she continued, perceiving that Harold was about to speak, "our time is short and I have somewhat yet to say. Believe me, dear Harold, I shall not be unprotected. I go hence to the convent of St. Winifred, the good abbess of which is my near relation.

"And," she continued, lowering her voice, "if brighter days should ever dawn Sir Harold Rookby shall find Violet Hamlyn the same in sunshine as in sorrow."

Just then Myra appeared at the window and held up a warning finger to the lovers.

"The signal !" said Violet, anxiously, observing the face of her foster-sister at the window. "Fly, Harold, fly !"

"Must it indeed be so, my Violet ?" said the young soldier, sighing deeply. "Then fare thee well ! But, trust me, those brighter days of which you speak may dawn sooner than you wot of."

"Heaven grant that it may be so !" she fervently exclaimed. "Believe me, dear Harold, that although my lips cannot express what my heart does indeed deeply feel towards you, my first and fondest prayer shall ever be for your prosperity and happiness. Farewell, Harold ! and may He by whom all things are ruled ever watch over and protect you !"

These last words were uttered in a low, tremulous voice—so low as to be scarcely audible.

The young soldier caught her to his heart, and, pressing her sweet lips again and again, exclaimed—

"Farewell, dearest Violet ! We shall meet again when you dream not of it."

His voice trembled with suppressed emotion, and he turned aside as if he did not wish to prolong the pain of parting.

But almost before the words had passed his lips Violet had disappeared.

For some seconds the young soldier continued to gaze at the doorway through which she had vanished, as if half hoping that she would appear again.

But the firm, collected voice of Myra soon recalled his scattered senses, and, starting forward, he was about to retreat by the same door at which he had so lately entered, when the strong grasp of Myra was laid upon his cloak.

"Not that way, Sir Knight, if you would avoid those who thirst for your blood," she exclaimed, as she led him towards a door which he had not hitherto observed, in a remote part of the chamber.

Pressing her finger upon a secret spring a narrow passage was disclosed to view, through which she conducted the young soldier.

It was terminated at the farther extremity by a long winding flight of stairs.

These Harold and his fearless conductress rapidly descended.

At the extremity of a second passage was a strong iron-plated door, the fastenings of which Myra, with a steady hand, undid.

Issuing through its portals Harold Rookby found himself in the open country.

"Farewell, Sir Knight," whispered his stately guide, as she closed the door and again replaced its many bolts and bars. "Farewell ! Be prudent and cautious."

CHAPTER XXVII.

GUY FAWKES AND THE DANCING-GIRL AGAIN.

THE remains of the unfortunate Sir Godfrey were placed in their last resting-place with due solemnity, and Guy Fawkes was conveyed to the romantic haunt of Will-o'-the-Woods in the forest, where his wounds were attended to. A soothing draught having been administered to him, he fell into a deep and refreshing slumber.

Guy Fawkes awoke next day considerably better, though it was evident some time would elapse ere he would be fit to pursue his vocations.

On the fourth evening, whilst he sat musing and alone, and wondering what could keep Leo so long away, he fancied he heard a knock without.

He listened attentively. Presently the door was cautiously opened and a light step ascended the stairs.

Then his chamber door was thrown open, and instead of the page he saw enter, to his surprise, Evelyn, the dancing-girl.

She was pale, except a small hectic flush that burned on either cheek.

Her beautiful hair, dishevelled and glittering with rain-drops, fell in profusion over her neck and bosom.

Her faded dress, ill-suited to resist the wild storm she had passed through, looked travel-soiled, poor, almost wretched, yet it could not destroy the beauty of the slight delicate form it so ill protected.

In spite of the poverty of her guise—while with her graceful little hand she swept back the straggling tresses from her fair brow, and turned her deep expressive eyes with timid earnestness on Guy Fawkes—her aspect was most bewitching.

"You are betrayed!' she exclaimed, glancing fearfully for an instant round the room. "You are betrayed by one you trusted!"

"Betrayed!" repeated Guy Fawkes, fixing his keen eyes upon her. "By whom am I betrayed?"

"By the boy," cried Evelyn. "The page that I told you was faithful. Oh, look not thus!" she continued, wildly, burying her face in her hands, and sobbing as if her heart would break.

Guy Fawkes's expression at that moment was indeed fearful.

His face, pale from recent sickness, became ghastly pallid, and his features showed intense surprise and agony.

"What has he disclosed and to whom has he betrayed me?" he inquired at length, in an unsteady voice.

"The letter Sir Everard Digby wrote, bidding you attend the next secret meeting of the conspirators—a letter which he was the bearer of to you—was ere to-morrow to have been placed in the king's hands."

"The viper!" shouted Guy Fawkes, furiously. "And Sir Everard and my companions?"

"Are safe," said the dancing-girl, her eyes brightening through her tears. "I obtained the letter and destroyed it. The boy has been taught his treachery by another, and will himself suffer deep remorse for his wrong-doing. The evil can go no further?"

Guy Fawkes looked the very impersonation of the Furies.

"Nay, calm yourself," she continued, drawing nearer to him, and raising her soft, eloquent eyes anxiously to his.

"I have been a madman and a fool!' exclaimed Guy Fawkes, in a tone of frenzy, breaking from her and moving hurriedly up and down the room.

"My blindness," he continued, "has made me a villain—a traitor, unfit to herd with men. The lives of hundreds—one whisper of whose acts would bring them to the block, the gibbet, and the rack—are in that vile boy's hands! But it is to you," he added, turning fiercely towards the girl, "it is to you I owe all this! I trusted you—I believed you when you told me the boy was faithful. You have surrounded me with a labyrinth of craft, and the blood of innocent men will now be on my wretched head."

The poor dancing-girl commenced to weep, and hid her face in her hands in silent agony.

"Madman as I was," pursued Guy Fawkes, "I trusted you—the companion of vile, con-temptible spies—the mysterious follower of a villain!"

"Spare me!" shrieked Evelyn. "Oh, spare me words like these!"

"Hence, begone!" shouted Guy Fawkes, in terrible wrath. "Go back to the vile herd to whom you belong and help them make market of true men's blood.

"And tell them that one whom others trusted was outwitted by a well-atuned voice and a suppliant air to receive the spy that brings the rich harvest in—tell them that he deemed you virtuous and the victim of an unhappy lot—that he took your words without a warrant and considered a woman's tears the test of truth!"

Sobbing as though her very heart would break she held out her hands beseechingly towards him.

"Hence!" cried Guy Fawkes, with wildly-swelling breast. "Leave me! Nay, linger not! I will hear no more!"

He waved his hand as he spoke—his eyes kindled with redoubled fury, and checked her imploring look.

The dancing-girl meekly obeyed as she drew the thin mantle over her shoulders.

But ere she reached the door she staggered and fell senseless on the ground.

CHAPTER XXVIII.

IN WHICH THE READER IS INTRODUCED TO JAMES THE FIRST OF ENGLAND—SIR SIDNEY SEEKS AN AUDIENCE WITH THE KING - THE RESULT.

WE will now ask our readers to accompany us to another scene.

In an old-fashioned apartment of the royal hunting palace, with its carved and massive ornaments, its rich and finely-chiselled oak ceiling, divided into many compartments, each adorned with the crown and cipher of monarchs who had long returned to their kindred dust, sat three persons, apparently engaged in a discussion of weighty import.

The first of these in rank was the reigning monarch of England, James the First. He sat at the upper end of a small table, on which a few loose papers were carelessly scattered.

His face was handsome and kingly, and his dark blue eyes at times softened into an expression of poetic sweetness. At other times, with a bright and piercing glance, they seemed to search the inmost recesses of the heart.

Yet the brilliant lights of his character were not unaccompanied by their corresponding shades.

His passions were of the most violent kind, his resentment implacable, and there was a tendency to avarice in his character, which effaced the brightness of many of his more amiable qualities.

Of the two persons who were with the king one was the renowned Lord Cecil, his principal minister and adviser—a man of sound judgment and superior genius, and still in the prime of vigorous life.

The other, who was sitting on the king's left hand, was Sir Edward Coke, the Attorney-General.

We must not in our enumeration, however, forget a fourth party, who, although deeming the business occupying the King's attention not worthy of his notice, had his own important occupation in hand.

It seemed to consist in a strenuous and continued exertion to capture a swarm of bluebottle flies that buzzed in the recess of the window where he stood.

This renowned individual was Johnny MacKilrie, the king's favourite jester.

The party had not sat for any length of time in consultation when the door of the apartment was opened and a stranger was ushered in—a long dark mantle enveloping his figure.

In his hand he held a smart Spanish hat, adorned with a profusion of dark feathers, and, his head being left uncovered, a set of harsh and unbending but not unhandsome features were observed.

He made a deep obeisance to the king as he advanced, and bowed slightly to the Lord Chancellor and the Attorney-General.

James bent one of his keen and searching glances on the new comer as he approached, then said, coolly—

"Approach, Sir Sidney, and state your object in thus demanding audience."

"I would crave a boon of your gracious majesty," was the recreant knight's answer, uttered in steady, unmoved tones.

"Name it," said the king, "but be brief, distinct, and concise."

"Your majesty," answered the knight, "may not be aware that I come in the character of a suitor. The Lady Hamlyn—I crave your highness's pardon for the introduction of a name that must be allied in your majesty's feelings with so many bitter reminiscences and——"

"Nay, nay, do not dally, man," exclaimed the king, impatiently. "Proceed, in Heaven's name!"

"The Lady Hamlyn—peace rest with her ashes—was, perhaps your majesty is aware, related to me in no distant degree——"

"Sir Sidney Wildbrook, we know it, man," again interrupted the king, testily, "and now what have ye to say, sirrah, to that?"

"Simply," replied the knight, bowing, "that your majesty would not, in the exercise of your just rights, extend the penalty of her faults to those who have no connection with them?"

"Heaven's grace, man!" exclaimed the king, "we shall never extend it to you—to you who, under Providence, hath been the instrument o' communicating the foul conspiracy to our gracious self. Nay, nay, man—that were but small thanks to return for the affection ye have shown to our royal person, and the sore mischief ye have prevented by the timely disclosure of the diabolical and most unholy plot."

This reply, though spoken in a tone veiled by natural politeness, conveyed beneath its smoothness the existence of a bitter feeling of sarcasm and contempt.

Sir Sidney did not observe it, however, and answered, in the same unwavering tone that always marked his speech—

"Under Providence, your majesty, I was indeed the means of disclosing that most abominable conspiracy——"

"And I wish," said James, aside, "your tongue had clung to the roof o' your mouth, or that your ten fingers had been blistered to the bones when ye said the words."

"It was indeed my duty," said the arch-hypocrite, not hearing what the king had said, "as it would have been that of every faithful subject, forthwith to warn your grace of the hellish practices by which your royal life was so far endangered."

"Doubtless, man, doubtless, and we are most thankful for your zeal. God wot that we had many sic faithful servants around our throne. Having thus afforded the information ye doubtless thought it behoved ye also to give evidence against your unfortunate relations."

"That, please your majesty," said the knight, bowing, as he heaved a deep sigh, "that the laws of my country compelled me to do."

"Aye, Sir Sidney," said the king, while the flashing of his eyes and the compression of his lips told the agitation of his mind, "very true. But we would gi'e the best jewel in our crown that these matters had been conducted with less speed, and God wot they might never have mischanced at all. Then you, Sir Sidney, might hae been spared a kind relation and I a faithful subject."

"I cannot," said Sir Sidney, "place my own feelings in competition with my country's weal."

"Perhaps your feelings may have sped ye this way," said James, "for methinks we move but slowly to the object of your visit."

"It is simply this," said the wily schemer. "Your majesty is aware of the near relationship I bear to the unfortunate family of Hamlyn?"

The monarch bowed.

"As nearest of kin," proceeded the knight, "the protection of the hapless Lady Violet now falls to my lot, and as her guardian I would humbly beseech your highness in your clemency to bestow a grant of her forfeited estates on your humble suppliant."

"And on what grounds would Sir Sidney Wildbrook urge us to give away so fair a heritage, either to himself or to the daughter of an attainted lord and his guilty lady?" demanded the king, bending a searching glance upon the knight.

"Simply on the grounds of that justice which doth not extend the punishment of the guilty parent to the innocent and unprotected offspring."

"God wot, man, but ye say true!" exclaimed James. "In good sooth ye have given us a rare homily on charity and morality, and as we cannot allow ourselves to be outdone in generosity by Sir Sidney Wildbrook, we will even take the poor lassie under our own especial care, and see that her bits o' acres be well nursed till she comes o' lawful age or we can provide her with a good and fitting lord."

Sir Sidney bit his lips with rage, but it passed unnoticed, and in a somewhat hesitating voice he resumed—

"Your majesty will pardon me, I trust, but in consistency with my duty as guardian to the orphan I could not avoid applying to your majesty's Exchequer for a signature of her lands and——"

"Now may the foul fiend seize your impudence!" cried the king, dashing his clenched fist violently upon the table. "Ye come here to ask an especial favour frae our ain royal

THE DOOR WAS BURST OPEN AND A BURLY RUFFIAN SPRANG INTO THE ROOM.

person, and then ye have the presumption to tell us that ye have already applied to our Exchequer about the matter, as if we were a pack o' nobodies."

"Sir Edward," he added, turning to the Attorney-General, "see that a message be forthwith sent to our Exchequer that the matter o' Hamlyn be not meddled with except by our ain especial advice and consent."

Sir Edward Coke slowly bowed his head.

"And now, Sir Sidney," continued James, "I think we have gratified your utmost wish. We shall ourselves look to the puir bonny lassie, and free ye frae the responsibility o' wardship and the management o' the land, which to a gay gallant like yoursel' must hae been a sair and serious grievance. Eh, Sir Cecil?"

Sir Sidney bowed low, but in the lineament of his scowling face was a fixed expression of disappointed malice and cunning

Suddenly, however, a new hope seemed to spring within his breast, and looking up he thus spoke—

"Your majesty is very good and gracious in your kindness towards my unprotected kinswoman, but I fain would have been spared a confession——"

"Tut, man!" exclaimed the king, impatiently, "we have had confessions and testimonies enough for a while to come."

"The confession I would make," resumed Sir Sidney Wildbrook, "is one of a different nature from those your majesty has of late been accustomed to hear."

"Aye, man, and what in the name of all the saints in the calendar may it be?"

"A tale of love," said Sir Sidney, bowing.

"Whew!" whistled the monarch in astonishment. "A tale o' love, and the gay Sir Sidney the bearer of it. Weel, let's hae it, man!"

"Your majesty is perhaps not aware that the youthful lady, Violet, has placed her affections upon one in every way unworthy of her accomplishments and beauty."

"We hae heard something o't, I'm thinking," said the king, with a significant look at the Chancellor Cecil.

Sir Sidney looked surprised, but continued—

"If the unworthy servant of your majesty might be permitted the suggestion, would not the object of Lady Violet's choice, when united to her by your majesty's gracious permission, be the fitting person to invest with the management of her wide demesnes?"

"We'll not say ye're far wrang there," James replied. "Faith, man, but ye hae got an inkling o' common sense aboot ye after all."

"Then, your majesty, the character of legal guardian would be lost in that of the husband of the fair Lady Violet, and as such I, Sir Sidney——"

"You—you the husband of the Lady Violet!"—exclaimed the king, with a voice and look of the utmost astonishment.

While the Lord Chancellor Cecil, with equal curiosity depicted on his fine countenance, turned his eyes upon the speaker. Sir Edward Coke could not refrain from smiling.

"You, Sir Sidney Wildbrook, the husband of the fair winsome lassie?" continued the king, after a moment's pause. "By the beard o' my ancestors but ye have been speaking of your ain over-matured person all this time!"

The knight cursed inwardly at the way in which his confession had been received.

"Methinks," went on James, "ye said ye were the object of the Lady Violet's choice—are ye weel advised o' that, Sir Sidney?"

"I could not mistake the declaration from her own lips," rejoined Sir Sidney, with an injured air.

"By the crooked mouth o' St. Bartholomew see that ye be so," said James, "for to tell ye the honest truth we oursel' have been somewhat advised to the contrary—eh, Sir Cecil?" giving the chancellor a familiar jog with his elbow.

Sir Sidney felt like a man treading upon thin ice, and, in nautical phrase, determined to try the king on another tack, so, with a graceful inclination of the head, he said—

"Should your majesty wish to put my word to the proof, from the lady's own sweet lips shall you hear it."

The crafty nobleman, in his secret heart, however, had determined that the king should never have an opportunity of even seeing the maiden if he could help it.

"Weel spoken," said the king, "weel spoken, and fairly too, by the bones of our ancestors. And now, Sir Sidney," he added, "if it please ye, we shall defer the final decision o' this matter till we see the bonny bairn, poor thing, and hear what she has to say aboot it."

"Your majesty's will is my pleasure," replied the knight, with a hypocritical smile, while inwardly he thought, "May all the fiends in hell sink you to perdition!"

"We bid ye good e'en, Sir Sidney," said the king, with a slight inclination of the head.

"There is," ventured Sir Sidney, lingering—"there is yet another subject in which I feel too deep an interest to leave your majesty in ignorance of it."

The king looked in astonishment.

"Already I have been an humble instrument in the discovery of a foul conspiracy and hellish plot, and when the safety of your majesty's person seems concerned it were treason in me to seal my lips."

"Vera true," said the king, "and what new conspiracy has Sir Sidney now brought to light?"

"Harold Rookby is in England," was Sir Sidney's reply, delivered in a low, compressed tone.

"And where heard ye this intelligence, Sir Sidney?" asked the king, with provoking calmness.

"I have seen him, an' it please your majesty."

"Indeed, an' in this town, say ye, man?"

"Even so, your majesty, and methinks the presence of a base attainted traitor within your majesty's realms can bode but little good."

"And ye would, Sir Sidney," exclaimed the king, "that this young branch of a noble family should be cut off—that this last scion of an honourable race should perish on the scaffold, and his very name, like an unclean thing, be blotted from the earth!

"Bluid—bluid," continued the monarch, with emotion, "they say is thicker than water, but with you, Sir Sidney, the veriest puddle i' the street is of more substance than the red current that flows in your ain veins. Yet, supposing such a measure to be in our mind, who would take this same Sir Harold Rookby?"

"Who would take him, your majesty?" said

Sir Sidney, still somewhat dubious as to the ground on which he stood. "While Sir Sidney Wildbrook wears a sword it is at the service of his king."

"And what," demanded James, in a tone of bitter sarcasm, "would Sir Sidney say were we to tell him that we know Sir Harold Rookby is even now within the four walls of the city, and that little time has elapsed since he was cheek-by-jowl and side-by-side with our ain royal person?"

"Awa, awa, Sir Sidney," concluded the monarch. "We are obliged for the proffer of thy services and the loyalty ye have expressed, but in the present instance they appear to us to be both alike—needless. We bid ye once mair good e'en, and heaven prosper ye according to your deserts."

This was spoken in a tone which admitted of no reply.

And Sir Sidney, making a somewhat haughty obeisance, withdrew, little satisfied with the unexpected and wholly unlooked-for turn affairs had taken.

When the door had closed behind him the king fell back in his chair and indulged in a long and hearty burst of laughter, in which he was joined, although in a more moderate degree, by the two statesmen and the jester.

"By the mass, Sir Cecil," James at length exclaimed, "we have scraped him till his hide is raw. Sir Edward, saw ye ever man get sic a dressing?

"By the bones of my sire," he added, more gravely, "it is weel we had an inkling o' this affair, and were made masters of the truth beforehand, or the consummate, insinuating knave, with his weel-favoured tales would have gone awa' and left a flea in our most royal lug. Ha, ha, ha!"

CHAPTER XXIX.

THE MAD MAID OF KENT—THE PREDICTION— THE DANCING-GIRL'S WARNING—THE RENDEZ- VOUS BY THE RIVER—IN DEADLY PERIL.

THE night was dark and louring, and the keen, chilly wind swept mournfully through the deserted London streets as Guy Fawkes hurried along the narrow turnings leading to the river, on his way to attend a secret meeting of his brother conspirators.

The locality he traversed was the haunt of desperadoes of the worst and most ferocious type. Its long narrow alleys, dim courts, and secret passages to the river, its sanctuary and means of concealment, made it the resort of the most desperate and abandoned of mankind.

An old building of considerable size, the irregular proportions of which were magnified by the dim light and the narrow alley, stood in the centre of Whitefriars.

It was part of an ancient religious house—its walls were thick and massive, its gateway narrow and arched.

The windows were protected by bars of iron, and the place had altogether more the look of a prison than the chosen abode of peaceful men. The back part reached to the river's brink, with which it had communications in various ways.

In short, the whole formed an irregular mass, intricate in its windings and a stronghold of crime, perhaps the securest that ever stood within a populous city in peaceful times.

Guy Fawkes, looking cautiously round, now stood before this gloomy building.

The bleak wind from the river whistled through the vaulted passages, and the deepest and most perfect silence reigned around him.

With noiseless tread a female form suddenly glided towards him.

She was dressed in white, and her long dark hair fell luxuriantly over her neck and shoulders.

Her eyes were dark and sparkling as his, her step was queen-like, and her look was fixed upon him with an expression which riveted him to the spot.

It was the crazed maid of Kent—a poor religious fanatic.

"A feller spirit or a more ruthless heart than thine, Guy Fawkes, never beat," she said, with an air of prediction. "You are come here to league with the enemies of Christendom and exult in the false doctrine of the heretic.

"Is it zeal for the purity of religion and concern for benighted souls that makes thee wander thus far at this lone hour and in secret?

"No!" she added, fixing her wild, piercing eyes upon him. "A meteor has drawn you to the precipice's brink—an all-absorbing ambition, an unholy love for vulgar notoriety and the vain applause of the multitude."

"Silence, mad wench!" cried Guy Fawkes, sternly. "By whose licence do ye wander here?"

"By the licence of that charity and protection which this sanctuary granteth even to the vilest. The heretic leaders thirst for my blood because a poor peasant girl has courage to preach openly against a power which seeks to chain soul as well as body to a despotic will— against a power which, aided by thy impious hand, would wreak desolation and destruction around, and again deluge the land in the blood of good and brave men. I could curse thee, Guy Fawkes," she continued, in a tone of frenzy, "did I not see that thy doom will be a bitter and a terrible one, and that a weight is already on thy heart which human power can neither lighten nor remove."

"Base shrew! what mean ye?" demanded the conspirator, ruffled at her scathing words.

"Thou art in love! You start, but it is so— passionately, fondly—every kindly feeling of your fierce soul is centred in that love—and yet that passion is your bane, the poison of your happiness, the curse of your existence."

"How, madbrain, how?"

"The pang which on earth is keenest is thine. You know that she whom you so madly dote on can never be yours—that she is another's!

"Hold!" she continued, lifting her hand on high, while her wild but beautiful features glowed with fervour. "Yours is the deepest curse of manhood. You feel—you know that my words are true. You love as only souls like yours can love—it is deathless, quenchless —yet your judgment mocks it!

"There is a scorpion at your heart, and its sting rankles—rankles! Heaven's justice is already fulfilled in thee. Life has no punishment keener than that in store for thee, and the world no crimes deeper than those you meditate!"

She waved her arms with a frenzied gesture, and, muttering a maniacal laugh, fled noiselessly from his side.

He saw her white robe wave for an instant

in the darkness of the street, and the next moment she was gone.

Guy Fawkes was again alone, but there was a gloom on his spirit which he had not felt before.

The maniac's words, which still rung in his ears, had found a response in his bosom, and awakened thoughts which had long lain there, although they had not burst into life till now.

Violet, the idol of his heart—the being whom his whole soul worshipped, on whom every fond thought of his stern nature hung. How different would have been his career if blessed with her precious love, he thought.

"Yes, yes," he mused, "to win that priceless gem I would forego my wildest dreams of ambition—aye, the great purpose of my life."

"But the wench was right," he added, with a sigh that seemed to come from the very depths of his heart. "Her love can never—never be mine. But I must not think on it—it unmans me. I must act—act !"

He gave a hasty glance around. The dark buildings stood in tomb-like silence—there seemed to be no one near.

Guy Fawkes laid his hand upon the scabbard of his sword, and, raising the belted weapon within easy grasp, entered the dark passage.

The pavement of the archway was broken in many places, and its walls had recesses and angles where lurkers might have stabbed at ease.

Someone suddenly touched his cloak.

He started aside and clapped his hand on the hilt of his sword, but the same instant his keen eyes met the earnest glance of the dancing-girl.

Guy Fawkes could not check an exclamation of surprise.

The girl put her finger to her lips, and by a sign implored him to follow her.

He did so, and in a few seconds found himself by her side in a retired and protected portion of the exterior of the building.

"You parted harshly from me when last we met," said Evelyn, laying her little hand timidly on Guy Fawkes's arm. "Do you doubt me still ?"

"I parted not from you," returned Guy Fawkes, "until I saw your eyes look upon me with consciousness, and I left you in hands that tended you well."

"Yet still it was harshly done. You doubted —you suspected me. Do you do so still ?"

The light from a window shone upon her pale face—its look had the touching eloquence of misery.

"No," answered Guy Fawkes, drawing her shrinking form to his side, "I do not doubt you, Evelyn. I had rather be betrayed by you than again doubt."

"It is noble !—it is as I would speak were I a man !" said the dancing-girl, with enthusiasm. "Now listen to me. Your retreat in London has been discovered, and officers from the Star Chamber are lying in wait for you there."

"How know you that ?"

"It is an evil hour for questioning; but I must answer you. It was I—it was through me it was discovered."

"You—you knew it not !"

"A price was was set upon your head," continued Evelyn "officers of justice were on the alert, and men left their business stalls to search for you and win the reward. You eluded them but not me. There was no pause in my search—day and night I followed you."

"But why ?"

"To look upon the house," cried Evelyn, promptly—"to be near you, though you knew it not—to catch a glimpse of you as you passed from it—to follow your footsteps like a chastened dog, that dares not approach its master whom it loves—to know you were safe—to watch at your threshold, a weak but faithful guardian—to pray for you when you slept—and warn you, if I could, had danger come nigh."

She paused, and Guy Fawkes, obeying an almost irresistible impulse, pressed the lowly but lovely speaker to his bosom, and imprinted a passionate kiss upon her flushed and burning brow.

Tremblingly she withdrew from his embrace, and, deeply embarrassed and confused, she stood hiding her blushing face between her hands.

"Nay, shrink not from me, little one," said Guy Fawkes, earnestly. "By the Virgin, I meant not to offend ye."

Reassured by his tone, the dancing-girl again timidly approached, then continued—

"But while I thought only of you I forgot myself. I, too, was watched and followed by one who is your enemy, and is now a prisoner in the power of the king.

"He told me yesterday he knew of your retreat—that he was on a desperate errand, and if he failed would buy his safety by betraying where you might be found. This morning I saw the officers arrive. I heard them speak of the rack," continued Evelyn, shuddering, "as the means by which the names of your accomplices would be extracted from you."

"Enough !" said Guy Fawkes, gravely. "I know too well the fate of those who stand before the Star Chamber on a charge like mine. But, sweetheart, it is a bitter night, and I do ill to keep you here. I have a meeting to attend, after which I must crave concealment of Sir Everard Digby for awhile."

"He is more than suspected, and his house by the river will be searched to-night. To-morrow you may go there, but now you must hide elsewhere. Come with me—I will take you to a place where, for the night at least, you will be safe."

Guy Fawkes gladly accepted her kind offer. The night was dark, and they proceeded in perfect security.

Reaching the river they took a pathway that led through gardens bordered by fields, until passing Savoy Palace, when the place became desolate.

Close to the water's edge, and at the extremity of a vacant space between the river and the Strand, there was a house—old, rambling, and variously tenanted.

The lower part was said to be occupied by smugglers, a name sometimes employed to cover the harsher term of pirates, for in those days enterprises on the open sea were by no means rigidly inquired into, and adventurers of this class often landed their booty within gun-shot of the Tower.

The building in question was admirably situated for the purpose for which it was said to be employed.

From the Strand to this part of the river there was no house, but the distance was mainly by marshy fields, within view of which were several wooden crosses, erected over spots where murders had been committed.

The Thames ran under the very walls of the building, with the fields of Lambeth on the other side. Here and there only stood a solitary farm house, while if escape could not be made in that direction there was an easy retreat behind the house.

The dancing-girl proceeded along a narrow passage, the door of which she had unlocked.

Guy Fawkes followed, and as he passed through the place remembered the retreat to which he had pursued Evelyn's ruffianly taskmaster; who had attacked him at Charing, and doubted not that this was the same.

It was, however, too dark to judge accurately, and he continued to follow his gentle guide, directed by her soft footfalls on the paved floor, until she entered an apartment, the door of which she also unlocked.

Taking a pistol from the wall she struck a light, and set fire to some chips piled upon the hearth, then lit a small lamp that hung over the fireplace.

"You are safe here," she said, handing him a seat, while her eyes brightened with delight. "You are safe here for a season."

Guy Fawkes looked around the place—it was scantily furnished—only a few rough weapons hung upon the walls.

But what attracted his attention most was a strong iron-studded door, under which the cold air blew, showing that it was in the outer wall, while a sound of the bubbling of water below made him imagine that it opened on to stairs leading to the river.

Evelyn seated herself, her eyes still fixed with timid joy on Guy Fawkes, on whom the spirit of adventure had in some measure caused to forget his desperate position.

The appearance of the room, the arms on the walls, on which the blazing firewood was casting a fantastic light, coupled with the bleak poverty of the abode, formed a touching contrast to the delicate, graceful figure of the beautiful dancing-girl.

"My lot is a gloomy one, sweetheart," said Guy Fawkes, thoughtfully, "but yours is as strange and sad. What has one of your beauty and tender years to do in a place like this—more fitted for a guard-room than a domicile for such as you? In good sooth, Evelyn, your life is a riddle to me."

"And its reading is bitter," said the girl.

"My arms are tied at present, and I cannot shield you now, Evelyn, but your life seems to be one of suffering—even ignominy."

The dancing-girl did not reply.

"Why, then, do you not quit it?" continued Guy Fawkes. "Followed and hunted as I am I might yet find you an asylum where——"

"No more of this! I need no monitor to tell me what I am, and the hope of rescue now is vain. If I have a hope left it is for you."

"All this is hard to account for," said Guy Fawkes. "You have saved my life—you have followed me like a guardian angel—you have done for me more than devotion itself might compass."

"And is not its memory dear to me, think you?" she said, with touching pathos. "Oh, the past would be a blank indeed but for you. What I have done deserves not to be named with what my heart tells me I could do for you."

"Yet I have never merited it," said Guy Fawkes, with a sad smile.

"Say not so. The look you first gave me is fresh and warm in this poor bosom—a bauble, you will say, to be treasured there, but it is even so. Not that alone, but many a gentle look, kind word, and noble deed. I have seen the tears start to your eyes—yes, you once wept for me. No one ever wept for me but you."

Guy Fawkes was about to interrupt her, but she added, rapidly—

"Nay, you forced me to speak. The good I have done you, the sleepless wish to serve you, recalls me to purity again. You are the only sweet memory in my dream of life, and to watch—to serve—to save you—is dearer to me than the proud estate which makes woman, however humble, a mate for kings."

Guy Fawkes did not reply. His mind for a moment was disturbed by her words, but thoughts which he could not check soon carried him from Evelyn and the scene around him—from his own desperate fortunes and the danger he was in to his last parting with Violet Hamlyn.

Evelyn seemed to read his thoughts. She covered her face with her hands and sat in her usual attitude, with her elbows resting on her knees.

She was silent too, but the quivering of her slight back showed that she was weeping.

There was a sudden sound of oars from under the door that opened to the river, and the next instant a low whistle was heard.

The dancing-girl started to her feet—grief, horror, and despair depicted on her countenance.

She stood like one transfixed—her fair brow wrinkled, her beautiful features collapsed, and her little hands clenched in agony.

Guy Fawkes was already up. He hastily examined the priming of his steel-hilted pistols, and, grasping his sword, slackened it in its scabbard.

There was a pause of perfect stillness for a moment, then came a louder whistle, clear and shrill.

Evelyn strode forward, and, grasping Guy Fawkes's arm, by sheer strength alone thrust him behind the heavy hangings of the bed, while by a look she enjoined silence.

"Stir not," she whispered, "or you are lost!" then glided from his side.

The visitor without seemed to have become impatient at receiving no answer to his signal.

He threw himself violently against the panels—the next moment the door was burst forcibly open, and a burly ruffian in a steel cap and armed with a boat-pike darted into the apartment.

Had Guy Fawkes time to speak he would have refused the conditions of such concealment.

As it was, notwithstanding the dancing-girl's warning, he slipped unobserved from behind the curtains of the bed through a door into a dark passage beyond.

The spirit of chivalry urging him on, he retraced his steps softly back again to the door, with some vague idea that evil was menacing the devoted girl who had sheltered him.

The door was partially ajar, and he could see a man advancing towards Evelyn, habited in a half-pirate, half-sailor garb of the period—the same who had entered by the stairs leading to the river.

The man's features flashed on Guy Fawkes's recollection, and he recognised in him the person who had commanded the boat in which he had escaped from the vault by the river's side.

The memory made his blood run cold, for the associations of the rack, even to the bravest, were painful.

The dancing-girl stood at the iron-fastened door, and the cold wind rushed into the apartment and almost extinguished the lamp.

Torchlights glimmered from under the walls, shooting fantastic beams on the dark water, while the dipping of oars and the sound of voices showed that a boat lay there.

"Ah, my little queen of hearts, 'tis a plaguey testy night to be kept waiting in the cold," said the pirate, shutting the creaking door, and taking the girl's small white hand, which he locked in his bronzed and jewelled fingers.

"I greet you well, my bonnie White Rose of England. How fare you? Saint Mary! your cheek is pale, and you tremble as if you had another mine of gunpowder to fire again. 'Twas a bold act, Evelyn. Nay, one kiss," he continued, as his strong arm wound round her and he pressed his lips to her cheek.

"Shudder not, my pretty shrew. Come, the fire wanes," added he, tossing another log on the hearth and seating himself on the stool where Guy Fawkes had lately sat. "Why did you not answer my first summons?"

Evelyn crept to her seat, but said nothing.

"This is a cold greeting, sweetheart, after a long cruise. Hast nought to ask?"

"How fares my brother?"

The pirate burst into a loud laugh.

"He is well," he said, "and, by our lady's grace, will one day be as great a knave, as ready to shed blood, rob a church, kiss a nun, seize a merchant's venture on the high seas, or do any fair deed of manhood which a wench could wish——"

The dancing-girl heaved a deep sigh.

"You are ill at ease, my fair one; but cheer thee. I have brought thee robes that a queen might wear, and jewels for which a city dame would commit any crime in woman's compass to deck herself withal.

"I heard of my comrade's mishap," he continued, "and knew you would be alone. My ship is anchored below London Bridge, and I have as sweet a nest for you as ever the bride of a sea king revelled in—gay music—dancing—the ripe wines that dark eyed, and fair-eyed maids, too, i' faith, wax merry over.

"Come," the pirate continued, "the cabin is trim. There are no more blood spots to startle you. This has been a holiday cruise—we got spoil without dinting a blade."

"I cannot leave this place," said the dancing-girl, her blanched lips quivering as she spoke.

"Not leave it! Go to. You wait for one whom you will never see again. He is a prisoner on a State charge, and that is a death-warrant in any country where there is a headsman and a king."

Evelyn was silent, yet her looks were expressive of increased agony and alarm.

"Now this would make some men grow stern," said the sailor, "but not me. You have lost your mate, poor dove, and must needs be sad. Would I had the art of minstrelsy, I would sing ye a love-song till your eyelids drooped, then change the strain to amorous joy, until you smiled and your heart waxed wanton in the joyousness of mirth.

Evelyn held up her hand beseechingly, but he went on—

"Your mate is lost—give him tears and a sigh or two, it is woman-like, and, by heaven, I like thee for't; but you have found another, and a wise wench wears weeds no longer than she can help. Come, Evelyn, the boat waits for us, and the knaves that sit in it have found out ere now that there is a biting frost on the river."

"I am glad that my brother is well, and that you have returned safely," said Evelyn, "but I may not leave this place."

"And why not? Who is there now to control you?"

"Myself," said the dancing-girl—with her natural impetuosity. "'Tis enough—I will not go with you."

The swarthy features of the pirate changed their expression in a moment.

His merry bright eyes lost their coyness, and he fixed them on the girl with a glance which made her shrink from him.

"It is too late to play the prude, pretty one," he said, with a forced laugh. "They say a lion will crouch before a maid in the pride of her purity and innocence—a thing I am inclined to doubt—but even were it so, by Heaven! you were a jay in peacock's plumes. Nay, a sweet night—wine, music, and love; for to-morrow rich robes, bright gems, and yellow gold. You are a woman—go to!"

Evelyn fixed her mild eyes mournfully on the ground, but did not speak.

"Men learn patience by watching the sea storms," said the sailor, "and wit by toying with woman's will. He is mad who bends not to the one—he who is swayed by the other is a fool.

"I have thought of you, Evelyn," he went on, "in the midnight watch, in the stormy night, and when the white spray danced in the sunrise under my vessel's bow. The first glance I got of England brought you back to my heart again.

"By the bones of Becket I become apt at a love-tale! I say, sweet wench, I have thought of you and also of the night when at your entreaty I permitted that hawk-eyed, soldierly gallant, whom you called Fawkes, to escape."

At that moment there were the sounds of oars without.

"They grow restless—and small marvel, for the air is pinching, and warm revels wait for them. Come, my girl," said he, seizing her rudely by the arm, "the use of words has lasted longer than a wise man would have dallied with them."

Evelyn started back and raised her beautiful head, while her spirituelle countenance beamed with defiance.

Her very figure, slight, graceful, and pliant, had an expression of its own, as with her scattered hair falling in rich clusters over her fair brow, and her loving eyes now flashing with the indignation of woman when her heart is stung, she stood confronting the pirate like one whom passion has inspired.

The instinct of manhood made him pause for a moment, but the very check excited him the more.

GUY FAWKES

Or Gunpowder, Treason, and Plot.

THREE ARMED MEN SUDDENLY DARTED UPON HAROLD ROOKBY AND BORE HIM BACK.

No. 8.

"This is idle!" he said, sternly. "This bold air is lost upon me. You are bound by your own pledge—by your own act, and the compact, which some might blush for, to——"

"It is false!" cried Evelyn, impetuously. "I will not obey your beck to feast or revel, and dispute the right which you or anyone has to exact my compliance. I am no slave even of thine."

"By Satan! not of mine alone, but of——"

"Hear me!" exclaimed Evelyn. "I am a weak girl and you are an armed man; we are here alone, and it is idle to bandy words. You may kill me if you will, but not to save myself from death will I enter that boat with you!"

"Brave words and boldly spoken," observed the pirate, his malignant eyes sparkling fire, although his manner was sarcastic and calm; "Such would sound well in an old play or a minstrel's chaunt, but love has rough tricks which the poets tell not of."

"Come," he added, "or, by the mass, I will carry you to the boat like a fluttering bird! Men's patience, like women's virtue, sweet one, has its limits."

He grasped her as he spoke.

Evelyn was in the very act of uttering a cry when a noise at the inner door made her look towards it.

She got a glimpse of Guy Fawkes, and her whole manner changed as if by magic.

She suppressed the shriek, laughed hysterically, and said, with a forced smile—

"Unhand me—I go willingly."

Even the pirate looked surprised.

"Yes," continued the dancing-girl, evidently striving to hide a tumult of conflicting emotions. "Were rescue at hand I would refuse it. I go willingly, and will return ere daybreak."

The arm of the pirate captain was twining round her slender waist—there was a laugh on his lips as he was about to speak, when suddenly, like a shot from a cannon's mouth, he was hurled with terrific force backwards against the granite wall, and Guy Fawkes stood between the startled pirate and the dancing-girl.

The suddenness of the act and the violence of the blow for an instant stunned him, but it was only for an instant.

Drawing his sword and uttering a wild yell he sprang towards his assailant with a bound.

Guy Fawkes received a heavy cut on his trusty blade, and the swords flickered and leapt like lightning streaks.

All this passed so rapidly that it seemed like a single act.

The mist that rose to Evelyn's eyes on the entrance of Guy Fawkes had not yet left them.

The deep respiration which follows a sudden alarm had hardly passed away when the ring of steel fell on her ears.

In those days it was a frequent sound.

The girl stood like a statue, her eyes fixed, her small hands clasped, and her features expressing alarm and agony, save the lips, which moved as though in prayer.

As we have said, Guy Fawkes was a splendid swordsman, and the headlong fury of his adversary was repelled with a skill and force that speedily checked the recklessness of the assault.

The man had met his match—strength and fury were wasted here, and Guy Fawkes in turn became the assailant.

Now it was that his dark eyes glowed, and that volcano of passion which for good or evil was seated in his nature aroused the bitterness of his heart. The hellish energy of action in which the very war-horse is said to exult seized his mind.

The passes of his blade were rapid and his adversary lost ground inch by inch. The keen, basilisk glance fixed thirstily upon him made the pirate feel he was the other's prey.

Onward, closer and closer, Guy Fawkes pressed, his active arm and his strong sinewy frame readily obeying the instincts of impulse.

The pirate saw his danger, and, on his part, it was no longer a fight but a defence.

Twice he attempted to raise his whistle to his lips, but as often Guy Fawkes, who saw the object of it, prevented him by the rapidity of his passes and the manner in which he pressed upon him.

He knew his only chance of escape was in destroying his adversary before he could give the alarm to his crew, and he needed no monitor to urge him to do this.

Guy Fawkes could have shot him with one of the pistols in his belt, but the report would have been heard without. Besides, it was an advantage—his adversary had no firearms— which he scorned to take.

Nearer and nearer he forced him to the iron door.

Twice the conspirator's sword's point had been turned aside from the pirate's throat, but now the conflict seemed nearly at an end.

But again the bright blades glimmered—the sailor struck fiercely, yet still he lost ground.

He retreated till his back at length touched a corner of the panel, and Guy Fawkes's foot was within a short distance of his.

Another instant and the conspirator had pinned his opponent to the wall.

But the clash of arms had already been heard without, and the boat's crew were thundering at the door.

"Fly! fly!" cried Evelyn, springing forward. "The passage beyond is clear!"

"Not to leave you," muttered Guy Fawkes, holding his adversary at bay.

"Fly!" shrieked the dancing-girl; "the bars are bursting!"

And with a crash and a clatter they gave way.

Several men rushed into the room, and ere Guy Fawkes could defend himself he was felled with lightning speed to the ground.

"Pinion his arms," panted the pirate, savagely, "and throw that saucy jade into the boat."

He was immediately obeyed.

Guy Fawkes's arms were bound, and when he had recovered from the dizzy sensation caused by the blow he found himself gliding down the Thames with Evelyn by his side.

CHAPTER XXX.

SIR SIDNEY'S INTERVIEW WITH HORLOCK THE MAGICIAN—A DIABOLICAL PLOT OVERHEARD.

ON leaving the presence of the king Sir Sidney Wildbrook sought the most retired and sheltered way to reach his own dwelling.

There, throwing himself upon a settle, he

gave way to those angry feelings which had so long been suppressed.

"What!" he exclaimed, "am I, Sir Sidney Wildbrook, one of the first knights in Christendom, to be trodden under foot and spat upon by the grasping, greedy ruler of this bigoted land, who wields the sceptre's power with a rod of iron away?

"The cunning rogue! He would add Hamlyn, mayhap, to the Crown domains, under pretence of assuming the guardianship of its young mistress. But let them look to it. King and ministers alike shall feel that Sir Sidney Wildbrook is not the cringing, submissive slave they fancy him."

In wild and uncontrolled agitation he arose and paced the apartment with short and hurried steps, meditating on the injuries he had received, and revolving in his mind plans of deep revenge.

He was interrupted by the entrance of Zach Horlock, the magician, who gazed with a careless expression of surprise on the disturbed and agitated countenance of the knight.

"Ah, Horlock! this is well," said Sir Sidney. "You come at a fitting time. Let us get to business."

"What, in the name of all the Furies, aileth thee now, Sir Sidney?" demanded the magician, with more familiarity than the relative position of the parties seemed to authorise.

"By all the fiends! my very blood boils within me," exclaimed the knight, stopping short in his walk. "But listen, and thou shalt know it all."

And in a few minutes he made the magician master of everything that had passed between himself and the king.

When he had concluded, Horlock, with the cool calculation of one utterly unscrupulous, quietly answered—

"Just as I thought. Ye would not be ruled by me—to take the matter in your own hands, and let kings and counsel go whistle to the winds."

"Nay, Horlock," replied Sir Sidney, "it is not in that our schemes have failed. The train was well laid and so far hath exploded fairly."

"Aye," interrupted the magician, "but some deadly damp hath come across it. Methinks ye have but burnt your fingers and derived little vantage in the matter."

"By all the saints in heaven!" replied Sir Sidney, "'tis hard that so gentle a rain should yield so poor a harvest, and when the rich reward of all my plotting and toil lay within my grasp it is harder still to see it thus whirled away from me for ever!

"For ever!" he continued, after a pause. "No, not for ever. Violet shall yet be mine!"

"And what," said the magician, "will that avail thee? What is the puling girl without her lands?"

Sir Sidney turned short upon him, then burst into a fit of fiendish laughter, totally at variance with his usual stern, dignified manner.

"Ha, ha, ha! So thou, too, takest me for a witling. No, no! I would have the land without the girl, but without the land the girl may sink to the bottomless pit for aught I care.

"But hark ye, Horlock," added the knight,

"wherever she goes the land will follow. A man must perforce have been deprived of sense or sight not to see the deep and ready interest that James taketh in the Lady Violet.

"The lands are hers, and she will keep them, but once mine—and mine she shall be—then for her own sake and the sake of her maiden purity she will not deny the tale I have told the king, and he, believing her wedded to the object of her choice—ha, ha!—will straightway direct the wishedfor grant to be issued.

"The encumbrance of a mistress tacked unto the acres is no great thing, and besides, is one which may perchance be got rid of in a short space."

"A goodly scheme, truly," said the magician, significantly. "But how do you propose to bring the young falcon to the lure? Methinks she will fly a trifle beyond thy power if you use not the strongest means."

"Thou hast hit it, friend Horlock," said Sir Sidney, breathing through his closed teeth. "Thou hast hit it. Strong means must be used, and that, too, before James can have an opportunity to hear her tale.

"She is within reach, and unprotected, too," continued the knight, with fiendish exultation. "All worketh well, and ere many suns have sunk beneath the western wave she shall be an inmate of the most secret recesses of my stronghold.

"There she shall find every luxury that the east can boast or wealth procure to dazzle the senses and soften the heart of one who cannot, even in imagination, have dreamed of the scenes of voluptuous splendour she shall there behold."

"The Knights of the Temple lack not the consolations of the fair sex in privacy, nor ample means for their accommodation, I opine," said the magician, slyly.

This observation passed unheeded, and the knight continued—

"I cannot blame myself for delay, yet of a surety busy tongues have been before with the king and poisoned his ear against my well-varnished tale. Had it been otherwise my petition could not but have succeeded. Still," he added, pausing, "who could have told the tale, Horlock? Myra? Ah, by Satan! But —no, no! she could not have had access to the king. Who then could have whispered aught of this?"

"Canst thou not frame a guess?" said the magician, with a contemptuous curl of the lip.

Sir Sidney shook his head.

"One, I'll be sworn," continued Horlock, "whose whisper is somewhat of the loudest sort. What think you of the young knight fresh from Spain—Sir Harold Rookby?"

Sir Sidney started.

"Nay, nay, Horlock, thou dost but mock— it cannot be so. Thinkest thou one of his proscribed and banished race would dare to appear in the presence of his irritated sovereign?"

"And yet, in good sooth," responded the magician, with a quiet sneer, "did not James himself tell thee that he was here. Take my word for it, by book, bell, and candle, he hath had the king's ear."

"It may be so," said the knight, slowly, "it may be so. Yet it matters little."

"But, by the mass," interposed Horlock,

"It matters much, for while he liveth be assured thy schemes, whether with the girl or her lands, will ever be thwarted by some means or other. He is the rock upon which thou shalt yet split, at least so it is written, an' thou steerest not a safe course."

"And what course," said Sir Sidney, in the same stern and unmoved accents—"what course wouldst thou counsel me to steer?"

"A safe one," answered the magician, with a diabolical look, at the same time half drawing from its sheath beneath his vest a bright and gleaming dagger, the rays of which flashed for a moment in Sir Sidney's eyes.

"I counsel not murder," replied the knight. "Remember, Horlock, whatever may betide I counsel it not, but for thy past services and as an earnest of the future receive this trifling guerdon."

And he placed upon the table a well-filled purse of gold.

"Aye, aye!" exclaimed the villainous wizard, as he picked it up, "I understand thee. Thou counsellest not murder. but thou wouldst willingly see it done. If Zach Horlock succeeds 'tis well, if he fails there is none but Zach Horlock to answer for it. Well—so be it. A purse like this will outweigh the conscience of many a man. Fare thee well, Sir Sidney."

The magician turned to depart, but as he laid his hand upon the latch of the door a burst of laughter resounded through the room so loud and discordant that it could be likened to nothing save a deep and bitter howl of hatred and contempt.

The magician started back.

Sir Sidney's features went as pale as those of a corpse, and the two villains continued to gaze in silence on each other's bloodless features.

"We have been overheard," Sir Sidney at length exclaimed, in a low and trembling voice.

"And if we have," said Horlock, recovering from his alarm, "by St. Barnabas I will make mince-meat of the cullion's ears."

Every nook and corner of the room that could have concealed a living creature was searched, the adjoining passages were ransacked, but all in vain. No trace of a human being could be seen.

And the wily plotters were compelled to separate, writhing under the apprehension that their secret and abominable plans had been overheard.

CHAPTER XXXI.

THE CONVENT OF ST. WINIFRED S—A MYSTERIOUS ADVENTURE—THE SECRET ASSASSINS—THE ENCOUNTER—NEW SCENES AND STARTLING EVENTS.

A FEW evenings later Sir Harold Rookby was making his way along the wild and rugged woodland track that led to the convent of St. Winifred's, which, rich in ruin and architectural beauty, stood at the foot of a beautifully-wooded eminence.

The young soldier had received a mysterious communication the previous day from some unknown hand, informing him of Sir Sidney's attempt to obtain possession of his beloved Violet's person and property from the hands of the king, of the knight's galling failure, and of the monarch's avowed intention of protecting the possessions and person of the young heiress himself.

Harold was overjoyed at the intelligence, and, notwithstanding the lateness of the hour, as he came within sight of the convent he could not rest till he had informed Violet of the blissful news.

He knew that the tidings would be those of joy to her, at least, in so far as she could now rejoice in anything.

Impelled by this and a dozen other motives, besides a lover's fervent desire to behold the cherished image of his heart's devotion, Sir Harold hurried onward, though not without many a fear, as the increasing darkness surrounded him, that the gates of the convent would be closed for the night.

Fortune, however, in this instance favoured him, for, as he approached the building, the melody of the vesper hymn swelled upon his ear, and the light in the windows told him that the evening service was not yet concluded.

He hurried onward, and had nearly reached the precincts of the little garden that surrounded the monastery, when his attention was attracted by a group of figures advancing hurriedly along the margin of the lake.

The nodding plumes and glittering armour of one of the mysterious party betrayed him to be of military rank.

As the figures advanced Harold could perceive that they bore in their arms what appeared to be a female form, but so muffled up as scarcely to be discerned.

The place, the hour, the appearance of the group, all awoke suspicions of a vague and foreboding kind within his breast, and retreating behind some stunted bushes he determined to watch their movements.

They advanced, and, rapidly passing the place of his concealment, made towards a clump of cedar trees that overhung the upper end of the lake.

They were on the point of entering the shelter of the drooping foliage when the figure which had hitherto lain motionless in the arms of its supporters suddenly appeared to struggle violently, and the young soldier thought he could distinguish a suppressed cry for help.

Nay, more, he fancied he could hear sounds resembling his own name.

But the head of the figure was again instantly muffled, and the sounds died away ere any distinct utterance was heard by Harold.

The young soldier, in whose breast the spirit of knight-errantry burned like a lambent flame, darted forward with all the impetuosity of youth.

Speedily would he have overtaken the base abductors, for such he deemed them, had not the increasing darkness of the hanging trees prevented him from observing the path he strode, and, stumbling over a straggling root, he fell heavily to the ground.

For a few seconds Harold lay stunned by the fall.

But, quickly recovering, he sprang to his feet and darted forward in the direction he imagined the party had taken.

On emerging from the shadow of the trees, however, no sound met his ear, and he could not descry a moving object within sight.

He paused a moment, uncertain what course to pursue—like a hound at fault—totally ignorant of the direction in which the chase should be followed.

He took a few steps forward and then again paused to listen.

At that instant the splash of an oar was heard in the water.

Turning towards the lake, he had the mortification to behold the objects of his search crossing it in a boat which was being propelled swiftly through the still waters.

He rushed forward to the margin of the lake, but the boat was already beyond his reach.

He called aloud, but no answer was returned to his call.

The echo of his own voice had scarcely ceased when the last dying swell of the vesper hymn burst upon his ear, and again all was silent.

Instinctively he glanced towards the convent.

The lights were fast flitting from the chapel, and, recalled to recollection by their disappearance, Sir Harold, forgetting the figure, boat, and crew, quickly proceeded to regain the path he had quitted in his fruitless chase.

A short space of time sufficed to bring him to the gate of the convent.

His thundering application for admittance was speedily answered by an old nun, whose thin and pinched visage appeared at a small wicket in the gate.

She demanded his business, which was soon disclosed, and, with an assurance that it should be immediately communicated to her superior, she disappeared.

After the delay of a few minutes the gate was unbarred and the young soldier was admitted to an outer apartment of the convent provided for the reception of male visitors, it being against the rules of the community to admit such within its interior.

Here again he was doomed to wait for a long time, and his patience was somewhat put to the test.

Suddenly his attention was roused by what appeared to be a very unusual commotion within the convent.

Lights danced to and fro at the different windows of the building, and from time to time the name of Violet, uttered in varied tones of apprehension and alarm, reached his ears

A vague, undefined idea seized upon his mind that all was not right.

Uncertainty was what he could not bear, so, determined to know the worst, he rushed from the apartment, and in another moment stood in the midst of the alarmed and timid nuns.

The lady abbess, a mild, venerable-looking being, but on whose pale features consternation was now visibly depicted, approached the young soldier.

The words that would have fallen from her white lips died upon her tongue.

Harold's impatience was at its height when the old nun whom he had seen at the gate approached him with trembling steps.

The winter of old age had almost frozen up the channels of her grief, but the tears stood in her dim and sunken eyes as she addressed him.

"The young lady hath disappeared, Sir Knight," she said, in a faltering voice—"the convent has been searched from top to bottom, but Lady Violet is not within its walls."

A strange fear seized upon the young soldier's heart.

No one could say whither his beloved one had gone, nor could the cause of her disappearance be traced.

She had retired to her apartment previous to the evening service, and there part of her upper garments still remained.

One chair was overthrown, her prayer-book lay upon the floor, and beside it was a small silver crucifix, which Harold well remembered to have seen suspended from her neck.

The ring of it was broken, as if from the use of violence.

Sir Harold snatched it from the hands of the old nun and pressed it fervently to his lips.

The remembrance of the boat—the muffled figure, and the suppressed cry for aid, all rushed upon his mind with lightning speed.

Without tarrying to ask further questions he darted from the place like an arrow from a bow, and stood once more on the brink of the still and placid lake.

The moon had risen and was shining in full splendour from above the tall hills.

By its light Harold Rookby could distinguish the boat as it reached the opposite shore.

He saw the white garments of the female-like form flutter in the breeze as two of the crew lifted their apparently inanimate burden out of the boat.

The young soldier's eyes nearly started out of their sockets, so fixed and eager was his gaze.

A few minutes elapsed while the treacherous abductors were making some necessary arrangements, then they bore their motionless burden in the direction of the ruined chapel on the other shore.

Harold again shouted aloud to the presumed robbers of his beloved Violet, but they vouchsafed no reply.

The marauding party were fast disappearing from his sight.

Without further delay he rushed with frantic speed towards the upper end of the lake, and, rounding its extremity, rapidly neared the spot where the villainous horde had landed.

The boat lay there, rocking idly upon the waters, deserted like a friend whose services are no longer required, but the daring abductors had vanished.

Harold proceeded hastily towards the ruined chapel, calling in a frenzied manner upon the name of Violet as he advanced.

But ere he reached its exterior his progress was intercepted.

Three armed men suddenly darted from behind a clump of dwarf shrubs, and, drawing their swords, attacked the young soldier in a manner which showed their intentions to be of the deadliest kind

The violence of the assault at first bore him back.

But, quickly recovering himself, the young knight drew his weapon, and in his turn became the assailant.

Harold was an excellent master of the sword, but the odds were fearfully against him.

One, at least, of his adversaries was distinguished by skill almost equal to his own.

Harold succeeded in grievously wounding the other two, but though he tried every feint, every stratagem, all his attempts on his third foe were unavailing.

His attacks were parried with a coolness and precision not to be surpassed, although his opponent, aided as he was, seldom ventured to become the assailant in his turn.

But alas! the fury of Harold's attacks was beginning to exhaust him.

He became weaker and weaker, and, divided as his attention was by the desperate assault of so many assailants, in an unguarded moment he received a severe thrust in his side.

Almost at the same instant a blow upon his sword-arm nearly deprived him of its use.

Skill and valour, urged as they were by desperation, were now of no avail.

Weakened by loss of blood and pressed by so many powerful opponents the young soldier was upon the point of being borne to the ground.

Just then, however, a new and unexpected ally appeared upon the scene.

The new comer was an extraordinary creature, and looked more like the denizen of another world, being a stunted, hairy, and hideous dwarf.

He scudded forward with the rapidity of lightning, and, as if possessed with the strength of a Samson, darted upon Harold's principal assailant.

Twisting his long, muscular arms around his neck and body he gave him a bear-like hug that nearly drove all the breath out of his body, and thus rendered him utterly powerless. At the same time the dwarf's shrill and piercing shouts for assistance struck familiarly on the young soldier's ear.

The tread of feet was now heard advancing, but whether of friends or foes Harold knew not.

The unearthly cry and appearance of the dwarf had so completely thrown him off his guard that his opponents, taking advantage of the circumstance, made one furious effort ere the approaching aid could arrive, and stretched the gallant young soldier, apparently lifeless, upon the ground.

The triumph of the cowardly assassins was, however, of short duration.

They were attacked in turn, and it is scarcely necessary to say that the dwarf and his companions soon put the ruffianly abductors to flight.

But to all appearance their well-meant aid had come too late, for the young soldier lay upon the turf weltering in his blood.

By the directions of Othus, which was the name of the dwarf, a litter was formed from the rough branches of the neighbouring trees, and, the cloaks of some of the rescuing party having been spread over them, the wounded youth was laid upon the litter and as gently as possible carried from the spot.

The *cortége* proceeded in a southerly direction, under the guidance of the dwarf, and in the space of an hour arrived at what appeared to be the place of their destination.

It was a retired and sheltered spot, buried in the midst of many hills, in which a strikingly picturesque and apparently untenanted cottage reared its humble head.

But the signal of the dwarf soon caused the latch to be undone.

And a moment later the door of the cottage was opened by a sweet damsel, whose bright and sunny looks even in that light might have put to blush the rosy dawn of day.

A few hurried words were exchanged between Othus and the beauteous inmate of the hut, and Harold was then conveyed into the interior of the cottage.

The rescuing party were rewarded with a liberal supply of money and some words of caution from the dwarf, and were then dismissed.

There was an air of profound mystery in the whole proceeding, and the scene that now occurred did not derogate from the general character of the events of the night.

At the further end of the apartment the young soldier was extended, still apparently lifeless, upon the only bed the place could boast of.

Near the window, at the opposite extremity of the room, the charming and blushing maiden of the cottage stood trembling like an aspen leaf.

While the dwarf, having first ascertained that Harold was past the power of observing anything that took place, stood confronting her with a stern and steady gaze.

"Janet," Othus at length said, "this is none of my seeking. I would not have brought yonder wounded knight hither unless I had been compelled so to do. I owe no favour to him or any of his race, and if I could utter a prayer from these scorched and blasted lips it would be that he should never move hence alive."

The gentle girl trembled—as much at the manner as at the violent language of the wild, grotesque imp—and seemed to shrink with loathing from him.

The dwarf regarded her with a most peculiar and almost diabolical expression.

"Nay, maiden," he exclaimed, "shrink not thus from one who loves you. By the bright stars above my love is no more like that of mortal man than these crooked and distorted limbs resemble those of a human being. But the heart that beats within this compressed carcase, like the fierce struggles of the imprisoned lion, throbs with greater violence the more it is confined, and every throb it tells Janet, is a throb for thee!"

The unhappy girl covered her eyes with her hands and mournfully shook her head.

The dwarf approached nearer. Seizing her white and shapely arms in his long, misshapen fingers, he drew her hands from her pretty face and stared greedily and triumphantly upon it.

A faint sickness seemed to fall upon her as she closed her eyes, and with suppressed horror she turned shudderingly away.

"Janet," exclaimed the dwarf, and his shrill voice rose to its highest pitch, "Janet, I tell you this is vain. I love you, and by the foul fiend you shall be mine.

"The power that at present compels me to acts of kindness," he added, "yet which my heart rebels at, I know protects you, but the day will come, maiden, and it is not far distant, when that power shall be shaken to the ground.

"Meanwhile attend to what I say, since I must be the servant of another's will. See that you tend yonder knight till his accursed

A BAND OF SOLDIERS BURST IN UPON THE CONSPIRATORS.

wounds be healed, and mind that there be no foolish passages of maudling fondness betwixt you and yonder would-be gallant churl.

"Look upon him as one you will never meet on earth again, for assuredly ye shall not, and remember that although Othus the dwarf may be absent his eye is still upon you—his ear open to your slightest word. Remember, therefore, and beware."

The dwarf turned to leave the cottage, muttering to himself as he went—

"Yes, yes, but I would that the fool were bound to me by the ties of gratitude alone."

Janet, the very image of despair, gazed after him as if his absence were a great relief.

The beauteous girl, although in other respects a sensible and enlightened being for her rank in life, was not free from the terrible superstition of the age.

So, while she could not help inwardly loathing and regarding with a species of horror the malevolent being who had dared to address her in the language of affection, she had a trembling fear of offending him, and, under the influence of that powerful bane, in many instances blindly followed whatever orders it was the dwarf's pleasure—for the time—to issue.

The power of Othus, too, might be accounted for by his unlimited exercise of that influence which strong minds invariably possess over those of a weaker character.

It was, accordingly, amid the existence of varied feelings, but with a heartfelt wish to do good uppermost in her mind, that the maiden proceeded to discharge the duty which had been assigned her.

In it she was ably assisted by an experienced leech, who, despatched probably by the dwarf, soon arrived at the cottage.

And ere long Janet had the satisfaction of seeing that the joint efforts of herself and the man of medicine had partially recovered the handsome stranger from the fearful state of stupor into which he had fallen.

CHAPTER XXXII.

THE MIDNIGHT JOURNEY ON THE RIVER—THE PIRATE SHIP—EVELYN PLEADS FOR GUY FAWKES'S LIFE—THE SEVERED BONDS—A LEAP FOR LIFE—AT THE MERCY OF THE WAVES.

THE boat containing Guy Fawkes and the dancing-girl continued its progress down the river.

The boatmen rowed in silence, and the light barge, aided by the tide, shot over the turbid stream gallantly.

Dark was the sky, but fretted with the purest stars. The winking cottage lights shone here and there over the broad Surrey fields, and London, although the hour was late, had many a glimmering beam issuing from its huge masses of buildings, where high revels were being held.

The sharp night wind curled the rushing waves as the boat dipped among them and made the white spray dance from the moving oars.

"What boat?" shouted the watch on old London Bridge as they darted under one of its peaked arches.

"Cast thy buff doublet, Charlie, swim after us, and we will answer thee," replied the commander of the party, laughing at the puckered cheeks of the shivering guard, who stood with his clumsy musquetoon in his arms by the lantern on the parapet. "Marry, my bold nighthawk! come hither, and we will reckon with thee."

"What boat?" repeated the guard, his eyes half-shut with cold, and satisfied with doing his literal duty, which was to challenge every boat that passed after curfew.

Guy Fawkes was half inclined to call out to the useless functionary, but a moment's reflection showed him that to escape thus from his captors would place him perchance in worse hands.

"What boat?" reiterated the guard in the distance, faithfully discharging the duty he was paid for, the answer to the question being the duty of those he challenged.

No notice, however, was taken of his question, and long after the boat was out of musket-shot a faint "What boat?" was still heard in the extreme distance.

On the pirates sped, London was passed, and the lights of Greenwich Palace were becoming more distinctly visible, when a long-hulled, taper-sparred vessel was seen floating sleepily on the stream under the shadow of the land.

The boat glided to her side.

A low whistle was heard from the sailor on watch, bulwarks were opened, ladders were lowered, and the boat's crew sprang up the dark sides of the vessel.

Guy Fawkes stood upon the deck, and the dancing-girl in her old attitude was already seated at his feet.

"Now, my fair bird, you are nested rarely," said the commander of the pirates, addressing Evelyn, and gently raising her from her drooping posture. "Get thee below, sweet one. I have a rough reckoning to make with your companion. Nay, you will not go! You have then some whispered word, some gentle souvenir for him who cheered you in the absence of your mate.

"But what is this?" he added, intently regarding Guy Fawkes. "By Heaven! I thought I knew the face. It is the dark-browed knave for whose rescue I had well-nigh worn shackles in a Spanish mine! Go to, go to! It was at your prayer I saved him. Your warm words, your honeyed kisses, then, were false, your——"

"No, no, no!" cried Evelyn, with a cry of agony, springing up and confronting the speaker. "You are a man, and people say you are a bold one! Is it manly to crush——"

"Crush thee!" shouted the pirate, furiously. "By the foul fiend you are an adder, with a smooth skin and a sting of hell! I have been duped and fooled! Throw the black doublet into the river!"

"Hold!" shrieked the dancing-girl. "I am your slave, and will yield—nay, I will—love you—obey your slightest wish, but spare one who has never injured you, and whose only crime was the gratitude I bore him for a kindly act."

"Gratitude! You are apt. Go to—you love this dark-browed devil. Gratitude! Women seek not the haunts of privacy to tell that they are grateful. The king holds one rival, and I hold the other, with his arms pinioned on my deck. Men of action deal fairly, false one, and plead for pardon instead of love.

"Saint Mary!" added the pirate, "this wind pierces to the bones. Get thee below—there is a nest for you there that the daintiest dame might recline in, and robes that a queen might wear. Come, lads, pitch our prisoner into the river!"

Two or three of the ruffianly crew promptly advanced towards Guy Fawkes to execute the order of their chief, when Evelyn sprang forward, and, again throwing herself at the pirate's feet, uttered passionate entreaties for mercy.

But they were unheeded by the fury-roused chief.

The men were sullen with their cold watch, and in no humour to be stayed in their purpose.

Guy Fawkes was already seized, when the dancing-girl, seeing all hope of forbearance over, suddenly snatched a dagger from the pirate's girdle.

Then, quick as the lightning's flash, she bounded towards Guy Fawkes, cut the cords that pinioned him, and the next moment his arms were free.

Until now Guy Fawkes had been passive. He had made up his mind to die, but hope at once burst upon him, and the active energies of his nature returned.

The first man that had seized him lay stunned upon the deck from a terrific blow of the conspirator's fist, and ere the others had recovered from their surprise Guy Fawkes dived head foremost into the river, and was swimming for the shore.

A cry of baffled rage burst from the pirate ship.

The report of a fire-arm was heard by him above the rushing sounds of water in his ears, then another and another.

But still he made for the shore, the hissing bullets making the water white around him.

The distance, however, was considerable, and the tide was strong. Although a stout swimmer, he felt himself swept away by the violence of the current, and drawn into the middle of the stream.

Guy Fawkes was rapidly wafted out of gunshot of the pirate ship, and found himself, when the first shock was over, struggling with the cold rushing water far from the land—the banks on either side hidden by the darkness.

The sullen surge-like sound of the deep current was alone heard, and the dark swelling waves around him were the only objects his eyes fell upon.

Again and again he strove to make for the bank, but the rapid swirl of the current bore him on in sportive mockery. The rough bursts of wind fretted the rolling waters and obstructed the strenuous efforts which he made.

There was no light but that which the stars gave.

Once or twice Guy Fawkes turned his eyes towards them, and saw them twinkling afar in the dark sky, with a feeling that cannot be described.

He became faint. The icy chillness of the water numbed his limbs, and his saturated clothes seemed to have the weight of lead.

He struggled more and more feebly.

Strange, unearthly noises rang in his bewildered ears—fantastic shapes and lights danced and flickered before his strained and aching eyes.

His brain seethed and reeled, and he felt himself sinking down, down into those dark, cold, terrible depths below.

* * * * * *

Many days elapsed before Sir Harold Rookby awoke to a sense of the situation in which he was placed, and even when he did so his perceptions were fearfully bewildered and confused.

He found himself in a rudely-formed bed. His wounds had been severe and attended with high feverish symptoms, which left him in a state of extreme weakness.

In vain he tried to arrange his ideas. His remembrance of the past was very faint, but he had the recollection of a form that was like a pleasing dream, for it was fair as fancy's brightest picture.

But ever and anon the remembrance of another shot across his mind, and it frowned like the demon of the wilderness when a bright angel sheds a passing light athwart his dreary dwelling.

CHAPTER XXXIII.

THE COTTAGE IN THE GLEN—THE KNIGHT AND THE WILD MOUNTAIN ROSE—A DAINTY NURSE— LOVE UNBIDDEN.

WITH youth and a good constitution on his side Harold Rookby fast recovered his usual strength and spirit.

Drawing aside the thick curtains that encompassed his bed Sir Harold perceived that the sole inhabitant of the hut, except himself, was a sweet looking, comely girl, whose dress bespoke her to belong to the better rank of burgher's daughters.

When the young soldier first spoke to her the deep blush that overspread her cheek and neck told how little she had been accustomed to such addresses.

But every attempt to extract information from her as to where he was or to whom he had been indebted for his life was in vain.

When he spoke on these subjects she pressed her finger upon her rosy lips, but her dimpled smile, disclosing two rows of even, pearly-white teeth, and her laughing blue eyes, in which a mingled look of archness and kindness dwelt, told him that he had little to dread from his imprisonment.

She would turn playfully away, and, carolling a light air, resume her wonted occupation, till some question of the wounded knight again called her to his side.

Janet would sit for hours singing plaintive ballads, in a voice of enchanting sweetness, or listen to her companion's tales of the olden time, wherewith he would seek to beguile the weariness of his confinement.

On these occasions Janet would gaze upon his handsome countenance till every other feeling seemed lost in admiration. Her rosy fingers would forget to ply her task, and the unfinished tapestry would remain untouched upon her knee.

But when Sir Harold asked if she was the sole inhabitant of the cottage a deep tinge of scarlet overspread the maiden's cheek, and shaking back her clustering ringlets she would change the subject.

Once, when the maiden had left him for a few minutes, Sir Harold thought he could perceive through the half-opened door of the room the long bare arms and huge misshapen head of Othus the dwarf.

But the door was instantly closed, and although Harold heard the voices of several persons whispering he could not distinguish the subject of their conversation.

Upon this occasion a tear stood in Janet's eyes when she returned to the young soldier.

But Sir Harold spoke, and, like an April shower, the tears gave place to a soft and sunny smile.

When the young soldier had nearly regained his strength he was impatient to be gone.

The image of Violet, her mysterious disappearance, and the position of peril in which she undoubtedly was, filled him with a feverish anxiety to hasten to her aid.

But how to proceed, even were he at liberty, was a question he could not solve.

Another subject likewise gave him considerable uneasiness.

His arms and armour were nowhere to be seen, and, when pressed upon this last subject, his lovely nurse at length told him they were in safe keeping, and that when he was perfectly restored to health and strength they would be returned to him.

With this assurance Sir Harold was obliged to rest satisfied.

Having entirely recovered, the young soldier was allowed to walk occasionally in the enclosure by which the hut was surrounded.

The cottage was situated in a wild and solitary glen, the broken and precipitous banks of which precluded the possibility of approach from either side. A wild, brawling stream leapt from rock to rock, and foamed from crag to crag, as though rejoicing in its liberty.

No other dwelling appeared in sight, nor did a human foot ever seem to tread the solitary and sequestered glen.

In his walks Sir Harold was generally accompanied by his fair attendant, whose artless beauty and simplicity had already strongly impressed her in his favour.

It was a strange sight to see the stalwart knight leaning on the arm of the graceful, tender maiden, which was always ready to help support his faltering steps.

But this soon changed, and the sturdy young soldier became the supporter of the delicate trembler, who at times appeared almost to cling to his side.

She had been kind—more than kind to him. His every want, almost his every wish, she had anticipated, and in the fulness of his heart the young knight had repaid her devotion with equal kindness.

Impelled by a sense of gratitude, and a knowledge of all he owed her, there was a softness in the young soldier's manner towards the maiden that irresistibly made its way to her heart, and the simple guileless girl already more than half loved the youthful knight.

It was the joy of her life to wander by his side and listen to him when he spoke.

Eagerly did she drink in his gay tales of lords and ladies, and court belles and beaux, with wondering ears. But when he talked of depart-

ing she would remind him of his wounds, and, turning towards him with an innocent and confiding look, beseech him not to think of going till they were completely healed.

Then, as her eye caught his, she would blush deeply, and turn aside her head to conceal the starting tears.

Sir Harold smiled at her emotion, and pressing her hand in his vowed to remember the sweet maiden who had wrought him so kind a service.

In one of these playful moods the young soldier slipped a ring of some value upon the maiden's finger, while talking to her within the cottage, and told her to wear it in remembrance of him whose life she had been so instrumental in saving.

It was set with turquoises, and Sir Harold laughingly said—

"When I cease to think of thee with gratitude and affection, sweet Janet, the colour of these stones will change."

The maiden blushed and trembled. She fondly pressed the precious gift to her rosy lips. Then her eyes filled with tears, and, as if afraid she had done too much, she laid her face upon his shoulder, exclaiming in an ecstasy of emotion—

"Forgive me, Sir Knight, for we shall not soon meet again!"

Sir Harold, in his most winsome tones, strove to reassure her, but in vain.

The pearly tears still continued to flow, and to all his inquiries he could only obtain the sobbing answer—

"Oh, do not, do not ask me! but believe it to be true!"

Her pretty head still reclined upon his shoulder, and her soft, comely form rested in his arms.

Her liquid-blue eyes glanced upwards, and, meeting Harold's, she seemed for the first time to be conscious of the impropriety of her situation, and sought to withdraw from his ardent embrace.

The young knight stooped and just touched her pure white forehead with his lip.

A deep blush overspread her beauteous face and neck, and rose mantling to her temples as she cast her eyes upon him, this time with a half reproachful glance, and, disengaging herself from his arms, turned away and pretended to occupy herself with some domestic duties.

The young soldier gazed for an instant at her light and graceful form, and then silently leaving the cottage proceeded thoughtfully towards the extremity of the enclosure by which the dwelling was surrounded.

It was plain to the young knight that he had made an impression upon the heart of the gentle Janet—a very unwished-for impression upon his part.

No idea of dishonour towards a being so pure, so innocent, and confiding, ever entered Sir Harold's mind, but even had his affections not been otherwise engaged the difference of their rank precluded the possibility of their ever being united, and he now felt it to be imperative upon him to depart from the cottage on the very first opportunity that presented itself.

Occupied by such reflections the young soldier had nearly reached the termination of the enclosure, and had entered an almost impenetrable clump of trees, when the well-known figure of Othus, the dwarf, suddenly burst upon his view.

It started from behind the trunk of a broad and gnarled oak, and waved its long hairy arms on high, as if it had been the evil spirit of the woods warning a benighted traveller from its path.

The young soldier was startled by the suddenness of the apparition.

But, quickly recovering himself, he sprang forward, and at once seized the dwarf with a firm and determined grasp.

But the creature seemed to be endowed with strength and agility beyond those of a human being, and with apparently slight exertion he shook off the knight in a manner that convinced him force with a being so formed would be useless.

The dwarf tossed back his huge jolter-head, and, opening his immense jaws for a few seconds, rent the air with shouts of most discordant laughter.

But at length he spoke, and the tones of his voice broke upon the ear in the same shrill, inharmonious sounds, which Harold had now heard twice before.

"What oh, Sir Knight, and you would tilt it with Othus the dwarf! Put on thy armour of tempered steel, don thy bacinet, and, with a gisarme in hand, thou may'st run a chance. Without them thou wouldst fare but scurvily. But wherefore dost thou set upon thy friend?"

"In good sooth, Sir Dwarf," answered Harold, "I know not as yet in what thou hast proved my friend, for thou wouldst coop me up here till I lose that which is dearer far than either life or limb."

"Nay, good Sir Knight," replied the dwarf. "It is that thou may'st recover that which is dearer to thee than life or limb that thou hast been somewhat constrained of late. I wot well that I needed not to have preserved thee from the assassin stroke of Sir Sidney Wildbrook and his gang to let thee run another tilt ere the gangrene of thy former wounds have yet been covered o'er."

"What! my preserver?" exclaimed Harold, as the recollection of past scenes rushed dream-like upon his mind. "My preserver! Nay, then, a thousand thanks, Sir Dwarf, and I pray thee to forgive the rudeness of my first assault."

"And I pray of thee, Sir Knight," rejoined the dwarf, "to forgive the rudeness of its reception, the which, I opine, was the rougher of the two."

The knight smiled.

"And Sir Sidney," continued the young soldier, "was the perpetrator of this base outrage?"

Othus nodded.

"'Twas, then, as I suspected," pursued Sir Harold, "and dearly indeed shall he pay for it. By all the saints in the calendar I——"

"Swear not at all," cried the shrill voice of the dwarf. "But now thou knowest me for thy friend, listen to that I would impart to thee. Thou must hie thee hence."

"But how shall I accomplish that?" inquired the young soldier, eagerly.

"Hark patiently," returned the dwarf. "With man I have little or nought to do; with their manners and customs I have less.

Brought into the world a mis-shapen and distorted thing, I am made the laughing-stock and scorn of the meanest varlet that boasts a straighter form or limbs.

"I shun the haunts of my fellow-men with loathing and contempt. I meet with no kindness at their hands, and in return they meet with none from me. But when this foolish heart would do a service it must be done in its own way, and at its own time, or remain undone. So choose thee now, Sir Knight."

Sir Harold gazed upon the strange creature with newly awakened feelings of interest and compassion.

In the mis-shapen and grotesque being before him he thought he could trace all the workings of a heart whose warmest affections had been repressed because scorned by those on whom they would have been bestowed.

The dwarf observed the emotion of the young soldier and his harsh features softened for a single moment.

As if ashamed, however, of having betrayed a symptom of human feeling, he turned away, and his wonted expression was immediately resumed.

His tone, however, had lost much of its bitterness when he again addressed the knight.

"Now, Sir Knight, as I have already told thee, thou must forthwith hie thee hence. With the means I will provide thee, and, leaving this place, thou must proceed straightway to the shrine of our Lady of Walsingham. There thou wilt learn somewhat of the Lady Violet, but seek not to approach the preceptory of Sir Sidney Wildbrook unharnessed in thy Milan steel, or it may fare ill with thee. This recreant knight dare not harm thee in open guise, but in secret he would slay thee, for thou art as gall and wormwood unto his heart, so look to thyself in that, young sire. And now follow me."

As he spoke the dwarf darted away with the rapidity which characterised his movements, and with which Sir Harold found difficulty in keeping pace.

Othus threaded the mazes of the wood with incredible dexterity, and through many intricate windings and passes at last brought the young soldier to a spot where a large rock, overhanging the earth at the height of many feet, and surrounded by trees and shrubs, formed a natural cavern of considerable extent.

On a rough bench, hewn from the solid rock at the farther extremity of the cave, Sir Harold observed a heap of arms and armour.

The dwarf approached, and, selecting various pieces, presented them to the young knight, who instantly recognised them to be his own.

His trusty sword felt like the hand of a familiar friend within his grasp, and as he once more arrayed himself in his burnished breast and thigh-plates, which bore the dint of many a hard-fought day, he felt a sense of security that he had not enjoyed for weeks.

Leaving the cavern, they continued to push on through the wood in an opposite direction to that by which they had entered.

Toiling up a steep ascent on the opposite side, they now stood gazing on the wooded banks and brawling stream far down below.

As the young soldier's eyes wandered unconsciously over the scene they were arrested by the appearance of a figure in white seated at some considerable height on the opposite bank.

Harold at once recognised the maiden of the cottage, and she, too, seemed to be aware of the recognition, for she waved her kerchief in the air, and, as if she had only waited for that last look—that parting sign—darted into the thicket and was instantly lost to view.

The dwarf observed the action, but no voice gave utterance to his feelings.

He turned hurriedly away, and approaching the outskirts of the wood on which they now stood, whistled a shrill and peculiar note.

This was soon after answered by a similar whistle, coming from no great distance.

The dwarf again impressed his cautions upon the young soldier, and again urged him to make his way speedily towards Walsingham. There, he assured Sir Harold, he would hear news of the Lady Violet and meet with aid and assistance.

At this juncture the attention of Harold was arrested by the heavy tread of a war-horse close at hand.

He turned and beheld his own steed, in fresh and excellent condition, led by a ragged, keen-eyed lad.

The young knight sprang forward in an ecstasy of joy, and the noble animal neighed with pleasure as he received the caresses of his delighted master.

Sir Harold then turned to where he had left Othus, and opened his lips to again assure him of his gratitude.

But no dwarf was there—no footstep sounded upon his ear—and the leaves of the trees waved in melancholy cadence, as if the recesses of the wood had never been disturbed.

The young soldier, somewhat alive to the superstition of the age, felt a chilling sensation of awe flit across his mind, but it was awe mingled with curiosity.

He therefore turned towards the ragged equerry who had led his horse, and whom he rightly judged to be a creature of the dwarf, in the hope of extracting information from him.

But he too had vanished.

Vexed and disappointed, the youthful knight mounted his steed, determined to follow the dwarf's advice of forthwith hieing over hill and dale to Sir Sidney Wildbrook's estate in famed Walsingham.

CHAPTER XXXIV.

A FRIEND IN NEED—A DESPERATE VENTURE—THE ATTACK UPON THE PIRATE SHIP—AN OLD ENEMY SENT TO HIS LAST ACCOUNT.

As if by magic the hollow, rushing sound in Guy Fawkes's ears aroused the instinct of self-preservation, and he fought with the merciless torrent again.

Suddenly his breast touched some floating object, and he grasped it with all his remaining strength.

It was a narrow plank, which had drifted from the beach. Then eagerly he clutched at it, and it supported him.

The lights of Greenwich Palace were now falling in long quivering streaks on the dancing river, and he looked upon them with what he deemed his dying gaze.

The sound of music also reached him, for a grand bal masque was being held at the palace,

mingled with the dull murmur of the rapid stream, as he clung to his frail support.

Then, to his boundless joy, he discovered a boat—a duke's barge—crossing the river, and advancing towards him.

He tried to shout, but his voice failed him. He kept his eyes fixed upon the boat—at one moment it seemed as if he were seen, at another the boat's head turned away.

Again he tried to shout—the sound was feeble, but it appeared that it was heard.

The boatmen rested upon their oars, and a voice which seemed familiar to him hallooed in answer to the challenge.

After a short pause the boat began to move slowly forward.

Two men holding torches were now stationed at the bow, and Guy Fawkes saw to his despair that it was leaving him.

At length, weakened by his supreme efforts, and exhausted with the struggle, his head drooped in that prostration of nature which seeks for death.

A dreadful lethargy began to steal over his mind, his sight grew dim, and as the icy water gurgled around his head he ceased to heed it.

He felt the languor of ebbing life, and dreamy visions came, as if, instead of being tossed like a sinking weed, he had been sleeping on a bed of down.

He saw the sunny bank which, when a boy, he had happily reposed upon—the sweet, green hill-top—the old, mossy church-spire, rising above the blue, misty woods, with the rooks floating idly round—and the clear, musical streamlet, that had murmured at his feet.

Voices, too—the kind familiar tones of long-forgotten days were heard again—but the well-beloved sounds grew fainter and the visions waxed dim.

Nature rallied for a moment and consciousness returned. Reality now seemed a dream.

He strove to awake from it—to shake it off.

He struck out his numbed arms on the cold flood that was overwhelming him, in an agony of horror, which was more bitter than death.

At that moment he heard again the measured sound of oars, and his dimmed eyes could discern a faint stream of light shooting and widening near him.

A loud shout followed, the light increased, the dash of the oars became louder, and he felt himself grasped by a strong arm, as the bows of a boat glided by his side.

Guy Fawkes had been drawn to it, and it bore him along.

More hands aided him, and, dizzy with rapid changes of feeling, he found himself on board a barge manned by some twenty men.

"Saint Mary!" exclaimed a familiar voice, "this is master Guy—row men, row! he is exhausted and hardly breathes. Let us but reach the Jolly Trooper, and, by St. George, a flagon of spiced wine will make his heart beat lightly, for mine host can mix it well."

"By'r lady, 'tis a cold night to swim in. Row, I say, row! Am I not your commander, you lazy varlets?" added Ralph Roley (for he it was) authoritatively, as the creaking boat made the cleft waters boil again.

Guy Fawkes had sunk down weary and half dead. Honest Ralph supported him and continued to cheer him, and to excite the men to renewed exertions.

GUY FAWKES

Or Gunpowder, Treason, and Plot.

GALLANTLY HE FACED THE ARMED THRONG.

No. 9.

"This is a bitter night, in Heaven's name, to buffet with the Thames, but mine host of the Jolly Trooper hath ever a blazing hearth and goodly drinks to warm the sinking heart, and make the chilled blood mantle kindly. There is not a butt of Rhenish rolled into his cellar that is not blessed by a priest, who drinks the first cup for conscience sake, that there may be no poison in it.

"Good, my master—comfort ye. Yet you make no moan, but bear it bravely. Ha! I can see the lights. Hasten, for the love of the virgin, or his limbs will stiffen. This may be a king's councillor for aught we know," added Ralph, in an undertone to the boatmen, "and if he die on our hands we may go hang ourselves, for not one of us will live till Shrovetide. Row, ye lusty varlets—well done, stout knaves, well done! Now—softly, softly."

The barge was brought alongside of a bridle path leading from the shore to a small hostelry, the same from which Guy Fawkes, with the aid of Leo, had escaped when in the power of Oliver Blackstock and his creatures, the lights of which shone brightly in the distance.

To this place Guy Fawkes was conducted by Ralph, who first threw a dark cloak over his former master, to avoid detection, which he knew would be as bad for Guy Fawkes as the fate he had rescued him from.

"Now, canst thou call to mind, good Master Fawkes," said Ralph, as they proceeded together to the inn, the boat having left the place on landing them, "that we two met even here at a former time, the night thou wottest, when we were taken down the river, and I was thrown into it, bound neck and heel, like a boar pig dead of the pest, rather than a living Christian man. Trust me, I have not forgotten it!"

"Let us push on," said Guy Fawkes, faintly. "I am weak, and my limbs tremble under me. A brief rest, and I will guide you to where we shall both be revenged. Do you carry pistols?"

Ralph's countenance fell.

"I knew it!" he exclaimed. "I knew it would be thus. But, by my grandam's virtue, I am a man of peace. Even though I be a yeoman of the guard, and wish all heretics in the devil's net, I would strike a shrewd and goodly blow for thee, Master Fawkes, were my ears cropped for it. But, I pray you bring me not into trouble, for I am a simple man. So the pope and the king agree I am content, and leave my creed to their care in all humility, but as long as I have my own way I will neither make nor meddle with such dangerous matters."

"Nay," said Guy Fawkes, "I do not ask you to do aught that you may not avow tomorrow in the palace courtyard. It was wrong of you," he muttered, after a pause, "to let your boat leave us."

"I durst not detain it," said Ralph. "We lost much time in searching for you, and a party waits for it on the opposite side of the river."

"There are many yeomen at Greenwich Palace who would doubtless assist you."

"I think not," replied Ralph; "one half is on duty and the other is drunk. Saint Mary! it is ball night."

As he spoke they reached the door of the inn, which was lighted up at every window, and loud sounds issued from it.

The noise of the wine-cup and trencher, the bustle of the kitchen, the song and laugh of the guest-chambers, the din of voices, of gaiety, jest, and controversy, all mingled their babel clamour, as though it were carnival time.

Pulling his looped hat over his brow, and drawing his cloak closer round him, Guy Fawkes, followed by Ralph, entered the inn kitchen, which was thronged with guests.

Such was the bustle around them that they had to wait several moments ere they could catch the eye of the stout host, as, with a joyous professional smile on the lower and utter confusion on the upper part of his rubicund visage, he moved his round, aproned figure about from place to place.

Catching sight of the jolly yeoman and his companion, he pushed his way through the throng, exclaiming—

"Right welcome, worshipful Master Roley. I cry you mercy, but does your companion wear a mask? How fares my sovereign lord the king?"

"Marry! his gracious health," he added, "has been drunk a hundred times within my poor house to-day by, the chalk-scores on the wall. I pray you let it be reported to his majesty, for I trow I am in bad countenance with the court, because I serve Protestant and Catholic alike with equal respect."

"Now, in that," said Ralph, "you have done well—honest——"

"Prithee peace," interrupted Guy Fawkes, impatiently. "Ha! you know me," he continued, as the innkeeper started back in surprise. "You will not betray me. But let me enter a chamber where there will be no eye on me, where I may cast me down for a few moments, and bring me a flagon of warm wine, for, weak as I am, I must needs go forth again."

"Aye, in sober truth, you seem sorely in need of rest," said the kindly host.

"My time presses," returned Guy Fawkes. "So no more of this, as it needs must be."

The landlord said no more, but conducted him to an inner apartment, where a cheerful fire was blazing.

Divesting himself of his wet clothes, Guy Fawkes wrapped himself in a warm cloak, and threw himself down on the long dais by the hearth side, while his garments were drying.

The wine was quickly brought. He drank, and, in spite of his numbed and stiffened limbs, felt himself refreshed.

The warm blood again played freely in his veins. He arose, and attiring himself in his dry things he, all heedless of honest Ralph's remonstrances, called upon him to go forth.

The yeoman did not refuse. The landlord gave Guy Fawkes weapons, and conducted both by a back passage from the house, bewailing the hard fortunes of his whilom companion-in-arms.

"They say, Master Fawkes," said mine host, "that you are in league with a number of Catholic gentlemen to kill the king. Now, were it the first peer in England that said so under my roof-tree I would tell him that he lied!"

"Aye, marry, so also would I," said Ralph, stoutly, "for that I would never believe of Master Fawkes."

"That you are conspiring with your companions to bring about some measure of reform I can well understand," resumed the landlord, "but I will never believe you capable of the other vile charge. However, let me warn you, come not near Greenwich, where you are known. It is death to harbour you. Leave England. Your life here is not safe an hour, and even now methought a strange man that sat in the kitchen started when you passed him, as if he knew you. I pray you take good heed of——"

"Thanks, thanks, my good host," returned Guy Fawkes, waving his hand. "You have done me fair service to-night, and if I live I will requite it."

He passed out and made again for the river side, followed by Ralph, who moved with evident reluctance.

"I am a quiet man, Master Guy Fawkes, and am now the husband of sweet Dolly Rosebud. Moreover, I am a yeoman of the king's guard. I pray you, for the love of heaven, lead me not into heresy or sedition."

"Fear not, good Ralph," returned Guy Fawkes. "It is a true man's quarrel, and against knaves, with whom you, as well as I, have a reckoning to settle."

"I would willingly leave this reckoning till another hour," muttered Ralph, ruefully, "for I much dread it bodes me no good. Here am I, again on a blind errand, and may thank Heaven if I escape with no other danger than a broken head. I would give ten silver James's had I the wit to run away."

"By Heavens, you stir not from my side!" cried Guy Fawkes, fiercely. "It is rough courtesy, but what a piebald varlet art thou to shame your good deeds by such words as these!"

"I would willingly strike a blow in your quarrel, Master Fawkes," said Ralph, embarrassed, "for I have received many kindnesses at your hands, but, in honest truth, I like not this business. You were ever fond of desperate hazards, and held life too cheap for many days."

"Do you mark that long, dark vessel under the shadow of the bank?" said the conspirator, pointing towards the object in question.

"I do. But what of that?"

"It is at present poorly manned, but those on board are old friends of ours. You remember the men that threw you into the river?"

"Shall I ever forget them?"

"They are there," said Guy Fawkes. "So let us hasten. I doubt if there is anyone on board we need fear to meet."

"Under favour, not so fast," said Ralph. "I will back to Greenwich and get assistance."

"It is too late. Besides, I should be detected. No—we must do it ourselves."

"But—good Heavens—why this haste?"

"There is a girl on board whom I will rescue or die in the attempt!" exclaimed Guy Fawkes, determinedly. "She has been taken there by force. We have lost much time at the inn. It is a full half-hour since I sprang from the vessel's side. Would I could see a boat."

"This is a venture which no wise man would take," said Ralph. "Two men, if they had the prowess of St. George himself, are no match for the crew of a vessel like that."

"The crew are on shore except a few, and we have both swords and pistols," urged Guy Fawkes, unmooring a small skiff that nodded on the full tide. "Let us on board—nay, pause not now. If you hesitate I go alone."

"This is sheer madness," remonstrated Ralph, stoutly. "There are lights enow in the ship to show that there are more on board than you reckon on. Would I had asked some of those revellers to accompany us. Good Master Fawkes, bethink you awhile."

Here a loud, piercing shriek was heard from the ship.

"I will save her at any cost!" cried Guy Fawkes, springing into the dancing skiff.

"Hold!" cried Ralph. "By my Dolly's blue eyes, but I will e'en join you in the venture, though it is a desperate one."

"And, by my halidome, look!" resumed the worthy yeoman, "here is my own barge. A few dozen strokes of the oars will bring us to her side!"

Ralph stepped hastily into the skiff. They seized the oars, and worked vigorously at them. In a few minutes they were on board the yeoman's barge.

"Row for that vessel moored by the bank!" shouted Guy Fawkes, furiously, standing up in the boat all heedless of detection.

Ralph seconded the order, and the boatmen pulled lustily towards the pirate vessel.

The barge's torches had been put out, the night was dark, and the restless sounds of the fretting wind drowned the noise of their oars.

They reached the vessel unperceived. No watch seemed to be on deck, and Guy Fawkes at once sprang up the vessel's side.

He was followed instantly by Ralph—still no one appeared to oppose them.

The noise of boisterous revelry broke from under the fore part of the deck, and the clamour of voices showed how wild and fruitless the attempt of two men would have been to have attacked such a body.

Sternward there was less noise, but there, too, were evidences of revelry.

The cabin door was open, and through it and the long iron-guarded window Guy Fawkes caught a glimpse of the interior of this part of the vessel.

The cabin was gorgeously furnished.

Rich hangings of crimson velvet, embroidered in gold, between which plates of burnished silver multiplied the numerous lights, were hung around the sides, whilst soft couches and ottomans covered with leopard skin were placed here and there. Quaintly-shaped instruments and crooked Moorish scimitars were also suspended from the walls.

The board was covered with luxury—choice fruits and richest wines, in vessels of gold, set with rare gems. Two swarthy boys, in the dress of Moorish pages, waited on the pirate and his beautiful captive, who sat some distance from him.

Evelyn looked as if she had been weeping. A gay robe lay, as if tossed from her, and priceless jewels glittered before her on the table.

The pirate chief looked flushed and angry.

"I pledge thee yet again, my fair one," said he, "and may this wayward humour cease anon. You shrink from me, and scream like an unweaned babe when I would draw you to my side.

"You spurn my presents—eat not, drink not. Now, mark me, you are false as water and full of art as a courtly dame. But look around you and consider where you are. I am in no mood to be ruffled longer. Join me in this festive hour—smile, pledge me in the cup, and twine you to my side."

"Come," he continued, caressingly, "smooth that sullen brow—be false as you are frail, and look as if you loved me. Nay, you will not. Then, by Satan! I must needs teach thee a lesson in the art of love."

He seized her roughly as he spoke.

The dancing-girl struggled wildly, but her frenzied shriek was only echoed by a more boisterous shout of mirth from those in the fore part of the vessel.

Guy Fawkes darted at once to the cabin.

The pirate, with a bitter smile, wound his strong arm round the shrinking girl, while with his other hand he was in the act of raising the wine-cup, when a startled cry from the pages made him turn.

He sprang furiously up, and threw back his thick black hair from his forehead, as if his eyes deceived him.

The next instant, however, he tore down a sword from the wall and shouted lustily to his ruffianly crew.

But other sounds—the sharp detonation of a matchlock, a cry of alarm, and the deadly ring of steel—warned the pirate that his vessel was attacked in another quarter.

Maddened with rage, heated with wine, and thwarted thus in a loving hour, he met Guy Fawkes with the fury of a tiger bearded in its den.

"Have at thee, dog!" hissed the pirate, while the white froth flew from his lips.

He made a furious thrust, which Guy Fawkes with difficulty parried.

Another and another followed, with reckless and rapid force.

Guy Fawkes was weak and ill—a burning fever was already in his veins—he felt his right arm was feeble, and called out to Evelyn to fly, but she refused to do so.

A few more rapid passes and Guy Fawkes was struck down and disarmed.

With a cry of savage satisfaction the pirate knelt over him.

His knee was on his enemy's breast, and he shortened his sword to strike. Guy Fawkes thought his last moment had come, but the pirate's arm was grasped suddenly from behind.

It was the dancing girl who had interposed, uttering passionate appeals to the would-be destroyer for mercy.

The ruffian strove to shake her off, but the wildly-excited girl twined round him with the energy and strength of a serpent's folds.

This delay, however, was only momentary. The pirate flung the screaming girl violently from him, uttering a volley of fearful oaths, and a prayer trembled on the half-swooning conspirator's lips as the pirate, with frenzied determination, once more raised his weapon to dispatch him.

CHAPTER XXXV.

SIR SIDNEY AND HIS FAIR CAPTIVE—VIOLET PROVES HERSELF A HEROINE—THE ATTACK UPON THE CASTLE—A FEARFUL ENCOUNTER—FIRE.

WE must now conduct the reader to the princely residence of Sir Sidney Wildbrook.

If the exterior of that splendid building was gorgeous and magnificent in the extreme the interior was not less so.

But passing over the more public parts of it we must at present confine our attention to one of the private apartments.

The walls were decorated with the richest tapestry, and the floor was covered with a carpet of the same material.

The soft breeze stole through beautifully painted latticed windows mingled with the perfume of rare and lovely flowers. The chairs, table, and couches were heavy but magnificent, and bore evident traces of having come from a far distant land.

But perhaps the most striking piece of furniture in the room was a low ottoman, supported on the backs of four gilded tigers, whose glancing eyes, each formed of a single gem of surpassing beauty, gave somewhat of the appearance of life to the animals.

On this ottoman reclined the graceful, sylph-like form of a young and lovely female.

But the ineffable sadness of her sweet countenance, and the sorrow in her large and liquid eyes, ill accorded with the magnificence by which she was surrounded.

A slight noise at the door of the room caused the lady to start from her recumbent posture.

Next moment Sir Sidney Wildbrook entered the apartment.

He advanced with the air of one who knew that there was nobody near to dispute his will, and essayed to take the lady's hand, but she coldly and silently withdrew it.

"Be it so, lady," said Sir Sidney, "but the time allowed you has elapsed, and I now await your final answer to the proposal I have made."

"You have had it," said Violet—for she it was—calmly. "Sooner than wed a base and perjured knight—a foresworn and recreant champion of the faith he has disgraced—I would submit to be torn to pieces by wild horses."

"And is this, Violet," asked the knight—"is this all the return I am to meet with for the care that has been taken of you?'

"Care!" retorted Violet, in a tone of bitter contempt. "The care that the gorged wolf takes of the lamb it cannot yet devour. No, no, Sir Knight, I am not thus to be deceived. I thank you not," she pursued, "for forcibly tearing me from the protection of my friends and guardians. I thank you not for depriving a helpless orphan of the only solace that remained to her in life

"But know, Sir Sidney Wildbrook," she added, with impressive vehemence, "that if justice remain in this realm—if the sceptre our royal sovereign wields is aught but a child's bauble, you shall yet have cause to dearly rue your unmanly conduct."

"Yes," answered Sir Sidney, sneeringly. "When Lady Violet Hamlyn obtains speech of our gracious sovereign—— But a truce to this folly. Bethink you, fair Violet, of the wealth—the splendour—the magnificence that will be yours!

"By Heaven!" he resumed, with increased fervour, "I swear, Violet, that no wish of your heart shall remain ungratified! Speak but the word and gold and jewels shall be showered upon you like summer rain.

"The vast revenues of this princely retreat shall minister to your enjoyment—its servants shall be your slaves, and its proudest knight, who never bent the knee but to his Maker, will be willing to worship thee."

The beauteous girl looked at the dissolute knight for some minutes with a calm and fixed regard.

"I would not," she at length said, "seek the enjoyment of that wealth gained by base treachery, rapine, and murder. The boasted riches you possess, Sir Knight, are but the price of blood, and your most precious gems are all discoloured by its hue."

"By the rood, lady!" exclaimed Sir Sidney, frowning darkly, "you spurn my offered wealth as if it were the gold of some degraded artisan."

"All the splendour of the east," answered Violet, "could not bestow one hour of joy upon a crushed and broken heart. But," she added, with startling animation, "know, Sir Knight, that if offered to Violet Hamlyn, coupled with the conditions you propose, she would spurn it with utter loathing and contempt."

"Ah!" cried Sir Sidney, "this does indeed surpass belief—the gentle Violet transformed into a termagent! Well, well, be it so! I love you not the less for this show of spirit. But," and he advanced a step, "I would that it had been spared, for force must now——"

"Keep off!" exclaimed the terrified girl, as she sprang from the couch and darted to the opposite extremity of the apartment. "Off, villain! or by the eye of Heaven, which now looks down upon us, I vow to plunge this, not into your base heart, but into my own, for I would rather trust to His mercy than to yours!"

As she spoke she drew a glittering dagger from her breast and held it aloft in the air.

Her eyes sparkled, her bosom heaved, and the gentle girl appeared at once transformed into a being endowed with that fearless courage which desperation alone can bestow.

Sir Sidney gazed upon her, while she stood confronting him, with a keen and steady look.

"Away!" she commanded—"quit this apartment, unless, indeed, you would rather see it flooded with the blood of her you profess to love."

"Nay, Violet," said the knight, still regarding her with fixed attention, but not daring to move a step from the spot on which he stood, "this is downright madness. Throw aside that weapon and I promise you I will quit the room."

"I trust you not, Sir Knight," returned Violet. "Broken vows are well known to men of your calling, and some obliging father could, doubtless, soon be found to shrive your polluted conscience ere yonder sun shall set."

"Hear me, Violet," cried the knight—"hear me while I swear——"

"Swear not!" exclaimed Violet, interrupting him. "Add not another sin to the long list of crimes that already weigh upon your soul. You have heard my oath, and unless——"

"Well, well, Violet," said Sir Sidney, while a grim smile passed over his dark, handsome face, "so be it. You will have your way, and I now quit you in the hope that time may yet work a change upon your mind. Farewell. You will apprise me when you wish that I should again visit you."

As he spoke he proceeded towards the door. Violet watched his movements with a keen and suspicious glance.

When he had reached it he paused a moment and turned round.

"When you would summon your attendants," he observed, "sound yon silver call."

He pointed to a table in a distant part of the room.

Violet, thrown off her guard, turned for an instant to look in the direction to which he pointed.

With lightning speed Sir Sidney sprang upon her, like a tiger upon his prey, before she was aware of his intention, and wrenched the dagger from her hand.

"Ha, ha!" shouted the well-bred ruffian, as he cast the weapon away, while he held Violet with a grip that made her wince with pain. "Now, my brave maiden, now you are disarmed, and, by all the laws of battle, must yield to the victor's will."

The terrified girl cried aloud for mercy and for help.

"Shout away, my bonny heroine!" cried Sir Sidney, mockingly—"shout to your heart's content. But know, lady, that no human ear can hear you, and no human hand can aid you here. Fair means have failed, but now—now you are mine, and by Heaven——"

At that moment a loud and appalling yell, accompanied by a terrific crash, like thunder, broke upon the knight's startled ears.

Instantly seizing the terrified girl's wrist, he thrust her into a small ante-chamber, and turned the key upon her.

He had barely done so when the huge folding doors were thrown violently open, and a score of armed retainers, with an officer at their head, appeared before the startled noble.

"My lord!" exclaimed the officer, with energy, "the castle is besieged—your followers call on you to lead them against the enemy—your presence is required below."

"My presence shall be given when it suits myself," answered Sir Sidney, haughtily.

"Now, by the saints!" exclaimed Horlock, as he entered the apartment, "but this surpasseth belief. The fabric of his power trembles to its foundation, his life and honour are at stake, and he quietly talks of moving when it suits himself."

"What mean you, sirrah?" demanded Sir Sidney, in the cold, stern demeanour that marked his every word and action.

"Mean!" repeated the magician. "Gaze from yonder window and satisfy yourself."

The knight moved towards the casement, and, looking from it, beheld a sight that might have shaken stouter nerves than his.

The castle was surrounded by a strong division of the royal archers, headed by a herald, who had summoned the place to surrender in the king's name.

A motley crowd of artisans and idlers, and a large gathering of Freerangers, concealed by quaint disguises, led on by Will-o'-the Woods, attended in the rear, yelling and hissing as tho spirit moved them.

In the courtyard and on the ramparts of the castle a number of armed knights, retainers, and vassals of Sir Sidney were assembled, a stern and resolute defiance glowing upon the countenance of each.

Sir Sidney looked for some seconds upon the scene.

But, excepting a slight curling of the upper lip, not a muscle of the knight's countenance changed.

"Await me at your post," he said, turning to the captain of the guard.

The officer saluted, and, giving the order to march to his men, hastily left the spot.

When their footsteps had died away, without taking his gaze from the scene below, he addressed the magician, saying—

"I have looked for this for some time, and am prepared to meet it."

"The deuce you are !" exclaimed Horlock, in surprise. "Then methinks you had better to your post and head your knights."

"No," replied Sir Sidney, carelessly, "if the fools choose to fight let them do so. The royal mandate shall meet with no resistance from me."

"And your friends——"

"May go to the devil in their own way," said the knight, interrupting him. "My own safety I have cared for, and each of them may do the same."

"Then, by the rood ! Sir Knight," cried the magician, "I stick by you, for I doubt not, were I out of sight, the old proverb would be verified, and you would consign me to perdition with the rest."

"No," replied Sir Sidney, "I have further use for you, and cannot yet dispense with your services."

"And when you can," sneered the wizard, "I suppose I shall meet with little consideration or reward at your hands, but be turned from the door like a scurvy hound."

"Doubtless," laughed Sir Sidney, all heedless of the magician's dark and menacing look, as he proceeded to barricade the door of the apartment.

Having effected this he next released Violet, and led her, trembling like an aspen leaf, to the couch from which she had formerly risen, and on which he now replaced her almost passive form.

"Sweet maid," he said, mockingly, "remain there, for a time at least, and if nought else can be accomplished you shall accompany us in our retreat."

"Retreat !" exclaimed the magician. "Why the castle is surrounded, and all retreat cut off."

"Fool !" replied Sir Sidney, as he again advanced towards the window. "There are more ways of escaping from the preceptory of Wildbrook than you dream of.

"Ah !" he continued, as he once more gazed upon the scene below, "by Heaven, they mean to resist ! Then there is still a chance.

"No, no," he added, after a moment's hesitation ; "they may protract the blow for an hour or two, but more they cannot do."

A loud shout now burst from the assembled multitude, as a volley of huge stones and other missiles were hurled against the great gate.

This was succeeded by the rattling clang of hammers, as they rang tremendous blows upon it.

"Aye, bang away ! bang away !" exclaimed Sir Sidney, contemptuously. "The gates of Wildbrook were ne'er meant to be broken down by beardless churls."

"Beardless !" exclaimed the magician, who

had again joined him. "By the mass ! yonder fellow in the garb of the Prince of Darkness handles his long battle-axe with telling effect."

"'Tis the daring knave Will-o'-the-Woods," said Sir Sidney. "I know the bold miscreant despite his disguise, and mark him well. A day of reckoning with the hell-hound may yet come."

"And see," continued the magician, in an undertone, "your youthful and comely rival, Sir Harold Rookby, is amongst the churls !"

"Ha ! by the foul fiend !" yelled Sir Sydney, "this accounts for much. 'Tis he, then, that has sprung this train ! Let him look to it that the ruins crumble not on his own head."

"How the fool presses forward !" muttered Horlock, in the same low tone. "Would to Heaven yon barbed arrow had rung against his heart in place of rebounding from his helmet."

"Look, Horlock ! how is this ? The assailants pause. By St. Jago ! they retire !" cried Sir Sidney, triumphantly.

"No, no," said the magician, mockingly. "They only pause to receive instructions from their leader how to prosecute the siege afresh."

"True," answered Sir Sidney, with a fiendish smile. "There are two among them who would not yield to the devil himself."

The magician gave utterance to a blood-curdling laugh.

"By my faith," he exclaimed, "yon sturdy Freeranger chief now tries his eloquence on the archers—now he is at their head—he presses by your rival's side—they reach the gate—they place ladders against the wall, and he mounts with the agility of a squirrel. Down, down with them, brave lads ! There they go ! Well done—victory, victory !"

His cry of triumph at the temporary discomfiture of the assailants, however, was not of long duration.

All was still and silent for a few seconds—then another loud shout from without proclaimed a renewed attack.

"Ha !" cried the knight, as a volley of arrows from his own battlements whizzed through the air and stretched many of the attacking party lifeless upon the grass, "well shot, my brave knights. Another such volley or two, and King James shall have little left to boast of."

But the sight of their killed and wounded comrades inflamed the royal archers, and a flight of cloth-yard shafts soon told the knights that their armour of proof was not defence enough against the flower of England's bowmen.

A loud cheer from the besiegers proclaimed the success of this volley, and another flight was directed towards the battlements. Then the renewed crash of the hammers rang merrily against the gate.

"That's right, Jock Ironsides ! Go it, lad, go it !" shouted Will-o'-the-Woods, cheerily, scattering all before him.

"Bang away—bang away, boys !" roared another lusty voice. "The devil himself couldn't hold out long against that."

"By our lady, locks and bolts give way !" cried a third.

"A thousand curses ! The gate totters !" yelled Sir Sidney, furiously, as the massive portals shook, creaked, groaned, and finally burst open with a crash, like the thunder of many guns, amid the deafening roar of the triumphant assailants.

The motley crew—archers, men-at-arms, and rabble, all mingled together—now rushed yelling into the courtyard, and a fierce and sanguinary conflict ensued between them and the knights and vassals of Sir Sidney.

"Well struck, my brave Raymond," cried Sir Sidney, as he watched the progress of the savage encounter below. "Well struck! But it matters not. Should the miscreants be beaten, like the hounds they are, they will only rise like hornets, in a larger swarm on the morrow.

"So be it," mused the knight, "so be it. Let them fight it out. 'Tis some comfort at least to see so many of them biting the dust from which they spring. For the temple, ho!" he shouted, as the knights gained a momentary advantage.

But his voice was unheard amidst the mad, fierce din of the conflict.

"On, on, my brave Raymond! Down with them like chaff before the wind! Ha! by the fiend! they waver! they turn! they retreat!"

"Who? Who?" exclaimed the magician, eagerly. "The archers?"

"No!" roared Sir Sidney, clasping his hand to his head with passionate violence. "The recreant knights. Holy Mary! the temple's pride is gone!"

The last words were uttered in a subdued tone—the pride of the temple was indeed laid low, and her vanquished knights were compelled to retreat before the pressure of an overwhelming force.

A few brave spirits among the besieged soldiers still held out.

But these were soon slain, and their comrades, beholding their fate, threw down their arms and surrendered at discretion.

The work of destruction then commenced.

The fairest ornaments of architecture were pulled down and broken in pieces.

The rich and costly furniture was strewed and scattered like the fragments of a wreck, or piled in heaps and burned.

The most sacred repositories of the knights were plundered of their gold and jewels, and loud shouts of ribaldry echoed through the vaulted chambers as the long curling wreaths of dense smoke and fierce darting tongues of flame wildly ascended the richly carved pillars and stole ominously along the groined and fretted oak roofs, enfolding all in its destructive and deadly embrace.

CHAPTER XXXVI.

THE END OF THE FRAY ON BOARD THE PIRATE VESSEL—THE JOURNEY OF EVELYN AND GUY FAWKES DOWN THE RIVER—THE MYSTERIOUS HOUSE—THE CONSPIRATORS AGAIN.

AT the very moment when Guy Fawkes thought all was over the pages of the pirate uttered a cry of terror.

The pirate chief paused a moment in his murderous work, and, turning at the cry, beheld Ralph Roley rushing down the cabin steps with a blood-stained sword in his hand.

At the startling sight the pirate let go his hold of his enemy and Guy Fawkes was free.

Evelyn, clinging to him, and all heedless of the din around them, gave utterance to sobs of passionate joy.

Others of the yeomen now entered the cabin. The pirate fought bravely and well. Ralph wished to spare him and take him prisoner.

So, taking advantage of this forbearance, the pirate chief darted from the cabin and gained the deck.

He saw his ship was in possession of the king's guard, and cursed his fate when he remembered the rich spoil which would now be theirs.

He sprang to the bulwarks, and was in the act of leaping overboard when a bullet from the matchlock of the solitary yeoman left in the barge pierced his brain, and he fell dead into the river.

The current swept his body rapidly down the stream.

The stout yeomen now looked with delighted eyes upon the gorgeous cabin and the cups of gold. They had already bound with ropes such of the crew as were not wounded.

A few nasty cuts had been given and received, but these were lightly regarded in those hardy days.

In the confusion Guy Fawkes, who was apprehensive of being detected by the king's yeomen, took hasty farewell of Ralph, and, commending the dancing-girl to his care, descended to the small skiff, which had been moored to the barge.

As Guy Fawkes was pushing off, Evelyn glided down the rope, sprang from the barge into the boat, and seated herself at the conspirator's feet in her usual attitude, with her mantlet drawn over her pretty shoulders, and her fair brow resting on her white, shapely hands.

Guy Fawkes clutched the oars eagerly, and the little boat was propelled rapidly down the river.

For some time after leaving the ship there was not a word spoken.

Greenwich lights again were passed—they were fewer now. The open country lay in darkness on both sides of the river, but still the little boat careened over the restless waves and floated on.

"Beshrew my heart!" exclaimed Guy Fawkes, "this is the most bootless course I have ever ventured on. This boat, which, Heaven wot, is none of mine, is too frail to carry us across the channel, and where to land I know not."

"On, on!" muttered Evelyn, without changing her attitude. "We shall find a landing-place anon."

"Aye. But at this rate we must first run into the German Sea, and how to cross it puzzles me. Besides, morning will dawn upon us before we leave the river, and there are king's ships prowling about that, out of sheer charity, will not permit us in this trim to go out to sea. Known as I am to most of the captains, it is a desperate hope to expect to escape. I am wet and ill, too. A murrain on that night swim! It has made me long for rest."

"You will have it soon," replied the dancing-girl, feelingly. "Do you see yon light, that begins to glimmer by the water's side?"

"Yes," replied Guy Fawkes. "'Tis a good mile away."

"Direct the boat towards it," said Evelyn—"there you will find rest and security."

"They will be welcome both," sighed the conspirator, wearily. "I have learned to trust you, Evelyn, and will not scruple now."

The boat ran on.

Guy Fawkes, weak and exhausted, allowed it to drift on the rapid tide, but did not move an oar to accelerate its progress.

By-and-bye they approached the light.

It proceeded from a lone stone cottage on the low shelving bank.

The small windows shone brightly, and showed that there was a watcher within.

The house was strongly built—its firm, peaked gables looked thick walled and massive, and the low porches and iron-bound door gave the solitary dwelling an aspect of security, with something of a suspicious air, as if its inmates needed it.

One or two strange vessels were anchored near the cottage which Guy Fawkes and Evelyn were approaching in the boat.

There was a convenient landing-place, to which the boat was soon moored by Evelyn. Then the dancing-girl sprang to the beach, and Guy Fawkes followed her to the cottage-door.

It was cautiously opened, though not at the first summons.

A shaggy wolf-hound rushed out fiercely, but, suddenly uttering a yell of joy, fawned upon Evelyn.

Towards Guy Fawkes its savageness remained. It growled and showed its teeth, and although not daring to attack, it was easy to see how willingly it would have obeyed such a command.

An old woman had unbarred the door, and Guy Fawkes soon stood by the side of a cheerful fire, in a neat and orderly apartment.

Utensils used in cookery, also swords, pikes, and burnished pistols shone upon the walls.

The well-swept floor was scrupulously clean, and the empty oaken seats ranged around the place were elaborately carved.

The table by which the old dame had sat was of ebony, richly inlaid with ivory. The hearth had the needless extravagance of being of black marble, and the mantel was of walnut-wood.

The woman had a foreign countenance—her wrinkled brow was high and calm, and her large black eyes were brilliant still

Her brown fingers were hooped with various gems, a sarcenet of gold was twined in many folds around her neck, and a large cross of silver hung from her girdle.

Evelyn addressed her in Spanish, with fluent energy, as Guy Fawkes, wearied and heedless of ceremony, threw himself into a seat.

The dog watched him closely, and the old woman seemed to hesitate.

Evelyn redoubled her entreaties, but the language spoken so rapidly was imperfectly caught by Guy Fawkes.

Threats followed persuasion—the pale, agitated girl drew herself up to the full height of her beautifully-moulded figure, and her eyes, usually so dove-like, now flashed with anger.

Her clenched hand, the small foot that unconsciously beat the ground, the flush that struggled on her cheek, and the passionate tones of her tuneful voice, formed a strange contrast to the scoffing and cold aspect of the other.

But the dancing-girl at length prevailed, and the old woman, taking a taper from the wall, left the apartment.

Evelyn crept to Guy Fawkes's side.

"You will find rest and security for this night," she said, in a whisper ; "on the morrow you must depart early. One of those vessels you saw moored opposite the house is bound for France."

"France !" exclaimed Guy Fawkes. "Nay, by St. Mary, I quit not England ! I have a destiny to fulfil," he added, with his old dreamy look.

"Think no more on it, but fly while the chance offers," urged Evelyn, passionately. "Warrants against you have been sent to every sheriff in the country, and Oliver Blackstock and his bloodhounds are seeking you night and day in all directions.

"Stay not in England, I beseech you !" she continued, pleadingly. "The very stones you walk upon may rise up against you. Your name is execrated by the Protestants, and there are several of your own closest friends who are jealous of your bravery and power. Moreover, many of them are scattered and in hiding, and Tresham and Rookwood have already fled. There is a chamber being prepared for you—sleep in security. I will watch here all night, and when I hear the boatswain's pipe you will be called. I counsel thee well."

"Now hear me," said Guy Fawkes. "Since the first day we met you have been a riddle to me. I have found you in my path when I had forgotten you, and in the hour of danger you have been near me. Your presence grows familiar, and I trust you—a poor, wandering girl

"Say, fair one," he continued, "by what means have you compassed this ? How know you designs which statesmen hide, the secrets of courts, and the haunts of desperate men ? How comes it that in this late whirl of life, which seems to me a dream, you are ever thus, like my good angel, leading me from peril ? In sooth, I would fain learn this. A ship, as if by a spell, awaits me in the morning. You tell me that it is unsafe to remain in England. Yet this very night you thought I might do so with safety."

"But since then I have learned that the chase is hotter than I dreamt it was," returned Evelyn. "Your escape from the pirate ship was regretted as the loss of gold."

"And there, too, the path is tangled," observed Guy Fawkes. "Why did you consent to go on board the ship and say that you went willingly, when your own agony at the demand, and your shriek when you obeyed it, gave your words the lie ?"

"I can answer you that—I wished to prevent you from——"

"It is well," said Guy Fawkes. "But of what promise, of what pledge——"

"Sir Cavalier," replied Evelyn, in an excited tone, "I would give my life to save you, but if you question me thus——"

"Nay, then let it rest," said Guy Fawkes, stroking her silken tresses. "If I went to France for a space wouldst go with me, sweetheart ?"

"And wherefore ?" demanded Evelyn, curtly.

"To mark the tedium of your languid hours, to see you sad and melancholy, to hear you whisper the name of the one you love, to be repulsed by coldness from your side, or stung by looks of pity that would tell me I was endured—not wished for.

"To find the kindness of your heart the bitterness of mine, your smiles a mask to pleasure me? No! The beggar fondles his dog and shares his crust with the dumb brute joyfully, but the man who loves has no smile for another that is not wrung from him by feelings which the heart he sheds it on revolts at.

"Nay, hear me yet a little," she continued, as Guy Fawkes attempted to interrupt her, "for I would fain speak now as I have never spoken before. You love me not. You believe me vile—the bauble of some light-houred fantasy, the slave of——"

"No!" exclaimed Guy Fawkes, with passionate fervour. "No, by my hopes of Heaven!"

"What then?' asked Evelyn. "The dancing girl you saw first at Charing, the companion of a villain, the sister of one who betrayed you, the abandoned wretch who smiled at a pirate's beck——"

"Still you wrong me, Evelyn," said Guy Fawkes, reproachfully. "Rather than believe you that base degraded being, or that your heart, so rich in kindness, had ever nourished falsehood or impurity——"

He paused.

"Even while you speak your judgment wavers," cried Evelyn, "and the fervour of your voice is chilled. But no more of this. You have need of rest. It is enough, Sir Cavalier. I go not to France with you."

"Neither go I there," returned the conspirator, as though speaking to himself.

The old woman here returned, and Guy Fawkes, obeying a signal from Evelyn, took the taper she offered him, and entered a sleeping apartment to which the old woman pointed.

A fire burned on the hearth, a small game pie and a cup of warm wine was on the table, and a soft couch invited him to repose.

Guy Fawkes unbuckled his heavy sword, and, taking it off, seated himself at the snowy cloth, to partake of the repast which he so needed.

He was scarcely seated when Evelyn entered, hurriedly, and said, in eager, excited tones—

"Master Catesby and several other gentlemen having learned, I know not how, that you were here, are waiting below, and desire to see you on a matter of the most vital importance."

"Might I see them here in this apartment?" said Guy Fawkes.

"Need you ask it?" returned Evelyn, readily.

"Then would you be kind enough to conduct them hither?"

With a willing smile Evelyn withdrew.

Another moment and the footsteps of his brother-plotters were heard ascending the stairs.

Just then, however, other footsteps were heard. The opposite door was forced violently open, and a band of soldiers burst into the room upon the conspirators.

Oliver Blackstock, the hated pursuivant, was at their head.

"At last I have thee, juggling traitor!" he cried, with demoniacal triumph. "Surrender, in the name of the king!"

"Never to thee, vile slayer of my sainted sister!" cried Guy Fawkes, springing to his feet. "It is *I* who *have thee!* Thus—thus do I avenge her!"

And, snatching a petronel from his belt, he fired point-blank at the advancing pursuivant.

The bullet penetrated his brain. He threw up his arms wildly, gave a short, sharp scream of agony, and fell crashing at the feet of the avenger—dead!

———

CHAPTER XXXVII.

FACE TO FACE WITH HIS FOE—A MYSTERIOUS EXIT—THE LONE HUT—THE ATTEMPTED ASSASSINATION—A PERILOUS JOURNEY—ENGULPHED IN THE OCEAN'S WILD FLOOD—PARTED.

WHEN Sir Sidney Wildbrook beheld that the fortune of the day was against him, and heard the loud shouts of the victorious crowds echoing through the many winding passages, he speedily descended from his station at the window.

And, touching a spring in the ornamented wood-work of one of the huge pillars, a portion of that which appeared to be the solid wall sprung back and disclosed a secret passage.

"Now," he exclaimed—"now for a safe retreat. Come, lady, come!"

He approached the shrinking, terrified Violet, and rudely seized her in his arms.

The unhappy girl struggled and screamed aloud for help, but her cries were unheard, and appeared to be in vain.

Such, however, is the strength which desperation sometimes lends even to the weakest, that in her frantic struggles Violet had nearly overcome the knight, and escaped from his restraining arms.

With a muttered curse he called his coadjutor in villainy to his aid.

The magician advanced, and, springing upon the hapless girl like an eagle on its prey, the two betwix them dragged her towards the secret passage.

Violet fought desperately, again filling the vast chamber with her piercing cries.

But all to no avail, and she was on the point of being forced into the passage and hidden from the light of day.

Just then, however, the door of the apartment was shivered into a thousand pieces, and Sir Harold Rookby, Will-o'-the-Woods, and half-a-dozen others rushed into the room.

The surprise occasioned by the sudden entrance of his armed foes caused Sir Sidney and the magician to turn round, and for an instant to loosen their hold of Violet.

Taking advantage of their momentary confusion, by an effort she escaped from their grasp and darted behind the heavy tapestry for safety.

Like a flash Sir Sidney drew his sword and stood on the defensive.

Two long and rapid strides and Sir Harold stood face to face with his hated foe.

"Have at thee, villain!" cried Sir Harold, aiming a sweeping blow at Sir Sidney's head, which would have cleaved him to the chine had he not received the cut on his guard.

As it was it shivered the false knight's

weapon like glass, and he stood at the mercy of his enemy

"Down with the miscreants!" cried Will-o'-the-Woods to those in his rear, waving his sword.

Sir Harold again raised his sword to deal Sir Sidney his death blow.

But the astonishment and awe of the assailants may be conceived when they beheld that nothing but the solid wall met their young leader's sword thrust.

Sir Sidney and the magician, seeing all resistance useless, had sprung into the secret passage, the door of which immediately closed behind them.

"They must be in league with the Evil One, by all that's infernal!" said the Free-ranger, recovering from his fright and crossing himself. "Holy Mary preserve us!"

All at once the tapestry became violently agitated.

The onlookers tightened their grasps on their swords.

Then a female form suddenly appeared before them.

It was Violet Hamlyn.

Uttering a loud, glad cry, she rushed forward into Sir Harold's outstretched arms, and the next instant lay clasped to his wildly-beating heart, shedding tears of joy.

* * * * * *

Late on the evening of the same day on which the stronghold of Sir Sidney Wildbrook had been so effectually assailed, the baffled knight and his sinister partner in guilt were seated in an inner compartment of a rudely-constructed inn, in a wild and solitary glen.

Sir Sidney frequently arose from his seat and paced hurriedly to and fro.

On passing the window a bright red glare burst upon his vision from the distant horizon.

He paused in his walk, and gazed steadily from the window. The light continued to increase, till every feature of his swarthy countenance was plainly visible.

Its workings were fearfully distinct, but, making a strong effort to suppress all appearance of passion, he said, half aloud—

"By the rood, the old rafters make a goodly blaze!"

"Aye, and the rich furniture," said Horlock, with a nod.

The knight turned to his companion with a look of contempt.

"Fool!" he said, "think you that those hell-hounds would leave one article of value to become the prey of yonder blasting flame? No, no! they know their trade better. But if Sidney Wildbrook lives a day of reckoning shall yet come."

"I doubt it not, Sir Sidney," returned Horlock, "if ye but watch your hour, for never man who has sworn revenge was yet disappointed in his object if he but patiently waited for a fitting time."

"True, but I am somewhat weary of waiting. You have seen the manner in which I have been foiled by a pale-faced, sickly chit. I never loved her, but I loved her broad lands. I would willingly have taken them, even under an encumbrance that—that might soon have been removed."

Again he paced the apartment with restless step.

"Failing the Lady Violet and her issue, Sir Sidney," said the magician at length, "are you not the nearest heir to the Hamlyn estate?"

"Why do you ask that question?" demanded Sir Sidney. "What devilish thoughts are now passing in your mind?"

"None, by the rood!" exclaimed the magician, with a grim smile. "But as you *only* are the next heir, and as you care not for th maiden, there may be ways and means of—of——"

He hesitated.

"Of removing the encumbrance without first acquiring a lord and master's right over it?" muttered the villainous knight, in a voice scarcely above a whisper.

The magician nodded.

"Most unrelenting and accomplished villain," continued Sir Sidney, "you have pointed out a clear and ready path to vengeance. I hate this pining girl now she has foiled me, and since she has thought fit to despise my proffered love. But one way remains to gain her broad lands, and, by the soul of my ancestors, she dies!"

"Hush!" hissed the magician in an undertone, as the distant sounds of the tread of horses' feet broke upon their ears.

The sounds approached nearer and nearer, till, at length, turning a bend in path of the glen, they were distinctly heard approaching the door of the lonely inn.

"By the saints!" exclaimed Sir Sidney, gazing cautiously from the window, "the bird has run into the fowler's snare. 'Tis the Lady Violet!"

Horlock grasped the handle of his dagger and whispered to his accomplice in crime—

"Then the matter may be settled here. The dead tell no tales, and the tarn in the glen is deep and still."

"Yes," replied Sir Sidney, "the matter may be settled here—that is, if you wish the sword of Sir Harold Rookby to rasp against your ribs, or the blade of his companion—that cursed Freeranger, Will-o'-the-Woods—to crack your skull, which I promise you he would willingly do, without wasting a thought about the matter.

"No, no, Master Horlock," continued the knight, "there is a time for all things. They are bound for the south, and thither *we*, too, must proceed. But stay! By Heaven, they have gained an entrance! Away! this is no place for us. Away, I tell you, or we shall be done to the death!"

With rapid steps Sir Sidney and the magician retreated through the back entrance of the hut.

They had scarcely disappeared and closed the door behind them when Lady Violet, Sir Harold, and Will-o'-the-Woods entered the apartment.

Violet was pale and fatigued, and leant heavily on the young knight's arm as he strove to comfort her with the assurance that ere long he should place her under the care of those who were both able and willing to protect her.

"Alas, dear Harold, I fear I shall never reach our destination," said the fair girl, in a desponding tone.

"We will stay here, dearest, till to-morrow's sun shall rise," replied Sir Harold, lightly. "A light refreshment and a night's sweet rest will work wonders in restoring your wasted strength and spirits."

Violet shook her head, while the Freeranger chief muttered—

"As to the refreshment in this vile hole, it is likely to be light enough, and as to the sweet repose, I have ever found it a forlorn hope attempting to sleep on an empty stomach."

At this point, however, the worthy forester's meditations were interrupted by the entrance of the mistress of the inn, bearing a more solid and savoury mess of provisions than, at first sight, it would have been supposed that the place could produce.

Of these provisions Violet partook sparingly.

But it will readily be believed that the goodly stew of venison, obtained perhaps by no very creditable means, was not lost on the Freeranger chief, and truth compels us to confess that it was not lost upon Sir Harold either.

"It is strange," said Violet, with a melancholy smile, turning to her lover, "that when I ought to be happy, and to feel confidence in your protection, an unaccountable depression should overshadow my mind."

"Believe me, Violet," returned the young soldier, gazing fondly upon her, "the depression of which you complain is merely the effect of bodily fatigue."

"No," said the gentle girl, laying her hand affectionately upon his arm—"no, you must not attempt to deceive me thus. There are hours when the events of after years seem to rise in prophetic guise to the mind, and the heart too truly feels that icy chill of misfortune press upon it long, long before its actual approach."

"Violet," said Sir Harold, "dear Violet, these are dull words. Surely you cannot believe that an all-wise Providence sends such messengers of His to the heart of man?'

"I know not," answered the lovely girl, sadly, "but were you to ask me to interpret my present feelings I would prophesy that ere many days—nay, many hours—elapse all that remains of Violet of Hamlyn will be but the poor casket that now contains the germ of life."

"Violet," exclaimed Sir Harold, starting, "for Heaven's sake do not talk so mournfully! But come, come!" he added, cheerily, "you are wearied—worn out with fatigue, and I cannot wonder that all you have gone through should weigh upon your spirits. Believe me, when you behold the morning sunlight gild yonder hills you will talk in another strain. In the meantime, however, repose will be your best physician. Compose yourself, then, dearest, and may a sound sleep and pleasant dreams be yours. Rest in security under the guardianship of those who will protect you with their lives."

Sir Harold and the Freeranger then retired.

But Will-o'-the-Woods, with the precaution which his wild, adventurous life had taught him, first examined the apartment, observing that in an enemy's land the means of security to the citadel should be looked to.

The door through which Sir Sidney and the magician had departed did not escape the forester's penetrating eye.

And, observing it to be unfastened, he forthwith set to work, and soon secured it in a manner that precluded the possibility of attack from that quarter.

This done, he laid his powerful length on a rug in front of the door, so that no one could enter the apartment without stepping over his prostrate form—an undertaking which few acquainted with the bold outlaw would have ventured to attempt.

Ere the night had passed away Will-o'-the-Woods had reason to congratulate himself upon the precaution he had adopted, the use of which probably saved the life of Violet.

The early grey dawn had scarcely began to tinge the east with the soft mystic light of coming day when the watchful Freeranger was aroused by a slight noise at the outer door of the hut.

Without moving from the spot on which he lay, he turned his eye in the direction from whence the sound proceeded.

A few seconds elapsed, then he beheld the door he thought he had so securely fastened slowly and cautiously recede upon its hinges, and a figure in a dark flowing mantle enter.

Will-o'-the-Woods did not move a muscle, but again half-closed his eyes, feigning slumber, while he kept a strict and rigid watch upon the movements of the intruder.

Ere he proceeded further the first object of the early prowler seemed to be to prevent the door from closing, so as to secure his retreat should retreat be necessary.

Having effected this the nocturnal intruder advanced with a slow and stealthy step.

When he came within arm's length of the spot on which the apparently sleeping Freeranger lay he paused a moment, and drew a bright and glittering dagger from his vest.

He then seemed to listen for a few seconds with the most profound attention.

But no sound met his ear, not a breath stirred, and he approached one step nearer to the prostrate but still watchful outlaw, and raised his glittering poniard in the air to strike.

In an instant Will-o'-the-Woods was upon his legs.

But he had one to encounter as ready-witted and nearly as well-skilled in the arts of warfare as himself.

The blow descended, but the dagger struck in vain against the well-tempered breastplate, that rung again beneath the stroke.

Its violence, however, for a moment disconcerted the tiger-like spring the Freeranger made at the throat of his cowardly opponent, and gave the latter an opportunity of escaping through the open door.

But Will-o'-the-Woods had seized upon the long dark cloak, which the would-be assassin left in his hands.

To gaze at the spoils of the encounter, however, was no part of the forester's present occupation.

Quicker than thought he threw the garment aside and darted after his retreating foe.

But his adversary, less encumbered and less in need of rest, gained ground rapidly, and, speedily plunging into a thicket, was almost instantaneously lost to view.

Cursing his stars the Freeranger returned to the cottage to secure his spoil, as well as to prevent the risk of surprise to the defenceless garrison from any other quarter.

On arriving there he found Violet and Sir Harold—both of whom had been disturbed by the struggle, short and passing as it was—not only awake, but nearly ready to depart.

"Sir Harold, I beg of you a moment's delay," said the Freeranger, as he lifted the garment which lay unnoticed upon the ground. "I have small relish for these pedestrian exercises. But had there been glory to be obtained by following a retreating foe Will-o'-the-Woods is not the one that would have returned from the pursuit. And after the hour of victory, to lose the fruits of it by running into an ambuscade, were an act of folly I was scarcely likely to commit."

The speaker had been quietly examining the garment as he spoke, and when he beheld the small golden cross upon the left shoulder he sagely exclaimed—

"Yes, yes; I deemed as much. No one but a shaveling templar—half-soldier, half-monk—would have practised an art of war so villainous, unknown save amongst the most barbarous and uncivilised nations."

Sir Harold's exclamation, as he looked at the garment, was of a shorter nature.

He turned aside and muttered to himself—

"Another score added to the account. 'Twill be long and black ere it be wiped out."

There was enough, however, in this incident to show that danger was at hand, which served to expedite the motions of the party.

Accordingly, ere many minutes had elapsed, they were moving at a rapid pace across a long rugged stretch of moorland that lay before them.

Sir Harold, mounted on a powerful black charger, held Violet firmly on his saddle-bow before him, grasping the reins tightly with his right hand, while Will-o'-the-Woods, on a mettlesome roan, brought up the rear.

During the day their progress met with no interruption.

But they were still far from any habitation where they could remain for the night when the sun began to cast long and increasing shadows towards the east.

The young soldier felt somewhat vexed and annoyed, not for his own sake, but for that of Violet, whose slight and delicate frame could but ill bear exposure to the night air on a bleak and barren moor, without other shelter than the covering of the blue sky.

Availing himself, however, of his knowledge of the country, he left the more direct paths and made towards the coast, in the hope that, by directly crossing the sand that lay betwixt two projecting headlands, he might save a distance of several miles.

His determination was most unfortunate.

But the wisest of mankind cannot dive into the events of futurity.

And Sir Harold could not foresee the result that was destined to attend upon his well-intentioned movement.

He led the way in descending towards the sea-shore by a rough and broken path, and, rounding one of the headlands spoken of, a long and wide stretch of level sand extended before them.

At the farther extremity another bluff appeared, and around the upper end of the bay the hazy and indistinct outline of the land rising here and there into something like cliffs appeared but dimly in the increasing mistiness of night.

The party rode at a rapid pace across the hard and level sands for some time, during which there was but little spoken.

They had, however, passed over more than one half of the space between the headlands, when their attention was attracted by a solitary figure upon the tall summit of the distant bluff.

He seemed striving to catch their notice, and repeatedly waved something resembling a small flag in the air.

But if he spoke his voice was lost in the roar of the breakers, and his motions became less and less visible as the twilight faded more rapidly than the travellers had any reason to expect.

"I like not the appearance of the night," said the Freeranger, after a pause of some duration. "Yonder rising mist bodes us no good. Take a fool's advice, Sir Harold, and spare not the spur for a brief space."

Harold Rookby looked in the direction towards which the forester had pointed, and he saw a thick mist rising from the bosom of the sea.

It seemed to quickly expand from east to west, and it then advanced rapidly towards the shore, first passing the travellers in a thin vapoury form, and then coming down with racehorse speed, in a dense and heavy mass, till even the wild headland they were approaching was concealed from view.

At the same time a melancholy sighing sound, like the feeble moanings of departing spirits, fell mournfully upon the ear.

In a brief space the awesome sound arose to a louder pitch, and came in fitful broken blasts, till the wild wind blew upon the travellers, and the drizzling rain fell in cold and piercing showers around them.

Sir Harold pressed onward as rapidly as the steed could move, in the hope of passing the extremity of the sands, and thus attaining some shelter ere the fury of the storm burst fully upon them.

But another sound now mingled with the shrieking wind.

At first it seemed as if the feet of a numerous party of horsemen tore along the sands, and Sir Harold deemed they were pursued.

But this was only the delusion of a moment.

Soon—too soon—did the deafening rush of many waters break with fearful distinctness upon the ear.

Wave after wave reared their crested heads and rolled onwards in a manner that seemed to bid defiance to human art or power to cheat them of their destined prey.

The swiftness of the wild horse or the speed of the mountain wind would have been of no avail.

With feelings of the most desperate and despairing agony the young knight recognised, at one glance, the situation in which they stood, and that the help of man was vain.

Violet sat in front of her lover, pale as chiselled marble, and looked on the young knight with an inquiring glance.

Without uttering a single word he dashed onward with a speed that seemed, for a time, to give a slight hope that escape from the devouring jaws of the ocean might be possible.

But their panting steed, encumbered as it was by its double burden, could not long bear the continued exertion necessary to carry them

GUY FAWKES

Or Gunpowder, Treason, and Plot.

SIR HAROLD HELD VIOLET HAMLYN FIRMLY ON HIS SADDLE-BOW BEFORE HIM.

No.10.

through the now damp and heavy sand at the rate at which they were proceeding, and his speed soon slackened.

Then came the increasing roar of the ocean, and the proud, leaping waves touched the horse's feet.

The affrighted animal started back with instinctive dread, and became nearly unmanageable.

It reared and pranced, and, neighing loudly, bolted.

Violet screamed, and Sir Harold called aloud for help, but no human aid was near.

The Freeranger muttered something like a prayer.

But he had seen too many days of danger to tremble when death even in its present terrific shape stared him in the face, and his bronzed, stern-set features remained unmoved.

"It is hard to die without the chance of a struggle," he murmured, calmly. "Aye, doubly hard to one who has witnessed so many stoutly-contested battles. But no mortal help an reach us in our present peril."

This was, alas! too true.

The treacherous sands almost immediately became like quicksilver, and slid from beneath their feet.

The waves rolled onward, as if rejoicing in the capture of their prey, and the spirit of the storm rode with fearful mutterings upon the blast.

One plunge—one wild cry—and the terrified steeds were floundering in the sea.

But their riders were calm, for the calmness of despair had taken possession of their souls.

Deeply did Sir Harold regret the blind and inconsiderate haste that had led him to adopt so perilous a path.

But regrets for the past were unavailing now, and his whole efforts were bent towards making a last struggle to save his beloved Violet.

For himself he cared nothing—to him life was of little value; but the desire of his heart was to save one whom he had placed in so fearful a strait.

He speedily extricated himself from his plunging, screaming animal, though with difficulty.

Violet still kept her seat.

He stretched out his hands to receive her.

At that moment exhausted nature gave way, and she fell from the horse, apparently senseless, into his arms.

It was then that, nerved with new vigour, Sir Harold battled most desperately.

The current of the mad flood and the direction of the wind both favouring, he entertained the hope that he might yet accomplish his object,

But, encumbered as he was with Violet's lifeless-like form, his strength soon began to fail him.

With a feeling of the most hopeless despair he clasped the pale, beauteous girl more firmly in his arms, and resigned himself to his fate—a watery grave.

It was hard, very hard, to be thus cut off in the prime of life, vigour, and youth.

But they had loved in life, and in death they were not destined to be separated.

It was in this moment of apparently certain and unavoidable death that a strange cry burst upon the young soldier's ear.

A new hope sprung up for an instant within his breast.

Alas! it was only the cry of drowning agony that emanated from his own brave steed.

Then all was still—still as death—for the very winds seemed to have been hushed by the appalling despair of that awful sound.

And in that dreadful stillness there was yet another sound borne upon the wildly-heaving waters.

He could not be mistaken. Human voices and the dash of oars broke upon his eager ear.

Exerting his remaining strength to its utmost he shouted aloud again and again with all the force of his lungs.

Joy! For a moment he fancied he heard an answering shout.

He might, however, have been deceived.

Strangely-mingled and confused sounds and sights now burst upon his bewildered senses.

And in the agony of approaching death the thought flashed like lightning across his seething brain, that even if the voices he had heard were those of human beings, and not the mocking gibes of the spirit of the storm, all aid, however near, was now too late.

Once more, by a stupendous exertion, he recovered for a few passing seconds from the stupefaction that was rapidly coming over him.

Then Violet's sweet plaintive voice fell upon his ear, and he heard it murmur a last farewell hope that they would meet where no storms and no tempests could ever separate them more.

The thought of her prophetic forebodings at the inn at the same instant flashed into his mind.

Again the numbness of approaching dissolution returned.

And then he felt her cold form slip gently from his grasp.

Bright rainbow-tinted objects danced before his fading vision.

A kind of dreamy sleepiness fell upon him.

He fancied that he lay on a bed of down, in the midst of bright, glorious-looking, and wonderful things.

At last he seemed to quietly fall asleep, as if all he had gone through had been but the remembrance of some beautiful and pleasant dream.

CHAPTER XXXVIII.

THE CONSPIRATORS VICTORIOUS—TO LONDON—THE FLIGHT—THE PURSUIT—CONCEALED IN THE WOOD—STEALING A MARCH ON THE ENEMY.

RETURN we now to the cottage by the river.

The soldiers, on witnessing the fall of their leader, Oliver Blackstock, at the hands of Guy Fawkes, dashed into the apartment with mingled cries of—

"Upon him, lads! Down with the miscreant!"

"Fools!" thundered one of them, making his voice heard above the rest. "Secure, but do not slay the daring traitor—the reward will be double if we take him alive."

"Aye, aye!" was the reply of one of the soldiers. "Roger is right, secure him!"

Guy Fawkes had snatched up his sword and stood on the defensive.

In a moment he was surrounded by the troopers.

Rapping sharply with his heel upon the floor, Guy Fawkes furiously attacked his weary foes.

His hasty summons was immediately answered by his brother conspirators, who rushed in a body into the room and fell upon the startled troopers with vengeful fury.

The contest was sharp and deadly.

The scuffle of feet and the ring of steel, the report of firearms, the cry of mortal agony, the half-muttered oath, and the falling of heavy bodies—then all was quiet, save the hoarse panting of the victors as they wiped their blood-stained blades, or bound up their wounds.

Evelyn, with painfully-beating heart, peeped timidly into the room and gazed a moment upon the fearful scene.

All save two of the troopers, who had taken flight, lay dead or badly wounded about the room, the white boards slippery with the dark, awful stains of the deadly conflict.

Several of the conspirators were slightly wounded, but, save a few scratches, Guy Fawkes himself appeared to have sustained but little injury.

On observing this Evelyn murmured a fervent thanksgiving for his safety, and glided noiselessly and unseen away.

"Why have you been absent from us so long?" now asked Catesby, addressing Guy Fawkes. "Father Woodruff grows impatient at the delay."

"His reverence regrets it not more than do I," returned Guy Fawkes, with a troubled look, "but I have been a slave of circumstances—hunted by night and day, like a wild beast—every attempt I have made to approach our place of rendezvous of late has been futile."

"The time is ripe for action," observed the impetuous Percy, brother-in-law to the conspirator Wright. "Parliament sits within the month."

"Say ye so?" returned Guy Fawkes. "Have any measures been taken during my absence?"

"We have lost little time, I promise ye," replied Percy. "A dwelling have we taken adjoining the House of Parliament, from Sir James Whinneard, the keeper of the king's wardrobe, on pretence that my office of gentleman pensioner compels me to reside part of the year in the vicinity of the court."

"You have done well," observed Guy Fawkes, his dark eyes lighting up.

"The commissioners appointed by the king," continued Percy, "to play the dull farce of considering the union of the two kingdoms, have been occupying it for some months past, but fortunately for our great purpose we take possession to morrow."

"Though, in order not to lose time," interposed Catesby, "we have hired another house in Lambeth, where we have ample stores of wood, gunpowder, and other combustibles, which we can remove by night across the river to this house in Westminster."

"Good! Excellent!" exclaimed Guy Fawkes, with kindling enthusiasm. "I am all impatience to begin the good work. But this is scarcely a fit place to hold conference," he added, glancing round with a shudder. "Let us away from here."

"Aye," returned Ambrose Rookwood, "while we can do so in safety. The palace of Greenwich swarms with the king's guard, and ere long this house will be surrounded by them, for by this time I opine the cropped-skull villains who escaped our blades will have reached the palace and told the story of their defeat."

"You advise well, Sir Ambrose," said Catesby; "let us away at once. On, on, gentlemen, to London."

"To London and the House of Parliament," returned Guy Fawkes, with his old fanatical look, rushing from the room.

The other conspirators speedily followed.

On gaining the open no sign of impending danger was visible in the witching silence of that lovely starlight night. All nature seemed at rest.

For a moment they missed the presence of Guy Fawkes.

He had been searching for Evelyn and the dame, in order to recompense them for the trouble he had brought upon the house.

But they were nowhere to be found. They had fled.

Joining his companions, they took the most unfrequented paths, and keeping well in the deep shadow of the tall trees and bosky hedge-rows, moved rapidly in the direction of London.

"How knew you my hiding-place?" asked Guy Fawkes of Catesby, in a low voice, as they proceeded.

"We had been seeking for you along the river, and were about to take shelter for the night at the Old Ferry House, below Woolwich, when we chanced to meet your late page, the boy Leo, and he told us where you had taken refuge," returned Catesby.

"Ah, the viper—cub!" cried Guy Fawkes, fiercely. "Is *he*, then, dogging my steps?"

"He is," said Catesby, "though not for any sinister purpose, I trow. In sooth, he seems most anxious to regain your good opinion."

"I will never trust him more," returned Guy Fawkes, gloomily.

"Is there no other means of reaching our destination, gentlemen, save on foot?" here asked Thomas Winter.

"A conveyance at this hour, I opine, is out of the question," observed Rookwood.

"Utterly so," returned Catesby. "But I have bethought me of one Martin Wrackford, who keeps the Old Cross Farm on the Deptford Marsh. In his stables he hath at least half a score of the finest horses in all Surrey, and I think for a consideration he might be induced to loan them to us for a space."

"Then let us push on to Old Cross Farm with all speed," said Percy, "for methinks I hear the faint clatter of pursuing hoofs on the distant road."

They paused a moment to listen.

The speaker was right. The rapid beat of horses' hoofs on the hard road was now distinctly heard—coming nearer and nearer every second.

"Forward, gentlemen!" cried Catesby, in an undertone.

To the right the country, though broken

and rugged, was open, and offered but little shelter to the fugitives, while to the left there was a dense and matted wood.

Towards this the conspirators made their way with all possible speed, for the approaching horsemen were now in sight.

And the clank and jingle of their arms and accoutrements told that a party of armed men were in pursuit.

In a few minutes half-a-dozen mounted troopers, with an officer at their head, came into view riding at a furious pace.

Brandishing his sword the officer called loudly on the flying fugitives to "Stand!"

"To the wood, gentlemen!" exclaimed Catesby, determinedly. "To the wood!"

Another hundred yards and they would be penetrating its dark and sheltering recesses.

Nearer and nearer came the clatter of the horses' hoofs, louder and louder the triumphant shout of their pursuers.

The wood is reached at last.

But so matted and tangled are its approaches that the conspirators only succeeded in forcing their way into it with great difficulty.

Thomas Winter is the last to enter. His cloak, streaming in the wind, is suddenly caught by the interlacing and thorny branches, and wrenched from his shoulders.

He pauses not to recover the garment, but leaves it hanging to the bushes.

Then he darted through a gap and followed in the footsteps of his companions a few yards lower down.

He had barely rejoined the others when the soldiers came thundering up.

"Halt!" cried the officer, pulling up short.

The command was instantly obeyed.

He then dismounted, and approaching the cloak, which partly hid an opening in the matted foliage, said, as he drew it aside—

"They have entered here, the murdering traitors!"

Then turning to his men, he added—

"Dismount! Merribren, look to the horses. On guard—forward!"

Almost as quick as the order was given was it executed.

The officer now entered through the gap concealed by the cloak, followed by five of his men, while Merribren took charge of the horses.

By entering the wood through the gap in question the troopers had put a wall of matted branches and foliage between themselves and their prey, to follow the windings of which would take them five or even ten minutes.

Standing under the spreading branches, their masks on and their naked swords clutched with a determined grip, the conspirators listened to the advancing footsteps of their foes.

Nearer and nearer came the dread sounds, and the snapping of each dry twig found a responsive echo in the conspirators' anxiously beating hearts.

They were not aware that a thick hedge divided them from their pursuers.

Presently the footsteps of the troopers died faintly away in the distance.

"They have passed us," whispered Catesby.

All breathed freely once more.

"I have a plan," suddenly said Guy Fawkes, in the same low tone.

"What is it?" asked Catesby.

"Follow softly and I will tell you," answered Guy Fawkes, stepping with cat-like tread towards the gap by which they had entered. "Keep close."

Promptly did the conspirators obey the bidding.

As they proceeded cautiously and stealthily on their perilous way Guy Fawkes briefly and quietly unfolded his plot.

They now stood silent and breathless, peering through the branches at the trooper who had charge of the horses.

His face was towards theirs, but suddenly he changed his position.

"Now!" cried Guy Fawkes, in a loud whisper.

He darted forward and felled the man at a blow with his clubbed petronel.

The soldier uttered a single sharp cry of agony and remained on the ground unconscious.

In an instant they were all in the saddles.

"Just the required number," laughed Catesby, as he mounted.

"Now, gentlemen, spare not the spur," exclaimed Guy Fawkes, "but on—on to London."

In another instant they were flying along the dusty road, with the mad cries of their baffled and enraged pursuers sounding loudly on their fearless ears.

CHAPTER XXXIX.

THE FISHERMAN'S HUT—SIR HAROLD'S RESCUE— A SAD STORY—VIOLET'S LOSS—THE YOUNG SOLDIER'S DESPAIR.

ON awakening from the state of insensibility into which he had fallen Sir Harold found himself stretched on a hard, rough bed, and he was the inmate of a crazy cottage.

The curling smoke from a huge fire in the centre of the hut found its egress through the chinks and crannies of the old walls.

A stout, hale-looking man, weather-beaten, and having the appearance of a fisherman, hung over him, and appeared to be engaged in administering such restoratives as his skill or his means afforded.

At a short distance, seated on a stool near the fire, Will-o'-the-Woods was polishing his sword and firearms, rusted by his late immersion in the sea.

But there was another form which the young soldier looked for—yet looked in vain.

Violet was nowhere to be seen. He closed his eyes and tried for some time to recall his scattered senses, and listened with a strange, mixed feeling, while the voice of the Freeranger, addressing the fisherman, broke upon his ear.

"It is useless, I tell you—it is useless. The lamp of his life is extinguished—drowned— quenched in the merciless ocean, and the sun of heaven will never brighten it again. Alas! 'tis a sorry end for so brave, so comely a youth, and I cared for him as though he were my brother!" concluded Will-o'-the-Woods, sadly.

While he yet spoke the past rose with dreadful distinctness to Sir Harold's mental view.

Feeble as he was he started from his bed, and uttered the name of Violet in accents of the most fearful apprehension.

At the sound of his voice the Freeranger

chief threw down his work, seized his hand, and clasped it within his own.

Traces of deep feeling were marked upon his bold features, but in answer to the repeated inquiry of Harold concerning Violet he only shook his head.

Sir Harold staggered back as though from some heavy blow.

The whole building seemed to swim around him. He tried to speak, but no sound issued from his cracked and blackened lips.

Insensibility again overtook him, and for a time he lost all consciousness of his woe.

It would have been well for him had he remained in this state, for he would have been spared a deep and bitter suffering.

But the exertions of the generous Freeranger, aided by the master of the cottage, in a short space again restored him to his senses.

And the dreadful truth could no longer be concealed.

Violet was no more.

"I stood upon the rock, and I waved to you to turn," said the fisherman, "for I saw ye approach the quicksands, and I knew how 'twould be.

"The wind and storm were brewing in the offing, and when the east wind rises a gossamer thread would sink in these sands. Many is the one I have seen perish—aye, within sight and well nigh within reach, yet the hand of mortal man could not save them, and my only wonder is that ye are now where ye are.

"But ye would not be warned," he added, gravely, "ye would not be warned, and I trow ye have paid for your obstinacy."

Sir Harold groaned in agony, but the speaker scarcely heeded him as he continued—

"Aye, aye, many is the one I have seen lost in these fearful sands, but I trow my heart sank within me when I saw the white garments of the fair lady floating upon the broken surf. I would have saved her—aye, at the risk of my own life, for what else could have tempted me to the shore! But just then a scour of mist came on, and when the next gust cleared it up a bit the lady had disappeared—deep, deep, I warrant me, in a watery grave."

There was a silence of some minutes, for none wished to intrude upon Harold's grief, which appeared too deep for utterance.

The tears stood in Will-o'-the-Wood's eyes, and it was with a trembling hand that he sought to efface a single spot of rust that stained his cuirass.

Far different and more powerful were the emotions which struggled within his breast from those that dwelt in the bosom of the master of the hut.

Sir Harold was the first to speak.

"But how," he demanded—"how, then, comes it, that I am here and safe—my friend, too?"

"This gentleman," replied the fisherman, indicating the Freeranger, "had got on the firm shore, somehow or other, and was crawling along it like a crab.

"As for you, Sir Knight," he pursued, "the death struggle had been strong, and ye had clutched at the mane of the powerful steed that brought ye nigh the spot where Jack Bowline had ta'en his stand, and it was not the part of a Christian to keep his hands idly by his side when the life of a fellow-creature was in jeopardy."

The young soldier pressed his hand upon his burning forehead. The hope of many years had gone. The sun of his existence had vanished from his view, and the cold future seemed clad in the dark and dismal garments of the grave.

In the days of his sorrow, however, the generous-hearted Freeranger chief seldom quitted his young friend's side, save to rejoin his band for a few hours in the Forest of Bleam.

But Sir Harold knew him not, and when the Freeranger spoke he only gazed upon him with a vacant stare, or answered with the wild ravings of delirium.

At times, indeed, he tried to leave his bed, and it required the united strength of Will-o'-the-Woods and the fisherman to hold him down.

It was a fearful sight to see—a strong and gallant young soldier thus laid prostrate, day after day sinking under the wasting and desolating stroke of sorrow and disease.

But so it was for a time.

At length, however, youth and a powerful constitution gained the victory, and after many days the violence of the fever subsided.

It was during these periods that the Freeranger rejoined his companions in the woods, or wandered on the beach, as was his habit, in the hope that he might recover some trace of Violet.

He could not bring himself to think that one so young and beautiful could have perished thus.

His labour of love, however, was all in vain. Day after day passed, and the devouring sea still kept its own dark secret.

"I tell you," said Jack Bowline, "ye may look till ye are blind. These yellow sands never yet quitted grip of aught that came within their reach."

"She was marvellously sweet and fair," said Will-o'-the-Woods, in a mournful tone, for Violet's gentle manner and loving, generous disposition had made a deep impression on his kind but rugged heart.

"And think ye," continued the fisherman, "that the raging ocean heeds a fair skin? No, no, it's all fish to its net, and the prettiest lass that ever stepped in leather is held in no more reverence by it than the broken plank of a rotten coble."

"I would give my best bow, my brightest sword—aye, a dozen years of my life—if she were alive and well," said the Freeranger, earnestly.

"And were ye to add your life itself to it," answered his companion, "it would be of no use—the deep sea will not give up its dead at the bidding of mortal man."

A silent tear rolled down the Freeranger's bronzed cheek as he turned from the beach and murmured brokenly—

"Poor youth. The blow is a sad and bitter one, and will last him all his life."

They reached the cottage door at last, and the Freeranger resumed his watch upon the sick knight.

In the intervals of pain and ever busy memory a more calm and resigned spirit had come upon the young knight.

And he desired to quit a spot that could be productive of no other feeling than that of a vain and useless regret.

As he lay one evening upon his humble couch, meditating upon the course he should pursue, the letter he had received from the king, offering him service in Spain, recurred to his mind.

Having no other object now in view—for he was not a conspirator at heart, and had never taken their dreadful oath or even understood the diabolical nature of their plot, beyond its supporting the rights and liberties of the Catholics, which he even yet hoped to do in the capacity in which he was about to embark —he determined, when sufficiently restored to health, to proceed to the court of James to deliver his credentials.

Many weeks, however, elapsed before he was able to carry this resolution into effect.

So time passed, and after liberally rewarding his kind preserver, and taking an affectionate farewell of his faithful friend and companion, Will-o'-the-Woods, he proceeded with a heavy heart to his destination, totally careless of what might befall him.

CHAPTER XL.

THE LONE HOUSE ON THE MARSH—THE CONSPIRATORS AT WORK—THE RIVER MYSTERY—THE LANDING OF THE POWDER.

GUY FAWKES and his brother conspirators were soon safely ensconced in the lone house by the riverside, on the skirts of Lambeth Marsh.

Its wretched appearance, difficulty of approach, owing to a deep and muddy ditch which partly encompassed it, and its solitary situation, rendered it a place to be shunned at all times, but more especially at night.

Catesby had induced his servant Bates to join in the plot, and to his entire charge the cottage was entrusted.

The conspirators were all assembled in the lower room, together with Father Woodruff and Father Garnet, the Jesuit priest.

"Let us go into the vault and ascertain the state of the powder," said Guy Fawkes, addressing all present. "I fear it must have become damp, from the exhalations of the marsh, after having been for so long a period in the cellar."

The conspirators assenting to the proposal, Catesby immediately made a careful reconnoitre at the front and back of the house, through the partially-opened shutters.

Then securely bolting them, and barring the doors, he and Guy Fawkes approached a large cupboard beside the fireplace.

This was unlocked, and the pair stepped in. The floor of the cupboard proved to be a large trap-door, for on Guy Fawkes touching a hidden button in the wall they began to sink, till their heads disappeared below the flooring.

Soon after the trap rose to the surface again, two more of the conspirators took their stand upon it, and in this manner the whole of them descended.

The vault below was lighted by a single lantern stuck in the wall, and its lurid glow revealed a strange, fantastic, and sombre picture.

The masked and stealthy conspirators grouped together, their mysterious movements, the glimpses of their rich dresses and arms seen beneath their voluminous cloaks, the venerable priests, the many barrels of powder ranged against one side of the wall, while the other portion was occupied by piles of halberts, matchlocks, rapiers, lances, pikes, corslets, &c.

Guy Fawkes, approaching one of the barrels of powder, burst open the top, and taking some of it in his hand rubbed it between his fingers.

"How is it?" asked several of the group, eagerly.

"Sound, and dry enough for the work in hand, I trow," said Guy Fawkes, with a grim smile. "I would we had every barrel of it safely stored in the cellar beneath the Parliament House. That apostate and tyrant, James, and the faithless time-servers who surround him would then not much longer prove obstacles to the advancement of our holy cause."

"Amen to that, my son," said Father Garnet, solemnly.

"Marry!" replied Catesby, after a brief pause, "we have much to do, Brother Fawkes, ere the consummation of your wishes be accomplished."

"Alas, I sometimes fear Heaven is angered with me, and that they never will be accomplished," observed Guy Fawkes, with his old gloomy look and manner.

"Is this your boasted courage?" retorted Catesby, with a sneering frown. "Would you turn traitor and draw back on the very eve of coming success?"

"*You* know me better, Catesby," answered Guy Fawkes, sternly, drawing himself up to his full height, and instinctively laying his hand on his sword, "than to deem me capable of either cowardice or treachery. But you also know my belief—I have a presentiment that I shall fail in my set purpose, or that when my hand doth fire the train I shall be hurled into eternity with our enemies. More than all, I have again seen the vision of my sister, warning me to desist."

"These idle fears, my son," said Father Woodruff, "are unworthy one so brave—so eminently fitted for the great purpose for which an all-foreseeing power has chosen you."

"Exactly, your reverence," rejoined Catesby, "and, moreover, they are calculated to intimidate others of our brethren, some of whom, I trow, already begin to doubt the wisdom of our plans."

"You are right there, Catesby," observed Sir Ambrose Rookwood. "I certainly do begin to doubt the lawfulness of our plot, because innocent people must perish with the guilty, Catholics amid the persecuting Protestants."

"For my part," said Catesby, readily, "I have no qualms as to the justice of the measure; but, as a captain of the Archduke Albert, I might be called on at any moment to make an attack in which the innocent might fall with the guilty—women and children with armed soldiers. I would fain, like yourself, Sir Ambrose, be resolved by our holy father Garnet, whether I can do these things lawfully in the sight of Heaven."

"Undoubtedly, my son," returned the priest, "otherwise an aggressor could always defeat the object of the party invaded by placing innocent persons amongst guilty ones in their ranks."

This was enough for one and all. The principle was admitted and their scruples satisfied.

"And now," observed Guy Fawkes, his old energy returning, "I propose that as the night is favourable we transport as much powder across the river as possible."

"This sounds like business," said Catesby

THE CONSPIRATORS LISTENED INTENTLY TO THE FOOTSTEPS OF THEIR FOES.

gleefully. "Bates," he added to his servant, "have you the wherry ready?"

"I have, your worship," returned the man. "It is moored in the ditch at the back of the house."

"Excellent," rejoined his master. "I wish you to accompany me to the cottage adjoining the Parliament House. Will you oblige me with the key, Mr. Percy?" he added, addressing that conspirator.

"With pleasure," said Percy, handing it to him as he spoke. "But don't you think it would be best for your servant to proceed there first, in order to see that the coast is clear?"

"I would rather myself be the first to enter the place," replied the indefatigable plotter, "and that my hand be the one to place the first of the regenerating element under the feet of our hated foes."

"Be it so, and I will join you," said Guy Fawkes, readily.

They cautiously viewed the night again. It was still favourable to their plan.

Dark murky clouds obscured the waning moon, and a thick and chilling mist lay upon the river, which was ruffled into tiny wavelets by the mournful, gusty wind.

With the aid of Bates and Guy Fawkes, Catesby brought from the cellar as many barrels of gunpowder as the boat would hold.

The wherry was then steered up to the back door by Bates, and the powder lifted quickly in and carefully covered over with sacks.

Catesby then desiring Bates to get another cargo ready by the time they would return, took his seat beside Guy Fawkes in the boat, and the latter, seizing the oars, pushed off.

The mist was so thick on the river that they experienced the greatest difficulty in keeping in the right course; indeed, they found it utterly impossible to steer direct for their destination.

Having reached the centre of the stream Guy Fawkes exerted his utmost strength, and the skiff darted along with gratifying swiftness.

As yet they had not met with a solitary boat.

But all at once, above the shrieking wind, they thought they detected the splash of oars.

The next moment they came into violent collision with another craft coming in a contrary direction, which, rebounding from the shock, nearly capsized.

"'Sdeath and fury!" hissed a passionate voice, which for the instant Guy Fawkes thought was familiar to him, "you nearly had us all into the stream, ye clumsy knaves."

"Heed them not, but on—on," eagerly whispered Catesby in his companion's ear.

Guy Fawkes, recovering from the shock, strained his powers of vision to penetrate the mist, and perceived that the boat they had run foul of contained two persons, muffled to the eyes in thick cloaks, the hoods of which were drawn far over their heads, in order to conceal their features as much as possible.

The conspirators vouchsafed no reply to the angry outburst, and the strangers, righting themselves, were in the act of rowing away, when a white figure started up in the boat and uttered a stifled cry, as though for help.

But one of the muffled strangers immediately sprang forward, and, thrusting his hand forcibly over its mouth, instantly checked the half-uttered appeal.

"That voice!" cried Guy Fawkes, starting so violently as to almost let go his oar, "whose music is the only joy my sorrowing soul ever knew!—am I mad or am I dreaming? No, no," he added, calmly, after a moment's pause, "it cannot be she—impossible."

"Come," said Catesby, in an undertone, "these delays are fraught with danger and death," plucking him by the sleeve.

Guy Fawkes obeyed, and, dipping the oars in the water once more, was about to pull off when another stifled shriek for help burst above the swirl of the wild wind.

"'Tis there again!" exclaimed Guy Fawkes, excitedly, stopping to listen. "By Heaven, I'll satisfy myself whether it be she whom I suspect it is, even at the hazard of my life."

"Madman—would you ruin all," exclaimed Catesby, passionately, "by this reckless exposure of our persons in pursuit of a mere phantom?"

"Phantom or not," returned Guy Fawkes, firmly, "I would rather a thousand times forego the great purpose in which I am embarked than pass unheeded that appeal, should it proceed from the dear lips of her of whom I speak."

Catesby uttered an impatient oath, but Guy Fawkes pulled vigorously in the direction from whence he fancied the cry proceeded.

But after pulling down stream for some time and not meeting with the object of his search, he turned the head of the boat round, and began to cast about, but though he scanned the river right and left, up and down, not a trace of the strange boat nor its mysterious occupants could anywhere be seen.

Guy Fawkes, giving up the search, now resumed the journey, dispirited and in silence.

Did the cry in reality emanate from the sweet vision he had secretly cherished in his bosom so long, or was it only fancy—a mere coincidence of sound?

Alas for his hopes! Had he only known the fatal truth!

By this time they had reached the other side of the river.

Running the skiff into a kind of inlet Catesby moored it to one of the old wooden steps of the landing-place, then assuring himself that no one was about to watch their movements, he desired Guy Fawkes to hand him out the powder.

This was speedily done. Then, each taking a barrel under his cloak, they cautiously proceeded to the dwelling adjoining the Parliament House, and, entering the same, deposited the powder therein.

Returning again to the wharf few times they soon had the whole of it securely stowed away under lock and key.

Then they rowed back to the house on the Marsh for another consignment of that awful cargo without meeting with further adventure.

CHAPTER XLI.

SIR HAROLD'S RETURN—OTHUS THE DWARF—NEWS OF VIOLET—A WILD STORY—HOPE AND FEAR.

DURING a three months' sojourn in Flanders, where he proceeded after delivering his credentials to King James, Sir Harold reaped a glorious harvest in the many and desperately-contested battles there with the Archduke.

But when, ultimately, the young soldier saw through the masked and cunning policy of James—how that, instead of granting the ill-used Catholics exemption from the excessive fines imposed upon them as recusants, and the recognised right of public worship in their monasteries and churches, he was carrying on a warfare against them of still greater oppression and persecution—when Sir Harold saw this, and that *he* had been fighting against instead of *for* the cause so dear to his heart, he threw down his arms in disgust, and returned to his native land.

On the evening that we again introduce him to the reader he was seated on a projecting stone at the base of a ruined tower, standing on the margin of a bold precipice, which commanded a magnificent and romantic scene below of silvery stream, smiling fields, and rugged rocks, clothed with trees and mingled with flowering furze, in the neighbourhood of Hamlyn.

It was a favourite haunt of the young soldier, for here he had first won the young and virgin affections of his lost love, Violet.

Sir Harold gazed upon the beauty of the setting sun with feelings listless and undefined.

Gradually, however, his thoughts took shape, and the dim, shadowy past assumed a vivid aspect. The forms he had once seen, redolent of life and health, again rose like spectres to his view.

Horlock the magician—that dark and mystic man—stood before him.

Violet, too—his fair, his beautiful Violet—and the thrice-accursed Sir Sidney Wildbrook were there. Then his faithful friend and brother-in-arms, Guy Fawkes—then James, and the promises he had made.

A dark shadow fell upon his heart when he thought how vain they were now.

Few, indeed, would have recognised the once gay and gallant Sir Harold Rookby in the apparently toil-worn and weary soldier who sat at that turret's base.

The setting sun was fast disappearing, and the west was covered with a beautiful crimson hue, with here and there a fleecy gorgeous cloud resting upon the surface of the sky.

In the long vista, stretching forth in burnished beauty, the imagination might almost have pictured the golden gates of Heaven, and Sir Harold gazed upon it with high and excited feelings.

Suddenly short and hurried whisperings fell on his ear.

And the many strange tales of the ghostly old place being haunted flashed like lightning through his mind.

"Ah! a stranger blocking the way to our secret retreat," murmured one of the low, spectral-like voices.

"Come, lads," said another, "silence him or we are lost. The officers of the coast follow on our track!"

Then came the rush of many feet.

The danger of his position came upon Sir Harold with sudden and startling force.

Quickly he drew forth both his sword and dagger, and, springing round, stood boldly on the defensive, his hat falling off as he did so.

In front of him stood Othus the dwarf, with a gleaming knife in his hand, leading on four ferocious and fully armed ruffians to the attack.

Two of the number carried a small keg of brandy each—plainly telling the illicit nature of their calling—and one of them had rolled on the ground.

"Hold! Put up your weapons, brave boys!" exclaimed the dwarf, on recognising Sir Harold. "I know this gay cavaliero, and have news for him."

The scowling, bravo-looking crew returned their weapons to their belts, and one of them picked up the brandy-cask.

Othus, saying he had important intelligence to communicate, requested Sir Harold to accompany him to a more retired part of the ruin.

The young soldier, curious to learn the nature of the communication, quietly obeyed.

Meanwhile one of the half-smuggler, half-bravo-looking band, by a secret and peculiar movement, raised the projecting stone upon which Sir Harold had been sitting.

A flight of dark steps was disclosed, down which they all rapidly descended, the last man carefully replacing the stone behind him.

"And now, Sir Harold," queried the dwarf, when they had reached a retired spot, "why tarry you here in this lone, haunted spot, when those you profess to love may want your aid?"

"My cause and my country demand my aid here," said the young soldier, despondently, "and no one now exists who has a stronger claim for any poor assistance I can render."

"Say you so," answered the dwarf, bitterly. "Aye, aye, it is ever thus. Pride of heart and a reliance upon our own knowledge will mislead the wisest amongst us, but a single ray of light will sometimes break upon the mind, and we then see that our boasted wisdom is but folly, and wonder, forsooth, how we could have been deceived."

"What mean you?" said Sir Harold, turning to the strange creature in astonishment.

"You believe," returned the dwarf, "that the Lady Violet perished on the sands. Aye, perished, Sir Knight, when *you* were at hand to save her."

Sir Harold buried his face in his hands, and groaned audibly at the recollection thus abruptly forced upon him.

"Aye, you, Sir Knight—you, with your straight and well-formed limbs, and your boasted strength and gallant bearing—you could not save her, and the world pities you. But," he added, with a shriek, "had the misshapen dwarf been there, obloquy and curses would have been heaped in full measure upon his head, because he could not do that which the gentle and the brave failed to perform."

"Misshapen wretch!" exclaimed Sir Harold, frenziedly, "would you drive me mad?"

"No, Sir Knight," said the dwarf, in a tone of bitter irony, "I would not drive ye mad. I come to you as the bearer of good news."

The young soldier stared at him vacantly yet wonderingly.

"Do not think, Sir Harold," he continued, "that I bear aught of favour to you or any of your race—no! I *hate* mankind, and had I the power I would crush and trample upon them as I despise and scorn them.

"I come because I am sent by one whom I must obey. But Satan and his angels grant that the intelligence I bring may yet prove to be a curse and bane to you and others. Listen, Sir Knight. The Lady Violet lives!"

"Lives!" repeated Sir Harold, gasping for breath. "'Tis false—I saw her perish."

"You thought so, brave knight, but the intelligence I bring is true nevertheless. I would not speak a word of comfort to the heart of a single human being if I could help it, far less to you, who have come betwixt me and the dearest object of my life."

"How, in Heaven's name?" asked Sir Harold, in astonishment.

"How!" exclaimed the dwarf. "Have you forgotten the fair Janet, or the scene in the cottage garden, when she rested at your knee, and you pressed your hated lips upon her pure, fair brow? Had Othus the dwarf dared to do the deed shouts of derision and of laughter would have echoed after him, as if he, forsooth, has not the heart and feelings of a human being—the same passions that animate the breasts of the accursed race!"

"But you—you, Sir Knight," he added, after a pause of passion—"you who have stolen her from me, who would have ruined her if you could—you—ha! ha!—oh, I could crush trample, tread upon your whole race!"

"Unhappy wretch!" murmured Sir Harold, compassionately, "what can have thus instilled so many evil passions in your heart against your fellow-creatures?"

"Fellow-creatures!" yelled the dwarf, stamping upon the earth with impotent rage and fury—"and who, I pray you, would acknowledge this maimed distorted frame and these hideous features to be those of a fellow-creature? I tell you no! I have been reviled, despised, spat upon by all, and in return I hate, scorn, and detest every being of the human race!

"Oh! that I had my will!" he added, extending his long, claw-like hands. "I would even strangle the vile mass of clay to which I owe my being."

The young soldier started back with an undefined sensation of horror.

The hideous and distorted features of the dwarf, and his bent and misshapen limbs trembling with the violence of his passion, were something terrible to behold.

The awful creature, observing the effect of his appearance, shouted with scorn and derision as he pointed his long, lean fingers at Sir Harold.

But almost immediately becoming calm again, he drew nearer, and spoke in an altered tone, though with that shrill, unearthly voice that ever took from him the semblance of a human being.

"But enough of this," he continued. "My errand is not yet done, and although I would fain leave the rest unsaid I may not do so. Listen, then, and let the truth of what I have already said be impressed upon your mind.

"Those fellows who have just left us," he went on, "are, as you may have surmised, smugglers. One evening, some three months since, when off the South Coast in search of plunder, they were alarmed by loud and repeated screams, apparently rising from the bosom of the deep.

"At the same time the death-cry of some drowning animal in its last agony was borne across the wave. A boat was immediately lowered, not with the hope of saving life, but with the expectation of gaining plunder, and four stout rowers soon brought it to the spot from whence the cries seemed to proceed.

"But a thick mist had fallen upon the waters, and nothing was to be seen. After rowing about for some time, therefore, they prepared to return to the ship, when their leader, who was on board, suddenly descried something white floating upon the surface of the waters, within two or three oars length.

"They made for it and found it to be what they at first mistook for the corpse of a female. But the captain, who could boast of some little skill as a leech, observed symptoms of life in the apparently dead body, and prevailed upon his companions to return to the ship.

"This they did, and proper means being used, Lady Violet, for it was she, was soon restored to life. But meanwhile the wind had arisen, and they were compelled to quit the coast, and ere the lady had acquired sufficient strength to enable her to narrate the particulars of her catastrophe, or to say who her companions had been, the vessel was far enough away, tossing in the wild sea.

"Perchance, Sir Knight," grinned the dwarf, mockingly, "it would have been a mercy to have concealed your fate—your supposed fate, I mean, from her.

"But she was among those who had not been bred in the lap of luxury, and who knew nothing of refinement or delicacy of feeling, and it soon came to her ears that of all the party the insatiable ocean had spared but herself.

"Oh," he concluded, with fiendish glee, "that I had been by to witness her agony at the tale!"

"Fiend!" exclaimed Sir Harold, springing towards him.

But the creature eluded his grasp with wonderful agility, and, standing at a little distance, cried, in jeering tones—

"Nay, Sir Knight, hands off or I tell no more. So let that be understood. But if you are disposed to be quiet I will continue.

Sir Harold of necessity sat down quietly, and the dwarf went on—

"In a few days the smuggler chief, who possessed a good deal of power over his rough companions, persuaded them to steer northwards, and to land him and the lady at the village of Ravensbury.

"From that to Hamlyn was but a short journey, soon performed, and there the lady took up her abode sorrowfully enough, as I have heard.

"But a maiden's sorrow soon departs," he leered, "and perchance her's might have been far away by this time had not the fame of your doughty deeds, Sir Knight, lately reached England. As spirits seldom perform exploits like those you have done, conjecture arose that you, too, had escaped the fate ye well merited, and were still alive.

"Nought then," snarled the hunchback, "would serve the turn of that devil's hag Vera —a curse upon her!—but I, forsooth, must be dispatched here to you with the tidings of which, praise be so the fiend, I am now well rid."

"And Violet—where is Violet now?" demanded Sir Harold, quickly, for the tale of the dwarf was too connected and too consistent to leave a doubt of her preservation on his mind.

"Here, at Hamlyn," said the creature, with a malicious grin, "and I well ween she might be in safer quarters."

"How—what mean you?" exclaimed Sir Harold, with an indefinable sensation of alarm.

"Nay, nay, Sir Knight," said the dwarf, retreating, "my mission ends here, and may the foul fiend seize me if I utter another word!"

"Then, by the Heaven above us, I shall rip it out of your misshapen carcase!" cried the young soldier, fiercely, springing towards him.

The dwarf uttered a loud yell of mingled derision and contempt.

With inconceivable agility he sprang upon a projecting fragment of the ruin, far beyond Sir Harold's reach.

From his post of vantage he looked down upon the knight, and with cutting irony in his shrill voice exclaimed—

"Excuse me, Sir Knight, but I care not to trust these fair and delicate limbs in hands that are more fitted to handle a shark's skin than velvet "

"The hide of a shark!" shouted a deep voice behind him, while a strong hand seized the startled dwarf with an iron grip—"a smuggling shark. So, I've got you, my——"

But with a sudden and violent exertion of what appeared to be a species of supernatural strength, the dwarf shook off the grasp that had been laid upon his neck, and in an instant hurled his assailant to the ground.

"How are the mighty fallen!" cried the dwarf, shrieking with laughter, as he tossed his long arms on high. "Come and take me now, Mr. Coast Officer."

The discomfited Ralph Roley—for he it was—arose with the evident intention of renewing the assault, but he essayed in vain to scale the position on which the dwarf stood, which greatly provoked the creature's horrid laughter.

"What, Ralph, is it indeed you?" said Sir Harold, in pleased surprise, shaking the delighted yeoman's hand. "How comes it that you are here?"

"I am on a holiday trip to my cousin Launce, Sir Harold," replied Ralph, "who is a coast officer down these parts, and I have been amusing myself by joining him in a hunt after a party of smugglers in hiding among these ruins. But excuse me awhile, Sir Knight—first let me lay that devil's cub by the heels," he added, pointing to the dwarf.

And without more ado he proceeded to roll a huge fragment of stone to the foot of that part of the wall on which the dwarf had taken his station.

The latter watched his motions in silence for a few seconds, and then turning towards Sir Harold, said—

"Nay, then, Sir Knight, if it is thus ye would treat the bearer of good tidings I must e'en say fare thee well. You will soon hie thee away, Sir Knight, with saddle and spur, but see if these distorted limbs bear not this misshapen carcase to Hamlyn long before the boasted strength of your fleet and powerful steed will transport you there. Again fare thee well, and may the blessings of St. Peleg, which are curses, light on thee."

As he concluded, the dwarf sprang backward, and was immediately lost to view in the obscurity of the deep shadow that overhung the interior of the ruin.

"'Tis a spirit," cried Ralph, when the dwarf disappeared, "and as such its want of knowledge of the rules of civilised warfare must be admitted. Nevertheless, had it but waited the regular advance——"

"Which it by no means seemed inclined to do," interrupted Sir Harold, laughing.

"True, Sir Harold," rejoined Ralph, testily. "But had he fought, I say, according to the rules of war, I should undoubtedly have come off victorious and——"

A loud, shrill yell, echoing from the ruins, startlingly interrupted the worthy yeoman's speech.

The loud yell came from the dwarf, and Sir Harold rushed forward to the part from whence the sound emanated, but the creature was nowhere to be seen.

A diligent search was made, and the young soldier came to the conclusion that be he where he might the dwarf was no longer within the precincts of the ruin.

The intelligence he had communicated, however, was too important to be neglected, and although the obvious malice of the creature undoubtedly tended to throw a shadow of discredit upon his narrative, yet it was too well connected to be altogether false.

So, without troubling himself to inquire by what impelling motive the dwarf could have been urged, the young soldier determined forthwith to bend his steps once more to Hamlyn Court.

CHAPTER XLII.

DIGGING THE MINE—TRESHAM'S TREACHERY—AN EVIL OMEN—THE MYSTERIOUS BELL.

As it was only on dark or misty nights that Guy Fawkes and his companions could, with any degree of safety, prosecute their dangerous work, a full week passed away before the whole of the powder was landed in the cellar of the building adjoining the Parliament House.

When all were assembled, Father Garnet offered up a fervent prayer of thanksgiving for having so far succeeded in their purpose.

Then he addressed the conspirators, adjuring them to be faithful to their vow, and to stand by each other to the last extremity.

Each and every one of the fanatical plotters drew their swords, then, bending the knee before the reverend father, and kissing the upraised blades, repeated after him their solemn and fearful oath.

The group formed a rare subject for the pencil of the painter.

They had laid in a store of eggs, dried meats, biscuits, cheese, wine, &c., so that no suspicion should be excited in the neighbourhood by their going in and out, or from their having brought in provisions for so many persons.

All were provided with a password, and the greatest secrecy and caution was used by the ever-watchful Bates in the admittance or departure of any of the members of the league.

Guy Fawkes had assumed an effective disguise, in order to pursue his onerous and multifarious duties without recognition.

Having talked over and arranged their plans, the conspirators sat down to a frugal supper.

This done, some wine and drinking-cups were placed upon the table.

"Gentlemen," said Catesby (who sat at the lower end of the table), as he poured himself out a cup of the ruby liquor, "I am proud to inform you that fresh converts are joining our league daily.

"John Grant, of Norbrook, who has suffered severely as a recusant, has become one of us, and, besides money, has offered us the use of his house, which is large and strongly fortified, as a good depot for horses, arms, and ammunition."

"Long life and prosperity to him!" cried several of the conspirators, and all drained their cups.

Catesby proceeded—

"When the great and final blow is struck I can place myself at the head of over five hundred armed and disciplined men, all good and true, to enforce our rights. Then why should we hesitate—what should we fear?"

"That our cause is a just and righteous one," observed Sir Everard Digby, reflectively.

"Croaking again, Sir Everard," sneered Catesby. "Have I then failed to satisfy your unseemly scruples? If not, let me further add that the storm of persecution against our downtrodden brethren rages fiercer than ever, despite the fair promises of that false and lying tyrant, James.

"In the shires and provinces, and even here in London itself, the violence and insolence of the heretics' continual searches have grown to be intolerable.

"Scarcely a night passes but what soldiers and catch-poles break into quiet men's houses while they are asleep, and not only carry away their persons and thrust them into prison, except the villains be bribed excessively, but whatsoever they like best in the house besides.

"Furthermore," continued Catesby, "our gentlewomen are dragged out of bed by these shameless dogs, to see whether they have anything there concealed. The gaols are crammed with Catholic prisoners, because of their openly avowed love of Holy Church, and who, instead of obtaining redress, are placed in the pillory to be insulted and pelted at by the coarse and brutal rabble. Our priests and missionaries are also murdered or condemned to death.

"Are these acts of right and justice?" concluded the speaker, with telling emphasis. "If they are not, I consider our measures for redress cannot surely call for condemnation."

A murmur of applause came from the assembled conspirators.

"I am answered," said Sir Everard, bowing and resuming his seat.

"And now let each man fill his cup to the brim," added Catesby, rising and filling his goblet, "and drink to the success of our great enterprise."

All rose to their feet, and, raising their wine cups on high, drank the toast with a burst of frenzied enthusiasm.

Guy Fawkes waited till quiet reigned once more, then, holding aloft his goblet, he exclaimed, in low, startling tones—

"And here I solemnly swear that not only shall my hand alone fire the train, but that I will not leave my place of watching until the explosion has taken place, even though I should be hurled into eternity with our enemies."

And he drained his cup of wine to the dregs.

The conspirators now retired to rest, with the understanding that they would commence operations the following day.

Next morning Sir Charles Percy, who had not yet visited his fellow-conspirators at their new quarters, presented himself at the garden gate, and gave the required sign.

He was cautiously admitted by Bates, who, striking three times on the wall, caused the conspirators to emerge from their place of concealment.

His confederates greeted him warmly, and they proceeded to an apartment below, in order to converse in safety.

When they were seated Percy said—

"I am rather inclined to suspect our brother Tresham of treachery towards us."

All started in mingled astonishment and apprehension.

"Your reason, Sir Charles?" demanded Catesby.

"In my capacity of gentleman-pensioner," answered Percy, "I hear many secrets touching the court, and among other matters it is whispered that my Lord Monteagle hints vaguely at a plot in operation on the part of the Catholics against the king."

"The false, fickle trickster!" cried Catesby, wrathfully. "Deeply do I now regret admitting him to our league or entrusting him with our secrets."

"'Twas an evil day for us when he joined," observed Thomas Winter.

"Evil indeed," rejoined Catesby, sternly. "Fool and madman that I was ever to bring him among us; but I was won over by the two thousand pounds he promised to lend us towards our urgent need of funds to carry out our plans."

"Let us not judge him too hastily, gentlemen," interposed Ambrose Rookwood.

"If I find he has played the traitor," cried Guy Fawkes, with suppressed passion, "he shall answer for it with his life."

It was growing late. The abbey clock had long since struck the hour of midnight.

Seizing a mattock and spade, Guy Fawkes said—

"To work, brethren, to work."

"Aye, aye, to work," each responded, taking up some implement.

"Yes, to work," cried Catesby, shouldering a heavy pick. "I will strike the first blow."

"And I the last," muttered Guy Fawkes, as they all descended to the vault beneath.

One side of the cellar lay in a straight line with the Parliament House.

On this they now prepared to work.

Raising the pick on high Catesby exclaimed—

"Would that this stone were the heart of the heretic James. Thus would I pierce it to its inmost core!"

And, throwing his whole force into the blow, he struck the hard wall with such violence that sparks of fire and huge splinters of granite flew about in all directions.

One of the jagged fragments struck Guy Fawkes under the left eye, inflicting a severe wound, and narrowly depriving him of sight.

"'Tis an evil omen," he muttered, staunching the flow of blood, his superstitious nature

GUY FAWKES

Or Gunpowder, Treason, and Plot.

SIR HAROLD DREW BOTH SWORD AND DAGGER AND STOOD BOLDLY ON THE DEFENSIVE.

No, 11.

attaching more importance to the incident itself than the danger he had escaped or the pain of the wound.

This circumstance, simple as it was, cast a gloom upon the whole party, and considerably damped their ardour.

Upon Guy Fawkes, however, assuring them that the injury he had sustained was a trifling one, the work of excavation was resumed.

Guy Fawkes, in his disguise, now passed as one James Johnstone, the supposed servant of Sir Charles Percy.

To him was allotted the task of keeping watch in the garden, armed to the teeth, and wearing a long cloak, for concealment.

Three of the conspirators worked whilst the fourth rested—each and all taking their spell in turn.

The work was of the most laborious and arduous nature, such indeed as the sturdiest excavators would most reluctantly have undertaken.

But, undaunted by such considerations, they toiled with unceasing assiduity during the day at undermining the wall.

And during the night they buried the rubbish under the earth in the garden.

They thus laboured indefatigably for many days.

One night, when they were toiling with all their energies to complete the passage through the wall, all were startled by the solemn tolling of a bell.

"It seems to proceed from inside the very bowels of the earth," said Guy Fawkes, in a fearful whisper.

All listened, when again came the clear, solemn, blood-freezing sound.

They stood for a space spell-bound with awe. What did it mean?

Was it a warning from above to desist? Were they braving the wrath of high heaven, or did it proceed from an infernal agency?

"That unearthly warning has rendered my arm nerveless," at length said Guy Fawkes. "I can do no more."

And he threw the mattock shudderingly from him.

Each in turn dropped his implement, and stood aghast, listening to the mournful tolling of that awful and mysterious bell.

Even the bold and unscrupulous Catesby stood silent and apart, evidently affected by its sepulchral-like tones.

"Arouse ye, my children," observed Father Woodruff. "If, as I think, it should prove to be the work of the arch-fiend, Sathanas, the dispersion of holy waters shall stop it!"

All gazed in wrapt curiosity and wonderment.

A vessel containing the sacred fluid was brought, and the priest, uttering a grave and impressive exorcism, sprinkled the stones liberally with it.

The bell instantly ceased.

Nor was it heard again.

So the conspirators once more took heart, but no more work was done that night.

CHAPTER XLIII.

THE HOME OF GREGORY THE GOLDSMITH—THE MAIDEN OF THE COTTAGE—THE DWARF AGAIN.

WITH a lighter heart than he had felt for many weary months Sir Harold pursued his way in the direction of Hamlyn Court.

Dreams of bright days in store danced before him, and the image of Violet, more lovely than perhaps even she, fair and beautiful as she was, could in reality boast, rose in view.

In this happy mood he entered the town, and, catching sight of Gregory Goldpurse's swinging sign, he determined to pay the worthy old goldsmith a visit.

In truth his weary steed and himself alike needed repose, and even the iron frame of Ralph Roley, who insisted on spending his holiday in company of the young knight, began to acknowledge the power of forced marches.

Arriving at the portal Ralph dismounted, and knocked loudly on the iron-studded door.

In answer to his summons the door revolved on its hinges, and in the light that shone from above Sir Harold recognised the pretty face of the maiden of the cottage.

The surprise was mutual.

Sir Harold sprang to the ground and clasped the hand of the blushing maiden within his own.

Ralph winced, ogled, and chuckled, and muttered something about "the beauty of the flesh."

And as Sir Harold relinquished the maiden's hand, Ralph approached, with the evident intention of snatching a kiss from her ripe, tempting lips, in conformity, as he said, to the fashion of more polished lands, when a new actor appeared upon the scene.

With a wild and rapid stride he made towards the yeoman, and, raising his hand on high, would soon have finished his career.

But Ralph's quick eye caught the gleam of naked steel, and, swift as thought, arrested the assailant's arm and wrenched the dagger from his grasp.

"How now thou misshapen imp of Satan," cried Ralph, hotly. "Art gone mad that ye set on folks in this fashion. Were ye but a head taller I would teach——"

What more he would have said is not known, for the dwarf, Othus, his features rendered more hideous than ever with high-wrought jealousy, uttered a wild and fearful shriek, and dashed past him, at once laying the redoubtable yeoman prostrate on his back.

With the dwarf this was but the work of a moment, and ere Ralph had recovered his perpendicular the mysterious being had darted up the winding stairs, and was quickly beyond his reach.

"The vile cockatrice of the devil. to serve me so scurvy a trick!" cried the ruffled yeoman. "An may I never see my Dolly's blue eyes again if I do not make him——"

"Stay," said a calm voice, as a restraining hand was laid upon Ralph's shoulder—"stay, and threaten not with condign punishment one who, for aught ye know, hath more to do with the affairs of another world than of this."

"A spirit!" exclaimed Ralph, starting back. "Then he may go to his father in his own way, for aught that I will ever do to send him there. With flesh and blood I would hold my own, but with the outcasts of another world I have no wish at present to become acquainted."

"Ah! Sir Harold Rookby," said the worthy goldsmith, with pleased surprise, now recognising the young knight. "No ill wind surely hath blown thee hither *this* time?"

"My worthy preserver!" exclaimed Sir

Harold, grasping the goldsmith's extended hand.

"Nay, nay, odds, hammers and anvils," said Gregory Goldpurse, good-naturedly, and, ordering their horses to be stabled, he led the way to his cosily-furnished parlour. "No more," he added, "an thou lovest me, as the maskers say."

Order and comfort reigned throughout the apartment of the goldsmith.

At opposite sides of a highly polished oak table, on which was placed a huge measure of spicy canary, flanked by two long and slender glasses, sat Sir Harold and the master of the house.

On one side, and removed to a little distance from the board, Ralph stretched his stalwart form, turning with eyes of glowing interest upon the maiden who was seated by his side.

The amorous Ralph had already begun to whisper in her ear sundry anecdotes about his adventures with Guy Fawkes, when his attention was attracted by the words of Sir Harold and his host.

"Nay, Sir Knight," exclaimed the goldsmith, in answer to a question of Sir Harold. "I can tell you little about him, save that the misshapen whelp is the plague and torment of my house, and also of my niece the pretty Janet here."

"Indeed, uncle, and he is," earnestly exclaimed Janet. "And would to Heaven you would show him the outside of your door."

"A—well, Janet," answered her uncle, "and I am sure I wish I could, but it's uncanny meddling with such folks. And, besides, to say the truth, the creature has been useful, although, no doubt, against his own will."

"He has indeed been of service," said Sir Harold, musing. "And that, too, upon more occasions than one. But if, as you say, against his own will, why should he ever have done any act of kindness at all?"

"That," said the goldsmith, as he swallowed a glass of his rare canary—"that I must e'en leave to Janet to explain."

Sir Harold turned an inquiring glance at the maiden.

"It is no use to conceal it," said Janet, in answer to his look, "for he has ever acted under the direction and control of Vera Horlock —one whose kindness is yet impressed upon my mind, and who did more than a mother's part to me when I had the misfortune to lose my own."

"Aye, aye, my poor sister," sighed Gregory Goldpurse.

"Vera Horlock!" exclaimed Sir Harold, thoughtfully. "But from what source can her power and authority over that unhappy creature flow?"

"That I know not," answered the goldsmith, "but that she does both possess and exercise a certain power of control over him is certain, and from mutterings I have heard the imp of darkness—Heaven forgive me—use in moments of wrath and disappointment, which are of no rare occurrence, there seemeth to me to be some sort of close and intimate but mysterious connection betwixt them."

"But why?" continued the young soldier, only half satisfied with this explanation—"why does Vera Horlock work by such means?"

The goldsmith shook his head.

"She is a strange woman, Sir Knight," said his host, "and comes of a strange family, for, among many other things, 'tis said her father is a wizard, and, although her wilder passions have long been melted down in the crucible of misfortune, ye may as well try to hammer a golden noble out of a silver crown as to discover the secret impulse that moves the actions of Vera Horlock. She has the interest of you, Sir Knight, and of the Lady Violet, much at heart. And it may be she has good reason for that, too, but she loves to do things in a mysterious way, and will be guided by the advice of no one."

"But what need," asked Sir Harold, "of so much mystery when none seems to be required? Surely in aught which the Lady Violet and I have been concerned a plain communication from herself would as well have served her end?"

"Perhaps it might," replied the goldsmith, "but further explanation is beyond my power to give. She ever moves in mystery. It is her pleasure, and she always takes the bye-ways and lanes even when the wide and open path lies straight before her. In truth," he added, "I have often thought that early misfortunes have turned her brain, and she wants something here, Sir Knight, as a body might say."

And the worthy man, with a knowing look, touched his forehead with the tip of his finger.

The young soldier sat deep in thought for some time, but his thinking did not bring to light the hidden motives of Vera's conduct.

That she had been of service to him was clear. That the dwarf had acted under her direction and control was also certain. Yet why she should have chosen so extraordinary a messenger to fulfil her purpose he felt could only be accounted for by what the old goldsmith had advanced.

Sir Harold at length rose, and, thanking the worthy goldsmith for his hospitality, prepared to depart.

Meanwhile the host had ordered the horses to be brought from the stables to the front door.

It must not, however, be imagined that Sir Harold left until he had courteously saluted the gentle Janet.

Ralph saucily followed the young soldier's example, which the maiden received with a slight blush.

Wondering what his Dolly would think if she could have seen him, the amorous Ralph hastened with rapid step after Sir Harold, who had descended the long stairs leading from the mansion of the worthy goldsmith.

As the evening was now drawing to a close Sir Harold and his companion took up their quarters at a pleasant inn in the neighbourhood, and, retiring to bed, were in a very short space of time in the full enjoyment of a sound and deep repose.

CHAPTER XLIV.

DIGGING THE MINE—THE MYSTERIOUS SOUND— THE CONSPIRATORS' ALARM—A BOLD RESOLVE —THE DISCOVERY.

NEXT day, after a hasty meal, the conspirators recommenced their work of excavation.

The earth was now soft and yielding. They worked with a will, and in a few hours made more headway than they had previously done with all their labours put together.

When Guy Fawkes descended from his post of watching, and saw the progress these gentlemen navvies had made, his heart beat high with hope, and he exclaimed, with enthusiasm—

"Nobly done, my brave brethren! Another such a day's work and we shall be right under the Parliament House."

The conspirators smiled at the well-merited compliment, and paused a moment to wipe their perspiring brows.

"You handle the mattock well, Sir Everard, for a hand so small and white," added Guy Fawkes, approaching that nobleman, whose rich hosen and velvet trunks were all besmeared and soiled with mud and dust. "Come, give me the pick, and do ye all rest awhile and partake of your well-earned repast."

Sir Everard smilingly complied, remarking, as he handed Guy Fawkes the pick—

"I trust, friend Fawkes, that ye will prove a true prophet, and that ere nightfall to-morrow this work of burrowing like so many blind moles will have been brought to an end, for, by St. Mary, I love it none too well."

The wish was re-echoed by all present.

Guy Fawkes having divested himself of his hat and doublet, began to work with such vigour and effect as to give promise of a speedy realisation of his prediction.

Driving his pick deep into the clayey soil he paused in the act of dislodging a huge mass of earth.

Then suddenly a jet of black water came rushing into the cavity, with a roaring, startling sound.

"Holy virgin!" exclaimed Guy Fawkes, leaping back, for the stream threatened to speedily inundate the place, "we have burst the bank of the river!"

"And our carefully constructed plan has turned out a wretched and hopeless failure!" cried Catesby, dejectedly.

"The labour of weeks swept away in a moment!" murmured John Wright, bitterly.

A lament in which all the rest joined.

"Quick, my son, shore up the hole, or we shall be flooded!" cried Father Garnet, in some alarm, as the inky flood came pouring in with increasing impetus and sound.

Guy Fawkes plunged through the icy pool—already up to his knees—and, with a few shovels-full of earth, quickly repaired the breach.

He returned to the others crestfallen and dispirited.

"I fear, holy father," he said, in mournful tones, "that our purpose is indeed disapproved of by the Almighty, and it would beseem us rather than incur Divine wrath to abandon, now and for ever, our apparently unholy design."

"Alas! it would appear so, my son," said Father Garnet. "Yet we must not give way to despair too readily. Our worldly wisdom hath clearly misled us, yet the all-seeing eye of Providence may have decreed that another channel shall be opened unto us, through which our great object shall yet be attained."

"Your words, reverend father," said Catesby, bowing, "inspire me with new hope. It hath occurred to me that were we to burrow more to the right we should thus avoid the bed of the river, and——"

"You would deviate too wide of the mark," interrupted Guy Fawkes. "Besides, were we able to penetrate to the desired spot, after the powder had rested there for a few days the damp from the river would render it utterly useless. No, the project is impracticable. Some other means must be devised, or, as I before observed, would it not be more seemly in the sight of Him we seek to serve to forget it for evermore, and leave Heaven to redress our wrongs in its own good time and way?"

As he spoke a sound louder than the thunder's mighty rattle crashed fearfully over their heads.

All started in the wildest terror and consternation.

Huddled together in the farthest corner of the vault, they stood in momentary fear of the entire structure falling in upon them, and burying them under its ruins.

"The blessed saints preserve us!" cried Father Woodruff, crossing himself. "In the name of holy Heaven what does it mean?"

But all seemed too paralysed by fear to reply.

Again came the dreaded sound—after a short interval.

This time, however, it resembled a rushing, rattling noise, as of falling stones.

"We are betrayed!" cried Catesby, in dismay—"caught like rats in a trap! and our enemies are entombing us beneath the ruins of our retreat!"

"'Tis a fearful thought," said Sir Everard Digby. "Let us make an effort to fight our way through our foes, and if we are to die let it be like soldiers, sword in hand, and not like vermin run to earth!"

"Let me be the first to go forward," said Guy Fawkes, "and see the nature of the peril by which we are menaced."

"Nay, my son," interrupted Father Garnet. "We can ill afford to lose your valuable aid at a moment like this."

"It recks not, holy father," replied Guy Fawkes, gloomily, "what becomes of me since all my dearly-cherished hopes have been so ruthlessly blighted. Your blessing, reverend father, for it may be that I go to my death!"

He sank on one knee, and the worthy priest having, in a voice of unusual solemnity, pronounced a fervent benediction upon him, he arose and ascended to the rooms above.

The conspirators listened to his departing footsteps in tormenting anxiety.

The sounds ceased, and all was again wrapped in death-like stillness.

In a fever of consuming suspense and dread apprehension they impatiently awaited the return of Guy Fawkes.

The seconds and minutes rolled on, but they heard not the welcome sound of his footfall.

An hour passed away, as the bell of the Abbey clock too plainly denoted, but still he came not.

Oppressed with dire and dismal forebodings as to his fate, they were almost on the point of giving way to despair when the clanking of spurs was suddenly heard on the steps leading to the vault, and the next instant Guy Fawkes stood before them.

"Your looks proclaim that you are the harbinger of good tidings, my son," said Father Garnet, at sight of the conspirator.

"I am, reverend father," answered Guy Fawkes. "You said that Heaven probably would open another channel for our deliverance, and you were right."

An exclamation of joy escaped all present.

"The noise that so startled us," continued Guy Fawkes, "proceeded from the cellar of one John Bright, a coal merchant, who was having his stock-in-trade removed, as he was vacating the cellar."

"Upon inquiry I learned that the cellar was to let, and I have taken it—taken it in your name, Sir Charles," added Guy Fawkes, turning to the wily Percy.

"But your object in so doing?" inquired Catesby.

"Need you ask?" returned Guy Fawkes. "It is directly under the House of Lords. Think of that, gentlemen."

"And therefore will make a splendid receptacle for the powder!" cried Catesby, with exultation. "Well done, brother Fawkes—victory, gentlemen, victory. The success of our enterprise is now certain."

CHAPTER XLV.

ON THE TRACK—THE ACCIDENT—DEFEATED—A FEARFUL LEAP—FOUND—A TERRIBLE SCENE.

AFTER a good night's rest, and having partaken of a hearty breakfast, Sir Harold and Ralph bade adieu to the host of the inn near the wood, and again set out on their journey.

During the heat of the mid-day hours they reposed at a small but pleasant hostelrie, where Ralph, who had plenty of prize money, made himself very much at home.

He treated, joked, and caroused with the men—he kissed the women—and he sang to all.

Indeed, he seemed for the time totally to forget that he had such a thing as a wife anxiously awaiting his home coming.

But pleasant things must have an end, and he was recalled from his entertaining duties by the sight of Sir Harold remounting his steed to proceed upon his way.

In another minute he was in the saddle riding by the young soldier's side.

Nothing particular occurred during the remainder of the journey.

Towards the close of the evening they reached the boundaries of the wide domain of Hamlyn-court, and about an hour, or it might be more, after sunset—for the shades of night were deep upon the earth—they ascended the steep and winding road leading to the village through which they had to pass in order to arrive at the dwelling of Vera Horlock.

The rumble of carriage wheels along the rugged path, and the repeated crack of the driver's whip, presently attracted the young soldier's eager attention. Soon on the brow of the ascent in front of him he observed a coach, driven at a furious rate, making direct for the village, and as he gazed he fancied he could hear a voice from within the vehicle urging the driver on to still greater exertions.

The speaker then thrust his head out of the window, ostensibly for the purpose of noting the progress they were making.

And in that brief moment Sir Harold felt convinced that he recognised in the traveller his deadliest enemy and bitterest foe.

Striking spurs into his steed he soon reached the steep entrance to the high street, in the track of the flying vehicle, leaving honest Ralph some distance in the rear.

At that moment a crashing sound, mingled with a female shriek, rang out on the still night air.

Urging his panting steed a few paces nearer Sir Harold beheld the nature of the catastrophe.

The coach was lying overturned on its side, with the unfortunate coachman partly underneath it.

But what attracted Sir Harold's attention most was a pale, senseless, female form, lying in the centre of the roadway.

His heart gave a great bound of mingled hope and fear as he gazed, and, springing from his horse, he drew his sword and rushed to her assistance.

"Merciful Heavens, Violet!" he exclaimed, on reaching her side.

He instantly sheathed his weapon, and was in the act of raising her up when two strong hands seized him from behind, and he was hurled with great violence some yards off.

Stunned by the force of the fall it was some seconds ere Sir Harold regained his feet.

When he did so, however, it was to find that his late assailant had possessed himself of Violet, and, darting down a side lane, was fast disappearing in the direction of Vera Horlock's cottage.

Sir Harold was now joined by Ralph, and, mounting his steed, they were soon on the track of the flying fugitive.

A deep ravine lay before them, and over it a slight rustic bridge afforded a most precarious footing.

The daring fugitive, with his fair burden, who had used his utmost speed to gain the opposite side of the bridge before his pursuers arrived, now placed the unconscious Violet upon the soft sward, and, exerting all his strength, dislodged the rude structure and sent it clattering down the abyss.

This placed a formidable barrier between him and his foes. Then, taking Violet in his arms again, he gave utterance to a mocking laugh, and, hastening on, was soon lost to view in the semi-darkness.

Sir Harold reined up his horse upon the dizzy brink of the ravine, and, though inwardly chafing, appeared calmly to measure the distance of the gap with his eye.

It was a fearful leap.

But maddened at being so easily foiled, and at the thought of Violet being again in the power of his hated foe, he determined to hazard the die.

Backing his steed for about twenty paces he urged it forward again with voice and spur.

The sagacious animal knew what was required of it, and, bounding madly onward, it sprang high into the air and alighted safely on the opposite bank.

"Bravo, Sir Harold, bravo!" shouted Ralph, in well-merited admiration.

And a moment after the fearless fellow had followed the young soldier's example, though he was within half a foot of being dashed to atoms down the deep ravine.

They pushed on for some seconds, perplexed and uncertain which direction to take.

But scarcely had they gone a hundred yards when they were startled and alarmed by one the most wild and fearful screams that ever rang upon the human ear.

It appeared to proceed from Vera Horlock's cottage.

The paralysed pair paused, and drew near each other, as if waiting for, yet dreading, a repetition of the sound.

It soon came, and, if possible, was a still more wild and unearthly cry.

They were not far from the dwelling, and without a moment's hesitation, therefore, Sir Harold set spurs to his steed.

Ralph followed closely on his heels.

Sir Harold's arrival at the house, and subsequent interference, seemed to be providential, for more than one life hung upon his speed.

He found the door of the house standing partly open.

Springing from his horse he rushed up the front stairs, and, guided by a glimmering light, made for the apartment whence it proceeded.

Merciful Heavens! what a sight burst upon his horror-struck eyes.

On a couch at the opposite extremity of the room lay the form of Vera weltering in her blood, and, standing over her, with the yet reeking knife in his blood-stained hand, was the magician Horlock, his features distorted by an expression too terrible for description.

But Sir Harold's attention was immediately withdrawn, even from that fearful sight.

A low and half-stifled cry fell upon his ear, and turning in the direction from whence it issued he beheld Violet faintly struggling in a ruffian's grasp.

Sir Harold's sword flew from its sheath like the lightning's flash.

But a fearful avenger was before him.

He felt something glide past him like a spirit, and Othus the dwarf sprang like a tiger upon Violet's assailant, and with his long, lean hands seized him firmly by the throat.

The released Violet darted with a wild sob into Sir Harold's arms, and, nearly maddened by the sight before her, clung with frantic fervour around his neck.

He, on the other hand, clasped her firmly to his heart, as if to shield her from an evil the nature of which he could as yet scarcely comprehend.

But the notice of all was drawn to the fierce and terrible struggle betwixt the dwarf and the ruffian he had attacked.

They rolled over and over upon the floor, and the wild cries of the deformed creature rang throughout the place.

His desperate opponent in vain tried to shake him off.

Othus clung with a fierce and deadly tenacity of purpose to his throat, and the struggle, though fearful and terrific, was of short duration.

In a few minutes all was quiet.

The dwarf quitted his hold and sprang upon his feet, uttering a wild and hideous yell, and the blackened and distorted countenance and staring eyeballs of his hapless victim told how well Othus had done his work.

Sir Sidney Wildbrook's long career of crimes was at an end.

His still quivering corpse lay before them.

The misshapen creature spurned it from him with his foot.

But as it rolled away the light fell strongly upon the awful countenance, and the dying Vera shrieked and covered her eyes with her hands.

"Wretched being!" she exclaimed, "it is your father!"

It was her last effort—her last words—and scarcely were they uttered ere her spirit fled.

Here an old woman hobbled into the room, exclaiming, as she bent over the knight's dead body—

"Alas, alas! it is fearful work! But it is all true—all true. He was the destroyer of my child when she was young and innocent, and they were the parents of yon distorted fiend!"

"Then," cried the dwarf, in his wildest screech-owl tones—"then have I avenged my mother's wrongs! And oh! that he had a hundred lives, that I might crush—crush—crush them all!"

While he spoke the whole form of the unhappy wretch seemed to dilate. His hideous features assumed an expression truly diabolical.

He stamped, he raved, and finally, tossing his long, lean arms on high, he uttered a wild, unearthly yell, and fled from the house.

He was never seen again in life, but the inhabitants of the district still maintain that his spirit haunts the deep glens, and is to be seen on stormy nights flying with wild and fearful screams upon the blast.

CHAPTER XLVI.

THE MINE LAID—NEW DANGERS—LORD MONTEAGLE WARNED — THE LULL BEFORE THE STORM.

THE mysterious bell, which had so startled and dismayed the conspirators, being no longer heard, their fears were now at an end, and they again became sanguine of the success of their project.

The following day Percy, having taken possession of the cellar under the Parliament House, he, in company of Guy Fawkes, examined it, and found it admirably suited to their purpose.

In a very short time, and, as before, under the cloak of night, they removed thirty-six barrels of gunpowder from the house adjoining, and transported them to the cellar, where they covered them over with faggots, coals, billets of wood, and old lumber.

All being prepared, they once more separated, intending to meet again a few days before the assembling of Parliament.

Guy Fawkes and Catesby, as the day drew near, retired to a romantic old house among the woods of Enfield, known as White Wells.

They were in deep consultation with several others, for a new and grave danger threatened them.

Many of the conspirators had friends among the members of Parliament, and, desirous of saving them, each wished to convey a particular warning to his own friend or relative, which should make their absence certain.

"Such a course," observed Catesby, referring to the above, "would endanger the safety of the whole scheme."

"Most assuredly," returned Guy Fawkes, "I am strongly opposed. In short, if it is persisted in, I will have nothing whatever to do with the matter."

Many protested, and Robert Keys, who had the custody of the old house at Lambeth, said—

"I pray you, gentlemen, let me send a guarded warning to that most honourable gentleman the Lord of Mordaunt, who sheltered and maintained my wife and children after my ruin at the hands of this accursed heretic monarch."

Sir Everard Digby, Ambrose Rookwood, and several others expressed their eager anxiety to warn the young Earl of Arundel, while Percy was equally anxious to save his relative, the Earl of Northumberland.

Catesby became extremely alarmed at these proposals.

"'Sdeath!" exclaimed Catesby, passionately, "are there not means enough in operation to keep all those who we wish to save away?'

"Aye, more than enough," responded Guy Fawkes, sternly. "Methinks our plans are already enfeebled and endangered by such careless publicity and unwise scruples."

"By the blessed Virgin!" cried Catesby, impetuously, "I swear that rather than imperil the cause by such unseemly acts of mad folly I would have all blown up, though they were as dear to me as my own son."

"And I am willing to sacrifice my very life rather than our glorious plan of regeneration should miscarry!" exclaimed Guy Fawkes, with his old fanatical look.

"Your sentiments do you honour, my sons," said Father Woodruff; "though I sincerely hope to see the fulfilment of our purpose without the sacrifice of a single son of Holy Church."

At this juncture Tresham suddenly made his appearance.

He appeared excited and embarrassed.

"I overheard your last remark, reverend father," he said, with a troubled look, "and I would strenuously urge that I may be allowed to put my Lord Monteagle on his guard, who is not only my kinsman—being the husband of my sister Cecily—but is, moreover, a true man, and a good and staunch Catholic."

"It cannot be," interposed Catesby, decisively. "Some base traitor has, I fear, already whispered abroad something of our secret," and he looked searchingly and significantly at Tresham.

"As Heaven is my judge I know nothing of these whisperings," cried the arch-traitor, with seeming sincerity. "Can you doubt my zeal and fidelity when I have embraced your cause at the hazard of my life and the sacrifice of my fortune?"

"Your zeal and fidelity have yet to be proven, Master Tresham," observed Catesby, with irony, "and, touching your promised *pecuniary* aid, we have not as yet seen the colour of your gold."

"I will reply to that anon," said Tresham; "meanwhile let me beg of you to grant my request with respect to my kinsman, Lord Monteagle. I would be most cautious, most secret and circumspect, in my manner and message to him."

"Enough!" exclaimed Catesby. "You plead in vain—the matter hath been fully discussed, and we are all resolved, brethren?'

"We are!" exclaimed the conspirators in a breath.

Tresham bit his lip, but, concealing his annoyance, he said—

"Touching the money which I have agreed to advance, I regret to state that I shall be unable to keep my promise until I have sold some property."

"He is deceiving us, I am convinced," whispered Catesby in Guy Fawkes's ear.

"He is a traitor, be assured," returned Guy Fawkes, in the same low tone.

"Believe me, comrades," urged Tresham, "this blind precipitation and hot haste is as unnecessary as it is unwise. The explosion will be just as effectual at the end of the Session as at the beginning."

"No, no! Delays are fraught with danger!" cried the conspirators. "We have had too many already; let us get the business over."

"Perhaps you will be kind enough, Sir Francis," observed Catesby, satirically, "to inform us how we, who are without funds, are going to exist meanwhile."

"I would advise," replied Tresham, "that for safety and economy we immediately proceed to Flanders, where we are sure of a hearty reception. I will supply the ship and find the necessary funds for maintenance."

"The wily, subtle traitor," muttered Catesby to Father Garnet. "He is trifling with us merely to gain time."

"I begin to fear your estimation of his character is correct, my son," returned the priest.

"Shall I plunge my dagger into his false, traitorous heart!" hissed Guy Fawkes, with passionate vehemence, his eager fingers closing on the hilt of his weapon.

"Nay, my son, leave his punishment to a higher power!" said the holy man, chidingly.

"Let us dissemble and appear to acquiesce," suggested Catesby. "That will help to throw him off his guard, and give us an opportunity of watching him and of learning the truth."

"You counsel well, my son," said Father Woodruff. "Let a close watch be kept upon his every action, and if he be a traitor we shall quickly know."

Soon after the conspirators separated for the night.

CHAPTER XLVII.

THE SECRET WARNING—THE SUSPECTED TRAITOR —THE KING AND HIS FALSE COURTIERS—GUY FAWKES AGAIN VISITS THE VAULT—THE GUN-POWDER PLOT NEAR ITS COMPLETION.

TRESHAM, on leaving the conspirators' secret haunt on the borders of Enfield Chase, returned to town.

On arriving in the metropolis it is supposed that one of his first acts there was to warn Lord Monteagle, and also Lord Mordaunt, who had married his other sister.

The movements of Lord Monteagle warranted the belief that he had received a warning of some kind, and that there was danger to be apprehended, for he immediately removed from his house in London to his country residence at Hoxton.

And a few days before the proposed opening of Parliament he, much to the surprise of his family, ordered a grand supper, to which he invited a large number of guests.

As Lord Monteagle sat at table about seven

o'clock on the evening in question a handsome youth, in a page's dress, entered hastily, and handed his lordship a letter.

"Where got ye this missive, boy?" asked the nobleman.

"I received it from a masked and cloaked stranger, my lord," answered the page, "who pounced out upon me from the shrubbery, and, bidding me, as I valued your lordship's precious life, deliver it immediately into your hands, vanished in the gloom like a spirit."

The guests looked surprised and interested.

Lord Monteagle opened the mysterious document, and, seeing that it bore no signature nor date, handed it to Thomas Ward, a gentleman of his establishment, and requested him to read it aloud.

It ran as follows:—

"MY LORD,—Out of the love I bear to some of your friends I have a care for your preservation. Therefore I would advise you, as you value your life, to devise some excuse to absent yourself from attendance at this Parliament, for God and man hath concurred to punish the wickedness of the times.

"Think not slightly of this advice, but retire yourself into the country, where you may expect the event in safety, for though there be no appearance of any stir, yet I say they shall receive a terrible blow, this Parliament, and yet they shall not know who hurts them.

"This counsel is not to be contemned, because it may do you good and can do you no harm, for the danger is past as soon as you have burnt this letter, and I hope God will give you the grace to make good use of it, and to his holy protection I commend you."

The astonishment of all the guests at the reading of this mysterious and remarkable letter may be better imagined than described.

After much discussion on the subject the party broke up.

And late as it was Lord Monteagle took horse and used the utmost dispatch in reaching Whitehall.

On arriving there he was ushered into the presence of Cecil and the Earl of Salisbury, and he immediately laid the important missive before them.

The king was again away at Royston hunting.

"Hum! This last piece of evidence," said Cecil, when he had perused the letter, "confirms my former suspicions of a Popish plot, having for its object the annihilation of a Protestant Government."

"Exactly so," observed Salisbury, "and the means employed, I opine, judging from the passage in this document, 'And the danger is past as soon as you have burnt this letter,' will be *gunpowder!*"

"My opinion, precisely," said Cecil. "We have, undoubtedly, had a most fortunate escape from a frightful death, thanks be to Providence and my Lord of Monteagle."

"True," rejoined the earl, "and I will see that his lordship loses nothing of his majesty's favour by the information."

Lord Monteagle gracefully inclined his head.

"We will take no steps in this matter till the return of the king," went on Cecil. "It would be highly flattering to his inordinate vanity to let him suppose that the means used was the result of his own bright penetration and superior sagacity."

"I entirely concur with you, Cecil," said Salisbury. "We will forbear to impart the news to him until a few days before the sitting of Parliament. Meanwhile, my lord," he added, turning to Monteagle, "extract all you can out of your informant, Tresham, and when he is of no further use I can doubtless find him a safe corner in the Tower, in order to prevent him using his tongue to our detriment hereafter."

"You counsel well, my lord," remarked Cecil, "and I would further advise that the suspicions of these bold plotters be not aroused by any forward or untoward movement on our part, so that they may be lured the more surely and completely to their fate. And now, gentlemen, good-night."

And they then separated—each one to his respective chamber.

* * * * * *

The next morning Ward, who had read the letter publicly at the supper-table of Lord Monteagle, met Thomas Winter as he rode through the village of Hoxton on his way to Tottenham.

Ward immediately communicated the circumstances of the letter to the conspirator, adding that the missive was now in the possession of Cecil.

Winter was thunderstruck, but, putting an easy and indifferent face upon the matter, said, laughingly—

"Depend upon it, my dear Ward, the whole affair is simply a hoax—an attempt to impose on the credulity of his lordship. Kindly commend me to his worship and family. Adieu!" and, raising his hat, he rode gaily off.

But no sooner was Ward out of sight than Winter urged on his gallant steed to its utmost speed, despite the wild storm of wind and rain, nor drew rein until he reached the conspirators' lonely rendezvous on the borders of Enfield Wood.

Wet and muddy with travelling as he was, he immediately sought an interview with Catesby, and imparted to him the startling news.

"The double-dyed traitor and villain!" exclaimed Catesby, alluding to Tresham. "That this is his vile work I would stake my existence."

"'Sdeath! there can be little doubt on't!" returned Winter, "when ye bethink on the manner in which he prayed to be allowed to warn his relative, Monteagle."

"The base double-dealer and craven!" cried Guy Fawkes, fiercely. "Curses on my blind folly in not crushing out the crawling reptile's life at our last meeting."

"I am quite agreed with you, gentlemen," observed Wright, "that Tresham is the guilty party. I cannot conceive from what source the information could spring but from him."

"Moreover," added Grant, "the fact that he has absented himself for several days on pretence of having business in Northamptonshire is another very suspicious circumstance."

"I am much concerned to know if this arch-traitor hath revealed the particulars of the plot, and whose names he has mentioned in connection with it," said Catesby, with a troubled look.

"To ascertain the extent of his treachery," remarked Guy Fawkes, "let us summon him to attend a meeting at the lone house on Lambeth Marsh."

SIR HAROLD DREW HIS SWORD AND RUSHED TO VIOLET'S ASSISTANCE.

"Be it so, Guy Fawkes," said Catesby, "and if we find Tresham guilty we will shoot him down like a wild dog."

They then decided that in the event of their fears being groundless Guy Fawkes was to fire the train with a slow match, which would allow of his escape before the explosion.

A ship was to be in readiness on the river to carry him over to Flanders, where he was to publish a manifesto justifying the deed, and calling on the Catholic powers for aid.

Percy, as a gentleman-pensioner, was to enter the palace and secure the person of the young Prince Charles, and, on pretence of placing him in security, convey him away to the appointed place at Dunchurch, where they expected the Catholic rebels to mass in great force.

Sir Everard Digby, Ambrose Rookwood, Grant, Winter, and others were to hasten with their armed followers to Combe Abbey, to secure Princess Elizabeth, whom, if the two young princes should not be saved, they were at once to proclaim queen; while the bold and ambitious Catesby was also to proclaim the heir apparent, whoever it was, at Charing-cross; and a declaration was to be issued abolishing monopolies, purveyance, wardships, &c. A Protector was also to be appointed, to conduct the Government during the minority of the Sovereign.

Surely there were circumstances enough in these regulations to have alarmed any but fanatics in the cause!

The endeavour to secure the royal children was full of hazard.

On their return to town Guy Fawkes repaired straightway to the cellar, containing the powder and other combustibles, under the Parliament House, to discover whether all was right.

Not a thing had been disturbed—not even the secret marks he had placed there were removed.

"All is precisely as I left it," he muttered. "Perhaps after all our suspicions are groundless. Yet again have I seen the shade of my sainted sister, Esmé, warning me to desist, and this time in company of the gentle and sweet-faced Violet. Ah! how different might have been my lot had she but have returned my love. Oh, for one last word—one last smile of those dear lips—ere I take my parting look of this sad world, which an inward voice is ever telling me is not far distant."

With a heavy heart he left the vault, and, watching his opportunity, glided like a spirit of darkness to the door of the house adjoining, let himself in with a key, then posted himself behind the curtains of one of the windows, and watched through the long, silent, dreary night.

On the 31st of October King James returned to town, and the letter was laid before him, with the particulars of its delivery.

James was greatly struck and inwardly terrified by the account.

He read the letter several times over, and discussed the matter at great length.

"Your majesty will observe," said the wily Cecil, at length, "that there is one passage in the epistle running thus, 'The danger is passed as soon as you have burnt this letter,' and it hath occurred to me that it might allude to an explosion."

"Mayhap it does," said the king, grasping the idea. "In good sooth there is little doubt but that these Papist rogues are conspiring to blow us all up with *gunpowder*."

"Your grace hath most assuredly defined the true meaning in a thought. 'Tis a Heaven-sent inspiration of a surety," observed Salisbury. "Such a thought never entered *my* mind."

"We are not all gifted alike, friend Salisbury," chuckled the monarch, flattered by the compliment paid to his supposed shrewdness. "Yet Heaven a mercy—what terrible villains and traitors to contemplate such a dreadful deed."

"Aye, your majesty," returned the earl, "none save these godless Papists would have conceived such a diabolical scheme. But just Heaven hath decreed it should fail and rebound on the heads of its base originators."

"Aye, by my faith, and it shall too, with a vengeance!" returned James, with an ugly look. "Have you any suspicion as to who these base traitors are, my good lord?"

"I have, your majesty," returned Salisbury, "but I would rather defer my opinion until after to-morrow, when I hope to be in a position to answer your grace with full confidence."

"A' weel, man," said the monarch. "Gad a mercy, we may have of late been walking over a secret mine with our lives in our hands. There are many vaults under the Parliament House, are there not?"

"There are, your majesty."

"Vera weel," said James, in alarm; "'tis in one of those the powder is concealed, depend upon it, man."

"We are truly indebted to your grace for your ready sagacity and invaluable information," said the insidious Cecil. "Indeed, I greatly fear me that but for his majesty's timely arrival and wondrous powers of penetration this detestable plot would not have been discovered till the fatal blow had been struck," said Salisbury, fawningly.

James's vanity was pleasantly tickled by these artful and fulsome remarks, and, bidding them search every hole and corner of the vaults, and to keep a strict and vigilant watch both by night and day till the sitting of Parliament, he broke up the council and retired.

CHAPTER XLVIII.

THE FIFTH OF NOVEMBER—THE WARNING OF DOOM—FIRING THE TRAIN—GUY FAWKES'S CAPTURE.

THOMAS WINTER, who still had access to the court, apparently unsuspected, learnt through Lord Monteagle's servant that the fateful letter of Tresham's was in the hands of the king, and that his ministers were in consultation on it.

Upon this Winter waited on Tresham at his house in Lincoln's-inn Walk.

Ushered into the arch-traitor's presence, Winter told him the alarming news, and asked him if he thought it was true.

"In good sooth, every word of it," returned Tresham, greatly agitated. "Moreover, they have discovered the existence of the secret mine"

"How know you that?" asked Winter, suspiciously.

"Through certain remarks let drop by my kinsman, Lord Monteagle," answered the traitor, with an air of truth.

"But cannot you venture a guess, Master Tresham, as to who the traitor is who gave them the information which has led to this unfortunate discovery?" questioned Winter.

"No, I cannot, as I hope for salvation!" cried Tresham, with seeming deep fervour. "But this I do know—that our plans are discovered, and that we are all hopelessly lost if we do not instantly escape."

"Is this your firm and decided conviction?"

"It is, most surely and candidly," returned Tresham. "The means are at hand for ready flight. My vessel, The Good Hope, lays off the Greenwich shore, ready to bear us all to Flanders. Go then, good Winter, to our brethren, tell them that our plot is discovered, and conjure them instantly to escape, while the chance offers, as to-morrow may be too late!"

"I will away at once, and do you, Tresham, meet us at the old rendezvous on the Marsh to-night, to make necessary preparations for our flight."

Tresham replied in the affirmative.

"And now adieu," added Winter, then shaking the cowardly craven heartily by the hand he hurried from the house.

The conspirators met that night at the old house on Lambeth Marsh.

After hearing Winter's startling news they sat down to decide on their plan of action.

Some of them advised instant escape to the continent, as suggested by Tresham.

Catesby, Winter, and others were perfectly convinced that Tresham was a vile traitor, and that he was in communication with Lord Monteagle and perhaps Cecil.

But some among them would not believe that such treachery was possible in a sworn son of Holy Church, and this, together with the arguments of Percy, nailed them to their fate.

This discussion took place on the 3rd of November.

"Gentlemen," went on the headstrong, impetuous Percy, "have patience and wait. In the name of our holy cause I conjure you wait and see what to-morrow brings forth—the very last day, remember, before the grand crisis."

"You advise well, and to the point, Sir Charles," said Guy Fawkes. "I shall not forego my set task, though you all resort to flight, and leave me to accomplish it unaided and alone."

"Well spoken, friend Fawkes," rejoined Percy, heartily. "I would we were all as staunch and true to our vows. By our Lady, it were most cowardly and contemptible in us, after all our terrible labours, the tremendous difficulties we have overcome, the ruinous costs we have incurred, the fearful anxieties and plannings we have gone through, to dream of abandoning our holy enterprise through the cowardly fears of a recreant colleague, who has probably described only what his affrighted fancy pictured to him."

"You utter my thoughts, Sir Charles, to the very letter," said Guy Fawkes.

"And mine," said Catesby.

"And mine!" cried Winter and several others.

"Furthermore, gentlemen," continued Sir Charles Percy, "there is my vessel still lying off London-bridge, at your service, and on the first positive proof of danger you have only to hasten on board and drop down the river out of the reach of our enemies."

These arguments prevailed, and they all agreed to abide by the result of the explosion, but they changed their plans.

Guy Fawkes was still to keep guard in the vault.

Percy and Winter were to superintend the necessary operations in London.

But Catesby and John Wright were to hasten to Dunchurch and put the youthful Sir Everard Digby and their fast mustering party on their guard.

On the evening of the 4th of November the Earl of Suffolk, in the prosecution of his duty as Lord Chamberlain, to see all necessary preparations made for the opening of Parliament, went down to the House accompanied by Lord Monteagle.

After they had been some time in the Parliament chamber they made some pretence to the king that some necessary articles were missing, and went down to the cellars to make a search.

They at length entered the vault where the dreaded mine was prepared, and where the disguised and dauntless Guy Fawkes was at his post.

Casting his eyes round the grim abode, the chamberlain said, addressing Guy Fawkes—

"Prithee, my good fellow, by whom is this vault occupied, and who, may I ask, are you?"

"This vault, your worship," said the bold conspirator, without a quiver of his iron muscles, "is rented by Mr. Percy, and I have the honour to be that worthy gentleman's servant."

"Your master has laid in a goodly stock of fuel," observed the chamberlain, in a careless, good-humoured way.

And he and Monteagle left the cellar.

No sooner were they fairly gone than Guy Fawkes hastened to the house adjoining, where Percy had resolved to stay till the stroke of midnight, and informed him of what had occurred.

But the warning was lost on the daring plotter.

"Your fears are all phantoms, believe me, my dear Fawkes," he said. "Were they acquainted with the secrets of our plot think ye they would wait till within an hour of the fatal blow being struck ere they made an effort to secure us? No, no! Depend upon it they have discovered nothing, and ere the first stroke of morning the enemies of our Church will be scattered to the four winds of Heaven!"

Guy Fawkes's spirits rose at these delusive words, and he returned to the vault to await till the fatal hour.

As the Abbey clock tolled the solemn hour of midnight, it being now actually the 5th of November, Guy Fawkes, with a blow of his petronel, stove in the head of one of the powder barrels, and, taking his powder flask, prepared to lay a train from the door of the vault to the open cask.

His eager finger touched the spring of the horn flask, and already a tiny black stream of powder began to fall upon the floor of the cell.

Just then a faint phosphorescent light illumined the opposite wall, and from out its pale, cloudy bosom the spectral form of a young and beauteous maiden appeared in flowing robes of spotless white.

"Shade of my sainted sister !" cried Guy Fawkes, in trembling awe and dread, on beholding the apparition, "why comest thou, and at a moment when by a stroke the great purpose of my life will be accomplished ?"

The apparition, with an expression of mute appeal on its angelic features, pointed to the door, and waved its white, spectral hand thrice.

"Is it to warn me even at the eleventh hour to abandon my dearly-cherished design, and leave the restitution of our wrongs to a higher power ?"

The vision inclined its head, while a sad, sweet smile seemed to irradiate its lovely countenance.

"My heart fails me, my hand falls powerless at my side," cried Guy Fawkes, uncovering and prostrating himself before the apparition. "Beloved Esmé, you have prevailed. I cannot do the deed."

And, springing to his feet, he moved towards the door.

He turned a moment to gaze once more upon the spirit of his beloved sister, but it had vanished.

Then, seizing a flaming torch from a niche in the outer wall, he dashed into the darkness of the passage.

He had not proceeded many yards when his progress was barred by an armed trooper. He was one of Oliver Blackstock's men.

"Surrender in the king's name !" cried the man-at-arms, "for I recognise you as that villainous traitor, Guy Fawkes."

Guy Fawkes never paused for reply, but struck his opponent down with one terrific blow of his lightning blade.

He was about to hurry on when, struck with a sudden idea, he placed his torch against the wall, and, seizing his victim by the armpits, dragged him into the darkness of a deep recess.

He then cautiously left the place and returned to Percy's house adjoining.

It was deserted.

He sat in gloomy silence for several minutes, then going to a press he took down a square black bottle, and poured himself out a cup of wine.

He drank it off, and it seemed to revive his shaken resolution.

"Pshaw, what a weak and piteous coward I am," he said with animation, "to be frightened by a mere shadow. What will my comrades think of me after boasting of what I would do ? They would dub me, and rightly, too, a braggart and craven. By Heaven ! I'll do it, though a thousand spectres warned me to desist !"

And, concealing a lantern under his cloak, he left the house with the usual caution, and made his way back again to the cellar.

It appeared just the same as when he had left it.

He was all booted and spurred, ready for a precipitate flight after he had lighted the train with a slow match.

Knocking in the heads of several barrels with the butt end of his petronel he made a train to each, all leading from the door.

He then lit a slow match with the light from his lantern.

While thus occupied a figure stepped from behind the piled lumber of faggots, powder, &c., though unseen by the busy conspirator, and, taking off his cavalier hat, with one sweeping wave of its long drooping plume fanned aside the powder, and thus broke and disconnected the train.

It was well he did so, for the next instant all would have been blown into eternity.

Guy Fawkes, in his haste, had omitted to prepare the powder properly.

And the instant he applied the match it exploded.

He leapt back, expecting in the same instant to be hurled into space.

But the flash of fire stopped short, midway between himself and the powder.

"Surrender, villain, in the king's name !" exclaimed a stern, deep voice, and the same instant Lord Monteagle faced him, sword in hand.

"Ah, betrayed ! Die, thou recreant son of Holy Church !" yelled Guy Fawkes, furiously, and he aimed a tremendous blow at Monteagle's head.

But, swift as the howling wind, half a dozen men-at-arms sprung out upon him from behind and seized his arms.

A terrific struggle now ensued, but Guy Fawkes was finally borne to the ground by his determined assailants.

Whilst there he suddenly wrenched his arm free, and, seizing the lighted lantern, threw it with great violence right into an open barrel of powder.

All uttered a cry of horror.

Like a hawk Lord Monteagle darted forward and secured the lantern.

A moment later and the awful catastrophe they were all so anxious to prevent would have been the result.

At this moment Sir Thomas Knewell and more soldiers rushed in, and between them Guy Fawkes was finally overpowered and bound hand and foot.

"Now, my men," said Sir Thomas, "lift the arch-traitor on your shoulders, and follow me into the presence of his outraged sovereign."

CHAPTER XLIX.

GUY FAWKES BEFORE THE KING—PUT TO THE TORTURE—THE EXECUTION—THE LAST OF THE DANCING-GIRL—CONCLUSION.

GUY FAWKES was conveyed through a magnificent enfilade of rooms by his triumphant captors to the king's bed-chamber in White hall, there to be interrogated.

Fast fettered as he was, the determined look of the defeated conspirator instilled terror into the hearts of the assembled courtiers, whilst the king himself sat in a state of nervous terror, although he was surrounded by a strong body-guard of armed soldiers.

Guy Fawkes stood before him calm and self-possessed, and, though bold, he was respectful in speech.

"A bold, daring traitor !" said the king, with inward misgiving, as he closely regarded the unabashed conspirator. "Your name, base wretch?"

"Johnson," answered Guy Fawkes. "I am servant to Mr. Percy."

"Beware, villain! You will do well to tell the truth," said James, sternly. "You were taken in the diabolical act of blowing us all up with gunpowder. Do you attempt to deny the fact?"

"No," cried Guy Fawkes, boldly, "my object was to annihilate both king and Parliament, as the only means of ridding our down-trodden Church of its persecutors."

"How could you have the heart," pursued the king, "to destroy my children, and so many innocent souls with them?"

"Dangerous diseases," replied Guy Fawkes, "require desperate remedies; gentler means had been tried and failed, but since Heaven has disapproved of my scheme I will not murmur."

"And pray, fellow," observed the Duke of Lennox, who sat opposite the Earl of Marr, on the left of the king, "what was your reason for having so many barrels of gunpowder?"

"To blow the beggarly Scots back to their native mountains," retorted Guy Fawkes, with a grim smile.

"This daring insolence surpasses belief!" fumed the king. "Listen, villain. Were I to spare your life would you divulge the name of your accomplices?"

"That would I, never!" cried Guy Fawkes, determinedly.

"Then the rack shall wring them from you," said Cecil, with inward fury.

"Do your worst. You will extort nothing from me."

"'Tis useless to question the stubborn traitor further," said James. "Away with him to the Tower, and there torture him till he confesses."

Guy Fawkes smiled contemptuously, and he was conducted by the guard from the king's presence.

* * * * * *

We must now retrace our steps to the hut of the magician, near the ravine.

Upon the flight of the dwarf, after having slain Sir Sidney, his reputed father, the magician, Horlock, attempted to escape.

But the strong hand of Ralph, who had stationed himself at the door, was laid upon him with an iron grasp as he cried—

"Oh, no you don't, Mr. Wizard."

Finding resistance useless the magician yielded with sullen indifference to his fate.

Ralph had just opened his mouth to make some disparaging remark touching the heinousness of his prisoner's foul deed when Will-o'-the-Woods, with half-a-dozen followers at his heels, dashed into the apartment.

"Heaven guide us!" exclaimed the Freeranger chief. "What creature was that that passed us on the stair like a flash of fire?"

"Hush!" said Sir Harold, as he pointed to a couch on which lay the lifeless form of Vera Horlock.

The forester looked in the direction indicated, and then, with a changed and serious countenance, added—

"This must be seen to. Who has done this fearful deed?"

"Here he is, noble chief," said Ralph, giving his prisoner a mighty shake.

"What!" cried the Freeranger, "taken red-handed? Then by the Heaven above us he shall hang as high as Haman by to-morrow's dawn."

"Well said, noble captain," cried Ralph, "and I trust you will not deny me the pleasure of a pull at the rope."

The Freeranger chief was much pleased to behold Violet and Sir Harold once more, and the welcome between them was a warm one, though brief.

For, suddenly recollecting in whose presence he stood, Will-o'-the-Woods turned with shuddering horror from the scene before him, and exclaimed—

"I cannot bear this terrible sight. To know that you, Lady Violet, and you, Sir Harold, are safe is my sole desire. Let us leave this place. See to your prisoner, lads," he added to his men. "Away!"

"One moment," said the magician, speaking for the first time. "Ere I quit this room let me say that the blow which has slain yonder unhappy woman was purely accidental. I would not have spilt my own blood. No, no! not so bad as that.

"'Twas intended for you, lady," he added, turning to Violet, "and done at the instigation of that false-hearted fiend whose carcase is blackening at your feet," indicating Sir Sidney Wildbrook. "But Providence directed the knife to my sister's heart, and, from the simple chance of you entering at the wrong door, your life has been saved. Now lead me to my doom."

"Aye, lads, away with him," cried Will-o'-the-Woods, "and let him swing ere dawn on the highest tree in Bleam Wood."

"Aye, aye, captain," was the hearty response, as the sturdy foresters led their prisoner away.

"I have news, Sir Harold, that I fear will sadden you," said the Freeranger, when they were a little distance from the house. "Your comrade-in-arms, Guy Fawkes, has been taken in his attempt to blow up Parliament, and to-morrow, at six of the clock, will be on his way from Whitehall to the Tower."

"When and how did you hear this?" asked Sir Harold.

"I overheard two of the conspirators, who were on their way to Dunchurch, talking of it in Bleam Wood not an hour since."

"This is ill news, indeed, that you bring me," said the young soldier, sadly. "Little did I think my cherished friend and comrade would have had a hand in such a dastardly and atrocious plot, yet I would give much to see him and take a last farewell."

"So also should I," rejoined Violet, with tears of pity in her gentle blue eyes. "He has often risked his life to serve us, and I loved him as though he had been my brother."

"He will go by water to the Tower," said Will-o'-the-Woods, "and if you would like to see him the means are at hand. A small vessel, bound for London, lays off the shore, and sails within three hours. Mention my name and a passage on board will be granted you at once."

"We owe you many thanks, Sir Knight of the Woods," said Harold, gratefully.

"Name it not," returned the Freeranger. "And now farewell. We may not meet again. My home is the green woods—yours the stately painted halls of stone. I trust that now your trials are over, and may every happiness that you wish yourselves be yours."

He clasped their hands fervently for a moment and was gone.

* * * * *

Sir Harold, following out the Freeranger's instructions, secured a passage on board the vessel for Violet and himself, and reached old London bridge at daybreak the next morning.

Here they landed, and, making their way to St. Paul's stairs, hired a boat. Harold ordered the waterman to row to Whitehall.

On reaching their destination they perceived a wherry filled with officers and soldiers, their arms and armour gleaming in the morning sunshine, coming towards them.

As the wherry drew near Violet could scarcely repress a cry on beholding Guy Fawkes heavily ironed on board.

Their eyes met for a moment, and the doomed conspirator's haggard features suddenly lighted up with an expression of almost celestial joy, while his lips moved as though invoking a blessing on the compassionate girl's head.

The boat swept on its way, and in another minute Guy Fawkes disappeared from their sight for evermore.

"Poor dear misguided Guy," said Violet, with deep emotion. "What a fearful fate for one so good—so brave!"

Tears checked her utterance, and she fell into the arms of the deeply-affected Sir Harold, sobbing bitterly.

* * * * *

Catesby and John Wright had left on the evening of the 4th for Dunchurch, as agreed.

Percy and others maintained their watch in London till they heard of the arrest of Guy Fawkes, and saw that all the town was in a state of terror.

Then they mounted their steeds and rode after the others.

On the journey they overtook Rookwood, Wright, Keyes, and Catesby, and the whole troop rode on together till they came to Lady Catesby's, at Ashby St. Legers, in Northamptonshire.

They arrived there at six o'clock in the evening, having ridden the whole eighty miles in little more than six hours.

A party of conspirators, with whom was Winter, were sitting down at supper when the fugitives, covered with mud and dust, and sinking with fatigue, surprised them.

"Our great scheme has failed, gentlemen," panted Catesby, sinking into a seat, "and our best and bravest member is taken."

"Guy Fawkes taken!" exclaimed the startled conspirators, in a breath.

"Alas! yes; and to-morrow he will be put to the torture to compel him to divulge the names of his confederates."

"And think you he will confess?" asked one.

"Need you ask?" returned Catesby, scornfully. "They may wring his heart out first."

The famished fugitives then sat down to a hasty meal and discussed their plans at the same time.

"My advice," said Catesby, in conclusion, "is that we strike across Worcestershire for Wales, where I flatter myself we might assemble most of the Catholic gentry and make a formidable stand."

In pursuance of this romantic plan they mounted and rode to Warwick.

All the way they called on the Catholics to arm and join them for the rescue of their faith.

But not a man would listen now that they had heard of the failure of the Gunpowder Plot.

On this the dispirited conspirators, instead of pushing on for the mountains of Wales, resolved on making a stand at Holbeach.

Meanwhile Sir Richard Walsh, the sheriff of Worcestershire, with the whole *posse comitatis* and a number of volunteer gentlemen, gave the conspirators chase.

And many a desperate hand-to-hand encounter took place between them, in which more than one valuable life was sacrificed.

The conspirators had considerably diverged from their original route, in the hope of being joined by the Catholic gentry, but they only drove them from their doors.

And no sooner did Stephen Littleton, the owner of Holbeach, learn the real facts, than, horrified at the certain destruction impending over these desperate men, he made his escape in secret from the house.

The remaining conspirators, who, with their servants, did not amount to more than forty men, set about to put the place in a state of defence.

But as they were drying some damp powder before the fire it exploded, horribly scorching and injuring Catesby and some others.

This appalling accident so impressed them with the belief that their enterprise was displeasing to the Almighty that Robert Winter, Bates, and some others, readily got away.

About noon Sir Richard Walsh came up with his troop, and, surrounding the house, summoned them to surrender.

"Never!" cried the undaunted Catesby, despite his injuries. "Let us rather die a soldier's death, sword in hand, than like criminals upon the scaffold!"

They one and all hurled a shout of defiance at their assailants, and resolved to fight to the last.

Upon this the sheriff ordered one party of his followers to set fire to the house and the others to batter down the gates.

Then a fierce and deadly encounter ensued.

The conspirators fought like lions, but they were greatly outnumbered, and their ranks soon became sadly thinned.

Blackened and nearly blinded as he was, Catesby fought his way, with his small handful of followers, into the courtyard.

Here they made a gallant stand, but were finally overpowered.

The two Wrights were slain, and Catesby and Percy were mortally wounded.

The former crawled on hands and knees into the house to a crucifix, which he seized in his hands, and expired.

Ambrose Rookwood, who was dreadfully burnt and wounded, was seized, as also was Winter, whose arm was broken.

Percy died from his wounds next day.

The rest of the conspirators were soon taken.

Whilst these events had been taking place Guy Fawkes had been put to the torture in the Tower.

Not all the devilish engines of torture, however, which the art of man could devise moved him to confess the names of his companions.

How this undaunted man endured for an hour and a half the excruciating agony of being screwed up double in the compressed iron band called the "Scavenger's Daughter," till the blood burst from his ears, eyes, nose, and mouth; how he suffered the terrible confinement of the "Little Ease," a wretched cell, scarcely wide enough to receive him, and in which he could neither lie, sit, nor stand, but remain with his head bent on his breast all night; how he hung suspended by his hands, crushed and screwed in iron gauntlets, for five hours, till his fingers were so lacerated that he could not use them; how he passed a night in the awful "Rat Pit," among thousands of these horrid, loathsome animals, and was only released at the very instant when they rushed upon him in a body to devour him; how his joints were started from their sockets and his limbs almost torn asunder on the grim and frightful rack, till he fainted; how he was stripped and strapped on a stone heated over a slow fire, until his skin was scorched and cracked, without so much as a groan escaping his parched and burning lips; and, lastly, how he and the rest of his companions were hanged, drawn, and quartered in Old Palace Yard, amid the shouts and execrations of the crowding thousands, their severed bodies flung into huge cauldrons of boiling pitch, and their heads spiked on Traitor's Gate, are matters of history, with which, probably, our readers are already familiar, and need not be recapitulated in detail.

In drawing this, our eventful history, to a close, however, we must not omit to mention that as Guy Fawkes was in the act of being assisted up the fatal ladder by the executioner—he was too much shattered by torture to walk—his attention was arrested by a piercing shriek from the surging, howling mass below.

A woman had fainted and was being borne out of the crowd.

"Evelyn!" faintly murmured Guy Fawkes, as he looked towards the pale, lifeless girl.

And with this name hovering upon his lips he was hurled into eternity!

The dancing-girl was never seen nor heard of after the execution.

And now but little more remains to be told.

King James kept his word to Sir Harold, and on the death of Sir Sidney Wildbrook not only gave to the young knight Violet's cherished hand in marriage, but restored to the happy young bride the broad lands and ample possessions of Hamlyn.

And one of Violet's first acts, on being reinstated in her own domains, was to reward the pretty Janet, who had tended Sir Harold in his hour of need, with a rich dowry.

Nor was honest Ralph forgotten, to whom the onerous but pleasant office of steward of the estate was entrusted.

And as the happy years rolled on, and the silvery frost of advancing age began to streak his chestnut locks, often round the blazing hearth would he delight the sons and daughters of Sir Harold and Lady Violet with many a wondrous tale of his own adventures during the period of the famed Gunpowder Conspiracy, and speak with moistening eyes and husky accent of his deeply-lamented and revered friend—Guy Fawkes!

THE END.